THE
100 YEAR
MIRACLE

Also by Ashley Ream

Losing Clementine

THE
100 YEAR
MIRACLE

Ashley Ream

FLATIRON
BOOKS
NEW YORK

This is a work of fiction. All of the characters, organizations, and events portrayed in this novel are either products of the author's imagination or are used fictitiously.

www.flatironbooks.com

Designed by Steven Seighman

The Library of Congress Cataloging-in-Publication Data is available upon request.

ISBN 978-1-250-08222-0 (hardcover)
ISBN 978-1-250-08802-4 (e-book)

Our books may be purchased in bulk for promotional, educational, or business use. Please contact your local bookseller or the Macmillan Corporate and Premium Sales Department at (800) 221-7945, extension 5442, or by e-mail at MacmillanSpecialMarkets@macmillan.com.

First Edition: May 2016

10 9 8 7 6 5 4 3 2 1

To Gamms

Prologue

The Last Day of the Miracle

When Dr. Rachel Bell turned, she saw the man who had pushed her. She knew she would fall, and she knew why. The certainty was oddly comforting. The compound that she'd been testing on herself, ground and mixed into a tincture, caused "auditory and visual hallucinations." It said so in her notebooks—not that anyone would be able to read them if she died. She'd had to write them in code to keep people from stealing them. "Possible paranoia" was written in those notebooks, too.

She had been clambering out in the dark and the cold to take one last sample from the waters of Olloo'et Bay, which didn't look like any water anywhere else on earth. A bright green glowing ribbon encircled the entire inlet like a water-bound version of the aurora borealis. The light came from the bioluminescent bodies of tiny arthropods, millions of them that pulsed in the shallow water. Their six-day life span was about to expire, and they were signaling one final time for a mate.

The footing was unsure. The wind and freezing rain were blowing harder than she'd ever seen. The slime-slick rocks were sharp and treacherous, and it was almost impossible to hear anything over the growl and hiss of waves rolling in and breaking against the shore. The night's high tide had made its stand and was beginning its slow crawl back out to sea, leaving pools of this glowing water among the rocky outcroppings. It was the very end of the very last day of the breeding, a thing that would not occur again for another century. It was so rare and so wondrous that comets and meteor strikes seemed workaday by comparison. Newspapers and television reporters had taken to calling it the 100-Year Miracle.

It did things to people, this miracle. Strange and not wholly wonderful things.

1.

The First Day of the Miracle

The Department of Fish and Wildlife had cordoned off the beach, wrapping the small half-moon bay in yellow caution tape. The mayor and the governor in separate press conferences—because even for this they could not share—had warned people to stay out of the water. They feared islanders and tourists would gather up so many of the glowing *Artemia lucis* into glass jars to wonder at like fireflies that the breeding activity would be compromised, killing the species forever. This fear was not, in Dr. Bell's opinion, unfounded.

She pulled the zipper of her waterproof jacket up a little higher. Gloves would've been nice, but she couldn't work in gloves. Winter on the San Juan Islands was cold, but only occasionally was it cold enough to snow, which meant the persistent drizzle didn't have to bother melting before it soaked into her clothes, boots, and skin. The light but unrelenting wet had not let up all that day and wouldn't until June. Apparently, people got used to it, but Rachel, who grew up in Arizona where the sun baked and bleached your bones while you were still using them, didn't think she would ever get used to it. She had been cold for two years running. It was a cold no wool socks and bulky sweatshirts could cure. It was the sort of cold that made a person irritable.

If it were not for the *Artemia lucis,* Rachel would never have considered such a place fit for habitation. But scientists have a long history of following their obsessions into the most unpleasant and treacherous places on earth, deep into jungles and out onto ice floes, so it would be a warm winter's day on this godforsaken bay before she would breathe a word of complaint to any of her teammates, some of whom had been raised on drizzle and moss and seemed to thrive in it, as though it were some sort of growth medium.

Her research team was led by Dr. Eugene Hooper, who had headed the biology department at the University of Washington for long enough that no one remembered who had done it before him. Hooper, who hated his first name and wouldn't answer to it, was a head taller than any other man in the department. Incapable of accruing body fat, his skin was shrink-wrapped to his frame, and he had deep lines carved around his mouth and eyes by too much sun on too many field expeditions. The work had taken its toll in other ways, too. A trip to Borneo early in his career had left him with a lifetime of reoccurring malarial bouts. It made for interesting "out of office" messages.

All of Dr. Hooper's seminars, office hours, and meetings are canceled this week due to feverish hallucinations. Thank you for understanding.

Hooper's team for this expedition had been assembled and waiting for a year. While the approximate time of the breeding could be estimated, the date could only be calculated within twenty-eight days, and even that was probability.

Each member carried a packed duffel bag in the trunk of his or her car. All the necessary laboratory and collection equipment was assembled and waiting at the university for transport. There had been training drills and practice scenarios and more meetings than Rachel cared to remember. No one, heaven forbid, let their cell phone battery die. It was as if they were all expectant fathers waiting for the water to break.

When the call had come that morning just after 5:30 a.m., Rachel, a biochemist, had been trying to bend over. Bending over was just one of the things that did not come easily to her. Everything tightened while she slept. No matter how many stretches she had done the day before, she had to begin all over each morning.

First Rachel pushed away the sheet, the comforter, the quilt, and the blanket and slid off the mattress like a woman balancing a glass of water on top of her head. Once on her feet, she let her head fall forward, which pulled at the ropey, knotted clump of shiny-looking scars at the base of her neck. She clamped her jaw tight and waited for the worst of that pain to pass before rolling her shoulders forward and letting her arms hang loose over her toes. With a series of deep, loud breaths that she pushed through her teeth, Rachel let her spine lengthen, one vertebra at a time. The thing here was not to pass out or throw up. Vomiting was a serious concern because she'd had her morning Vicodin, and it wouldn't do to lose whatever remained undissolved in her digestive tract.

Rachel was still doing her Lamaze breaths when her phone began to buzz and vibrate. It was a jarring sound in the predawn quiet when even the dusky blue scrub jays were fast asleep.

She reached up with one hand, feeling blindly for the nightstand and then for the top of the nightstand and then for her cell phone.

"Bell," she said into it.

"Rachel?" Hooper said. "It's time."

Understanding her brain's chemistry did nothing to control it. A jolt of epinephrine targeted her adrenergic receptors, stimulating the sympathetic nervous system and causing an involuntary start. She jerked up fast and phosphenes swam through her vision.

"Aargh." Rachel bit down and punched her thigh.

"You okay?"

Hooper often asked if she was okay, and Rachel always gave the same answer. The question and the answer had gone back and forth between them so many times that it no longer required a conscious thought. Rachel would, of course, never tell him about her scars because she would never tell anyone, but if anyone could ever be an exception, it would be him. This extreme hypothetical was the most trust Rachel had placed in anyone since she had been old enough to ride a two-wheeled bicycle.

"I'm fine," Rachel said on a breath. "I'm on my way."

She ended the call with her thumb but moved nothing else. "Dammit."

The thing she wanted more than she had ever wanted anything was happening—it was happening right then—and Rachel had no choice but to wait. She wiggled her fingers, scrunched up her toes, made fists and then released them, *fist, release, fist, release, wiggle, scrunch, wiggle, scrunch,* anything to calm her nerves. As each millimeter of scar tissue relaxed, her breath eased and then quieted. When it was all the way quiet, the stretches were done. She stood up, pulling off the baggy T-shirt she'd slept in.

Her back from her shoulders to her waist looked like dripping, melted wax. Rachel knew the scars well enough to pick out shapes as a child might see animals in the clouds. There was a tree just to the right of her spine about halfway down, a raven in flight was on the left a little higher up, and the face of an old man was etched between her shoulder blades. They stretched as she moved, and though they never seemed to get any better, she wondered if they did not change slightly over time like stars moving across the sky.

While Rachel did not find them horrible anymore, objectively, they were. They were the sort of scars that made people clamp their hands across their mouths when they saw them. The sort of scars that frightened people. And although an adult might say to a child that they—that she—was nothing to be frightened of, that was a lie. Any rational person would be and should be frightened because her scars were proof that things that should not be survivable sometimes are and that this is not good news. It was better not to know these things. Rachel wished she did not know them, which was part of the reason no one ever saw her scars. No living person, apart from her doctors—and there had been a lot of doctors—even knew they existed.

Keeping this secret did tend to interfere with interpersonal relationships but, then again, so did her tendency to think of them as "interpersonal relationships."

Hurrying, she reached into one of the two small fishbowls that sat on the nightstand. White pills in one, orange pills in the other. The Vicodin was a mixture of acetaminophen, which had begun to damage her liver, and hydrocodone. By her own calculations, her dosage trajectory would lead to heart and/or respiratory failure in less than a year. There were, she thought, some advantages to her default mode of detached analysis, not many advantages to be sure, but some. This was one. She knew how long she had to fix things. She could make a plan.

Rachel took three from the orange stash and swallowed them while pulling on yesterday's clothes, which she'd left on the floor the night before. Halfway into her pants, she stopped, debated with herself and then cursed, taking them off again. She found and put on a pair of clean underpants, pulled the jeans back on, grabbed her pre-packed duffel bag, and left without remembering to turn off the lights.

The underfunded, six-member team was to meet at the ferry that ran from Anacortes, a coastal town eighty miles north of Seattle, to Olloo'et Island, but when they arrived, hurriedly dressed and with to-go cups gone cold in their cup holders, there were seven of them. This made for some awkward shuffling of feet and discreet glances. It was like being halfway through a meal in a restaurant when a complete stranger decides to drag over a chair.

"This is John," Hooper said, clapping the stranger on the back. "John is an expert on the area's coastal ecosystem and comes highly recommended. He'll be joining us. I hope you'll all make him feel welcome."

Rachel made a noise. It was only after she made the noise that she realized she'd made it and that people were looking at her.

"Did you have something to say?" Hooper asked.

Even Rachel, who did not always judge these things accurately, suspected it would be best not to answer.

Hooper raised an eyebrow, but he went on, and she stewed. They were all experts. They had all come highly recommended. It was hardly reason enough to bring him on board at the last minute. But to object would not only have been rude, it would've required her to provide some sort of justification, which she was not, under any circumstance, prepared to do.

Rachel knew one very important thing about the *Artemia lucis,* one thing that, up until that singular moment, she felt sure no one else on the team knew. She'd been secure in this one-upmanship, and now, in the space of one introduction, she didn't feel sure anymore. If anyone else would know—could know—it would be John. She had never met him before, but she could read it on his face.

Rachel did not mean that as a figure of speech. Up his neck and ending just in front of his ear, John had the Olloo'et tattoo, the one hammered into the skin of all tribal men sometime after puberty but before taking a wife. Four rows of coal black dots. Eighty-eight dots in all.

The Olloo'et had always been small, much smaller than the better-known Snohomish whose national headquarters just off I-5 Rachel had passed on her drive. The Olloo'et were members of the southern Northwest Coast peoples, but they spoke neither Salishan nor Chemakuan nor Chinookan languages. They were culturally, linguistically, and geographically distinct. They lived on just the one island, the farthest populated island from the mainland. They were not known to other tribes as great diplomats like the Nimi'ipuu or great warriors like the Cayuses. In fact, the Olloo'et were hardly known at all.

Rachel had spent two years studying the handful of old photographs that still existed of these people, John's ancestors, a people she had come to think of as no longer a part of the world, as extinct as the Spectacled Cormorant. Of course, that was ridiculous. Languages died out. Religions died out. People did not. They assimilated and interbred, and the next thing you knew, you were on a team with John.

The rest of the team stepped forward. There were two or three handshakes and some polite nods, but later Rachel would be the only one to remember his name. For the rest, excitement and nervousness overrode everything. It zipped from scientist to scientist like static electricity, making them double-check cartons of equipment, bounce on their toes, and fiddle with zippers. Rachel was nervous, too. She clenched and unclenched her fingers inside her coat pockets, both looking and trying not to look at John, who stayed next to Hooper, the two of them leaning close when they spoke.

The ferry, which was rolling in the choppy sound waters, docked. Vehicles returning to the mainland were driven off, and the team hurried back to their cars. John, who had the build of someone who played rugby, bent to pick up his duffel. When he did, he reached his other hand out for the backpack sitting at Rachel's feet. She was on it before he could wrap his fingers around the straps.

"That's mine," she said, lifting the worn bag and shrugging it over a shoulder, well out of his reach.

"I thought I might help."

"I don't need help." Too many seconds went by before she remembered. "Thank you."

"Never?" he asked.

"Never what?"

"You never need help?"

Rachel directed her answer at his left ear. "Once. I electrocuted myself trying to rewire my bathroom light."

The last vehicles drove off the ferry, and a gull landed near their feet, attracted by an empty potato chip bag.

"I can't tell if you're kidding," John said.

"I had to get an EKG."

John didn't reply. Hooper called his name, and he peeled away from her without saying good-bye, which was fine, except that it was usually Dr. Bell who Hooper was calling for, and so she was left alone.

It was a two-hour ferry ride to Olloo'et Island. The seven-member team deployed workstations at both the water's edge and at the off-season summer camp where they were lodging. They worked as quickly and efficiently as a MASH unit setting up field hospitals. Some would work in the day. Some would work at night. Hooper would supervise both, sleeping when he could. By sundown, they were all standing in the rocky sand by the bay watching the water begin to catch a green fire, just a little at first so that Rachel had to blink and squint to be sure she wasn't imagining it.

Streaks and blooms of lime appeared along the water's edge, as though hundreds, perhaps thousands, of glow sticks had been cracked open and poured into the bay. The spots of phosphorescent neon grew and spread and joined together.

Awed murmurs came from the gathered locals standing side-by-side up the bluff behind the yellow tape. Rachel hugged herself, grinned wider than she wanted, and had to bite her lip to keep from letting out a whoop. If she'd been alone, she might have run down the whole beach hollering like a child who'd just been given ten years' worth of Christmas gifts all at once.

These tiny arthropods, related to brine shrimp, were some of the rarest living beings on earth. *Artemia* designated them as a member of their genus. *Lucis* is from the Latin *lux* for light. The lighted arthropod. Rachel loved the name. She always had.

As far as she knew, no one alive had ever seen one outside a specimen jar. They had segmented bodies, an exoskeleton, and twenty-two legs, which seemed an awful lot for something no more than eight millimeters long. With a life span of just six days, they hatched by the millions once a century and right away began to send out this bioluminescent signal. They thought—the biologists standing there at the shore—that it was for mating. (Almost everything is for mating in some way or another.) The light might be density dependent. It might be triggered by the movement of the water. They knew so little that it made Rachel's breath catch. It excited her, made her skin tingle and her heart pound. It made her feel like an explorer, a discoverer. She was about to know things that no one else had known before. Not one person. Not ever.

"All right," Hooper said to the six other scientists standing shoulder-to-shoulder on either side of him. He took a breath and seemed to be searching for something important to say. They all felt this and squared their shoulders in response, ready to absorb this fateful moment, even Rachel, who had never been one for speeches. But inspiration failed him, and they all had to settle for "You know what to do."

Rachel moved forward toward the waiting kayak with a plankton net attached to a specimen jar. This was it, she thought. This was what she was waiting for, the thing that could and would save her life.

2.

Tilda pulled into the driveway of the home that hadn't been hers for more than a decade. It was three stories with white trim and covered in weathered gray shingles. An interior designer would hire someone to "antique" shingles to look like these did. There was a porch around the front door, which was nothing compared to the multilevel decking on the back of the house that sloped right down to the narrow beach. Inside, almost every room had a bay view. It was the sort of house that people who went to wealth seminars pasted on "dream boards." There was even an honest-to-God library with a ladder that rolled along a track. At least, there had been some years ago. She'd had it installed.

Tilda turned off the car's engine and buttoned her coat. There were three newspapers in the driveway that had gone soggy in the rain, and she knew, if she opened it, she'd find a week's worth of mail in the mailbox. She pulled her collar up to her chin, and with a bag in each hand, she walked to the front door.

In the window just to the left so no visitor could miss it was one of her posters. "Vote for Tilda. U.S. Senate." It had faded, and the tape had come loose at one of the corners, which was as good a metaphor for her failed reelection campaign as anything. It was just like her ex-husband to leave it up months after it held any meaning.

She rang the bell. Shooby barked from the other side—just once to show he was on top of things.

It took Harry a very long time to answer.

She stood there, holding her bags, waiting. A car pulled up next door. She looked while trying not to look like she was looking. A man got out and didn't have to pretend he wasn't looking because he wasn't. He left the car in the drive—probably the garage was full of crap—and let himself in through the front door.

Tilda went back to staring at her own ex-door. Up close it needed a new coat of paint. The red on the trim was cracking. Around her feet she noticed the green, fuzzy lichen that took root in the pervasive damp. It was growing around the edges of the porch and had started to colonize the bottom six inches of the house. It would take a good power washing to beat it back.

Tilda thought about ringing the bell again but didn't. She thought about banging the brass knocker but didn't. That would've given Shooby fits. She thought about the neighbor who hadn't been the neighbor when she'd lived here. She wondered what happened to the old neighbors, the Feingolds. Were they the Feingolds? Maybe it was the Feinsteins. She couldn't remember and blamed it on age, which didn't make her feel any better about it. Whoever they were they'd had a cat with no tail that they'd let wander around outside until it got hit by a car. That she knew. The new neighbor was probably just as irresponsible.

He'd probably voted for the other guy.

He probably hadn't voted at all.

Apathetic. You could tell.

She'd had these thoughts about strangers a lot in the past month. Given the election returns, she was right most of the time.

Harry finally opened the door with the dog at his feet. "Come in. Come in," he said.

She hadn't seen Harry in six months. Still, he had called and asked her to come. It had taken a lot for him to do that, Tilda knew. Harry was not the sort of person who asked for help. He was the sort of person who, fully engulfed in flames, might try to operate the fire hose himself. That was, more or less, what he'd been trying to do since his neurological disease had been diagnosed two years before.

Their son, who was living in Seattle, had told Tilda what to expect. She'd heard him, but it seemed she hadn't listened. She did a poor job of hiding it.

"Harry," she breathed.

Harry Streatfield had been—still was—a classical composer. He worked at a piano and had long, spidery fingers that bent the keys to his will. Except now those fingers were wrapped around the handle of a footed cane, one of those aluminum ones hospitals and retirement homes issued. He leaned into it. His right knee was buckled, and his foot turned at an odd angle. He was putting almost no weight on that side, and the leg looked, even covered with his brown pants and sensible brown shoes, like that of a cripple.

"No." He lifted his hand off the cane and held it up between them like he was directing traffic. The other hand stayed on the door, holding him up. "If you're going to do that bullshit, you can damn well go home right now."

It was enough of Harry, even if he was trapped inside that mutilated body, to snap Tilda back into herself or the version of herself that she became with Harry.

"It's almost hard to believe you ran off all the nurses," she said.

"It was only two nurses, and they were both morons."

One side of his face was drooping slightly, pulling down the corner of his mouth and eye. Tilda tried not to stare and was grateful that it had not yet affected—although it would—his speech.

"Is that so?" she asked.

"Apparently, they're giving licenses to just anybody these days."

Harry turned around, which was a multistep process like a car executing a six-point turn, and headed into the house. Tilda followed, closing the door behind them and trying not to get impatient at the time it took for the two of them—three counting Shooby—to make it to the kitchen table.

Shooby had never been her dog. Harry had adopted him years after Tilda had been gone, but she was still fond of the mutt. Full name Schubert, he most resembled some sort of hound, but his lineage was anyone's guess. His legs were a little too long for his body, and his feet seemed like something he'd grow into, except he was as big as he was ever going to be. He was a medium brown all over but for a patch of white on his muzzle. His ears flapped when he ran and got wet when he drank. Adopted from the Humane Society, Shooby was as loyal as any dog could be. They'd met before, and he liked Tilda well enough. He liked everybody well enough—probably even that neighbor who didn't park in his own garage. But he was devoted to Harry.

Tilda dropped her bags, and Shooby sniffed them to be sure nothing dangerous was hiding inside before flopping down at his master's feet. Tilda was in the process of deciding to unload the rest of the car later and had yet to take off her coat or sit down when Harry said, "I'm hungry. What are you making for dinner?"

She blinked her most innocent look at him. "What? You're not cooking?"

The left half of Harry's face smiled.

God, Tilda hated smoke detectors. She was standing on a kitchen chair attempting to rip the guts out of Harry's, which dangled from red and blue wires from the ceiling. When she finally got the battery out of it, everything sounded muffled from the ringing echo of the screech still in her ears. Harry's hands were clamped over his like an overgrown child, and Shooby was so upset she was afraid he'd pee.

Tilda had attempted to brown some butter for a sauce to go over the chicken. It hadn't gone well. To be honest, it was no worse than the chicken, which was in no danger of giving anyone salmonella poisoning but would require big gulps of water just to get it down.

"You used to be better at this," Harry said, lowering his hands.

He was still sitting at the table. The crossword from the Sunday paper was in front of him, and he was doing it in pen. The letters were shaky, but he'd yet to ask for help with any of the clues. Almost all the squares were filled in.

"I was never better at this," Tilda said. "I have always been shit at this."

Harry knitted his brows together, something he could still do. "We ate."

"I brought home meals from the supermarket deli," she said.

"You did?"

"Of course."

"Did I know that?"

"I really don't know what you knew."

Harry tended to pay attention to only those things that interested him and had a remarkable ability to tune out those things that didn't, which often included wives and children.

"There was meat loaf," he said. "I remember there was meat loaf."

"Deli," Tilda repeated.

"It had tomato stuff on it. I liked that."

"Maybe they have meat loaf at Jake's," Tilda said.

"I don't think they do."

"Then order something else. Where's your coat?"

3.

Jake's had always been Tilda and Harry's spot. It was at the end of the road that curved around the bay, less than a mile from their house.

Harry's house, Tilda corrected herself.

Like the beachside homes, Jake's, too, took advantage of its waterfront position with an expansive and multitiered deck that they tried to keep functional in the winter with heat lamps and clear plastic tenting. It blocked the wind (mostly), kept out the rain (mostly), and made the whole place look like it was ready to be sprayed for termites.

It was early, but the restaurant had already started to fill. Strangers with cameras were tucked into burgers and piles of French fries, and the waitresses, young local girls with ponytails and small tattoos, looked overwhelmed by the influx.

Harry wanted to be out on the deck with a view of the goings-on down by the bay. Tilda said the cold would be bad for him and insisted they sit inside. Harry thought she was being ridiculous and motioned for the hostess to lead them out. The hostess looked like she wanted to be in the middle of an argument with a handicapped person about as much as she wanted antibiotic-resistant gonorrhea. If anyone could find and exploit the advantage in his disadvantage, Lord knew it was Harry, Tilda thought, and followed the two of them out onto the tented deck.

The outside temperature was in the low forties, but under the forest of heat lamps, Tilda needed to unbutton her coat. This did not remove the look of disapproval from her face.

"You used to be more relaxed," Harry said to the plastic laminated menu he was holding.

"And you used to be handsome," she said.

"You have to be nice to me. I'm dying. Besides, I'm still handsome."

Harry—and he assumed everyone else—knew quite well that he was not, which wasn't something he felt any sense of loss about. Tilda, on the other hand, had the sharp features and long limbs that tended to show up in Cubist paintings. It was a look that had not served her well as a young woman when her sense of herself was formed. Harry knew she did not understand how she had grown into her look and how arresting it could be to a certain type of man.

Tilda went on. "I don't have to be nice to you. You left me for a grade-schooler. But yes, if we're grading on a curve, I suppose you're still somewhat attractive."

It took all of her control to keep the corners of her mouth from turning up into something someone might mistake for a smile, so much so that she couldn't concentrate enough to read the menu. Her eyes just went through the motions.

"I didn't leave you for anyone," Harry said without looking away from the entrée section.

The conversation was scripted. They had some version of it every time they saw each other. It was like a favorite old movie, though the dying bit was new.

"I met Maggie six months after you moved out, and you know it," he continued with his lines.

"How is Maggie?" Tilda asked.

"Enjoying her alimony payments," he said. "She's really going to be pissed when I kick it." He changed subjects without pausing for a breath. "I'm going to have the fried coconut shrimp."

"That's terrible for you," Tilda said.

"The alimony payments or the shrimp?"

"The shrimp. It's nothing but grease and sugar."

"That's hardly a deterrent. I'm not going to live long enough to develop diabetes."

Their waitress stopped at the table to drop off water before disappearing again. She didn't introduce herself or mention any specials, and it was clear the service that night would resemble that of a drive-through window.

"Don't talk like that," Tilda chastised and then, in the next breath, "God, I want a glass of wine."

"I think I'll have some wine, too, now that you mention it," Harry said.

"No, you're not. It's not good with your medications."

A line had to be drawn somewhere.

Harry snorted. "Yes, how terrible it would be if anything interfered with my medications, which have done nothing but drain my wallet, interrupt my sleep, and upset my stomach. Let's not throw that off track."

"Imagine what things would be like if you hadn't gone on the regimen."

Tilda had kept in touch with Dr. Woo since the divorce. He had been a friend of theirs when they were still collecting mutual friends and was one of the few who managed to maintain an equal relationship with both of them. He had been the one to diagnose Harry and the one to suggest the battery of medications Harry was now taking. There had never been any hope for a cure. The best they could do, Dr. Woo had said, was try to slow things down.

The waitress returned. Tilda ordered a Chardonnay for herself and a tea for Harry before he could get a word out. He glowered, and she cut him off. "Screw with me, and I'll kill your dog just to watch him die."

Harry let out a bark of laughter so unexpected he coughed on his own spittle. He had to wipe his chin with a napkin and take a drink of water to get things under control. When they were, he said, "Quit talking. The show is about to start."

The sun, which was nothing but a pink flush on the horizon obscured by the low bank of clouds, would be gone within fifteen minutes. Yellow caution tape was strung up just at the end of the deck. Beyond it, scientists clustered under white canopies. Tables and chairs had been assembled, and laptops and microscopes were lined up and ready for use. From a distance, the researchers looked hurried and industrious, even if their movements meant little to Harry and Tilda.

Farther down the beach, a crowd had gathered to watch. They had been cordoned off, kept out of the sand, and forced to stand in the brush that grew up like a natural fence line. There were more people, including several film crews, than Tilda could remember ever seeing on Olloo'et at any one time. Two men in uniform kept an eye on things from the other side of the yellow tape, but anyone could see they would be useless if the herd decided to charge.

"You saw the news coverage?" Harry said without turning his head.

"Of course."

Tilda had worried there wouldn't be room for her car on the ferry. Tourists were flocking to the island to see the 100-Year Miracle. Rooms in the small local inns and B&Bs were impossible to get. If she and Harry had a fight and she stormed out, Tilda would have to sleep on the lawn.

Harry checked his watch. A minute passed. Two. Their drinks came. Tilda thought she saw a flicker in the water, but when she squinted, it was gone. Three minutes passed. Four. And then like someone switching on the Christmas lights, the whole bay began to glow. Just a little at first and then more and more, getting brighter and brighter. She had never seen anything like it.

"Jesus," Tilda breathed.

"I know," Harry said.

It was the sincerest conversation they'd had in months. Even the researchers, ever in perpetual ant-like motion, stopped what they were doing to look out over the water.

Harry and Tilda spent the rest of the meal watching. Generators out by the canopies were switched on, and bulbs spotlighted the workers. Those not sitting at laptops and microscopes were down by the water's edge, their movements marked by bobbing white lights from the head-lamps each of them wore.

Harry had been favoring his left hand since she'd arrived, leaving the other in his lap. But when his shrimp arrived with the tails on, Tilda watched him out of the corner of her eye use his right to pick up a knife. The utensil clattered against the plate when his hand shook. He wouldn't want her to see, so she pretended she didn't as he tried to use both knife and fork to trim off the tails. The simple coordinated effort proved too much. The shaking knife missed the shrimp and instead knocked a mountain of coleslaw onto the tablecloth. Harry cussed. Tilda didn't react, keeping her eyes on the beach.

One of the researchers moved away from the buzzing colony. She had a cell phone pressed to one ear and her hand pressed to the other to block out the ambient noise. Soon she was within ten feet of them, but she paid no attention to Tilda or the other diners. In fact, she gave no indication she saw the restaurant at all. Tilda had never seen someone so intent.

The woman caught Harry's attention, too. "Becca?"

Tilda's spine went rigid, freezing her in place. She breathed but just barely. Nothing else about her moved.

Harry's eyes went from the woman to Tilda, but he couldn't stop them from slipping back to the researcher. He opened his mouth and shut it again. Of course, it wasn't Becca. The young woman simply looked like Becca. They could have been sisters if Harry and Tilda had conceived another girl.

The pressure to say something, almost anything, was intense. "She looks a little like—a little familiar. Don't you think?"

Tilda didn't want to look at the woman, but Harry had made that almost impossible. There was, she saw from the corner of her eye, some resemblance to their daughter. They both had long black hair and the same fair but olive-tinged complexions. Most notable was the way they stood—or perhaps a way they simply were—that filled out the space around them, occupied it fully and without apology.

On the other hand, this woman looked as though she wouldn't know what a tube of mascara was for, while Becca had insisted on an extensive collection of ribbons, headbands, and barrettes and had kept them organized on her dressing table. There were similarities. Harry wasn't wrong. But they were not twins.

Tilda said none of this. She said nothing at all. They had agreed, in practice if not explicitly, never to speak of Becca. Violating that would be—Tilda didn't know what it would be. "Fatal" was the word that sprang to mind. She looked down at their food, concentrating on it.

Harry continued staring. The woman, still on the phone, moved stiffly. She had her back to the water and was looking down at the sand by her feet, her headlamp turned off. When she looked up at Harry, he turned back to his plate, embarrassed at having been caught.

His shrimp were different. Under his nose, the tails had been sliced off and the meat divided into bite-size pieces, the way you would do for a child. He looked at Tilda, but her eyes were on her own plate. With his left hand, he picked up his fork, and no one said anything about it.

Rachel hung up the phone without saying "good-bye" only because it hadn't occurred to her. The data she needed would be e-mailed shortly, and she headed back toward the tent, back toward the rest of her team, back, unfortunately, toward John.

The *Artemia lucis*'s bioluminescence was what was known as circadian. During the day, the bay looked as it would look any December, only to transform itself into a neon showpiece at night. For the next five days, they would all work in shifts. Three on days, three on nights. Rachel was assigned the night shift along with John. They would live as the arthropods lived, going dormant during the day and showing themselves only as the sun went down. Or at least everyone else would have the daylight hours off. Rachel had other plans.

That afternoon, back at the camp, Rachel had slipped two pilfered folding tables inside her cabin while the others had stopped to refill their mugs with coffee and eat cookies bought at the nearest gas station. After double-checking that the door was locked and secure, she'd set up three large aquariums like those that might hold goldfish at the local pet store, except these aquariums had been sterilized and outfitted with sensors and digital readouts to measure and track every variable that she could think of. She hooked up chillers, aerator tubing, UVA lights, and UVB lights, all to, as best as she could, reproduce a Pacific Northwest bay.

She'd first read of the *Artemia lucis* while finishing her doctorate. The mention, in a chapter devoted to animal bioluminescence, was brief but enough to lead her, after some months of digging, to the Olloo'et. Primary source material on the tribe was limited to the journals of nineteenth-century Catholic missionaries, who wrote down stories dictated by the Olloo'et, who had no written language of their own. When Rachel finally got her hands on the original diaries, she'd had to blow dust off the pages, and translating the papers, in even the most rudimentary way, took an entire summer. The priests were French, a language Rachel had gleefully abandoned after high school.

Buried in the minutia of land rights and the building of schools, which, among other things, instructed the Olloo'et people on European agricultural techniques, was a story of particular interest to Rachel. The Olloo'et man told the priest of the "lighted path from the land of the spirits." Although sometimes it was written as the "lighted path *to* the land of the spirits." Whether you were coming or going, the people reported that the arrival of the breeding was greeted with great ceremony. There would be dances and song and tents erected on the beach for the adult men of the tribe. It was the job of the shaman to walk out into the bay just as the glowing began and scoop up cups of water full of the creatures, not unlike what Rachel and the team were doing right then.

Details of the ceremonial preparation were vague, but the summary was they drank it. First the shaman and then the tribe's leader, whom they did not refer to as chief even though later historians would, and then eventually all of the adult men would have their fill. The men would go into the seaside tents, which would have been much colder and less hospitable than the cedar longhouses that were their permanent residence. For six days, they continued to replenish themselves with more and more cups from the bay, which resulted in a near-constant state of hallucinogenic trance. They reported seeing vision after vision of their ancestors and of the spirits that lived in the water and in the forest that surrounded them. They reported a feeling of great physical pleasure. The lame walked, the sick were well, and those who were injured ceased their pain. For six solid days, all of the adult males (never any women) lived in what could be compared to a modern opium den. Occasionally, the priests reported that someone died, usually by walking out into the water and never coming back.

It was not, however, the reported hallucinogenic properties of the *Artemia lucis* that interested Rachel. The world had enough LSD. What had caught Rachel's attention were the words "and those who were injured ceased their pain."

An analgesic. It had to be an analgesic. Some compound within the arthropods was a painkiller.

To say that this had gotten Rachel's attention would be understating it. Food, oxygen, sex—not that Rachel had ever had sex—nothing was more important to her than this.

It is impossible to describe what it's like to be in pain every single moment of your life. To wake up several times each night to take more pills because your nervous system won't stop reliving a single moment in time. To have exhausted every medical resource, to have death by overdose as your only way out. And then to find this. This vague, historic, impossible reference to a compound buried somewhere within the body of an ancient sea creature so small it was almost invisible. This hope—this tiny bit of hope—had kept her alive for the past two years.

And now she was here. She had the creatures in her hands, but still, the practical difficulties were almost insurmountable. Rachel needed to figure out how to keep the arthropod's eggs from going dormant, and she needed to figure out how to keep the adults alive. Then she would need to breed them in captivity and trigger the eggs to hatch, a new batch emerging every six days. Only then could she isolate the compound. If she could isolate the compound, everything would be different. She would live to see her next birthday and the one after that.

Almost insurmountable was not the same as actually insurmountable, and no one would work harder for an answer. Still, what she did not know about these creatures dwarfed what she did, and she didn't dare ask a question, not of anyone. Anything she did, the university owned. Anything she discovered, they could take away. They could take her lab, her specimens. And they would. She was sure they would if they knew. If there was something more valuable to the pharmaceutical industry than pain management, she didn't know what it was. If they knew, she would lose all control, and most important, she would not, under any circumstances, be allowed to experiment on herself. And that was all she wanted to do. That was all she wanted, and she intended to start right then.

4.

Only when the leftovers were stored in the fridge and Shooby had been let out to pee and the doors were all locked, checked, and double-checked, did Tilda climb the stairs to her room. She passed the second-floor landing, afraid to let her eyes so much as glance over the closed door at the very top of the stairs. She knew the inside had been scrubbed clean, rendered impersonal if not downright generic. She had insisted on it when no one, including Harry, understood.

Two of her cousins had come and boxed up the small pairs of underpants and the complete Little House on the Prairie series with the broken spines. They took the box of found seashells off the closet shelf and the chipped ceramic bank shaped like a puppy with three Sacagawea dollars inside. All of it was gone, but her mind saw it as it had been more than two decades ago. She knew where each dress had hung, knew the collection of stuffed bears and the names of all of them. And she had to hold much tighter to the railing to get her feet, one step at a time, to move up to the next set of stairs and away.

Harry did not understand what it took out of her to be here for him now. He did not know, Tilda thought, how much she must love him to do this. He really did not.

"Juno." Tilda hardened her voice in the way she would when dealing with an unpleasant and persistent lobbyist. "This is not your decision to make. It's mine, and I have made it."

Tilda had gotten plenty of warnings about the early years, about the midnight feedings and the toddler tantrums, but no one had warned her about having adult children, this adult child in particular. It was true that Juno had been difficult since birth. He was sensitive where his own feelings were concerned but willfully ignorant of others'. Tilda blamed herself and Harry for this. Becca's death had affected the parenting of their one surviving child. They had been overprotective and withdrawn, often at the same time. They had put Juno at the center of their world and then fell off the edge of it.

"I just think he's taking advantage of you," Juno said. "If Maggie was so much better, let Maggie come and take care of him."

Tilda wanted to set the phone down and walk away from it. She was tired, and it had been a difficult day. But Juno wasn't concerned about her feelings. He didn't get along with his father, and therefore Juno didn't want her to get along with him either.

"How's Anna Beth?" Tilda asked.

Anna Beth was a bright girl with a master's in architecture who made her living designing chain pizza restaurants but had greater artistic aspirations. Tilda had assumed she would tire of Juno. Instead she had gotten pregnant.

"She's fine. The baby's kicking."

"Right now?" Tilda wasn't immune to the lure of a new baby, as long as it wasn't hers.

"No, in general," Juno said. "Anna Beth is in the bathroom right now. She pees, like, twenty times a day."

"I see."

When the call ended, Tilda fell back onto the bed and tried to follow her yoga teacher's instruction about positive intention. She had to do something. Tilda was sure, if she kept up these thoughts, she'd end up reincarnated as one of the bright yellow banana slugs that crept through the island's leaf litter. She started by sending out good thoughts for Juno and Anna Beth's relationship. Tilda tried to imagine them happy. When she couldn't manage that, she tried to imagine them bathed in a warm light, but that reminded her of Chernobyl.

She opened her eyes and looked at the ceiling. If it weren't so cold, she'd open the window. The room hadn't been used in a while, and Harry's housekeeper had kept the door shut to save on the heating bill. It had to have been the housekeeper. Harry, if he had time to have every thought in the world, would never have landed on "reduce fuel expenses." And no one had thought to air out the space before Tilda's arrival. It was stale.

It might have been the guest room, but Tilda thought of it as her room. She had slept there for the last six months of their marriage when neither of them had liked the other enough to want to share a bed. So when she carried her bags upstairs, Tilda's feet guided her in without waiting for instruction, and she was relieved that much, if not quite all, of what she remembered about it remained the same.

It was a small room with a sloped ceiling tucked under an eave, which in another time might have been given over to some lower member of the household staff. It held a double bed, a tall dresser, and a small desk of the sort once used for ladies' letter writing. A stool that Tilda remembered purchasing at a flea market before Juno was born held the phone and could serve as a nightstand if she needed someplace to balance a glass of water or leave a book. But there was nothing else, and nothing else would fit. She liked it that way. It was simple, and it seemed whenever she ended up in this room, she needed for things to get simple.

The guest room had been the first stop on the way to moving out of the house and out of her marriage for good. Like training wheels, the room had supported her until the idea of being middle-aged and alone wasn't scary enough to make her topple over. In this room, she could try her aloneness on, and when she needed to, she could take it off until it fit well enough to wear out of the house and into the world.

Tilda wasn't sure what new role she was trying on this time. It seemed the old ones had fallen away and left her adrift without a sense of identity. "Tilda Streatfield is—" she said to herself, and fished around for an ending. She didn't have enough patience to stick with the exercise, and it concluded without success. Her new ventures in self-improvement still had a ways to go.

"I'm just tired," she decided. "It'll come to me tomorrow."

5.

Day Two of the Miracle

Some five hours later, almost to the point when night can fairly be said to be morning, Harry was downstairs in the library. It was where he kept his piano, and so he thought of it more as his workroom than a proper library. Still, the room held hundreds, maybe thousands, of books, all in white built-in bookshelves that went from floor to ceiling on three walls, with one of those rolling ladders to access them all.

Most of the books had been Tilda's. She'd taken only a few with her, leaving him with tangible reminders of her whims and interests. For quite some time, he wouldn't have thanked her for that, but he had never brought himself to throw them out either. So there they stayed. Politics, Pacific Northwest gardening, historical novels, several biographies of FDR. There were books on primitive art, chaos theory (that one, come to think of it, was his), and a farmer's almanac for every year they were married—Lord knew why. The books survived Maggie only because Harry was careful not to discuss their origins and because the library was understood to be his space and, therefore, off-limits.

When Harry was stuck on one composition or another, he would get up from the piano and walk over to a shelf, pick up a book at random, open it up, and read a page or two until sitting back down seemed the better option. The almanacs tended to hold his attention for longer. The historical novels were a sure path straight back to the keys.

It is something to be able to call yourself a professional composer without having to add any sort of hyphen to your business card. Harry did not also teach junior high band or clean offices at night. He made his living writing music, which was not nothing and was the thing, of all the things, he was most proud of. A lot of that music had gone into movie scores, and many of those movies had been horrible. But that wasn't Harry's fault, and the money came in just the same. Still, he did prefer the freedom of writing for musicians in concert halls—whole orchestras, when he could swing it—rather than trying to get the strings to come in just as the hero character crested the mountain with his army of warrior elves.

As Harry was dying, it seemed the right time to do the things he wanted while he still could, which was why he had agreed—promised, really—to compose for the Seattle Symphony Orchestra's next season. It would be Harry's fourth and last piano concerto. The promise had been extracted with not a lot of difficulty by Gerald, whose training at London's Royal Academy of Music was far more impressive than Harry's, which included leaving Juilliard without actually graduating. Gerald was the symphony's music director, now in his ninth year, and in a position to put Harry's concerto on the slate if he damn well felt like it. It was not clear to Harry if the four-night performance, which he might or might not live long enough to see, was something Gerald wanted or if it was a bone for a dying man. Harry didn't want it to matter, but on bad nights, it fed his insecurity and slowed his progress, which was the last thing he needed.

The trouble was that doing this thing, which shouldn't have been physically difficult at all, was turning out to be, and it was happening at a far faster rate than Harry had ever imagined. More often than not his fingers would not perform their digital ballet across the keys. It had even become difficult to hold the pencil he used to scribble notes onto blank scores as he worked.

Having a thought in his head that he couldn't perform and couldn't even get down properly onto paper for someone else to perform was the most frustrating thing that had ever happened to him. And while he would never tell Tilda, there had been nights before she came that the score sheets had been shoved off onto the floor, and his shoulders had shaken with sobs.

Harry knew his frustration was apparent in the music. It was only a question of whether he could consider that an artistic choice or an inevitability.

He looked down at Shooby, who was not the night owl Harry was and who had fallen asleep several hours before. The dog had long ago learned to sleep through Harry's piano playing, no matter how erratically the notes came. Harry listened to the waves outside, which were always audible even with the windows closed, and watched Shooby's chest rise and fall for a moment. The pup was on his side with his legs straight out, looking for all the world like he had fallen asleep standing up and had tipped over onto the rug. It reminded Harry that perhaps he, too, should try to rest.

One of the side effects of all the medications he was taking, of which there were many, was insomnia. When the pharmacist had first explained this, it didn't seem so bad. More time to compose while he could. What Harry hadn't realized was that induced insomnia didn't mean you weren't tired. Harry was tired all the time with the fuzzy-headed lack of concentration and clear thinking that came along with it. He simply couldn't fall asleep.

This night, however, couldn't be blamed entirely on the medication. Harry kept a small end table next to his bench. It was a landing place for the day's flotsam—plates with dried-out sandwich crusts, stained coffee cups, junk mail. But it also held the only framed photo of Becca in the house. It was difficult to see unless you were sitting at the piano bench, and no one sat at the piano bench but Harry.

Becca was nine in the photo. It had been taken just a few months before her death. She was out on the beach. You could see by her hair that the wind was blowing, and it was cold. She wore a red coat and rain boots and had her hands shoved deep in her pockets, probably because she hadn't taken her gloves, even though Tilda was always reminding her. Their old dog, the dog two dogs before Shooby, ran out in front of her, looking back to see if she was coming along. Harry had taken the photo himself, and Becca had looked up just as he did. The water, the sky, the beach, and the dog were all gray. Becca was the only thing that brought color to the scene.

And then Harry had killed her.

It had been an accident, but it was still his fault. Not metaphorically. Not in some larger, grander sense. He had done it. They had been driving to the pharmacy. Becca had asked to come with him, and he had let her. There had been mail to go out, bills. Harry had placed them on the dashboard, and they had slid off onto the floor during a turn. There was no reason they couldn't stay there, but he had decided to reach down under his seat and pick them up. He had left one hand on the steering wheel, taken his eyes off the road. It was so banal, so ordinary, a thing he could have done a million times without consequence. But this one precise, particular time, they crossed the center line. There was an oncoming car, a van. Harry had survived. The other driver had survived. But Harry had killed his only daughter. And for a moment that evening, when he'd sat at the restaurant table and looked across the beach, it was as if he had her back, all grown up. And then she was gone, morphed back into the body of a woman he'd never seen before.

Harry put his hand on the footed cane that sat in constant vigil now by his side and pushed up. It took some shuffling to make it to the other side of the room, which woke Shooby and brought him to his feet, ready to accompany Harry. He didn't have far to go. The room's only other major piece of furniture was a sofa. Across the cushions, he'd asked his housekeeper to tuck in a sheet and a quilt and bring down one of the goose feather pillows from his bed. He told her this was to save time, allow him to work through the night, nap, and be back up with a minimum of lost seconds in between. But the truth was that some days he was afraid to climb the stairs to his bed. Some days he was too weak, too off-balance, too scared to try for fear that he'd fall, and no one would find him. He would be crumpled on the floor in pain and with the crotch of his pants wet while he waited for someone to notice. It wasn't every day that this seemed a possibility. But it was some days, and there was no way to know what day it would be.

And it was painful. God, was it painful. Harry hurt most in the places he could control the least. At night, it felt like there was an electrical fire under his skin, and during the day, his limbs ached. It was like getting a bad shot when the needle doesn't go in right, and the vaccine is thick and hot, and you can feel it in the muscle.

Harry made it to the sofa, which was now his bed, and lowered himself down. Once he was settled and under the covers, Shooby lay down, too, head on paws and his eyes closed. Harry closed his eyes, too, but he wasn't at all hopeful about it.

The warm water was all around her, pressing down, so that Tilda couldn't hear anything else, couldn't feel anything else.

Stroke, stroke, breathe. Stroke, stroke, breathe.

The pool was enclosed in glass. Glass walls. Glass ceiling. Outside was black. It was morning but too early for the sun, too early for anyone but Tilda and the Y lifeguard, a teenager, who sat in the chair with his eyes closed, trusting she, the only member in the pool at that hour, would take care of herself.

Stroke, stroke, breathe.

She liked how warm they kept the water. Eighty-four degrees that day according to the white board next to the locker room. Nearly body temperature. Like amniotic fluid. So like her own skin, she could feel no temperature at all. Not hot. Not cold. No thoughts or feelings at all. Just water.

Stroke, stroke, breathe.

6.

"Rachel!"

Hooper was on the other side of the restaurant's parking lot waving to her. His hood was up against the early-morning drizzle, but John's was not. The two of them were standing next to the team van. It seemed every time Rachel looked up the two of them had their heads together.

She sighed and waited for a brown Cutlass to cross in front of her at a crawl as the old man behind the wheel inspected each empty space he passed. The wheels kicked up spray from one of the many potholes that had filled overnight, and Rachel jumped back to avoid it.

The team—or rather the other members of the team who were not Rachel—had all voted to end their workday at a diner for breakfast. The others were sleep deprived but full of energy. The switch in their circadian rhythm was painful but not yet unbearable, and the once-in-a-lifetime-ness of the work was still seeping enough dopamine into their brains to make them excitable. They talked too fast, laughed too fast, got angry and frustrated too fast, and they were all cooped up together. It was exciting to everyone but Rachel. It made Rachel nervous.

After the burns, her recovery, such as it was, had continued on and off for several critical years. Her schoolmates went on without her, their development bifurcating from hers at the age of six. It was not possible to return to the moment that they split—her from everyone else—and so she continued on her own path, evolving in isolation and adapting to her unique environment not unlike the platypus. A platypus that did not play well with others.

So here she was, a fifteen-minute drive from the study site and a tantalizing five from her bed, overfull on the early bird special—two eggs, two sausages, and fried potatoes served over a plate-size pancake. She'd taken the last two white pills from her pocket stash two hours before, which was too long, and now Hooper wanted to talk to her.

The Cutlass moved on, and Rachel crossed at a trot, anxious to get it over with.

"Exciting, isn't it?" Hooper said.

"Highly altered levels of dopamine are associated with schizophrenia," Rachel replied, shoving her hands in her pockets.

"What?" John asked.

"It's pathological," she said, even though she hadn't been talking to him.

John opened his mouth, but Hooper cut him off. "I think that's Rachel's way of telling us we're a little amped," he said, moving his body slightly, so he was between the two.

Rachel was pretty sure that's what she'd just said.

"You wanted something?" she asked, looking at John out of the corner of her eye and tugging on the collar of her jacket to make sure it was covering the uppermost parts of her scar, something she did so frequently it was an unconscious tic.

Ever since the ferry crossing, she'd seen John looking at her and not bothering to avert his eyes when she caught him. No one else seemed to notice this, which was unfair. Everyone noticed when she did something wrong.

"I was just telling John that you're one of the country's leading experts on bioluminescence," Hooper said.

Two sentences in, and already Rachel's palms itched.

"I've been studying density-dependent bioluminescence in bacterial colonies," she said, hoping it wouldn't interest him.

"It's a big jump from bacteria to arthropods," John said.

He stood with his feet a little too far apart, Rachel noticed. Even with hands in his pockets, his elbows were wide. Everything about him took up as much space as possible, and he spoke as though he regularly deployed the Socratic method. She did not like him. Even if he were not here invading her work space, she did not think she would like him. He was generally unlikeable. Not like Hooper. More men should be like Hooper. Her feelings for him existed somewhere on the fuzzy and incommunicable border between great respect and platonic love.

She took a small shuffle step closer to the professor and said, "No, the chemistry is the same. You're an ecologist. That's why it's confusing to you."

Hooper jumped in. "John's advisor at Michigan is an old mentor of mine. He told me John was making a big splash in their department and that his tribe is from this area originally."

Hooper looked to John for confirmation.

"The Olloo'et people," John answered. "They lived on this island until the 1920s when most of them were relocated. My parents still live in Tacoma." He paused and then said, "You're white. That's why it's confusing to you."

Rachel ignored this. She was studying his cheekbones. They were broad and flat in a way that might be mistaken for Asian along with a shorter-than-average nose that widened quite a lot at the nostrils. Textbook Olloo'et.

"I recognized the tattoo," Rachel said. "Was it done in the traditional way?"

John brought his fingers up to his jaw, and a flicker of something crossed his face. But it was too fast for Rachel to catch it.

"Most people assume I got drunk and made a bad decision."

A shot of pain ran up Rachel's back, and her hand, beyond her control, slipped into her pocket feeling for pills that weren't there.

"You didn't answer my question," she said.

"Yes," he said, "it was done the traditional way."

The Olloo'et tattooed by hammering charcoal into the skin with a bone needle. The pain, it was said, was excruciating. Pain being of particular interest to her, she had several gruesome follow-up questions, but Hooper—perhaps suspecting where this was going—didn't let her ask them.

"When I heard he had cultural, as well as scientific, interests, how could I not bring him along?" Hooper sounded jovial, like inviting another scientist on a once-in-a-lifetime expedition was akin to pulling up an extra seat at Thanksgiving.

"The more we can learn, the better we can protect the species," John said.

Rachel's thoughts made a hard turn. "You think the *Artemia lucis* are threatened?"

"I do."

"Do you have evidence of this?"

"I think anything that breeds once a century has to be considered threatened. I'd like to see this whole area protected in some way. If we can gather enough evidence, maybe we can figure out how to best do that."

He was talking like the whole team was on his personal mission. Rachel didn't like that. She found it was always best to assume that the only person who supported your findings was you. She looked to Hooper for backup.

"Well," he said instead. "I hope the two of you can get acquainted, share ideas."

Rachel thought this was overly hopeful, but it was Hooper, and so she nodded and turned back toward the truck, happy to dust off John's words like dirt from her boots.

7.

It had been easy not to notice the hours pile up as they worked, gathering and measuring and plotting through the night. But as she drove the deserted two-lane road to the camp, Rachel's eyelids began to develop a worrisome inclination to snap shut for longer than a blink and then reopen suddenly when her brain remembered that driving was something best done with the eyes open. When she pulled up in front of her cabin, the first thing she did, even before shutting the door of the borrowed pickup, was fifteen careful jumping jacks to keep the blood flowing.

In the truck's camper was a large red cooler marked "food." On the way to the worksite it had contained the team's allotment of sodas and deli sandwiches. For the trip back she'd stuffed it with pilfered containers full of her samples.

Until that day, she had only seen poorly preserved specimens of the *Artemia lucis* in the dim university basement. They had been gathered and dumped into formaldehyde solution during the last breeding, back before there had been such a thing as a World War, before women could vote, before antibiotics and the Spanish Flu, before her great-grandparents had even been born. It was hard to believe that those very specimens, ancient and rotting, were the parents of the creatures she carried with her now. All that time and only one generation had passed. There really was no margin for error.

Rachel lowered the tailgate and was reaching for the cooler when she heard the sound of running footsteps on oyster shell. She looked up and froze, as though hit with some sort of palsy. She didn't want to look as though she'd been caught, but it wasn't going well. She had read once about a bird called the Eurasian Roller that vomited a noxious, orange liquid all over itself to repel would-be predators. This did not seem, in the moment, altogether unreasonable.

"I believe," John said, not at all winded when he stopped less than three feet away from her, "that we got off on the wrong foot."

Rachel watched for signs of fatigue from the sprint but saw none, which made her uneasy. It meant that there was one more way in which they were mismatched, and she held the deficit.

"It's not important," she said.

Rachel hoped this would end the conversation. It did not.

"I should've done a better job of explaining myself," John said.

Rachel watched him take a deep breath, holding it in his diaphragm as experienced lecturers sometimes did. She thought about closing the back of the truck and walking away, but leaving the samples alone with him was impossible. She was trapped, unable to leave until he left.

"It would help you to know a little more about my people's history and their relationship to the breeding."

"It wouldn't," she said, stopping him before he could begin the next in what was sure to be a long line of sentences.

"It wouldn't, what?"

"It wouldn't be helpful."

"How could it not be helpful?" he asked, his prepared speech derailed.

"It's irrelevant." She tugged on the collar of her jacket.

"I don't understand," he said.

"When the arthropod's primitive neural structure receives circadian inputs, oxygen combines with coelenterazine, a luciferin. Unlike other species, I believe the *Artemia lucis* synthesizes coelenterazine—"

John cut her off. "What is your point?"

"I'm explaining the mode of bioluminescence and why anthropology is irrelevant."

"I can provide context," John said.

Rachel ignored this. "You are free to study the *Artemia lucis* in whatever way you choose. Hooper has made that clear by bringing you on, but please do not interfere with my work."

The day was warming, but she tugged at her collar for the third time, pulling it up near her ears.

John put his hands in his pockets. "You are a difficult woman to connect with, Dr. Bell."

Rachel knew this was probably true, but it was also true that she did not wish to connect with him. It didn't seem he had taken this into account.

"Is there anything else?" she asked.

"I don't suppose I can help you unload something."

"No, thank you."

"You're going to leave that out here?" he asked, nodding at the cooler.

"No, I just don't need help," she said.

"Right. I remember. You're the one who never needs help." His tone was sharp, which was fine with Rachel if it meant things were coming to a close. "But the offering and receiving of assistance is the basis of modern society."

He caught her off guard.

"It's what normal people do." He was still finishing the last sentence when he reached into the bed of the truck, grabbed the cooler's handle, and gave a tug. It barely moved.

Rachel seized his jacket and yanked his arm back. "Don't touch that."

John looked at his arm and then at her. "What's in there?"

"Nothing. It's empty."

"It feels like there's a body in there."

"I said it's empty."

"Do you expect me to believe that?"

"I don't expect anything from you at all," she said.

John took a step back. "Do you have some kind of disorder?"

Rachel felt herself redden. She knew who she was and how she came off, but his words were intended to be hurtful, and they were. "No, I just don't feel well."

"You should see a doctor," John said before turning and walking away.

It was nine a.m. before Rachel, finally alone inside her cabin, could take a double dose of whites, emotionally relieved, as much as physically, to have them.

She'd brought in the cooler, which took up much of whatever floor space had been left. The whole building was no more than twenty feet by thirty feet and consisted of one main room and a small bathroom, which hadn't been updated since the 1950s and gave nothing but lukewarm water. This hurt her more than the lack of sleep, and to add insult, the cabin's heat barely functioned.

Cold shower. Cold room. Few things made her scars hurt more than cold. She hoped she'd brought enough pills.

The main room, which had floor-to-ceiling wood paneling and a linoleum floor, held two beds, but only one of them had sheets and blankets. The other mattress was bare and looked like something that might harbor lice. The windows had ill-fitting, pull-down shades, and at the end of the room were two collapsible tables. They were identical to the ones in the makeshift lab in the empty mess hall, which still bore construction paper decorations from the summer before along with a 1943 advertisement for campers. "A training in self-reliance is a Godsend in wartime."

With the door locked—and after another fifteen jumping jacks to clear the slush from her brain—she opened the cooler and began removing container after container of bay water peppered with the tiny *Artemia lucis.*

8.

John was pressed up against Rachel's cabin. Hers was the farthest from the camp's entrance, which meant this eastern side had no neighbor. The foliage was dense here even in the winter, and with his dark green coat and brown pants, it was as if the trees had absorbed him and made him one of them. He had been out there for almost an hour, having walked away from Dr. Bell and her truck toward his cabin and then, once he was out of her view, right past it and into the woods.

He didn't think it was possible to explain to someone else—someone who was not a member of his tribe—what the breeding meant. It had been the central event in tribal life, something anticipated, as well as feared. It transformed those who experienced it, and then inevitably, took some of their lives as payment. It was something every generation was responsible for, even those who would not themselves experience it. Those members were duty bound to prepare the next generation, who would pass on their knowledge, and so it had gone until there were so few Olloo'et left—maybe no more than fifty now—that they had become something closer to a myth than a people.

The breeding had, it was said, come before them, and it would continue on after. But his elders had not been ecologists. They had not been given front-row seats to every major environmental disaster in the last decade. They had not seen whole swaths of ocean, whole sections of waterfront, whole colonies of animals wiped off the face of the earth in less time than it took to smoke a cigarette. He did not have the faith of his ancestors. He knew the breeding would continue only if it were allowed to continue, and it made him watchful, and being watchful made him distrustful, and being around Dr. Bell made him paranoid.

John knew about the hallucinogenic effects. All members of the tribe knew, but the breeding had been too rare for the news to catch the public's attention. If it became widely known, the effect would be devastating. And to become widely known, it only needed to be known by one wrong person.

Dr. Bell had recognized his tribe. She had known his tattoo, and she was, of all possible things, a chemist. So he stood there, and he watched.

The pull-down shades that were in each of the cabins, including hers, were at least thirty years old. They were ill-fitting, cracked, and torn and, in this state, provided him with perhaps three-quarters of an inch of clear glass to see through. The view was a small slice of the middle of the room, which was taken up by her camp bed. He could not see the door to his left or the back of the room to his right. It was not the best of eye lines, but it was the best that he could do.

He had seen her come in struggling to carry the cooler. It was clearly as heavy as he had thought, and his mind worried it like fingernails over a rough scab. Inside the cabin, she moved stiffly, something she had not done at the site, and he watched her do a few old-lady jumping jacks, which was odd but not interesting.

It was cold, and he was tired. The ground was wet. The trees were wet. The ferns that rubbed against his pant legs were wet. He wanted to go to bed, and then he saw it.

She crouched down by the cooler, and when she stood up, she was carrying specimen containers from the site, two large ones. She walked toward the back of the room, disappearing from view. Light from a source he couldn't see—something not overhead—switched on. Then the sounds came, the low hum of mechanical equipment. Within a minute, she had returned. Again she crouched down and again came up with more containers, more and more, over and over. Thousands, hundreds of thousands of *Artemia lucis* passed through her hands.

John's body went rigid. He knew it. He damn well knew it.

He pressed his face harder to the window desperate to see where she was taking the containers, what she was doing with them, but no matter how hard he tried, his three-quarters of an inch of glass did not get larger. He took a step back, his hands in fists. He would have to get inside.

Rachel tested the UVA and UVB lights, the fans, and the pumps. She made sure the chiller, which kept the tank water swirling around the flasks at forty-five degrees, was working, along with the probe thermometers. Each of those had an alarm that would beep if anything got too hot or too cold. She made small but different adjustments to each tank and placed the samples in. It was important that there not be too many creatures in each flask, or they would use up all their resources and die or cannibalize one another.

Once she was satisfied with the setup, Rachel made her notes, copious and exacting notes, which she kept in her bag at all times and the bag with her. It would be better if she could keep a closer eye on the tanks at night, if she could make measurements and adjustments. But the cabin was too far from the bay, and her absence would be impossible to explain.

She could not have carted all of this additional equipment unnoticed onto the ferry, and so she'd rented a box at the Olloo'et Mail-and-More that promised to accept and hold packages for as long as she continued to pay them. There was no limit on the size of the packages, and when she'd snuck off to retrieve everything shortly after arriving, the Mail-and-More manager was both relieved to be rid of her things and annoyed with her existence. She suspected that future box rental agreements would include more restrictive language.

Rachel stepped back and studied her makeshift lab. The room was not quiet. The fans, which she hoped would simulate breezes across the bay, hummed along with the pumps and chiller. The aerating lines gurgled. The two different light systems, one for each spectrum, shined. She wondered if the light was too bright and would kill the specimens. She wondered if the stress of relocating them to her lab would kill them. She wondered if the arthropods lived a symbiotic relationship with some other living thing in the bay that she had yet to guess at, and the lack of it would kill them. She wondered about all the things she hadn't thought to wonder about yet.

Standing there, scrutinizing her work, Rachel became aware of her smell. It wasn't a good one. She was still wearing the clothes she'd worked in all night. The layers of fleece and waterproof nylon, which kept her from freezing in the bay chill, held sweat to her skin, where it dried. What didn't smell of sweat smelled of the bay, like salt and fish. Sand coated her jeans. It was only this degree of filth, an uncomfortable degree, that kept her from collapsing onto the one made bed in her cabin. The insides of her eyelids itched with tiredness, but still she dragged herself into the shower. The water was cold, far too cold, and she had to move carefully to keep it from touching her back. She did the minimum amount of soaping before pulling on two layers of sweats and surrendering to her four allotted hours of sleep, trusting the alarm on her phone to wake her in time to go back to the beach.

9.

Harry still hadn't made an appearance when Tilda went downstairs to start the morning coffee. She'd showered and dressed and blow-dried and perfumed after coming home from the pool, but she could still smell chlorine if she put the back of her hand to her face. It was something she both loved and hated about swimming.

While the coffee perked, Tilda walked to the sliding glass door at the back of the house and looked out at the bay. The water was gray and choppy with no trace of the Miracle. It was like a tart who had returned home and washed herself clean of lipstick and eye shadow.

Tilda could see the waves lapping at the beach and the rocks, but when she slid the glass door open, the sounds hit her like a whoosh, washing over her and bringing with them the salty brine that sticks to your skin and gets in your nose. She breathed it in, and something in her loosened.

She stepped onto the deck. It was multitiered and as large as the great room inside the house. The wood was smooth under her bare feet, weathered and probably in need of some kind of sealant. Tilda padded across it, watching the scientists down by the water's edge. They seemed less hurried during the daytime, less frantic. They clustered under the canopy, which in the early-morning gloom was lit. She could hear the growl of the generator along with the crash and hiss of breaking waves, one not so different from the other.

She took the stairs gingerly, her feet already picking up blown sand. At the bottom, careful of the rocks and broken bits of shell, she curled her toes into the beach and let them sink down into the wetter, colder layers below.

With one hand on the balustrade, Tilda swung around to walk south and didn't make it a single step. Under the deck, up close to the house where the open area was more than a dozen feet high, stood a sailboat. It was a small sailboat. It couldn't have held more than two people. The wooden hull was painted white on the bottom and red at the top. Four jacks, two on either side, held it upright so that the keel dug an inch or so into the sand. From the hull jutted an outrigger on two arms, and it had a mast that nearly touched the uppermost decking above.

She stared at the hulk of a thing as though it were some sort of leviathan that had come up from the waves and beached itself here under the house.

"Tilda!"

She heard Harry shouting and then the *clomp, clomp* of his cane on the deck above her.

"In a minute!" she yelled back.

She took a few steps forward. Inside the hull was the sail. It had been lowered and stuffed into a bag with a long length of rope wound around it. She wanted to unwrap it, see what kind of shape the material was in. She touched the wooden edge of the cockpit with the tips of her fingers.

"Tilda!" Harry shouted again.

She closed her eyes before she could bark back something short-tempered and regrettable. "I'm coming!" she said instead, giving the thing one last look. "Hold your horses. I'm coming."

Tilda had climbed three-quarters of the deck stairs, her head not yet visible at the top, and already Harry was complaining. "You left the sliding glass door open."

Had she? If it was open, she supposed she must have. "So close it," she said, reaching the top of the stairs and then walking past him and into the house.

Harry was wearing the same gray sweatpants she'd seen him in the night before. His hair stuck up in a sort of spasmodic swirl in the back, and he needed a shave. Both of those things could be remedied in less than fifteen minutes, rendering him fit for public display. That was one disparity even the ERA had not attempted to address, and Tilda would carry that bitterness with her until the end of her days.

Harry followed her inside, and Shooby ran over, prancing a circle around their feet. She would need to walk him. She'd forgotten dogs needed walking first thing, having not had one of her own since leaving Harry. They were lucky Shooby was so well trained and had been doing his Kegel exercises.

She patted his ears, and he followed her through the house toward the kitchen. Harry brought up the rear.

"When did you get a boat?" she asked.

There was a pause, and Tilda knew he had forgotten it was down there.

"Maggie wanted it," he said when his memory caught up. "Bought it from the guy who used to run the hardware store but never did anything with it. Now it just sits down there eating insurance money."

"You could get rid of it," Tilda said, opening the cabinets and taking down coffee cups.

Harry shrugged. She knew he shrugged. She didn't have to look over to see it. It wouldn't occur to Harry to get rid of the boat. It just wasn't Harry's way. It would rot through and sink into the sand first.

"Is it seaworthy?" she asked.

"Doubt it. Been sitting there for years."

Tilda took a pause to think about the next sentence, but in retrospect, it probably wasn't a long enough pause. "I could take a look at it."

Harry snorted, and this time Tilda did look up. "What?" she asked.

"Nothing."

"I know about boats."

"Didn't say you didn't." It took Harry this far into the conversation to make it with his cane to the kitchen table. He seemed stiffer than yesterday, but there was no point in mentioning it.

"I grew up with boats."

Tilda took the half-and-half from the fridge and gave it a sniff before dumping it down the drain and throwing the carton in the trash.

"That was still good."

"It smelled like baby vomit," Tilda said and loaded the stainless steel four-slice toaster. The dials were unnecessarily complicated, a purchase of Maggie's no doubt. It was too early for that, so she just pressed the two plungers and let the crumbs fall where they may.

"Those sell-by dates are just there to get you to waste more and buy more. You're a cog in the consumer machine."

Tilda splashed plain 2 percent, which passed the sniff test, into her coffee and put the half gallon back. Harry took his coffee black. She poured it for him and placed it on the table along with a tub of margarine and a half-empty jar of orange marmalade that had formed crystals around the lid, making it hard to open.

Harry watched her struggle, which ended in victory, before saying, "I eat strawberry jam on my toast."

"Since when?"

"Since the past ten years."

"Don't be ridiculous. You love orange marmalade."

"If I loved it, the stuff wouldn't have turned to sugar in the jar."

Tilda didn't see a good reason to answer that. The toast popped, a little too light perhaps but serviceable. She dropped the hot pieces onto a small plate and brought both that and a jar of strawberry jam to the table.

"You're not eating?" he asked.

"I'm going to walk the dog," she said. "Don't eat it all."

"I'm not making any promises, and don't be long. I need a ride into town." Harry had stopped driving six months before and had sold his car. He had done it quickly and a little impulsively, but he was glad that he had. He wouldn't have wanted to have to look at it sitting in the garage getting dustier each week.

Tilda decided it was in her best interest to take something to go and snatched a plain piece from the top of the stack, making Shooby wait a minute more while she buttered it.

"A ride into town for what?"

"I'm going to church."

Tilda stopped buttering. "You don't go to church."

Harry was using a spoon to fish a glob of seedy jam out of the jar and onto his toast. Spoons had a larger margin of error than knives. "Why do you believe my life stopped when you moved out?" he asked, getting the glob onto the bread and using the back of the utensil to spread it around. "I eat strawberry jam. I go to church."

"What church?"

"Episcopalian."

Neither she nor Harry had ever gone to church during their marriage. They had never gone, and they had never discussed going. They had not, as far as she could recall, had a single religious conversation of any kind up until this very moment. It was one of their sincerest compatibilities. That and their love of orange marmalade.

"Well, don't expect me to go in," Tilda said.

"Don't worry. You've been banned. We had a vote."

"I thought churches were supposed to welcome everyone."

"Most of the time, but we made an exception in your case."

10.

Rachel woke to her alarm, feeling more tired than she had a few hours before. She sat up and groped for her hooded sweatshirt, the one with the university's husky mascot on the front. She was already wearing a long-sleeved thermal shirt, but the cabin's heater was anemic, and the doors and windows leaked.

This was the second night of the breeding. There were only four nights left. In the time it took fish to go bad, she would know—either everything would be different, or she would spend what savings she had left on her own burial plot.

She rolled over to the side of the bed, slid out, and performed her stretches, impatient at the time they took. When they were done, she padded over toward the glowing, whirring, hissing tanks at the end of the room. There was no doubt the machinery was alive, and it spoke to her exhaustion that she was able to sleep next to the growling, gurgling—

The thought froze Rachel before she could finish it.

She pivoted on her heel like an officer corps cadet, careful of her tender back, and opened the door of her cabin a crack then enough to stick her head out. The air smelled of rain and the rot of leaf litter. In another half hour or so, her colleagues would be waking up, too, but for now she saw no one and stepped outside, shutting the door behind her.

Cold in her stocking feet, she listened. There were birds and leaves that rustled. She heard those right away. No fans or sprayers though. She had half a second of relief and then stilled her breath and listened harder. Maybe there was something, or maybe it was the blood rushing in her ears. She pressed the side of her face to the cabin door. There. There she could hear something. She could definitely hear something. She pulled her head away. Still, Rachel could hear the sound, faint but there. Faint enough to wonder if she was imagining it but distinct enough to tell herself that, no, she just knew what to listen for. She pressed her ear to the door two more times and then walked around the side.

The ground was muddy with only a layer of pine needles over it that went from thin to downright sparse. She could feel her feet sinking in like pressing a handprint into wet clay. She'd never get her socks clean again. Almost to the window, she stopped. There were already footprints here, larger ones with the tread of a hiking boot. When and who? Careful not to disturb them, she tiptoed up to the glass and listened. It was thin, single-paned. It was easier to hear through the window. And maybe someone had heard, someone who had stood right there.

Her stomach roiled with worry like a snake in death throes.

Shit.

She needed to do something, and she had no idea what. She hadn't brought any soundproofing materials with her, and she didn't have time to find a hardware store and shop for something suitable. She tried to follow the trail of boot prints, but they disappeared in the leaf litter almost immediately. It was hopeless and a waste of time.

Rachel ran back around to the front, her feet sinking deeper in the mud.

And then she screamed.

She had been looking down at her feet, scanning the ground, and she had not seen him. The top of her head bounced off his chest, and

John reached out a hand to steady her then withdrew it sharply as though he'd been given an electric shock.

"What are you doing here?" Rachel demanded.

"Can I come in?"

"No." The single syllable came out fast like a punch. He started to respond, but she cut him off. "Wait, show me the bottoms of your shoes."

"What?"

She was looking at his feet, but he didn't raise one up. "Show me your tread."

He did not comply. "Dr. Bell, there are some issues I'd like to go over with you."

"I explained myself earlier," she said.

His were more like running shoes than boots. She thought the prints had been made with boots, but she couldn't be sure. She couldn't even be sure what the bottoms of her own shoes looked like.

"Well, apparently, I didn't explain myself."

He took a step forward, coming uncomfortably close. She stopped thinking about feet. Her heart, already jumpy, shifted into the next gear. He was too near her. She didn't like it.

"You can find me at the site," she said.

"I've found you now."

"Now isn't a good time."

"Really, why?"

Rachel wanted out of the conversation. She wanted him to go. "What I do on my off hours is none of your business."

John leaned in, closing the space between them that was too small as it was.

"What you're doing will destroy the breeding, which makes it absolutely my business."

"That's not true. You shouldn't lie."

"We are here to study," John said. "We take only what we need to understand and, by understanding, to protect. No more."

Anger bloomed beneath her nervousness. He was so conceited, so demanding and entitled. He had walked in off the street and dared to treat her as an underling to be dictated to. It was so like that kind of man to expect her to acquiesce.

"This is a biological phenomenon. It doesn't belong to anyone, including you, which puts you in no position to dictate how others work," she said.

"How are you working exactly?"

"I'm working right next to you," she said.

"No, you're not."

Rachel fought the blush that was threatening to spread up her neck to her cheeks. "Why won't you show me your shoes?"

"The *Artemia lucis* are part of our culture, not some cheap way for you to get high." His voice had started low and menacing but was rising with every word. Rachel started to object, but John continued right over her. "I shouldn't have to tell you how vulnerable this population of animals is. The last thing it needs is for you to be starting up a side business for drug heads. You open the floodgates, and the entire colony could be destroyed."

"You don't know what you're talking about," Rachel hissed, hoping her voice would lower his. It did not work.

"Then let me in."

"No."

"Why not?"

"Because I don't like you."

"You go inside then," John said. He tipped his chin toward the door but didn't move away from it.

"You leave first," she said.

"No."

"John!"

They both turned to look. Hooper was down the road, far enough away that he appeared as small as an action figure. He was yelling as loud as he could and waving his arm. Whatever he wanted from John, he wanted it right then.

John looked from Hooper to her and back again before blowing a sharp puff of air between his lips. "Not over," he said to her and took off down the road at a jog.

Rachel slipped back into her cabin, slamming and locking the door. She took little breaths, pushing her heart rate down. Her blinds were closed, but he had heard her experiments. Obviously, he had. She would need to work fast.

Her duffel bag of clothes and toiletries lay on the spare bed. It was unzipped, and bits of clothing hung out the gape like a panting tongue. She pulled out sweaters and fleece and all the thickest things and carried them over to the window, pulling the string that turned on the bare bulb in the middle of the room on the way. She stood on the end of her bed and leaned precariously over to the top of the window. With her roll of duct tape, she began to secure the clothes over all of it, covering the glass, the shade, and the framing.

She had to tear the tape with her teeth, and she wished desperately for a few more inches in height. She was leaning out too far, still in her muddy stocking feet, her footing shaky on those two measly inches of footboard, when gravity got tired of waiting.

Her hands scrambled for purchase, anything to slow the fall, but it was much too late for that. Her back caught the edge of the cooler, scraping all the way down. She landed with a clattering thump like someone dropping a hundred-and-thirty-pound bag of potatoes.

Rachel howled. It was the sound of an animal under attack. She brought her knees up to her chest and rolled to her side. The pain was so bad that she hoped to pass out. Instead she began to retch, dribbling down her cheek and onto the floor.

As soon as it stopped, she started to move, trying to get herself up off the cold linoleum. She kept her back as still as she could, moving like Frankenstein's monster. Once she had her feet under her, she went straight to the tanks. She knew the fright of the fall would have released adrenaline into her system, and it was dulling the pain. As bad as it was, it would get worse. It was best to move now and get the work done before the adrenaline drained away.

"Focus," she said aloud, colder and more demanding with herself than she had been even with John.

She peered through the ambient chilled water into the flasks. She picked one up, pulled out the aeration tubing, and held it close to her face. She could see them in there, her *Artemia lucis*. They were some of the smallest creatures on earth that were still visible to the naked eye, still recognizable as having bodies and parts. They were a reddish brown with an exoskeleton so insubstantial it was transparent in places. She could count their twenty-two legs if they held still. And they were holding still. They were dead.

Rachel went to the next tank and then the next, taking out flasks and inspecting them. Dead. All dead. Every one of them. She'd only been asleep for a few hours, and already they were gone.

She felt hot tears welling up behind her eyes, threatening to trickle out. She took a wet, ragged breath and ordered herself to calm down. She was overtired. She was in pain. She was frightened. She wasn't think-ing clearly. Maybe what the *Artemia lucis* needed were currents, tides. She didn't have a way in these tanks to simulate currents and tides. Some-thing like that would be a complicated build. Researchers might take a year to get conditions for a study right, run the tests, and write up the data. She only had a few days. The timeline was unheard of in her field.

God, her back hurt.

Rachel made herself be still. She imagined being back at the uni-versity lab. Hers was a sterile narrow room just wide enough for two black counters running down each side with cabinets above and stools below. The dingy white walls were decorated with safety procedures for fire and earthquake, along with biological and chemical accidents and bomb threats, which were mostly a problem in the primate lab. One small instruction sheet explained what to do in case of a mental break-down. Sadly, the instructions presumed it was a lab mate who was cracking. There were no self-treatment guidelines. She breathed in and out, and her heart rate calmed.

The adrenaline was draining out of her system faster than she'd anticipated. She stayed still. What would I do, she asked herself, if I were back in the lab under these conditions? Hurt. Failing. She would, she reasoned, deal with each problem in order, one at a time. She was in pain. That was the first thing. She was in pain, and she had an opportunity.

There was one box under the tables that was still sealed with packing tape. Moving as best she could, Rachel sliced it open and unpacked the contents. She pulled out an extra-fine mesh and separated the arthropods from the waste, algae, and other debris in one of the flasks. Then she deposited the dead *Artemia lucis* onto a digital scale accurate to one 1/1,000th of a gram.

Nothing in any of the original sources mentioned dosage. And without knowing what compound created the analgesic effect, she couldn't make meaningful measurements. She continued to scoop until the digital readout said one hundred milligrams. Assuming only a tiny fraction of the *Artemia lucis* was the compound, Rachel considered this to be a very conservative amount.

She took them off the scale and transferred them to a mortar, picked up the pestle, and started to grind. By the time she'd gotten the mixture down to a smooth, homogenous paste, she was sweating. It was harder than she thought it would be. In her backpack, she had half a bottle of orange juice. She took it out, opened it, and set it next to the mortar and pestle. Then, with a plastic spoon, she scraped up the paste, careful to get every last bit. The glob was smaller than a raisin, not much to hang her life on. There was no alternative plan. She had no other brilliant ideas, no discoveries, no chemical breakthroughs humming in the back of her mind. Either this would work or she would die. That was really all there was to it.

The pain was increasing her heart and respiratory rates. There was little time for sentiment. Rachel put the dose in her mouth and swallowed.

God, it was nasty. Fishy in the worst possible way. Rachel's mouth turned down at the corners, and she stuck out her tongue. "Oh, Jesus. Gah." She reached for the bottle of juice and chugged.

When that was gone, an unpleasant film of fishiness still coated her tongue. She was tempted to go brush it, but with such a small amount, she feared removing some of the dose. In her first aid kit, she found a few cough drops and popped one in her mouth. It helped, but the memory lingered.

She picked up her pen and documented everything she'd just done. Then she looked at her watch.

"Shit."

Hooper was going to be furious. She had to hurry.

Rachel stripped off her clothes, including the muddy socks, which she tossed in the bathroom trash on the way to the shower. She soaped the most critical parts in record time. In the cold cabin, she'd gotten used to speed dressing, and it wasn't until she stood in front of the mirror combing her wet hair back into a ponytail that she noticed the knot on the side of her head. She must have hit it when she fell. It had swollen up half an inch from her temple and was already bruising. It could have been worse, but it was bad enough, and it was noticeable.

With gentle fingers, Rachel touched the center of the knot. No pain. She leaned closer to the mirror and concentrated. She touched it again—harder this time, hard enough to hurt a wound like that. She felt the pressure. She felt her fingers against her head but no pain. That was then she noticed she'd showered, dressed, and combed her hair. She'd done those things like—like a normal person.

No pain.

No pain at all.

Rachel bent forward. Just did it—without taking a breath, without stiffening her muscles, without preparing herself, without anything.

No pain.

She stood up. She was almost afraid to think it, to think anything at all, lest that be the thing that burst the spell. But she couldn't stop herself. Rachel spun around. She spun around with her arms out. She spun like a little girl would spin. Rachel spun and spun, and then she laughed. She laughed until tears streamed down her face.

For the first time since she was six years old, Rachel was not in pain.

11.

Tilda had dropped off Harry at the Episcopal church. It was small with a newer addition on the back, painted white with a peaked gray roof and a bell tower perched like an afterthought on top. The sign out front with the moveable white letters that announced service times did, in fact, say VISITORS WELCOME, but Tilda was true to her word. She did not go in. Instead, she drove the quarter mile to the gentrified stretch of downtown, which had been far more down-on-its-heels when she'd lived there.

Now all the buildings had been painted the same shade of white, and all the plants were green and some even in bloom despite it being early December. A public employee was up on a ladder starting to hang large red ribbons from each light post. And there was a four-foot bronze rooster that had been yoked with a real evergreen wreath in front of a fancy garden shop. Tilda imagined the flower boxes would soon all be replaced by potted poinsettias. There was probably a schedule for it by which all the shopkeepers had to abide. It was as if her downtown had been taken over by a particularly strict condo board.

On top of it all, none of the stores carried anything practical anymore. You couldn't buy a jar of off-brand peanut butter or a book of stamps or get someone to clean your teeth. All of those things had been moved to the uglier utilitarian buildings that had gone up in the 1960s across town. Here your options were fair-trade coffee for four dollars a cup, a designer sweater for two hundred, or a plate of pasta with "basil foam" for thirty-five.

There was still the head-in diagonal parking that she remembered, but she was lucky to find a space, something that hadn't been an issue before. The hardware store she liked was gone. Probably run off by the pet accessories store that had taken its place. It seemed to Tilda that any creature lacking thumbs and speech did not need an accessory of any sort, and people thinking they did were ruining everything good and worthwhile.

In retrospect, this might have been overstating things a bit. But Tilda had used up her goodwill on thinking happy thoughts for Juno and accepting Harry's strawberry jam and sudden enthusiasm for the Eucharist, so she went right ahead and blamed the gentrification in general and rhinestone cat collars in particular for any of the changes that didn't suit her, which was most of them.

If Tilda were telling the truth, which she wasn't ready to do just then, she would admit that the changes made her feel as if she no longer belonged. This was not her home anymore. She was not a senator anymore. She was not employed anymore. It was as if her entire life had orphaned her, and she was left to stand alone holding a suitcase in the hopes someone might take her in. But Tilda was not thinking about any of that. In fact, she was actively and purposefully not thinking any such thing.

Tilda jaywalked at a jog, letting her open coat flap, with one of the two books she'd packed under her arm. The coffee shop was bright and full of people and noises. The baristas behind the counter wore mismatched, flowered aprons over their jeans. They had tattoos and easy smiles, and they brought peppermint tea and warm cherry pie to Tilda's table, which was the sort of thing Tilda liked in a person. She begrudgingly forgave the place for being new.

Like the aprons, none of the furniture matched, and the art on the walls was done by island residents. The unframed oil paintings had

low three-figure price stickers next to them. The work was unprac-
ticed and would be hideous in someone's home, but it was right for
foamy coffee drinks.

Tilda was lucky to get a seat. The Miracle tourists had found the
place, and she was surrounded by swirling red, yellow, and blue Gor-
Tex. Galoshes squeaked on the linoleum floor, and she was poked
more than once by an umbrella wielded by someone also carrying an
overfull latte and holding the hand of a toddler. Fortunately, the pie
was excellent.

It had been her plan to start her new book, but the shuffle of faces
and bits of conversation going in and out of hearing range were dis-
tracting. She found herself sipping her tea with an FDR biography
open but facedown next to her plate, which was naked but for some
crust crumbs and a few bright red smears of cherry filling. She was
thinking of nothing in particular, which was a rare pleasure that was
interrupted.

The door opened for what seemed the fiftieth time since she'd
come in, and Mr. Not-the-Feinsteins stepped over the threshold and
stopped. He looked startled and unsure of how to proceed. The line
leading up to the counter snaked all the way to the door, and by entering, he was already at the end of it and facing a twenty-person wait.
Probably, Tilda thought, they would be out of cherry pie by the time
he ordered.

Mr. Not-the-Feinsteins stepped to the side, and she thought he
would turn and leave, having decided the cost-benefit analysis for
his double espresso did not total in the bakery's favor. But instead he
walked right past the line of customers and up to the counter, a wake
of disapproving glares accumulating behind him. Tilda added hers on
principle. Some people.

She watched as he smiled and chatted with one of the baristas, a
brunette who might have been twenty-six and wore a head scarf
around her hair like Rosie the Riveter, her bangs nothing but a curl in
the center of her forehead. Mr. Not-the-Feinsteins was younger than
Tilda but had at least ten years on the barista, who did not send him to

the back of the line. He leaned forward, his arms folded over the glass pastry case, and cocked his hip.

Tilda made all sorts of judgments based on this. The barista disappeared into the back, and he stayed where he was, passing the time eyeing the hand pies, brownies, and croissants, both plain and with almond paste. When Rosie returned, she had two large brown paper bags like those from a grocery store. Both were filled with a rainbow of long baguettes, everything from the darkest rye brown to pale golden. She came around the counter and handed them to him, and he turned to leave without ever taking out his wallet.

Tilda was staring at him as he turned to go, and he caught her staring. She averted her eyes, but when she looked back, he was still standing there, holding an indecent amount of bread and watching her. To her irritation, he did not look away but instead came right toward her. Her shimmery soap bubble of solitude was about to be burst.

"I think we're neighbors," he said when he'd done a sliding zigzag through the crowd, looking a lot like a waiter used to navigating dining rooms. He set down one of the bags on her table and held out his hand. "I'm Tip."

"Of course you are," she said.

She could smell the bread. It was probably still warm, and it was hard not to touch the bag to see.

"Pardon?" he asked.

"Nothing. How do you know we're neighbors?"

He smiled, and it showed off expensive orthodontia. "Serious detective work. My front-of-house manager told me. That and I saw you show up yesterday with suitcases."

"Who's your—was it a front-of-house manager?"

"No one you know. She heard it from the bartender at Jake's, who's been around forever. Word on the street is that you used to be an islander. Welcome back."

"Thank you, but my stay isn't permanent," Tilda said.

Tip was making himself at home. He'd sat the other sack down and moved them both to the far side of the table, leaning them against the wall, before sinking into her empty chair.

"I'm glad Harry has someone staying with him," he said.

"You and Harry are friendly?"

Tip pressed his lips together and crinkled his chin. "Friendly might be pushing it. His dog dug up three hundred dollars' worth of brand-new plantings, and there was disagreement about their replacement."

"How do you know it was Shooby?" Tilda asked.

"That's how my disagreement with Harry started," Tip said. "I'd rather have a nicer conversation with you."

She repressed the urge to roll her eyes. Tilda had spent the past decade around men who flirted with any woman sitting across from them. They flirted in the hopes of sex, yes. But they also flirted to deflect meaningful negotiations. They flirted as a form of dismissal. They flirted to win votes, to curry favor, to assure themselves of their charms, and they flirted because they'd been at this popularity contest for so long that it came like breathing. Tilda didn't know how she'd ever be able to see any man flirt again and not wonder what highway project he was looking to save.

"Tell you what," Tip said, glossing right over her inner monologue. "Why don't you come to my restaurant tonight? It's just three doors down. You'll be my guest."

Tilda shook her head and opened her mouth to deflect the invitation.

"Please," Tip interrupted. "This island is too small for neither of you to like me. Besides, I already have all this bread, and someone has to be there to eat it."

"I'm going out," Tilda said. She delivered this news from the room's doorway, indicating her desire not to linger.

Harry was sitting at the piano trying to put the last ten or so notes he'd played in the right order. They were recalcitrant, and he was losing his patience with them. Shooby knew the signs and had retreated under a Shaker-style chair in the corner with the rawhide bone given to him by the last nurse Harry had run off. When the rawhide mixed with Shooby's drool, it made a paste that smeared onto everything the bone touched.

"Take that away from him," Harry said, pointing with his favorite Blackwing pencil at the dog.

"What for?" Tilda asked.

"It's disgusting."

"It's not hurting anything. It's fine."

"It's not fine. It gets everywhere."

This wasn't a conversation Tilda wanted to continue, so she decided not to. "I made you a sandwich. It's in the fridge. The chips are out on the counter along with the cookies. Don't eat too many of them."

"What are you eating?"

"I told you I'm going out."

"You didn't tell me that."

Tilda and the kids had learned not to talk to Harry while he was working. It wasn't that he didn't want to be interrupted; although he didn't. And it wasn't that he was in a foul mood when interrupted; although he was. It was that he remembered nothing of any conversation. He became a temporary amnesiac on every topic that was not the composition at hand. When he was thirteen, Juno had once interrupted Harry to tell him he needed to be picked up at the airport the following Tuesday. He was flying to Georgia to visit Tilda's parents, his first time on a plane by himself. Tilda would be away on state business when he returned, so Harry needed to take the ferry to Seattle, drive to the airport, and pick him up. Harry promised he would. Juno sat alone in the terminal for four hours before a concessions worker got concerned and called security, who called Tilda in Olympia. It had not been her task to pick him up, but Tilda had been mortified, and it had taken a long time to forgive Harry.

"I did say I was going out. I said it less than two minutes ago. You weren't listening."

Harry either ignored the criticism or didn't hear it. "Out isn't very specific. Where out are you going?"

"I'm going to a restaurant. I don't expect to be late."

"You're going by yourself?"

"I'm meeting someone."

"Who?"

"The neighbor." Tilda gestured in the appropriate direction.

"Why the hell would you have dinner with that jerk?"

"Because he asked me to, and it was the polite thing to do. He said he hoped to improve relations with us."

"Well, he can go suck a lemon." Harry had taken off his reading glasses and now put them back on. "He doesn't even have a real name."

"His name is Tip."

"Like I said."

Tilda wasn't in the mood to concede the point and, having imparted the information she needed to impart, turned to go.

"You're dressed up," Harry said to her back.

Tilda looked down at herself. She'd changed clothes three times and had only settled on the black cigarette pants and ivory ribbed turtleneck because putting on something else seemed even more absurd than what she was wearing. She wasn't at all sure ivory was her color.

"It's a dressy restaurant," she said.

"Tell me this is not some ridiculous date."

"Of course it's not," Tilda said and felt herself flush. It was not a date. She had already had that argument with herself, and having had the argument proved that she had entertained the merest notion that Tip might have been suggesting such a thing when he'd asked her. She had told herself that was ridiculous, but she didn't appreciate Harry saying it. When Harry said it, it sounded mean. It sounded like she was being silly.

"Some of us are simply capable of making friends," she said and walked out of the room.

On the way to the front door, Tilda stopped at the thermostat and turned it down. It was getting far too warm in the house.

12.

According to the missionaries, the glowing green ribbon that appeared around the island once every one hundred years represented to the Olloo'et either a path from the ancestral world to this one or the other way around, depending on how it was translated. So those who drank of the bay's waters would either receive spectral visitors—a sort of personal haunting—or their souls would be transported to a spectral plane, which is an entirely different kind of thing.

One of the missionaries recorded in his diary that several members of the Olloo'et tribe confessed to him that they feared being transported and never being able to return to their bodies—that the spirits were, in fact, actively working against their return—and, if they did manage to come back, the men feared they would be cursed for their impertinence. It was not the sort of thing Rachel had given serious thought to. A native tribesman in the 1800s had a number of things to be afraid of—starvation, small pox, and syphilis for starters. A soul coaxed across the spectral divide and forever trapped in a netherworld seemed, by comparison, overblown. But then again, those men had not taken magic mushrooms behind the Dumpster at the Stop-N-Go when they were sixteen. Rachel had, so the extra shimmer that the electric lights began to take on and the patterns that appeared in the sand while she worked at the research site were nothing more than pleasant flashbacks.

Compared to LSD, the visual effects were minor. There were no melting faces. She didn't suddenly see only in black and white. Time did speed up for a moment and then slow down. It wasn't easy to follow a lot of text on her computer screen. Side effects. They were side effects. A minor inconvenience she would happily tolerate if it meant feeling like this for the rest of her life.

"You want a soda?"

Rachel blinked. She couldn't clear her mind, but she could concentrate harder. She tried that. "What?"

Hooper was standing over her. She didn't remember how he'd gotten there. His face had more and deeper lines than usual. The wrinkles had turned to folds. It was, of course, the light. The white tents they'd set up on the beach just beyond the water's edge had the kind of lightbulbs hanging from the supports that she associated with mechanic shops. They plugged straight into an extension cord, which plugged into their generator, and each bulb had a little aluminum half shell around its backside. They made for odd shadows and pockets of light and dark under the tent. It made Hooper look strange. It probably made her look strange, too. Rachel didn't want to look strange. She tried to do a better job of arranging her face.

"I asked if you wanted a soda." He was holding out a can of Diet Coke he'd pulled from the cooler. Meltwater from the ice was dripping off of it and onto the table that held three of the team's laptops.

"Yes," Rachel said. "Thank you."

Hooper stood there while she opened it and took a drink. His presence made Rachel self-conscious of her movements. This was, she thought, exactly like taking magic mushrooms behind the Stop-N-Go, except this was the part when she had to go home and talk to her mother like she hadn't been taking magic mushrooms.

Rachel set the can down next to the laptop she was working on. Marcus, who had forgotten to pack a knit cap for his prematurely balding head and so had a hoodie up and tied under his chin, was sitting in the chair next to hers at his own laptop. She'd known him for a year or so. He tended not to say too much, which was what she liked about him. They were flash freezing a portion of the sample they had collected for future analysis. Another portion they were preserving in formalin for taxonomic identification. Rachel had taken detailed photographs of the preserved *Artemia lucis* under the microscope, and she was e-mailing the images back to colleagues at the university. Enlarged, the arthropods looked like B-movie monsters.

John had kept his distance, volunteering to take the kayak out and check the ADCPs that measured water temperature and currents. Once away from shore and the artificial light, he was invisible, out somewhere on the bay, paddling farther and farther away. If something happened to him, no one would know. Not until it was too late. This thought did not upset her.

Rachel let her hand move up to the knot at her temple. She didn't want Hooper or Marcus to notice her doing it. She pushed on the swelling. She pushed hard. Still nothing. No pain. It had been more than five hours since she'd taken the dose. This was excellent. She had to write it down.

Every hour, she'd been testing her pain responses in both her back and her facial bruising. She wrote it all down. It was still zero on a scale of one to five. She had estimated her back before taking the dose to be a four-point-five. She checked her watch, recorded the current time, and wrote in detail all the side effects she had become aware of. The last thing she needed to do was take her temperature and pulse rate.

Rachel stood up, and once she did, she wondered if she'd done it too fast. It felt like she'd exploded from the plastic folding chair like a pilot being ejected from a downed aircraft. But then again, it might be time getting elastic again.

Hooper had taken an interest in a spreadsheet open on someone else's screen. He didn't look up.

"I have to pee," she said.

"Thanks for the heads-up," Hooper said.

Marcus glanced at her and rolled his eyes.

Rachel gathered her backpack and hurried out of the tent. Earlier in the evening, she'd been out in the bay collecting samples close to shore and wearing waders up to her waist. But she was done with the wet work for the night, having deposited her portion of the team's samples where they belonged and secreting away her own new supply. Now in sneakers, it was easier to run up the beach, sidestepping the rocks and brush to the stairs and then up the stairs to the top of the cliff. The doing of it—the sheer physical ability—was exhilarating.

Porta-potties had been set up by the public parking lot. She ducked behind one, checking over her shoulder to see if anyone was watching. No one was. Rachel squatted down and leaned her back against the blue plastic wall of the toilet. It didn't smell, at least not too much.

Her shoes crunched. The asphalt was covered in a thin, blown layer of sand that scratched and scraped with every adjustment of her body weight. Near blind in the dark, Rachel unzipped the backpack. It was navy blue with a leather bottom. Loose change rattled around the small front pocket, along with some stray Tic Tacs and empty gum wrappers. It had accumulated ten years' worth of accidental pen marks and stains and was not the sort of thing anyone would so much as bend over to steal, but to Rachel it had become the most valuable thing in the world. She reached inside and fished around for the small, metal flashlight. When she found it, she twisted it on and put it between her teeth. Both hands free, she pulled out her notebook and started recording data.

"What are you doing?"

The flashlight clattered to the ground. Her balance failed her, and she fell the last few inches to the asphalt, slamming her notebook shut before looking up.

Even in the low light, she could see the tattoo on John's face. It made him look ancient somehow, like he was from another time. She didn't like it, and she wasn't sure if he really looked that way or if it was another side effect.

"Stay away from me."

Her flashlight had rolled over by his foot, shining bright as ever. He looked down at it but did not stoop to pick it up.

"What are you doing?" he asked again.

"Nothing." Her answer sounded childish even to her.

"People who aren't doing anything don't hide behind portable toilets."

"I'm not hiding."

"Yes, you are."

This wasn't a question, and Rachel didn't answer it. In the silence, the sound of the waves below seemed to get louder and closer. "I asked you to leave."

He moved his eyes down to her shoes and then back to her face. "This isn't like huffing paint under the bleachers."

"If you don't stop, I'll file a report with Hooper."

"I hope you do. I hope you tell him exactly what you're doing." John bent at the knees, dropping fast into a crouch. The quick move scared her, and she tried to skitter back, banging into the plastic toilet.

"My people have been living with this phenomena since the time of the creator. If you were as smart as you think you are, you would listen."

"If you had anything worth saying, you wouldn't have to corner people," she spat.

"I'm giving you a warning, Dr. Bell, the same warning that was passed down to me. The breeding opens a doorway. Souls can pass back and forth easily during this time. If one of your souls crosses into the spiritual plane, you may not get it back. You may be"—he paused to consider the word—"unwhole."

Rachel knew the Olloo'et believed in multiple souls. The loss of the bodily soul was death. The loss of either the immortal soul or the soul attached to their name would lead to something worse than that. The missionaries had used the word "damnation," but that was a Christian concept that the tribe lacked.

"If you believe those stories, we have nothing to discuss," Rachel said, trying to put more force behind her words than she felt.

"Don't be so damn literal. I am trying to help you."

Rachel held her notebook to her chest. "You have offered nothing like help—nor have I asked for it."

John pushed himself back up to standing. "Your pupils are the size of a cat's, Dr. Bell. Keep it up, and neither of us will have to say anything to Hooper."

And then he turned and walked back down to the tents.

Harry had no business being out on the beach alone, but it was a little late to be having that realization. Even Shooby seemed concerned. Harry had gotten on his shoes and his coat and gone out the sliding glass door to the deck all right. Even the stairs down to the sand weren't so bad. He had his cane in his left hand and the railing in his right. It was slow going but without incident. The beach, however, was turning out to be a different kind of thing.

Beaches on the island looked nothing like Florida postcards. The sand all but disappeared below the bits of driftwood and surf-worn rocks. Bits of feathery red seaweed and green kelp with floating bladders were scattered like trash after a concert. There was always something to step over or go around, and the sand beneath it shifted under his feet, which had not been fully under his control for several months. In fact, he couldn't always feel them. He could no longer trust that he would know where in the process of taking a step he was. It was as though he were always having that awkward moment of thinking there was one more stair and discovering too late and with a jolt up his shin that there was not. He could no longer watch the horizon but had to stare down at his shoes wherever he went.

The beach after ten o'clock on a cloudy night was a very dark place. Harry was looking down at his feet, but they and the landscape of sand, all of those treacherous miniature hills and valleys and trip hazards, was indistinct. He had to rely on his cane, which sank too deep when he put his weight onto it, and it took effort to pull it back up again.

It would've been hard not to be angry in a situation like that, and Harry wasn't trying. So he just went right ahead over the hump to furious. He couldn't even take a walk in what was, by all rights, his own backyard to clear his head. Harry's work was going miserably. No matter what notes he played they didn't say what he wanted them to say, which was certainly because what he wanted changed from moment to moment even when his fingers did cooperate. How was one to write about the end of life when life was ending? His emotions wouldn't stand still long enough to be captured, and he had no perspective. He had no perspective, and he would never have it.

Harry was furious that he had already agreed to provide Gerald this piece. It had been an arrogant thing to do in his state. He was afraid that it would turn into an embarrassment, that his career would end with people saying, "Well, he was very sick—" as an excuse.

Harry was considering pulling out. Gerald would argue, of course, but what could he really do? That was the one bit of freedom afforded to Harry these days. What could anyone really do to him?

With this morbid thought, Harry stopped trying to walk. He'd only made it a few dozen yards anyway. He had thought he might walk along the yellow tape toward where most of the looky-loos had gathered, down by the public stairs that led up to the road above, but instead he decided to give up and make the slow, unsteady trudge back to his sleeping place on the couch. Maybe he would watch *Law & Order*. It was bound to be on one of those channels. But first he needed to rest, so he looked up.

The bay was so much brighter than the day before. The green fluorescence stretched from the water's very edge, where it lapped a flat plane into the sand, all the way to the horizon. The ocean was lit from below, and the light shimmered two feet above the water like God rays. It was unearthly in the most literal sense. Harry had no context for this, no comparison point. The sight of it arrested him, and while it was hard to look at it and hold other thoughts in his head, he was, for a moment, grateful that he had lived long enough to see it.

And then he fell.

Harry let out a yelp on the way down. He had tried to catch himself with his cane, and Shooby, who never abandoned his post, was underfoot. The cane came down on Shooby's leg, and the dog let out his own miserable cry, which caught the attention of the crowd.

Harry wasn't sure if he had hurt himself. It didn't bear thinking about.

"Shooby? Shooby?"

Harry was belly down in the sand, only able to prop himself up with his left arm. His cane was out of reach, and so was the dog. He'd limped several feet away.

"You okay, boy? You okay?"

Shooby hurried to his master's side, showing as much concern for Harry, but he wasn't putting weight on his back left paw.

"You need a hand?"

Harry looked over, but all he could see from where he lay was thirteen miles of leg. The man appeared to be a giant. It was like trying to get a full look at a sequoia from up close. You just couldn't get it all in your view.

The man ducked under the yellow tape to the civilian side and crouched down in the sand beside Harry.

"I'm fine," Harry said, even though he hadn't been asked and ambiguity remained. "But my dog is hurt."

Shooby pressed his cool nose to Harry's neck. He had never been one for grudges.

"Well, we should take a look at him then, but let's get you better situated first."

Harry did not take an instant liking to most people. There were too many unknowns, but he was skewing positive on this man. He did not try to take away Harry's dignity—what was left of it lying facedown there in the sand.

The man, who was wearing rubber boots, jeans, and a jacket that seemed too light for the night, turned to call over his shoulder. "Rachel," he hollered. "Come take a look at this dog, would you?" And then back to Harry, he said, "I'm Dr. Eugene Hooper. Everyone calls me Hooper."

"Harry."

"Well, Harry, you have a good side?"

"The left is better than the right, but good might be an overstatement."

Hooper crab walked closer to Harry's left side and said, "Would you like to put a hand on my arm?"

And with that he let Harry clutch on to him and, using his thirteen miles of leg, slowly lifted both of them upright without it seeming like he was helping that much at all.

When they got themselves situated, Harry noticed Rachel. She had come when called, and once Harry noticed her, it was all he could notice.

"Harry," Hooper said, "this is one of my researchers on the collection team, Dr. Rachel Bell. Rachel, this is Harry."

Rachel held out her hand to shake. Harry was conscious of being covered in sand. He wiped his palm on his coat before offering it. "I'm concerned about Shooby. He's limping."

Hooper had fetched Harry's cane from the sand, and with it, Harry was standing under his own power. This final development was the last bit of interest for the looky-loos, who turned their attention back to the water.

Rachel looked uncomfortable. Whether she was uncomfortable with him or Hooper or just with herself, Harry couldn't tell. She looked down at Shooby.

"Dogs aren't my specialty," she said.

Another man had joined them. Harry hadn't noticed him before. He was young and darker skinned than the others with a tattooed pattern running up his neck and face, something, Harry was sure, he would regret in middle age. Rachel took a step away from him.

"My house is right over there." Harry gestured with his chin. "But

I'm afraid I can't carry him, and I'd rather he didn't put weight on that leg. If you wouldn't mind?" He directed the question to Rachel.

"I can do it," the tattooed man said. "I'm done recording the readings."

Hooper interrupted. "No, I need you. Rachel can go."

Rachel gave the professor a look and then scooped up Shooby, who offered no resistance. She didn't say anything, just stood holding the dog and waiting for direction. Harry gave one last look to the younger man, who'd set his mouth in a thin, stern line.

"This way," Harry said.

13.

They'd walked back to the house in silence, and the need to keep his eyes on his feet had kept Harry from staring, which was a small mercy. Harry was never so aware of how slow he moved as when someone was waiting on him, and Rachel had waited at the bottom of the stairs for him to clear them all before coming up.

"This is your house?"

She was looking up at it, much as Harry had tried to get all of Dr. Hooper into his line of sight. Watching her, he had the feeling that his home was garish. It was large, and all the lights were on and shining through the windows. It was like his house had gone and made itself gaudy while he'd been away.

"Yes." An apology seemed in order, but Harry didn't have one, so instead he said, "Would you mind bringing him inside? I'll call the vet."

Harry led her into the informal dining room off the kitchen where he'd eaten toast with Tilda. He picked up the phone and dialed from a list of emergency numbers Maggie had typed, laminated, and taped to the cradle. Fortunately, numbers on the island tended not to change much.

When he got through to an after-hours person, he described the situation and answered a short list of yes-or-no questions, after which he was told that it didn't seem like an emergency and that Shooby would probably be fine until Harry brought him in the next morning. Harry didn't like that answer very much. It wasn't that he wanted Shooby to be having an emergency as much as he felt the need to fix what he had broken as soon as possible. Harry wanted very much to do something. But there wasn't much for it, especially as Harry wasn't driving anymore. He hung up the phone.

Rachel had taken a seat at the table with Shooby in her lap. Shooby, who was a medium-size dog, filled the space and from his perch could reach the tabletop, which he was licking for crumbs. It should have gotten him a scolding but didn't. It didn't seem to bother Rachel either. She was looking around the room and into the kitchen, which was full of more garish things, most of them stainless steel and granite. Maggie had insisted on a full upgrade.

It took a moment for both of them to notice that Harry wasn't saying anything but that he was staring. She caught him and gave him her full attention.

"My daughter died when she was nine," Harry said, trying to find someplace else to put his gaze. "If she had lived, she would have looked exactly like you."

Rachel didn't say anything.

Harry tried making eye contact with the dishwasher. "That was probably more than you wanted to know."

"Not really," Rachel said. "How did she die?"

"A car accident," Harry said.

Rachel nodded and went back to inspecting her surroundings. Shooby nudged her neck with his nose just as he had with Harry on the beach. It seemed that was going to be a thing with him from then on.

"Would you like to take off your jacket?"

"No," she said. And then, as though it took her a moment to remember her manners, "Thank you."

Rachel had worn her hair in a ponytail that night. It was the obvious thing to do, keeping her long hair out of her face and her work, especially in the wind that blew constantly off the water. But wearing her hair up exposed her neck and the upper portion of her scars. Her jacket collar covered it. The house could have been 112 degrees, and she would have left it on.

"Are you hungry?" Harry asked.

"Yes," Rachel said, "but I can't stay. I have to get back. We're very busy."

"Of course," Harry said. "I'll make you something to go." He started off toward the fridge. "Who was that other man, the one with the tattoo?"

"John," Rachel said. "An ecologist." She was running both hands over Shooby's ears, and he was leaning into it.

Harry took out the plate Tilda had left him. He hadn't eaten yet. He'd been too worked up to eat. Now he was giving his dinner to her. He limped and shuffled around the kitchen gathering tinfoil and plastic baggies and a handled sack from his last trip to the pharmacy. Leaning against the counter for support, he wrapped up the sandwich and stuffed a handful of chips and too many cookies into baggies. The last time Harry had done something like this it had been for his kids, and Tilda had complained that he gave them too much food.

"They're schoolchildren not longshoremen," she'd said and took the lunch-packing duties away from him, which was what she did when things weren't done how she would have done them.

He put it all in the sack. "Do you want a bottle of water?" he asked.

"We have sodas back at the tents."

"Okay then." He handed her the meal.

"Was it a stroke?"

"Pardon?" Harry asked.

"You have reduced mobility on your right side, including slackening in your facial muscles."

"No, neurodegenerative."

She nodded. "Well, thanks for the food," she said. "I'm getting pretty tired of eating out of the communal cooler."

"I can imagine," he said. Although he hadn't really. She was getting up to leave, and he didn't want her to go. "It must be interesting, the work you do."

Rachel shrugged. "Most other people don't think so, but I like it."

"You get to see a miracle up close."

"The water glows due to the preponderance of bioluminescent arthropods. Lots of other animals do it. Some deepwater fish, a squid off the coast of Japan—which makes the water look a lot like this but more blue—certain kinds of bacteria. Fireflies. Everyone knows fireflies. You've been here a long time?"

Harry's brain lurched at the change of topic. It was like someone dumping the linguistic clutch. "We're not one of the original island families, if that's what you mean. We came with the first wave of gentrifiers."

"What happened to the original families?"

"A lot of them are still around, but it's getting harder to hang on. There aren't a lot of ways to make a living on the island, so when some of the larger land holdings got parceled up and developed, the only people who moved in were people who already had money. The cost of living went up. Most of the original folks—the Kalers, the Wests, the Abernathys—have jobs in town and small places away from the water. My pharmacist is an Abernathy."

Rachel thought about that for a moment. "So you're an invasive species," she said.

Harry smiled. "Don't say that to Tilda. She likes to think of the newer people as the problem."

"Who's Tilda?"

"My ex-wife. She's staying here for a while."

Rachel nodded, as though having one's ex-wife move in was nothing that needed further questioning. She might have been being polite, but Harry was beginning to suspect there were things in which Rachel took an interest and things in which she didn't, and those were not always the things other people would choose.

"Where are you staying?" Harry asked, still trying to keep her in the kitchen a little longer.

"At the camp."

Harry made a face. Juno had gone there one summer as a day-camper. Tilda had taken care of most of it, but Harry had a strong memory of a parents' night that involved a talent show and a spaghetti dinner cooked and served in the mess hall. The pasta had tasted like canned Chef Boyardee and came with a piece of white bread and half a pear, also out of a can. The next year Tilda sent their son to sleep-away camp on the mainland, possibly just so none of them would ever have to eat that food again.

"I haven't been up there in years," Harry said.

"It's cold, and there's almost no hot water."

"That doesn't seem very comfortable. Do you have to stay there?" he asked.

"The university won't pay for hotel rooms for all of us, if that's what you're asking."

"I mean is there a reason, a reason other than money, to stay there?"

Rachel pinched her brows together like she didn't quite follow. "There's nothing special about it. It's just cheap and big enough for all of us."

Harry had hit upon a thought. If the idea were music, he'd be scrambling for a pencil.

"I was just thinking that the camp is a bit of a drive, and it's not very comfortable."

Rachel waited.

"You could stay here."

"All of us?" Rachel asked.

"Oh, uh, no." Harry had not foreseen this leap. He could not have been less interested in the rest of the group. "I'm afraid the house isn't that big. I meant you. You could stay here. As repayment. For helping me tonight." He stopped talking and then with a jolt started again. "Not just with me. With Tilda and me. I'm not suggesting—I wasn't being inappropriate. I just hate to think of you out at that camp. It isn't very nice."

Rachel's eyes were brown but not dark brown. They were a swirl of fawn and woody green and something almost golden that reminded Harry of an animal. Her pupils were quite large, and behind them, a lot of calculations were happening. He waited for whatever it was to be tabulated.

"I have a lot of equipment," she said. "I can't come if I can't bring it with me."

"Of course, feel free."

"It's a portable lab. There are fans and aerators. It runs twenty-four hours a day and makes noise. And I'd need to have a place to set up. Some tables."

"I don't sleep much anyway," Harry said. "I can't imagine your work would make any difference."

"Then I accept."

"Good."

Rachel looked down. "We're getting sand everywhere," she said.

Harry was so pleased that it seemed a shame to concentrate on something as ridiculous as sand. But she was right. He could, now that he was paying attention, feel it crunching on the hardwood floor as he shuffled along. Tilda would be annoyed.

"I suppose I should've taken my shoes off by the back door," he said.

"Here," Rachel said. "I'll do it."

He did not resist. He sat and watched as she worked off first one shoe and then the other. The lamp behind him reflected in her shiny dark hair, making a circle of light on the crown of her head.

Rachel broke the reverie. "I'll knock these off outside and leave them by the door on my way out."

"Thanks," Harry said.

She didn't offer a platitude in response, just headed back to her work with his shoes and a bag full of his dinner.

"You'll be back?" he called after her.

"I'll be back," she said.

When Rachel got outside, she took the steps down to the sand at a jog. Her heart worked harder than it should have, and her hands were tingling. She would write that down in her notebook but with an asterisk. It could just be the adrenaline. She needed to get her work away from John, and now she could. It was like a piece of unbelievable luck that fell from the sky. It was like winning a contest she didn't know she'd entered.

She ducked under the yellow tape and took off toward Hooper. She would tell him she was driving the old man to urgent care and would be taking the truck.

The chef's table was capable of seating a dozen diners, which made Tilda feel all the more conspicuous sitting there alone. Only a bar separated the kitchen from this private dining area. It was intended to put a spotlight on the cooks, but in her state, Tilda felt instead that it allowed them to peer out at her. She tried to look very appreciative of each course and had taken to giving the waiters awkward smiles as they rushed in and out for plates. The whole thing was exhausting. The only saving grace was that Tip had appeared in the window only once to give her a nod and otherwise seemed to have retreated to the far side, which was blocked from view by shelves and pans and all manner of stainless steel things. She hoped if she couldn't see him then he couldn't see her.

It wasn't that the food wasn't good. The food was excellent, if unrelenting. Tilda had expected to be presented with a menu but instead had been informed by her waiter—a man so perfectly able to blend into the background that even then she had a hard time recalling what he looked like—that it would be a tasting menu of small plates all chosen by the chef. He hadn't even asked if there was anything she did not like, and there certainly was. Fortunately, it seemed Tip did not cook with cilantro.

As it was, she didn't think she could take one more course. She had lost count, but there had been at least fifteen. Small plates or not, fifteen of anything leaves the average person overfull. The arrangement had made it difficult for her to divide the meal into the usual parts. She'd begun with an olive, her waiter had explained, stuffed with a very particular kind of ham taken from a very particular kind of Spanish pig that was raised entirely on hazelnuts and given regular saunas while listening to Handel. Surely that would be considered an appetizer or maybe an *amuse-bouche*. But after that, things got murky.

Tilda knew there had been a croquette made of carrots, which hadn't tasted like carrots at all. And there was a Brussels sprout, just one, that had been pulled apart leaf by leaf and covered in a lemon foam, which looked a little like someone had spit on the plate. There had been fish, shellfish, beef, and more pork. It was a very good thing she wasn't Jewish. At one point there had been a pureed chowder served in a demitasse cup.

With the first course, the waiter had brought out wine to go with the food and had explained to her about it as he poured. It had been a short pour, which was fine. But after three, it became clear that he intended to do this with every dish. After the first few, Tilda had begun restricting herself to a small sip from each one just so it didn't all go to waste.

Finally, they'd made it to dessert, of which there were three. One of them had been a cookie that, when she picked it up and placed it into her mouth, crackled and zinged. She'd immediately removed it, unbitten, and stared for the two seconds it took her brain to retrieve memory of the candy Juno had eaten as a child. Pop Rocks. There were Pop Rocks in the cookie. If it had been meant to wake her from the food-induced stupor, well, she couldn't say it had been entirely successful, but it was a very good effort.

She was, at the moment, retreating into a shot of espresso, a drink she didn't enjoy, just for the stimulant effect. If she thought they offered it, she might have asked for TUMS. She even had some in her day bag, a sure sign of age, but they didn't fit in the small clutch she'd taken with her that night.

Tilda finished her espresso, and the cup was removed. In fact, everything had been removed, including her napkin. As a final service, the waiter took out a small scraper to clean up any crumbs before retreating for good.

There she was, alone at an enormous table without even a single piece of cutlery to fiddle with. The cooks went on with their business, feeding whatever diners were left in the main room beyond her sight. She looked at her watch. It was after ten o'clock, an unheard of hour for a restaurant on the island, or at least it had been when she'd lived there. During her days, everyone would be at home watching *Law & Order* reruns by then.

Tilda had no idea what the protocol for this was. Did she wait for Tip to come out to chat? Did she just leave? Could she interrupt one of the cooks and ask? She regretted not asking the waiter, and now he had no reason to return, not even for crumbs. She let out a sigh and then felt guilty about it. *We should all have such problems.*

"Oh, crap."

Tilda had almost forgotten to leave a tip. She pulled out her wallet and then stared at the money inside. She had no idea what her meal would have cost and, therefore, no idea how much to leave on the table. She pulled out a twenty and set it on the otherwise empty white cloth. It looked a little obscene lying there. So conspicuous.

"Hi."

Tilda jerked. "Where did you come from?"

Tip showed his dimples. "The kitchen. That's where we make the food."

He was wearing black pants that fit a little too loosely and a white coat with Brasserie, the name of the restaurant, embroidered on the breast. His hair was covered with a light blue bandana that tied in the back and reminded her of a pirate.

"I didn't see you come out."

"You looked a little lost in there." He pointed to his own head.

"I was trying to figure out how much of a tip to leave. Do you think that's enough?" She gestured to the money on the table.

"I do."

Tilda wasn't comforted by this. He probably would've said that even if she'd left three singles. She pulled a ten from her wallet and laid it on top of the twenty.

"Thank you," she said. "That was a wonderful meal. It was very kind of you to do that."

"It was my pleasure," he said, making a little bow, his hands clasped behind his back. "I hope you'll convey my goodwill to your husband."

"Ex-husband."

"Of course."

They looked at each other for a moment, and Tilda felt pressure to say something else. "I couldn't even tell that croquette was made of carrots."

"I'm sorry?" Tip said.

The desire to backpedal was intense, but there were no U-turns on compliment road.

"It was very meaty. Dense. Well, not dense like heavy, but dense like—" Tilda could feel the blush running up her neck. "Substantive. That's what I meant. It was substantive. And unexpected. For produce."

That hung in the air for a count of three, which was enough time for her to pray the building would catch on fire before this conversation could continue.

"Is 'thank you' the correct response here?" Tip asked when the moment had passed.

Tilda sagged against the back of her chair. "I really have no idea," she admitted. "I don't know what's wrong with me."

"I have those days," Tip said.

"This has been going on for a while."

"If you give me a second to change," he said, "we can go get a nightcap, and you can tell me about it."

He was walking away before she could answer. A younger version of herself might have found his self-assurance attractive. This version was older and wasn't so easy to impress. He had shown her a great kindness, but she was tired and didn't want a nightcap. There had been fifteen kinds of wine already. She didn't want to be rude, but it might be too late for that.

14.

Tilda had ordered coffee at the tavern, which turned out to be a mistake that could only be corrected with three packets of sugar and a whole pitcher of creamer. Still, she liked the place. In fact, she'd liked it for years. The Galley had been old and worn out even when Tilda had been local.

All the drinkers from the original island families sat at the bar or stood when the seats ran out. The men wore flannel shirts with their jeans and ball caps, and the women wore the same without the hats. Banana clips and scrunchies still held back their hair like 1985 had never left. Tilda's ivory sweater had no place at The Galley. Tip had done better but just, trading in his chef's coat for a pair of jeans and a blue oxford shirt. In the years Tilda had lived there, she'd never worked up the nerve to join the people at the bar, even when she could've matched them beer for beer. Tip must have felt the same because he steered her toward a booth.

Both the table and the cushions were cracked, and the condiments were displayed in a salvaged Heineken six-pack holder. The walls were decorated with ancient beer neon and taxidermy. Wagon wheel chandeliers hung from the ceiling, and plastic clothing hangers were hooked in the spokes, displaying the bar's logo T-shirts for purchase. More T-shirts were stacked on the pool table, rendering it unplayable, which was fine. Tilda had never seen anyone play it. An Oklahoma Thunder basketball game was on the television, but no one was watching.

The only thing new in the place was the cook Tilda glimpsed through the pass window behind the bar. She was a young woman just on the verge of not being so young, mid-thirties maybe. She wore heavy bangs and thick-framed glasses and had tattoos up both arms. She looked like she'd double-majored in women's studies and philosophy, and Tilda wondered how she'd come to work here where everything on the menu was passed first through the deep fryer and came with tartar sauce.

Tip was hungry. He'd spent all night cooking other people's food, including Tilda's, and had had almost nothing for himself. He ordered the fish and chips, which came out fast and was piled into a precarious mountain of golden batter on the plate. He offered Tilda some, but the idea of more food nauseated her. She waved him off, and he dug in. Tearing up the cod into bite-size pieces that still steamed and must have burned his fingers, he shoved the bits into paper cups of white sauce before chasing them with a handful of fries and a deep swallow of beer.

It was nice to see he wasn't a snob about his food, Tilda thought.

Over his shoulder, one of the local women sat at the corner of the bar with three or four of the available men standing around her. They were hovering like seagulls over a fisherman gutting a catch. She'd been there awhile. Tilda could tell by the looseness in her arms and the brashness of her speech. Whatever the woman said, she said it again and again, louder and louder until someone acknowledged each whiskey-soaked piece of wisdom.

"You can't tell you lost weight," she was saying to one of the older women. "You know what you need? You know what you need? You need to go shopping. You should go to the mall where they have the Chico's. You know the Chico's? You know it? They have good stuff. You get yourself some shirts and some pants. Chico's. C-H-I-C-O."

The older woman patted her on the back until she stopped talking, and the men went right on hovering. It made Tilda's heart hurt to watch.

When her mind came back to her table, Tip was watching her watch the woman.

"Seven-to-one no one tries to take her keys when she leaves," he said.

Tilda didn't want to talk about the woman. It was too uncomfortable. Instead she said, "How's the fish?"

"Better than you'd think. You sure you don't want some?"

Tip and Tilda stayed until all the food on his plate was gone, along with two beers for him and half the cup of coffee for her. Tip had been right. The woman had left, giving hugs to everyone at the bar on the way out, and everyone let her go, including them.

"You want to see my house? The inside of it, I mean," Tip asked when they got up to pay at the bar.

The wine had run off with more of her inhibitions than Tilda might have guessed. She was taking more liberty than she had any right to, giving herself a tour of the first floor of Tip's house. She left him to trail behind her, as though he were a Realtor and she were thinking of buying the place. She did everything but open the closets and test the faucets.

There were no planned developments on Olloo'et. Each piece of property had been purchased by an individual, who saw to it that a well could be dug and a septic system installed, and then the family built their own four walls in whatever configuration occurred to them at the time. It was the architectural version of a crazy quilt, which is to say that Tip's house looked nothing like Harry's, which looked nothing like any of the others, and some of them looked nothing like anything that should have been built at all.

There was a sliding glass door in the living room that opened onto a deck. With the lights on inside, the glass was a dark mirror revealing little of the outside but reflecting back to her the room, Tip, and her own full-length self. Her fingers itched to fuss with her hair, but Tip was watching her. So instead she cupped her hands around her face and pressed her nose to the glass.

She could see the green light from the Miracle. It was brighter in some places than others, less a continuous ribbon that night than a tie-dyed swirl. She could see the white tents on the beach all lit up and the scientists shrunk to the size of dragonflies by the distance, busying themselves with whatever it was that scientists did.

Tilda flipped down the little latch and pulled the sliding door open.

"Jesus." She sucked air in through her teeth and crossed her arms over herself. Had it been that cold earlier? She stepped outside to get a clearer look at things, and when she did a young woman crossed right below her, right below the deck she was standing on, walking at an angle toward the yellow caution tape and then under it and toward the commotion. Just then someone else stepped out of the shadows of Tip's deck, a dark-haired, darker-skinned man.

Tilda recognized the woman from Jake's, which wasn't so surprising. By the end of the week, any number of the scientists were bound to start looking familiar. Even if she never learned their names, she might give them nicknames, so she could discuss them with Harry. She would say things like, "That one over there, the one who looks like Ichabod Crane, certainly seems excited about something." And from then on they would call him Ichabod.

But the thing that was surprising was that the woman's trajectory made it seem for all the world that she had come from Harry's deck, just there to Tilda's left. Tilda felt a smidgeon of protectiveness, whether over Harry or his property she wasn't sure. Either way, it was her job to take care of things for him.

"Anything interesting going on out there?" Tip stepped outside and stood beside her.

"I think that woman was just at Harry's," Tilda said, nodding at her retreating form, already almost another indistinguishable Gor-Tex–clad dragonfly like the others. The man, who had been close on her heels, had peeled off and stopped to talk to someone nearer the water.

"A tryst, perhaps," Tip said.

"Don't be ridiculous."

Tip shrugged. "You never know. Women are very into the brooding artist type."

"She's young enough to be his daughter."

"Don't knock it until you try it." He was smiling and flashing his dimples at her.

Tilda rolled her eyes and went back inside, giving one last good shiver in the relative warmth of the living room. Tip shut the sliding glass door and clicked the little lock shut.

"You haven't remodeled," Tilda said. "It looks just like when the Feinsteins lived here."

"Feingolds," Tip corrected.

"Feingolds."

"That's because they still do," Tip said, stepping around her.

Tilda followed him to the kitchen. He opened the fridge and pulled out a bottle of beer, a microbrew that Tilda didn't recognize, which didn't mean anything at all. The Pacific Northwest had begun growing breweries like it grew moss. It seemed every man between the ages of twenty-seven and forty-five owned one. He tipped it toward Tilda in offering, and she took it. It was important to support the local economy.

Tilda twisted off the cap and left it on the counter, which, she noticed, had a circular red stain like someone had overflowed a glass of cherry Kool-Aid.

"Do you rent it from them?" Tilda asked. "The Feingolds, I mean."

"No," he said. "I inherited it after my parents died."

"The Feingolds died?"

He swallowed his pull of beer. "Well, just the two of them."

"Oh, my God." The memory came from behind and slapped into the back of Tilda's knees, threatening to take them out from under her. "I remember you. You were a little boy, and you had a cat."

"Goldie," Tip provided. "She got hit by a car."

"What happened to your parents?"

"Dad had a heart condition. We'd known about it forever, but his going was sudden. He was in Cincinnati when it happened. I had to fly his body back. That was just a year after Mom died. She had cancer."

"I'm so sorry," Tilda said, because she was. It was sad to be an orphan no matter how old you were, and he was not old enough to expect it. "They were my age."

"No." Tip shook his head. "They were definitely older."

"Not that much older."

Tilda decided not to provide a date to prove her point, and Tip didn't follow up, so they stood in his deceased parents' kitchen looking at each other. He didn't need alcohol to make him bold. He had youth and testosterone, which seemed to Tilda like walking around half bombed anyway. She saw that unsteady swagger in her son as he struggled with the powers that had been bestowed upon him.

Tip was older than Juno. Maybe as much as ten years. His swagger was more controlled. He'd had a little more time to get a grip on things but not so much that he was looking down at the slide ahead of him. It was something of a golden moment for him, and Tilda wondered if he appreciated it. Probably he didn't. No one ever does.

"Would it ruin the mood," Tip interrupted, "if I made us a bowl of ice cream? I'm still hungry."

"What mood?" Tilda asked.

"Well, I thought, if I worked at it a little, you might let me kiss you. But then my stomach might start growling, and you would hear it, and that might be awkward. So I'm hoping that if I stop to make a bowl of ice cream, you won't leave, and you'll let me keep looking at you a little more because I'm really enjoying that."

It was more than cold, it turned out, that could make her cross her arms over herself. "That's rather bold of you," Tilda said.

"It was, but in my defense, I've been doing all of my best stuff. It didn't seem to be working."

"That was probably a sign."

"I surrender," he said, holding up his hands, "and offer this microwaved fudge sauce as an offering of peace."

"I'm never eating again. That was, what, twenty, thirty courses?"

"I wanted to impress you."

Tilda pulled out a kitchen chair, knocked a few stray crumbs off the table in front of the seat, and let herself plop onto the gingham cushion. She was suddenly aware of how tired she was.

"You may have bit off more than you can chew," Tilda said. She wanted to kick off her shoes but didn't.

"I'm starting to see that." His upper half disappeared into the fridge, and he came back out with a jar of maraschino cherries and a can of whipped topping before taking a gallon of vanilla ice cream from the freezer.

Tip opened the lid and waggled the carton at her. "Last chance."

"Never again," she reiterated.

Tilda felt like a boa constrictor that had choked down a rabbit and needed to find a dark, warm place to digest for the next week before horking up a pile of bones and fur. It was time to go home. At home, she could take off her shoes.

"Well," she said. "Thank you very much for the dinner. You're very talented."

Tip didn't stop scooping. "It's really the only thing I'm good at," he said.

Someone else, someone not Tilda, might have opened her mouth and revealed that she, too, knew that feeling, the feeling of having one good skill and nothing else to fall back on. But such a person was not in the room.

"I'm sure that's not true," she said instead.

She shifted her weight to the edge of the chair, ready to push up to standing, a sort of punctuation on these last few good-night pleasantries.

"Oh, it's true. Ask anybody. Without the restaurant, I'd be selling ladies' shoes at some department store on the mainland. I'd be fetching those little flesh-colored footsies for the customers and carrying huge stacks of shoe boxes back and forth to the stockroom."

"How do you know about flesh-colored footsies?" Tilda asked.

"My mother took me shopping with her when I was a kid. I'd look all over for the little boxes of them. I remember they looked like white

Kleenex boxes. I'd try to stretch the footsies over my head, so I could look like a burglar and scare people."

"They couldn't possibly fit over your head."

"They didn't. I'd end up breaking a few before putting them on my hands instead and pretending my fingers were all fused together. Made my mother furious."

"I could understand that," Tilda said and then did stand up.

"What about you?"

"What about me?"

"What would your alternate future be if you weren't a senator?"

"I'm not a senator, so I guess we'll find out. But for now it's time for me to say 'good night.'"

Tip was putting the glass jar of store-bought fudge sauce into the microwave and setting the timer. "You can't leave yet."

"I'm almost certain that I can."

"Nope." The microwave dinged. "You can't leave because we're not friends yet. You've spent more time alone in my restaurant than you have with me, and the point of tonight was to convince you to be my friend."

"All of this because Harry doesn't like you?"

"No. I'm not that fragile." Tip dug a spoon out of the drawer and drizzled on the fudge with a generous hand. "I saw you in the coffee shop, and you looked like someone I would like to spend time with and maybe even someone who would like to spend time with me. Harry was just a good excuse. I guess I felt like I needed one."

Tip licked a drip of fudge off the side of his hand. "Are you sure you don't want some? It's really good."

He put the fudgy spoon into the bowl and topped everything with a good long squirt of whip and dug a cherry out of the jar with his fingers.

"Bring a second spoon over," Tilda said. "But I'm just tasting."

Two hours after they finished the ice cream, Tilda let Tip lead her to the bedroom. He turned the light on, and she took her hands from his shirt buttons to find the switch and turn it back off. He tasted like beer and chocolate, and the scars on his forearms from kitchen burns felt slick and taut under her fingertips. When she pressed her nose to his chest and breathed, she could smell that he had been sweating earlier, probably at work, and she could smell something else, the musk of his excitement, the smell that would be left on the sheets.

15.

Rachel grabbed her cooler marked "food," doing all she could not to reveal how heavy it was with a dozen of her full containers secreted away inside.

She carried it up to the parking area, loaded the cooler into the campered back, and shut the tailgate. Her heart rate and breathing were labored, and she bent forward with her hands on her knees, giving herself just one moment. Anyone might see her, so she raised herself up, refusing to pant from the effort, and came around to unlock the driver's door. She put in her key and turned. Something was wrong. The key turned freely in the lock. There was no telltale friction as the mechanism gave way, no click as the old-fashioned plunger popped up on the inside. Rachel opened the truck door and fiddled with the lock. The plunger moved up and down just as easily as the key had turned. She fiddled with the door handle and the key some more, looking for some configuration of maneuvers that would right this wrong, but there was no getting around it. Not only had the door been unlocked, but the lock had been broken.

With the door open, the small dome light cast a dim yellow glow in the cab. She looked all over the floorboards first and then climbed inside. She hadn't left anything important or incriminating in the truck. She was almost certain she hadn't, but the longer she sat there the less certain she became. She tried to push down the paranoia. This was ridiculous. Of course, there was nothing for anyone to find in here. What could there be? Everything was back at the cabins.

Jesus, the cabins.

She reached out far to grab hold of the wide-open door and slammed it shut, starting the engine with her other hand before the dome light could even click off. She couldn't get back to the camp fast enough, not even if she could fly.

It took two hours for Rachel to unhook all of her equipment and load it into the back of the camper. Thirty minutes of that was spent checking everywhere inside and outside for signs of disturbance. The door and window seemed secure, and her clothes were still taped up to block the noise. She tore it all down, shoving it into bags and hauling it out to the truck without even bothering to pull the duct tape off the sweatshirts. She was sweating, and her hair, which had started to fall out of the ponytail, kept getting in her face.

In the rush, she nearly forgot to grab her toiletries from the bathroom, which made her nervous about what else she might have forgotten. She checked her watch. The night team wouldn't be back—shouldn't be back—for another two hours, and the day team was asleep. But her stomach wouldn't stop clenching, and she worried she'd get diarrhea. It was the last thing she needed. Bad enough that the effects of the *Artemia lucis* had begun to wear off. Her back sent zings of pain up and down her spine, and the knot on the side of her head was sensitive to the touch. Just grazing it with her hand, which she kept doing as she pushed her hair away, made her wince, and a headache was coming on.

She locked up the cabin and wrote a note for Hooper, which she shoved under his door. The note said she'd decided to take her caretaking duties a step further and would stay at the old man's house.

Finally finished, she ran to the truck and backed up in a spray of oyster shell, feeling for all the world like she was fleeing the scene of a double homicide. At the bottom of the street, she stepped too hard on the brake. Her seat belt locked into place with a jolt, snapping her back and away from the steering column. Rachel wiped her hands on her jeans, made a loud exhale that only helped a little, and forced herself to drive the speed limit.

Later Tilda might wonder about her own judgment, but just then the bed was comfortable and her brain was operating on its lowest possible frequency. All she could manage was the general feeling that she should be home before sunrise for Harry's sake. And that general feeling was enough to get her to sit up and, with some reluctance, retrace the bread-crumb trail of clothing to get herself dressed again.

Tip groaned when she moved and was slow to follow her, but he did not object or ask her to spend the night. "I'll walk you home," he said.

"Don't be silly."

"I'm not being silly. You got me talking about my mother over ice cream, God rest her soul. How do you think she'd react if she knew I'd just let you out the front door in the middle of the night? You could be killed."

"I live less than fifty yards from this bed. I think that's unlikely."

"Ax murderers are very crafty these days."

At the door, Tip held up her coat while she slipped her arms in. Then he put on his own, and they walked across the grass, which had never grown well in the sandy soil, toward Harry's. They were quiet, and he waited while she unlocked the door.

"Good night," she said just before stepping across the transom.

"Good night," he said. "I hope you find your thing, whatever it is."

"Excuse me?"

"You heard me."

Tilda knotted her eyebrows. "What thing? Who said I'm looking for a thing?"

Tip didn't reply. He had already turned around and was heading back across the grass.

He really was a bold little shit, she thought, and went inside.

16.

Day Three of the Miracle

Harry was asleep in the library when the doorbell rang well before eight a.m. Tilda had woken up just after five o'clock like she did every morning. It had not been a joyous occasion. For a half hour, she tried to will herself back to sleep, but images of Tip kept intruding. There were whole story lines—what he said, what he did, what she did, what it would be like when she saw him again.

Tilda squeezed her eyes shut tighter. If anyone could see into her head, she'd kill herself rather than endure the embarrassment. These things probably happened to him all the time, and she herself was far too experienced to have expectations. Tilda tried to be without expectation. It sounded very Zen, which wasn't her at all. The night before was imprinted on her mind like letterpress. Tilda gave up and got up.

On three hours of sleep, a swim was out of the question. She had an exhaustion headache, and her eyeballs hurt. The alcohol had left her dehydrated and light sensitive. By seven, she'd been alternating cups of coffee—three so far—with glasses of water—two so far—which she'd used to swallow more than the recommended amount of ibuprofen. To keep it all down, she'd made two pieces of plain buttered toast but was only able to stomach one. The other sat on a small plate on the kitchen counter for later. She'd had a scalding shower, which she'd let beat down on the back of her neck for some time, and had put on jeans and a half-zip top more suited to the gym than going out in public, which was just fine because Tilda didn't want to be in public. Then the doorbell rang. Shooby barked at it for emphasis.

Tilda looked around herself, as though there might be someone else who could handle this. Finding no one, she walked to the door with Shooby at her heels and looked through the peephole. It was a woman. It was, if Tilda was not very much mistaken, the scientist woman from the night before, the one she'd seen coming across the sand from this house.

Tilda considered the possibility that Tip had been right. Maybe Harry had begun some sort of romance with this woman. One of Harry's male friends might have thought this good news. Why shouldn't he have one last bite at the apple? But Tilda was not one of Harry's male friends, and she didn't think that way at all. But she did open the door.

"Yes?" Tilda said and then added, "Can I help you?" because the first sentence had sounded snooty and short.

The woman stuck out her hand. "I'm Rachel Bell."

"Tilda," she said and shook.

Shooby stayed where he was but wagged his tail. Rachel stayed still. She seemed to be waiting for something. She did not ask for Harry. Perhaps she expected Tilda to have been informed of the dalliance already.

"Harry isn't up yet," Tilda told her. "He needs to rest whenever possible."

"Yes," Rachel agreed, not seeming the least bit uncomfortable standing there on the front porch. "I assume he's all right. The fall didn't seem serious."

"The fall? What fall?" Tilda forgot she was exhausted and put on the tone of voice she used with Juno when he tried to sneak unpleasant news into conversations.

"Harry fell last night on the beach. On the dog." She indicated Shooby, who seemed pleased to be made part of the conversation.

"He fell on the dog?"

"That's my understanding," Rachel said. "I didn't see it. My boss called me over to help. I carried the dog inside. It seemed like they were both more or less all right."

Tilda had let Shooby out to do his business earlier, electing to let him run around the front yard rather than go on an actual walk. She hadn't noticed anything wrong with him, but she hadn't been looking either. She looked down, but Shooby neither confirmed nor denied his injuries.

"He seems okay," Tilda said.

"Good."

There was that pause again like the young woman was waiting for some foregone thing.

"Did you come by to check on him?" Tilda was in danger of becoming annoyed. She remembered her head hurt. It was also cold outside, and her hair was wet, and now she had to deal with the fact that Harry had begun to have falls. Maybe he'd been having them all along. She really didn't know.

"No, I have everything in the truck," Rachel said. "If you could just show me where to put it, I can unload it myself. I prefer to."

"Unload what?"

"My lab equipment."

"Your lab equipment?"

"Yes."

"I seem to have missed something."

"Because Harry isn't up yet," Rachel provided.

"Apparently so."

"Last night, Harry offered to let me set up my equipment and stay here. It's much closer to the beach than the old camp. I imagine you have hot water, too."

"He asked you to move in?"

"Just for the next three days. I realize this is sudden, but I'm running some experiments, and it really can't wait. So if you could just show me where I can set up—"

In other circumstances, Tilda would have appreciated the woman's demeanor. She was forthcoming and didn't seem like the sort who would be dissuaded easily. She had started rocking back and forth from her heels to the balls of her feet, which was irritating to Tilda, but still, if the young woman had shown up at campaign headquarters looking for a job, Tilda would have given it to her. Not that any of that made any of this any better.

"Harry!" Tilda called out, walking back inside the house, no longer so concerned about his sleep.

She left the door open, and when she checked back over her shoulder to see if the woman was going to step inside, Tilda saw Rachel heading toward her truck to unlock the camper.

"Harry!"

It always took more than a little doing for Harry to get upright the first time each morning. He needed his cane in one hand, and the edge of a piece of furniture in the other, and still he might have to give a couple of heaves like a batter warming up before he got all the way standing.

"Yes," he said, annoyed that Tilda was watching these undignified contortions, jabbering on at him the whole time. He wished she'd stop talking. He wished she'd just stop all together, at least for the time being, which was a feeling he'd had often during their marriage.

"Yes, I did tell her she could stay. It was the least I could do, and it'll be interesting having her here. Perhaps," he said, cutting off another bit of jabbering before it could pick up any steam, "you might show her into the dining room. I thought she could put her things up in there, and then there's the guest room for her to stay in, of course."

Tilda did not appreciate being dispatched like a maid with her duties and opened her mouth to say so but shut it again when she heard footsteps in the entryway. There wasn't time to argue, but there would be time, she told Harry with her eyes, for discussion and soon.

There was no role for Tilda in the house, but now that they were hosting guests, she felt she couldn't go off and nap. Napping when someone had just arrived was rude, ruder even than leaving. Leaving was understandable. For all anyone knew, Tilda's plans had been long-standing. She could very well be a busy and important woman who could not be delayed. Feeling that she had to have this conversation with herself made Tilda even less happy about things.

She hissed at Harry the moment the woman walked back out to her truck that they would "discuss this later" and grabbed her purse from beside the front door. The two women did not acknowledge each other when Tilda climbed into her car and backed out of the driveway, and when she returned home half an hour later with two plastic sacks in the seat beside her, she did not go back in.

She sat in the driveway next to the old red pickup truck, which was in her spot. It was in her spot, and its driver was in her house. Harry's house. Her old house. It didn't matter. The truck and the woman were strangers, and they were in her space.

Tilda had a book from the marine shop on her lap. After she ex-plained her concerns, the clerk had dog-eared several chapters for her and then charged her forty dollars for the manual alone, which was something close to a mugging. She was skimming the marked sections, paying most of her attention to the photographs. Things were coming back to her.

She shoved the book back into a bag, gathered up the rest of her purchases, and climbed out, walking not into the house but around back. She stole glimpses at Tip's place as she went. His car was gone. She wondered if he was back at the bakery picking up bread or maybe already at the restaurant. Of course, there were a hundred other places he might be. She hardly knew him, she told herself. She certainly couldn't predict his schedule.

Having delivered this mental scolding, she continued down the sandy slope toward the beach, her tennis shoes slipping here and there on the sharp descent, forcing her to turn her feet sideways and crab walk down for better traction.

The boat was just where she had left it.

Tilda's father had owned boats his entire life, bass boats mostly.

Summers had been spent towing them back and forth from the house to the lake, then backing the trailer up into the water, which had excited and worried her as a child. The car is backing into the water! The tires are getting wet! And then her father would push the aluminum boat, which was not very much like Harry's at all, off the trailer and into the water.

Being the oldest sibling, she had been allowed, from time to time and when there were no other boats or obstacles like submerged trees around, to pilot. This was a good number of years before she drove a car and to be able to drive anything at all was terribly exciting. She was quite grown up, being a pilot and all, and she took the duty seriously.

The summer weekends her father didn't spend on the lake he spent in the driveway fixing the boat or, as often, the boat trailer. Things seemed to go wrong with an alarming frequency, and more often than not her father would say, "It's the damn wiring again. Bring me an iced tea." Tilda would, and then she would watch him work, fetching tools from the toolbox and holding the flashlight until it all got too boring, which it always did.

In college, Tilda had taken up with a boy whose family had owned a forty-foot sailboat, much larger than the one sitting in front of her. The boyfriend's boat had a below deck with galley and bunk and enough navigational equipment to sail from Florida to the Bahamas, which is exactly what he had planned to do. And she, more in love with the boat than with him, had spent nearly every weekend of her sophomore year helping ready it for the trip. When the school year was over, he had asked her to come with him for the final time, and for the final time, she had said no. He had left and had not come back, and she had married Harry and had her children and her career, and she did not regret that decision. She did not regret it, but that did not mean she was not very, very pleased to have found this replacement.

Feeling as though the boat watched her as much as she watched it, Tilda dropped her sacks in the damp sand under the deck and pulled her knit hat around her ears. From one bag, she pulled a box of cheese crackers and a diet soda. Not strictly boating necessities, they were medicinal.

There had been a lot of moving around that morning for a middle-aged woman with a hangover. Tilda rarely drank more than a glass of wine. She couldn't remember the last time she had drunk too much, but whenever it was, she felt certain she had recovered more quickly than this. She unscrewed the lid from the soda and took small sips.

She had moved on to the crackers when she heard footsteps on the deck over her head. She stayed were she was, listening as the feet, moving too fast and with too much assurance to be Harry's, went from the house to the stairs and then all the way down to the sand. The young woman, carrying two buckets, one in each hand, passed within fifteen feet of Tilda without ever seeing her. A Fish and Wildlife officer called out, but the woman waved him off. Tilda stopped chewing, watching as Dr. Bell skirted the work site, dipped her buckets into the water, and returned, moving more slowly, the weight of the buckets pulling at her arms.

When the woman had gone back into the house, Tilda put away the crackers, took another sip of soda, and fished around in her other bag. Adjusting the elastic band, she pulled the small headlamp onto her head, fitting it over her knit cap. All the weight was in the front, forcing her to adjust how she balanced her head on her neck, not something she had given a lot of thought to in the past. She dropped her shoulders, rolling them back, and settled into this new position before reaching up and pressing the small button once, which turned it on, and then again to make it brighter. The light was small, but the beam it cast was broad. She would have to remember not to look directly at anyone while wearing it. Reckless blinding was going to be a real possibility.

That done, she reached back into the bag and pulled out a pack of pens. She freed one and hooked it into the spiral of the small notebook she'd bought. She shoved that into the back pocket of her jeans, reached again into the sack, and came up with a stubby flathead screwdriver that she shoved into her other pocket.

With both hands free, she approached the boat. She approached it like she might have approached a strange dog, careful when reaching out her hand. Someone had built this boat, an actual someone, not an assembly line of someones. She could see it in the imperfections, lines not quite straight, paint that had gone on too thick and settled into the pebbled appearance of an orange skin. Across the back, obscured by the rudder fin that was flipped up for storage, was the boat's name, *Serendipity.* Not the name she would have chosen, but it would do.

She ran her light over the hull, the aft arm, the float. Her beam, the bright white of LEDs, cut a sharp line. The sun, somewhere behind the asbestos clouds, had risen, but its light was far too weak to penetrate the cave where she worked.

Tilda moved to the port side, opposite the outrigger. Standing dead center, she put her hands on the cockpit wall and pressed down hard, testing the jacks that held the boat in place. Nothing moved. She pressed harder, lifting her feet up off the sand. When the whole thing did not topple over on top of her, she tipped her weight forward and swung a leg up over the side. The boat shifted slightly, creaking. One jack dug deeper into the sand, and Tilda froze, her muscles tense, ready to fling herself clear of whatever imminent tragedy was about to occur. But none did. She gave it a full fifteen seconds, which she judged to be the maximum amount of time a tragedy could hang *in potentia,* before sliding the rest of her body into the boat.

A single bench spanned the cockpit near the rudder. She wrapped her hand around the tiller. It felt solid and smooth, as smooth as the driftwood that littered the beach around her, and she imagined the builder sanding it again and again and again, imagined the hands that gripped it, darkening the wood over time. Steering with a tiller was both rudimentary and counterintuitive, push left to go right and right to go left, shifting the rudder below accordingly.

Above her, the mast stretched up no more than twelve feet, and down by her sneakers was the sail bag. Whoever had stored it last—and a good part of her doubted it was Maggie—had had the sense not to wrap the sail around the boom and call it a day, which meant that just maybe it would not be in terrible shape. She lifted one end. It was like lifting a snake filled with sand, awkward and heavier than it looked. She eased her end over the port side and let the whole thing drop to the beach below. She would deal with that later. Underneath the sail had been a single orange life preserver that looked nearly as old as Juno. She tossed that over the side, too.

Ducking under the boom, she got on her hands and knees and got to work. Pointing her light with her forehead, Tilda looked first for a mud line, the high-water mark that would've been evidence of flooding. Finding none, she reached into her pocket and took out the screwdriver. Inch by inch, she worked her way over the boat. Anything that looked the tiniest bit suspicious got a good poke. Rot would give way easily, coming apart in splinters under pressure.

Inside the cockpit, Tilda found two sections, each a few inches across, that failed her test. She used the screwdriver to pry away the bad wood, working each spot until she had excised it all like a surgeon removing a tumor. Neither went all the way through the hull, and when she was satisfied, she stood, stretched, and dropped herself down to the sand. She took out her pen, made her notes, and then got back to work, performing the same test on the rest of the boat. She found more rot on the float and on both of the hiking boards, but the pivoting centerboard seemed in working order.

When she stepped back, shoving the notebook once again into her pocket, her relationship, their relationship, the one between her and the *Serendipity,* had shifted. They knew each other now. Not like they would. Not like it would be when she got it off the jacks and into the water. But they had begun things. They had been honest with each other about their faults and agreed to work on them.

With one more touch to the hull, Tilda reached up and turned off the headlamp. The sudden darkness blinded her and made her unsteady on her feet as she picked her way out from under the deck toward the relative light of the outside. She gathered up her plastic sacks, unscrewed the cap of her soda, and took another drink, this one deeper, her stomach having settled.

She was going to need epoxy, a lot of epoxy.

17.

When she'd first arrived, Rachel had refused to put her tanks in the dining room. While the room had no windows, it also had no door. It was out of the question. Mr. Streatfield had tried reassuring her that no one in the house would touch her equipment, but that wasn't the point. Although, once he'd brought up the possibility, Rachel added it to her list of worries.

She carried the tanks up the stairs to her bedroom and lined them up on top of dressers and bookcases. The tanks were large and heavy. She'd had to arch her back too far and feel each step carefully with her foot before ascending because she couldn't see around. The dose she'd taken earlier had worn off. She'd dry swallowed three of her white pills, the strongest ones she had, before leaving the cabin, but they'd been just enough to take the edge off. After the first tank, she was shaky with pain, so much so that her teeth started to chatter.

It went this way for all three tanks plus the algae setup, then the boxes and duffel bags full of her other equipment, and another trip with the cooler full of new water samples. It wasn't an ideal work space, but it was private—more private than the dining room and much more private than the camp—and that was the important thing.

She'd set everything up as quickly as possible, but her temperature gauges showed the bay water had warmed by seven degrees.

"Shit."

She did a visual check to confirm what she already knew. The samples had crashed. Rachel blamed the extended transport. She'd have to go back out and collect more before she showered or slept. She could, at least, do that from the house with relative ease and, with a view of the beach, could determine when her arrival would be undetected.

But she could deal with none of that until she got her pain under control. Rachel consulted her notebook and followed the procedure from the day before, measuring and grinding the dead *Artemia lucis* into a paste. This time she increased the dosage by fifty percent and swallowed, chasing it with a handful of raisins left at the bottom of a bag of trail mix.

"Gah." Rachel stamped her foot and pulled a face, sticking out her tongue, which was still covered in semi-chewed bits of raisin.

Once she'd collected herself, Rachel checked her notebook again. Yesterday morning, she had estimated the amount of time between taking the dose and noticeable pain relief was twenty minutes. She looked at her watch, noted the current time, and set about making herself at home for twenty minutes.

The walls were covered from floor to ceiling in wood panels that had been painted white, the same creamy white as the headboard and dresser. The comforter was plush and, when Rachel squeezed it, she realized, full of down. The fabrics in the room, including the two area rugs, were softly patterned with pinks and greens and yellows. The bedspread had tiny rosebuds, the curtains featured birds, and the rugs were printed with leaves and vines. It was the natural world as imagined by Beatrix Potter. It was the sort of room that could have been in a magazine or a bed and breakfast. It would've been the ideal room for a little girl—or at least it would have until Rachel had turned it into a laboratory.

She rubbed her eyes. She couldn't remember how much sleep she'd had in the past few days, but it wasn't much. When she stopped moving, her eyes pulled shut. Sitting on the edge of the bed, she was in danger of falling asleep. She got up and did her fifteen careful jumping jacks then went to hang up everything in her duffel bag, even though that which wasn't fleece was wrinkled beyond hope already. Then she checked her watch. Twenty-two minutes had passed. Rachel bent forward. She'd thought it would be fine, and so she'd done it quickly.

She let out a loud gasp and punched her thigh, her knees threatening to buckle. God, it hurt. It hurt. It hurt. Jesus. Why did it hurt? There was no reason, not with a fifty-percent increase in dosage, that it should still hurt. She pushed air through her teeth and forced herself to stand, feeling around desperately for a logical answer.

Rachel grabbed two of her sealed transportation containers from the cooler and ran down the wooden stairs as best she could, her shoes clomping too loud. Harry stood at the door of his library leaning on his cane and shuffling toward the source of the commotion. She had not bothered to grab a coat.

"What happened?" he asked.

But Rachel did not answer as she raced past to the back sliding glass door. She did not see anyone down by the white tents. They could be between shifts, on a break, collecting at another location. Wherever they were, they could come back and at any moment.

Rachel yanked twice before her shaking hands could make sense of the tiny flip lock. When the door opened, she threw herself out onto the deck as though making a dramatic escape. She was down the stairs and under the yellow tape, waving off the Fish and Wildlife officer fifty yards away who shouted something at her that she couldn't and didn't try to hear.

It is hard to run in sand. It is harder to run in sand with the December wind blowing in off the water and into your face, rocks and bits of driftwood reaching up their gnarled fingers to trip your toes. The wind whipped Rachel's hair in front of her eyes while her feet sank into the sand. She couldn't keep up her pace and had to goose-step, wasting energy and time. She needed to slow down. Rachel knew that, but knowing and believing are different. No amount of training in what was empirical could do anything against the adrenaline sloshing through her bloodstream. At the water's edge, her heart rate topped out, and she began to gasp.

She swallowed gulps of air. Standing there on the edge of the island on the edge of the continent with nothing but air, she still couldn't get enough. Water pooled in her eyes and dripped from the corners, which might have been from the wind.

"Go," she told herself before she was ready. "Move!"

Rachel waded into the water. It was too cold. Her nerves rebelled, turning temperature to pain. The joints in her toes ached. Her skin, right up to the crown of her head, shrunk tight to her body and broke out in goose pimples. Her muscles contracted. Her back—there were no words for her back. It was as if the wounds were happening all over again, happening on a loop she could not stop. It made her light-headed, sick to her stomach. It was hard to move, but she did. Through it all, she did it anyway because there was nothing else she could do, no one to turn to, nothing that could help. She went into the bay and skimmed her clear, plastic collection tubs across the water.

She had not brought the smaller containers that attached to the bottom of plankton nets. These were, instead, large tubs not unlike what off-brand rainbow sherbet might come in. She had to move more slowly on the way back. Water is heavy, and she was shivering and unsteady. She had to pay extra attention to her feet to keep from tripping and spilling. She made her way back up the beach, over the rocks and the driftwood and through the brambles near the stairs and back up the tiers of expensive decking.

Harry was waiting, standing just outside the door, which stood open, cooling the house and raising the heating bill. He was watching her with an intensity she did not appreciate.

"Excuse me." Rachel tried to step around him, but he filled too much of the space. "I really have to get these samples in the tanks," she said.

He was trying to back up and make way, and Rachel worried for a moment that he'd catch his house slipper on an uneven board or that his right leg, turned in at an awkward angle, would simply give way. But she didn't have time to help him. As soon as he'd moved just enough, she slid past, taking small but quick steps through the house, her eye always on the samples, careful not to spill. Up the stairs she went and into her room. She set the tubs on the floor.

Straight from the tubs, she harvested the *Artemia lucis,* measured, ground the paste, and swallowed it. She did not make a face this time nor did she wash it down with any sort of chaser. She did not have room in her mind for considerations like that.

She would fix this. She could and would fix this. She could never fix this. The previous test was a fluke. There was another benign explanation for the relief she experienced. Not true. She simply needed better, less decayed samples. She needed to stick to the protocols. What scientist, what scientist at all, would spend years of her life chasing a fairy tale?

Tears rolled down Rachel's cheeks while her neurons flung the competing messages, like tiny sparks, back and forth over their network. She carted the tanks into the bathroom one by one, stopping only to wipe her eyes and nose on the back of her hand. She washed and disinfected everything she could then used a long fireplace lighter to flame an alcohol mixture off the metal surfaces.

She did it because it had to be done, because this had to work.

Rachel had been six years old when it happened. It had been summer, and summer in the Arizona desert pushes everything down low. People and animals creep along with their bellies to the ground, slipping down into hidey-holes wherever they find them. Popsicles melt after the first bite, and public pools have to be topped off every few days for all the evaporation. Children have to choose then between the heat outside and the sharp-edged people inside, and you can measure the balance of things by how many little ones huddle in whatever shade they can find, holding on to basketballs and toy baby strollers they have no energy to play with.

Rachel had lived with her mother in a fourplex that was one of twenty other fourplexes all huddled together just behind the Taco Bell, which was open, and the dollar store that had closed. The buildings all looked identical, and visitors, not that there were many, often got lost. There were no helpful signs labeling one building from another or pointing the direction to any rental office.

On that day, Rachel had come down to the kitchen to find Darren, her mother's latest boyfriend, along with a pot of water boiling on the old stove. Rachel remembered some things very clearly and other things not at all. She remembered the wallpaper border by the ceiling pasted up by a former tenant. It had been mauve with flowers on it. Rachel remembered a stick of butter on the counter half melted in the summer heat. She remembered there had been dishes from the morning cereal and dishes from whatever the adults ate and drank the night before in the sink. She did not remember where her mother had gone that day or even, really, what Darren looked like.

He was by the stove, and Rachel must have been hungry, or maybe she had just been brave. The macaroni lunch wasn't progressing at all, and she could see the water had been boiling for some time, the level having dropped down in the pot, leaving a white line where it had started, as hard water sometimes does. Rachel had said something with what her mother had begun calling her "smart mouth"; although for the life of her, she did not remember what.

Darren grabbed her by the arm, which was bare. She remembered that. She had been wearing a little green-and-white-striped tank top that was small enough almost for a doll, and his hands were big enough to wrap all the way round one of her biceps. She had struggled, kicking and hitting as she tried to break free. And then she had. She had broken free, or maybe he had just let her go, but either way she had turned all the way around, her back to him. She had been intending to make for the sliding glass door on the other side of the room, but Rachel never got that far. Intending to run was all she managed to do before the water hit her.

Darren had picked up the pot and tossed the boiling water down her back. Rachel remembered the first moments. She remembered feeling the pain and not knowing what had happened. Then she'd seen the water at her feet, and she had known, and the knowing lasted for only one moment before the reel broke. Rachel had nothing else, nothing until weeks later in the hospital where she'd been forced to lie on her stomach for what seemed to be forever and certainly was. She hadn't known how she'd gotten there and had not thought to ask. The nurses had said that, in a small way, she was lucky. It could have been her face. She would still be beautiful from the front. And she would, after all, live.

Her mother would not. The guilt of it ate at her from the inside out. It took fourteen years, but it got her in the end. When she died, the doctors said it was cancer, but Rachel knew better.

In the present, Rachel wiped her cheeks and forced her mind down to the task in her hands. Wash, wipe, flame, acid rinse. Again and again until all the tanks and all the flasks and all the tubing were clean.

She set everything back up in her room. She prepared half the flasks with purified water, using a pipette to add the necessary nutrients and then a sufficient amount of green algae to feed them. In the other half, she filled the flasks with raw seawater, hypothesizing that some unknown element, some symbiotic relationship, might be necessary for the *Artemia lucis* to survive. Then she added in the new samples. It was only enough to fill a few flasks. She would need to make more trips. Rachel looked at her watch. Half an hour had passed since she'd taken the second dose. After a deep breath, she put her fingers to the bruising on her face and pushed.

It did not hurt at all.

She pressed so hard her fingers turned white, and still she felt nothing but mild pressure. Then she bent forward and touched her toes—careful this time. Results were promising. She could do it. She could reach them.

Rachel sagged onto the bed and took a shuddering breath. She gave herself a moment, just one, to be grateful. It would be okay. She was okay. She opened her eyes and pushed up. There was so much work to do. She picked up her plankton nets and sample jars. The two other tanks still needed to be filled and their settings adjusted and recorded and monitored. It was clear the analgesic in the *Artemia lucis* decayed very quickly upon death. She would need to keep them alive to isolate the compound. She would need to keep them alive and breeding. She had three days left.

Tilda climbed the deck stairs, tried the sliding glass door, and found it unlocked. Inside, she kicked off her shoes, setting off Shooby, who galloped out of the library to survey the situation, and then went back to alert Harry of her triumphal return.

In stocking feet, she headed for the kitchen. "Aww. Dammit."

She lifted up her foot and looked at the bottom.

"What did you do?" Harry called.

Tilda could hear him shuffling down the hall toward her. "I stepped in something wet. In my socks."

Tilda pulled off the offending item and then the other. And now that she was looking, the puddle, which was small, wasn't really a puddle at all. It dribbled all the way down the hallway.

"What did you spill?" Tilda asked.

"I didn't spill anything."

"Well, someone did."

Tilda knew exactly what the spill was and who had done it. She wanted to see if Harry would admit what had happened or cover for their new houseguest, but he, having said all he was going to on the subject, did neither. Barefoot, Tilda went to the kitchen for a towel. Harry followed her.

"You didn't come home last night," he said.

"Of course I did."

"I was awake."

"Well, if you were awake, then you should know I came home."

"You came home this morning. That is not the same thing."

"It wasn't morning."

"Three a.m. is morning."

Tilda took the towel from the drawer and went out to the hallway to mop. Harry and Shooby both followed her, and neither offered to help.

"This woman you've taken in," Tilda said, "that's a bit sudden."

"How could it be anything but sudden? She's only here for six days, and I just met her."

"Are you sure inviting a complete stranger into the house is a good idea?"

"What do you think she's going to do? Steal the silver?"

"I don't know what she's going to do," Tilda said. "I don't know her and neither do you. That's the point."

"She gave me a hand. We talked. I liked her. It seemed like she needed some help. I helped. End of story."

Tilda had made it all the way to the back of the house, scooting the towel along with her foot, using it to mop up each dribble as she came to it. Done, she bent over and picked up the damp towel. It was sage green with white checks. She remembered it from many years before. It was one of the few things Maggie hadn't replaced.

"It's not really the end of the story. It's the start of a new one, and I just want to be sure it's a good one. That woman seemed a little pushy this morning."

"Her name is Rachel," Harry said. "And she's not half as pushy as you."

"You need to be resting and taking care of yourself. You need a regular schedule. Dr. Woo has been very clear about that. If you have a parade of researchers coming in and out of the house, it's disruptive."

"It's my house. If I want a parade, I'll damn well have a parade. Not to mention that one person hardly counts as a parade."

"Harry—"

"This isn't a democracy, and you don't get a goddamn vote, Tilda. The only person traipsing in and out of here at odd hours, creating a disturbance, is you."

The hand Harry was using to grip the head of his cane was like a claw, and his knuckles had gone white. His neck was flushed red coming out of the collar of his white button-down shirt. He had missed a button, and Tilda couldn't help but notice the shirt needed a good bleaching and pressing. She wondered if it had been laundered at all before he put it on and if he needed help with getting it fastened or if the button was an isolated incident.

"My presence here is a disturbance?" Tilda demanded. "I seem to recall you asking me to come."

"Maybe that was a mistake."

Tilda drew herself up to her full height. She was just above average while Harry was just below, and when she did stand right up, putting as much distance as possible between every vertebrae, she could put her eye to his.

"Are you asking me to leave?" she demanded.

"Don't be hysterical."

It was clear that this conversation had gone further than Harry had intended, but he was unwilling to back down. A noncommittal insult did the trick. Harry turned away from her and maneuvered himself with two twisting clomps of his cane into a ninety-degree turn. Able-bodied, he would have stomped off in a huff. This was the slow-motion absurdist version, which might have been funny if Tilda weren't so angry. It was all she could do not to throw the towel at his head. She did the next best thing.

"She—Rachel—told me you fell last night while I was gone."

"It wasn't a big deal."

"She said you were down on the beach by yourself and that you fell. You hurt the dog."

Harry didn't answer. He was heading back toward the library, his safe harbor, to hide. Not that he needed a space to hide, Tilda knew. He had always been capable of hiding in his own head and locking up all the doors and windows once he was there.

"Did you call the vet?"

No reply.

Tilda was following him, and they'd made it to his doorway. Harry shuffled into the library, and she was on his heels. "You don't have anything to say about that?" she asked.

Harry was clomping toward his piano as fast and as forcefully as he could. "Carrying on with that damn kid next door makes you look like a bloody fool," he said and dropped down onto the bench in front of the keys.

A flush spread across Tilda's chest. She opened her mouth to throw something back at him, something equally hurtful. And then she didn't. Her mouth was open, but sound did not come out. She froze there, just for a moment, long enough for Harry to swing his head around to see what in the Sam-damn-hill was the problem now. Tilda closed her lips, and Harry followed her eyes.

Becca looked at them both from inside the photo frame. Her hair blew in her face, and the dog ran and the waves broke, just as they always had. Her coat was just as red and the scene just as gray, but just as it was exactly the same, it was completely different because Tilda had not seen the photo before. At least not in decades. All the other photos of their daughter had been boxed away, hidden in the attic or sent off to other family for safekeeping. Harry had thought the purge would be temporary, just until Tilda could breathe again, and he had not objected. He did not feel, given that he had done the most horrible thing that it was possible for anyone to do, that he could object to anything at all. But he had saved this one photo and hidden it here in his space where no one went but him.

Except now Tilda was here, and the three of them were together.

Tilda stood in place, staring at the photo. She said nothing. Harry said nothing, and then she turned and walked away with the wet towel in her hand, and nothing was said at all.

18.

Rachel had slept for three hours and was up and dressed in jeans and the same hooded sweatshirt she had worn on and off for days, scribbling into the notebook perched in her lap. She had completed another experiment, grinding a sample and running it through a small centrifuge that separated the animal body solids from the liquids. It had yielded important results. The liquids had no pain-killing qualities at all—she had tested that on herself—leaving the solids as the only possibility.

Rachel couldn't write fast enough. She was trying to hold twelve different thoughts in her head at the same time. It would take a lot to distract her, something like a bear falling down the stairs outside her bedroom door. At least, it sounded like a bear. It was enough to convince Rachel to put down the notebook and stick her head out.

Harry was halfway down the steps, having begun his fall from who knew how high. He no longer had his cane. It had clattered all the way down to the foyer below. Rachel shut the door tight behind her and took the stairs two at a time to reach him.

"I was going to take a nap," Harry said.

His hair, which was unkempt all the time, was even wilder. The bald spot on the crown of his head, which Rachel now had a clear

view of from above, was the size of a small egg and vulnerable looking, like it might be as soft and unfused as an infant's. Half of his collar
stood up, and his heavy fisherman's sweater was pushed up on one side.

"Did you black out?"

"No."

"Are you sure?"

"Yes."

Harry laid his head back against the wall. He wasn't even trying to
get himself up, and his right leg was turned below him at an awkward
angle that made her think of an ostrich with its knees bent the wrong
way.

"Are you hurt?" Rachel asked.

His eyes were closed. "I fell down the stairs."

"I inferred."

The corners of Harry's mouth turned up a little at the corners. The
woman was frank. You had to give her that.

"I fall all the time now," he said.

"Your disease is progressing."

"It would seem so."

They sat a moment in the quiet before Harry went on. "You know,
I have to grab the towel rack now to lower myself onto the toilet. One
of these days I'm not going to get back up."

"Yes," she said, "but the toilet is no more probable than any other
surface."

Harry looked at her.

She clarified. "A toilet is a chair like any other, functionally speaking. You might get stuck on a dining room chair or the sofa or in a
car."

"That really wasn't my point."

"I know."

"Do you know what it's like to be terrified of a shower?" Harry
asked.

Rachel did know. Unfamiliar showers sometimes had abrupt

changes in temperature, which hurt her back terribly, but she did not say this to Harry, who had continued talking without her.

"And I can't grip a pencil. I hold it in my fist like a toddler to try to put the notes I can hear in my head on the page because, Lord knows, I can't play them." He was quiet a moment. "That might be the worst part."

"The worst part changes from day to day," Rachel said.

He had closed his eyes, and now he opened them and looked at her. "That's true."

Most people, Rachel knew, didn't want you to talk about your pain, not unless it was temporary like a twisted ankle or hitting your thumb with a hammer. If you did not hold up your end of the bargain and get better, things fell apart quickly. People would avoid you. It was easier to keep hidden, and she felt sorry for Harry because he could not hide. There were not a sufficient number of high-necked jackets and fishbowls full of pills to get him through his day unseen.

"Where's Tilda?" Rachel asked.

"She went to the store. Well, she said she went to the store. She's probably just driving around, or maybe she went to go visit her boy-friend."

This information didn't fit well with the image Rachel had of the woman who had greeted her at the door that morning. She didn't seem like the sort of woman who would have something that sounded as girlish as a "boyfriend."

Harry glanced up at her and then looked back down either because it was embarrassing or the angle hurt his neck. "She and I had a fight. It was probably my fault."

"Okay."

"It was my fault."

"Okay."

"The good news is I don't think I messed myself, so if you could give me a hand, I'd appreciate it."

Rachel wasn't sure if that was supposed to be funny or not, so she didn't laugh. She just got hold of him under his armpits as best she could on the treacherous and uneven surface and lifted. His right leg did nothing but hang. He tried to get some leverage with his left, but it wasn't much, and it didn't help.

In the end, she half dragged him up the stairs, one agonizing six-inch rise at a time, with Harry pushing off from the wall and the handrail as best he could. At the top, she left him and went down to fetch his cane. When she returned, he had all his weight on his left leg and was holding up the right like an injured dog.

"Do you think it's broken?" she asked.

He shook his head. "It's just the knee. Torqued is all."

"You might have torn some ligaments," she offered, despite not being that sort of doctor. "Do you have Tilda's cell phone number?"

He shook his head again. "No need. Just gonna rest it."

"Are you sure?"

"I'm like an old dog with cancer," Harry said. "There's no point in going to a lot of trouble fixing things." He had to stop and take another couple of sips of air. "Just need one second here."

Rachel had done the same thing how many times? A thousand. More than a thousand. Her mind began to whirl, slowly at first like an engine warming up, but soon she was making calculations so quickly she thought for sure the zipping of her neurons would be audible. She could help him. She could alleviate some, maybe even all, of his pain, and she could—this was the important part—collect more data. A sample size of one wasn't really a sample size at all, but still, the risk was enormous. She would need to mitigate it. She would need to get information from him without giving any out.

"Stay here," she told him.

"Afraid you won't be able to catch me?" he asked, but she didn't respond. She was already down the hall and on the other side of her bedroom door, shutting it behind her.

When she came back, she had a white plastic spoon, the kind with sharp edges that can be found in every fast-food restaurant in the world. On it was a small lump of reddish-brown paste, not unlike the filling in the middle of a Fig Newton but a little lighter in color.

"I have this," she said.

He looked at the spoon and the lump.

"It's a new painkiller, one I developed. Am developing. Stronger than morphine."

Harry wrinkled his nose. "Did you find it on the bottom of your shoe?"

She didn't answer that. "It's experimental, and there are side effects. Some I know and some I probably don't."

Rachel had the feeling that she was stepping off a ledge into pure black, and Harry wasn't saying anything. She didn't know what that meant. She rarely knew what anyone meant by anything, and she was starting to feel very self-conscious standing there holding a plastic spoon with a disgusting lump in the bowl. Harry didn't know her from anyone, and it did look like something off the bottom of her shoe.

"Anyway," she said, lowering it. "I'd appreciate if you didn't discuss it with anyone."

She wanted to turn away and go. She could feel herself begin to blush, and the humiliation of blushing only increased the embarrassment and hurried the process. Harry would have to fend for himself. She backed a step away and went to spin on her heel.

"Have you tried it?" Harry asked.

"Yes," she said.

"Better than morphine?" he asked.

"Better is subjective. It's stronger."

He held his hand out. "When I was a teenager, I used to take things somebody cooked up in their bathroom. No reason to get cautious now," he said.

She handed him the spoon, and he took one long look at it before raising it to his lips.

"It has a rather strong taste," she warned him just as he was sliding it in.

"Gah—Jesus. Son of a—"

He made all the faces and exclamations she'd been through before. It was a little funny, she had to admit, when it was happening to someone else.

When he got control of himself again, he said, "You have got to make that smokable or something. God. It tastes like a fish's ass."

He handed her the spoon back.

"I need you to make notes," she said. "Anything you feel, even if you're not sure it's related or relevant, write it all down."

"Weren't you listening earlier?" he asked. "I can hardly make little musical notes on a page, and those are just dots and lines."

"You'll have to find a way," she said, holding him to the same standard she held herself.

She took a breath. It sounded wet and ragged filling up her chest, and she didn't expect that. Testing it on herself was one thing. Giving it to someone else—

"No one else knows about this," Rachel said.

Harry got his cane maneuvered around under his left hand where he liked it. At least he had hurt his right leg. The right leg was bad anyway.

"I know," he said, pushing his weight away from the wall but keeping his right hand out, as ineffectual as it was, to help with his balance. He started his many-point turn toward the master bedroom for that nap he'd fought so hard for. "First rule of fight club: Don't talk about fight club."

Rachel didn't know what a fight club was, but it sounded right. She nodded, but Harry wasn't paying her any attention. He didn't have any to spare. She watched until he made it to his bedroom door. Back in her own room, she scooped up the second half of the solids batch from the centrifuge. She took that herself and waited for it to kick in.

There was a bigger, newer Groceries "R" Us kind of place with full-size carts and eighteen kinds of orange juice on the other side of the island, but its presence irritated Tilda. Her market or, as she thought of it, "the" market, the real one, was downtown just a block from the bookstore. The sign said OLLOO'ET DRY GOODS AND GROCERY. It wasn't big enough to have or need wheeled carts. The shelves were made of real wood, and the whole store smelled a little like ripe cheese and patchouli, which might have also been the teenage clerks smoking weed in the back. There were two kinds of orange juice—pulp or no pulp—and that was fine with Tilda.

She wasn't in any particular hurry. In fact, she was trying very hard not to hurry and have to go back to the house too soon. She had known that coming back to take care of Harry would be a mistake. At least part of her had known it. Part of her remembered how he was— how insular and difficult and single-minded and so willing to do what he wanted when he wanted no matter what might follow later. Their friends had dismissed this as his "artistic temperament" during their marriage. Tilda had met plenty of artists. She was pretty sure Harry was just an ass.

The other part of her, the part that had agreed to come, felt that Harry was unfinished business or maybe just business finished poorly. It wasn't that she had stopped loving him as much as it had turned to something else. After Becca died, things had not been the same. Harry had blamed himself, and Tilda had blamed him, too. It had been an accident. No one thought that it hadn't been, but just because something is an accident, doesn't mean there isn't fault. And forgiveness, it turned out, was something that had to be given all over again, every single day. And it had to be accepted on that same schedule. There were probably people who could do it. People who were better than they were, but it had been easier to move away from each other, to stop bumping into each other's hurt parts quite so much.

But now Harry was dying. He needed her. He needed her to be close, and those hurt parts were still there, getting bumped all over again. And now she was in the grocery and dry goods store wandering up and down each of the aisles, so she didn't have to go back too soon.

She was in the personal care section even though she couldn't think of a single thing she needed there. It seemed the store did a booming business in overpriced boutique soaps and candles that she was sure were popular with tourists but were far too foo-foo for her to buy. She looked at them anyway and recognized little round lavender soaps that were in bathrooms on the second and third floors of Harry's house. Tilda wondered if the housekeeper bought them or if they were left over from Maggie.

Tilda was smelling some lemon verbena soaps—square and not wrapped in the floral paper like the lavender—which made them possibilities in Tilda's mind, when her cell phone rang.

"I think I'm supposed to wait a certain amount of time before calling," Tip said on the other end. "But I couldn't remember how long that was."

"Is that how you usually say 'hello'?" Tilda asked, trying not to sound too much like she was smiling.

"Not when I'm calling my dentist if that's what you're asking," he said. "Where are you, and what are you doing?"

"I'm thinking about buying soap, but only if it isn't wrapped in floral paper. And I'm at the little grocery downtown."

"Can you wait there for fifteen minutes?" he asked.

"Probably. Why?"

"Trust me," he said and hung up.

Tilda had the lemon verbena soap in one of the square wicker baskets the store provided for shopping. She'd also picked up some tomatoes on the vine, even if they were horribly out of season, and a pound of peppered bacon. She was trying to decide if she would walk down to the coffee-shop-slash-bakery for bread or if she would just buy it here. Part of that decision depended on what Tip had in mind, and she had no idea what he had in mind, and the uncertainty over whether or not to buy the bread was starting to get just a little annoying when she heard his voice over her shoulder.

"What's a pretty lady like you doing in a dry goods shop like this?"

She turned around. He was wearing a brown suede jacket with

off-white shearling around the collar, and he was holding a bouquet of flowers. They were white, and there were different kinds, none of which she could have said the names of with any certainty. They were arranged with bits of fern and greenery and a couple of sprigs of pussy willow, too. They looked natural and wild but still beautiful, which meant that someone with a lot of talent spent time making them look that way. He handed them to her.

She loved them, and she loved even more that he had surprised her with them, and she was afraid if she showed that a little too much that something vulnerable and bad would happen, so she took them and said, "Shouldn't you be at work?"

"Pay for that stuff," he said. "I want to show you something."

She did, and when they walked out the door together, she carrying the flowers and he carrying her groceries, she asked, "Are we driving or walking?"

"Walking," he said. "It's just around the corner."

They walked east, the opposite direction of the bakery and the bookstore and the restaurant he ran. This way was toward the end of the commercial strip, and if they went too much farther, they'd be on streets lined with old houses, most of them Victorian or something kind of like it, which had been turned into bed and breakfasts or dental offices. Just beyond those were the real houses—nice but less showy and historic—where real people lived. They turned left, away from the water, and went half a block.

They passed a children's clothing store called Two Birds. It had an old-fashioned Christmas scene done up in the window, but instead of ornaments, the tree was decorated with little socks. They passed a florist that didn't bother with a window display but just let you see right in to the buckets of flowers and potted plants, including red and pink and white poinsettias. Tilda wondered if that was where he picked up her flowers. And then they stopped.

Tip turned and faced this shop front. There was no sign over the door or on the windows, and in fact, the windows had been covered on the inside with newspaper. Tilda looked at the storefront, and then she looked at Tip, who looked at her with full dimples, as though this were the greatest surprise of all.

"This is it," he said.

"Okay."

He turned and faced her and did it so sincerely that she stopped looking at the shop and turned to face him square on, too.

"I want to rent this space and open my own restaurant. It used to be a café, so it already has a kitchen. The remodel would be minimal, and if I started now, I could have it open in time for the high season."

"That's great," she said. "I'm excited for you."

And she was. His food was delicious. The restaurant business was notoriously fraught, but that wasn't her business. It was his, and good for him for pursuing it.

"I'm working out the financing now. I really think this could be something."

"I'm sure you're right," she said.

"Anyway—" He shoved his hands in his pockets, the plastic bag with her groceries still looped over his wrist. "I just wanted to show you the space. I hope no one takes it first."

Tilda didn't know what to say. She hadn't been asked for anything, and the niggling feeling under her skin might be for nothing at all. "I hope they don't, too," she said.

"Do you have plans this afternoon?" he asked.

"Nope."

"Good," he said. "It's my night off, and I love bacon." He held up the bag. "Let's go back to my place."

19.

They had managed to get the bacon in the fridge, which meant that now, several hours later, they didn't have to worry quite so much about trichinosis. Not that anything so unpleasant was on Tilda's mind.

She'd picked up his denim work shirt from the floor and followed him into the kitchen, putting it on, buttoning a few of the buttons, and rolling up the sleeves. He hadn't bothered picking anything up from the floor or putting on anything at all, which was fine with Tilda. His wasn't a gym body. He didn't have a pack of anything or melon-shaped biceps. He was slender like a swimmer, and he had a small patch of dark fur at the base of his tailbone, just above his butt, but very little anywhere else. Everyone here lived under ten months of cloud cover and, because of it, had the pallor of the Irish, including Tip. But when her fair arm had lain across his fair chest, she had seen that his skin tended toward pinkish where hers was far more yellow. It made him seem vulnerable somehow, having that pinkish skin, like he would be prone to windburn and blushing while she would toughen in the out-doors.

Tip had scoffed at her out-of-season tomatoes and left them on the counter to ripen to whatever substandard level of flavor might be possible and instead laid the strips of thick, peppered bacon in a cold skillet and turned the fire up to medium to render. Tilda had never gotten around to buying bread, and he took a loaf of his own from the bread box and sliced off four pieces, neither too thick nor too thin.

"What kind is that?" she asked.

"Sourdough."

While his biceps were not large, his forearms were ropey, and the muscles went right down into his hands. It made Tilda consider for the first time that being a chef must be physical work—hard beyond the scars from cuts and burns she'd noticed before, some of which had gone white with time and some that were still new enough to be pink and tender looking.

He spread butter on one side of each of the slices and threw them into the oven to toast. His movements were economical, as though he'd practiced this meal in this kitchen and had spent time editing out every unnecessary step. When Tilda cooked, which wasn't often, she was forever going back and forth to the cabinets and the refrigerator and the sink and the drawers. He had everything he needed at his elbow and rarely, if ever, retraced his steps.

When the bacon was done—cooked but not too crispy—he removed it to a paper towel–lined plate and cracked two brown eggs into the still-bubbling fat. While they went to over easy, he pulled the toast from the oven, flipped the slices over, and spread a bit of sour tamarind chutney he had in the fridge on their naked sides. Then on went the egg and the slices of bacon and a small bit of greens she didn't recognize. Tip brought the two sandwiches to the kitchen table where Tilda had been watching, her knees pulled up with her feet in the seat of her chair.

When she bit into the sandwich, it was all she could do not to moan. The yolk ran and mixed with the bacon fat. The chutney was a tiny bit sweet but mostly sour and cut through the richness, along with the peppery greens, so nothing was too heavy. The bacon was salty, and the sourdough held up to all of it, keeping the whole thing together. Tilda had never put that much thought into a sandwich.

Tip had not sat but went back to the fridge and came out with a bottle of prosecco. He brought it and two champagne flutes to the table while Tilda wiped yolk from her chin.

"This is incredible. I don't think I've ever tasted anything this good," she said.

"I'm glad you like it."

He took the metal cage from around the cork and used a kitchen towel to pry the cork from the bottle. It was a subtle pop with none of the drink lost to an explosive burst.

"You should put this on your menu," Tilda said.

He poured the pinkish golden prosecco into the tall glasses.

"It wouldn't work," he said. "This is an after-sex sandwich. You wouldn't appreciate it quite so much otherwise."

Tilda didn't believe that.

He held up his glass, and she hurried to set down her sandwich and wipe her fingers before raising hers.

"To unexpected encounters," he said.

Tilda took a sip. She would have said that the sandwich needed nothing at all, but as it turned out, the crisp, dry bubbliness was exactly what it needed. Now it was perfect.

Harry was hunched forward, head down over the keyboard, shoulders up like a buzzard perched on a limb. He told his fingers to dance and roll across the keys, all of them, and they did. Like crickets hopping across a hot skillet, his fingers moved across the board, coaxing out notes almost too fast for Harry to remember them. He ended with a flourish and sat back. Giving himself just one breath before snatching up the pencil and getting all of it—as much as he could remember— onto the blank score sheets.

Once he had to stop to wipe his palms off on his pants. He was sweating everywhere. His palms, his armpits, it was running off his forehead, and he could feel dampness in his shoes. He didn't know if this was a side effect of the medication or a side effect of the speed of his work. Harry had done more in three hours than he had done in a month. It was like the surge of energy Tilda had described in the last weeks of each of her pregnancies. He felt there was so much to do, and finally he could do it.

The sun had fallen, and the room had gone dark around him. He stood up from the bench and reached for his cane. He took two steps with it, and then, just to see, he let it go. He left the four-footed thing sitting right there in the middle of the library, and he took a step away from it and then another and then another. He was stiff and stilted, and he still had some numbness in his right foot, but he could move. He did not fall but wasn't ready to trust that he wouldn't. Still he walked. He walked all the way over to the floor lamp next to Tilda's collection of American history books, and he turned it on. Then he turned and walked to the other lamp, the one next to the blue and white gingham couch where he'd slept so many nights, and he turned that one on. Just like that. It was possible, and his whole library was a soft yellow to prove it. Shooby sat by his feet, upright and alert and dragging his tail across the floor like a windshield wiper. Even he seemed to know that something unusual was happening.

Harry didn't know how long this would last, where Rachel had gotten it, and if she could get him more. It seemed terribly important to do as much as possible with what he had, and the desire to do everything was almost paralyzing. He could walk to the kitchen. He could make his own dinner and fill his glass all the way up without worry he would spill. He could change his clothes and not struggle with the buttons or take a shower, stepping over the lip of the tub like he did it every day. He did not have to wear slip-on shoes.

Shower, Harry decided, after a moment locking eyes with the dog. The shower was the most important thing. Harry looked over his shoulder at his cane still standing there in the middle of the room, alone and out of context, and with only a small niggle of doubt, he left it standing there and turned to leave the library on two rather than three feet.

He was still turning when he saw her, and it happened so fast that he wasn't sure he'd seen anything at all.

"Tilda?" he called out.

He went all the way to the door and leaned out to look down the hall. He heard the clock behind him in the library, and he heard the *shhhhh* of waves hitting rock out on the beach. He heard all the sounds he normally didn't hear because he had heard them so much, but no one responded to his call. Not even Shooby.

"Rachel?" He spoke softer this time, more convinced that there was no one there but not so convinced he wouldn't try one last time. "Dr. Bell?"

He walked down the hallway, his fingers trailing the wall along the chair rail. He didn't need it, not right at that moment. But it felt good to have something, even a chair rail, under his fingers. He wasn't used to being upright without training wheels anymore, and he was unsure of himself.

"Hey!"

He had made it all the way to the front of the house, the dining room, where they never ate, on one side of him and the entrance to the kitchen and the breakfast area, where they always did, on the other. And this time he had seen Rachel. He was sure he had seen her, and she was moving fast. He had just caught a glimpse of her out of the corner of his eye as she disappeared up the stairs.

"Dr. Bell?" he called again, his voice sure this time.

There was no answer, and he didn't wait for one. He kept right on going to the entryway and up the stairs. He climbed them one at a time with his hand around the railing. He raised one foot to the riser and then brought the other up next to it before mounting the next. It was the way a very young child might climb stairs, but he was not so brave as to try it any other way.

He called out Rachel's name two more times on his way up to the second floor, glancing up from his feet each time he did so. Her door was shut. He had not heard it open or close, but it was possible to open and close doors quietly.

He wondered why she had come back. She was supposed to be on her shift down at the beach, and she had seemed very anxious to go. She had stuck her head into his bedroom before leaving to check on him after his dose. Less than thirty minutes had passed, and he had felt better, although not as better as he felt right then. He had told her he was fine, good, no side effects yet. She had left her cell phone number on his nightstand and told him to call her if things went sideways.

He had wondered at the time how sideways it could go and if she meant to call her rather than 911 if it came to that. Harry didn't know much about this sort of thing, but he was pretty sure scientists weren't supposed to go handing out medications just like that. He didn't ask her what she meant. He didn't want her to have to answer if having to answer put her in an awkward position. He felt the two of them had entered into a pact. He had accepted the risk, and he would not rat if the odds did not turn out in his favor.

He had asked her when she was writing down the number what was on the agenda that night, and she had told him it was her turn to take the kayak out with the plankton nets for offshore collection.

"Don't drown," he'd said, meaning it as a joke. She'd nodded as though this were a serious instruction and was gone before he had time to follow up.

He wasn't at all sure he would like being out in a kayak at night. The island got very dark very quickly in winter. In town, there were shops that sold a joke postcard. It was all black, and in small white type it said, "Nightlife on Olloo'et Island." That black extended up to the heavens and down to whatever monster-ridden depths the ocean held. No, being out on a kayak in all that blinding inky-ness was not for Harry at all, and he was glad to be in his warm, bright house on shore.

At the top of the stairs, he knocked on her door and tried her name again.

When nothing stirred, it was a conundrum. This was his house, and under that reasoning, he should be able to open any door to any room he wanted. On the other hand, he had given her permission to use this room as her own, not just as a bedroom but as a work space, which was, to Harry, even more sacred. This permission extended to her certain rights of privacy.

Harry knocked again. "Rachel?"

It wasn't so much that she didn't respond as that he heard nothing at all. He put his hand on the doorknob and then, hoping for a way out, remembered to check over his shoulder to see if the door to the bathroom was perhaps closed and occupied. That would explain everything and make him feel both relieved and silly. Who wouldn't prefer to come back to the house in the middle of a cold, wet shift to use an indoor bathroom rather than those horrible plastic porta-potties?

"Rachel!"

She was climbing the second set of stairs. He saw her—the last bits of her anyway—disappear around the banister. He saw her dark hair swish down her back and her hand grip the rail.

How had she gotten past him? How did he not hear her on the wooden floors? Why had she not responded, and why was she going up to the third floor? There was nothing up there but Tilda's room and bath and a little storage nook. It had been designed for a live-in housekeeper, if you were the sort of person who had such a thing. It was an attic, really. And if he had limited rights in entering Rachel's temporary quarters, she had none at all that allowed her into Tilda's space.

Harry was confused, of course, but also he was just a little bit angry, just on the fringes, happy to have it explained away but far enough in that it had better be a very good explanation. He went after her, moving more quickly and not bothering—not even remembering—to hold on to anything at all down the hallway, and while his hand did rest on the rail as he ascended the second set of stairs, he took them like a man would take them, alternating feet on alternating risers, and he didn't take a moment to think of that at all.

She was waiting for him there at the top of the stairs, not at the very top but at the landing so that he didn't see her until he was all the way up and had rounded the final baluster.

"What do you think you're doing?" he said, getting it all out before looking her in the eye, which is when all the air went out of him and his blood stopped flowing and his bowels felt loose.

"Oh, my God."

20.

"Becca?" It was a question, but it was not a question because, for whatever terrible thing she had been through to be there, it was Becca. A man knows his daughter even like that, in the state that she was and all grown up.

She still had that terrible gash on the side of her face. He remembered it from the accident. Something, he did not know what, had sheared right through the skin and through the muscle and flayed it all open like something on a butcher's table until the white bone of her cheek could be seen, unmistakable and clear. God, how it had bled. It had pumped out right there in the front seat of the car. He had seen it, but he couldn't reach her, and he couldn't stop it, and there was so much blood around them both, he was sure that the whole car would fill with blood, that it would fill up the floorboard and then up to the seats and then up to the windows, and they would drown in it there was so much.

Of course, she was bleeding in other places, too. Her right hand had been nearly severed, and she was bleeding into her guts, but trapped in the car those years ago, he couldn't see those things. He had only seen her cheekbone, a part of his daughter he should never have seen, not if he had lived a hundred lifetimes.

It had been twenty years, and her face had not healed and neither had her hand. Harry saw it now. It was hanging from her wrist, still attached by a little bit of muscle and a little bit of skin and gristle and whatever else holds us together. It hung there off its hinge like a broken door on the end of her arm. And the bleeding had not stopped. It had not stopped in twenty years, and he had not been wrong. If the firemen and the police and the ambulance and the life flight helicopter and all the rest of them had not come, the car would have filled all the way to the top with her blood. He could see that now. She had so much of it. More than any other person had ever had.

"Becca."

"Dad."

She called him Dad. She had always called him Dad, even when she was very small. She was no-nonsense that way, like her mother. No Daddy for her. He remembered that about her. She had been born so frank and straightforward. She was full of "whys" and demanded clear explanations of the things in her world, things that she could touch and feel and know were true.

She was not a child for unicorns and fairy princesses, preferring games and books and teddy bears because bears were real animals that she could see in the zoo, and she had not particularly cared for her little brother. Not when he was born, which was to be expected, and not even three years later when she would die. She had never warmed to him. It wasn't that Harry or Tilda thought she might hurt him. Becca simply did not like him. He got in her way and interrupted her play and got the attention she would rather not have shared. And the truth of the matter was that when she was gone, it had always seemed that Juno was free of something and had grown to take up as much of the space his sister had abandoned as possible.

Of course, Harry knew this was not real. Even though she was right there and the blood was on the floor around her and he could smell the iron in it. He knew this was not real, and so he told her. He needed to be clear with her and with himself.

"I know you're not here."

Becca looked around herself. She looked at the small landing where they stood and behind her into Tilda's room. Tilda had left the door half-open and a lamp on inside. Tilda always left lights on, even in the middle of the day. When they were married, she used to say that she hated coming home to a dark house. It made her sad, and so Harry had stopped turning off all the lights she turned on.

When Becca had seen all that she could see from the spot where she was rooted, she looked down at herself. She was wearing jeans and dark blue wellies and a hooded sweatshirt with a logo on the front Harry did not recognize. Her hair was back in a ponytail, and were it not for those terrible wounds, Harry would have sworn she was home for a holiday break from whatever graduate school she had chosen. Surely, she would have gone to graduate school. An MBA or a JD or maybe she would be thinking about a PhD. She had been the sort of girl who would become the sort of woman who would think about doing that.

"Then where am I?" she asked.

"What?" Harry had distracted himself thinking about the young woman in front of him and what she would be doing if she were really and truly there and alive.

"If I'm not here, then where am I?"

"You're in my imagination," Harry said. "I'm imagining you."

"Why?"

Harry should have seen that coming. The girl with all the "whys."

"Because I am very sick. I'm going to die, too, pretty soon. So I imagine that's why. Maybe I think that when I die, I'll see you again wherever you are. Maybe my brain is practicing for that moment. This is the sort of thing you should practice for, don't you think?"

"My room isn't up here," she said.

The practicality of it pulled him from his thoughts. They were the first thoughts he had had of his own death that weren't all cold and full of blanks.

"No, your room is on the second floor."

"Why are Mom's things up here?"

"We're not together anymore, but she came back to be with me while I die."

"Why are you dying?"

"My brain doesn't know how to tell my muscles what to do anymore. My legs and my hands don't work so well most of the time—but I took something, and I'm a little better tonight. Most of the time it's very painful. And eventually my brain won't be able to talk to my lungs or my heart either, and that will be that."

Becca took a moment to think about that, and then she started to move. She was not rooted to the spot after all. She walked right toward him, right past him there on the landing, and she put her hand on the rail, and she started down the stairs. Harry would have sworn—he would absolutely have sworn—that the air moved when she went by, that it moved and tickled the hairs on his arm just below the shirtsleeves he'd pushed up earlier that night.

He was going to follow her, of course he was. He would follow her down the stairs and out of the house and across the way and around the world if that was where she was going, but before he did, Harry took three steps forward. The pool of blood that collected around her feet was still there on the hardwood floor. He was glad it was not real, could not possibly be real, because there was a terrible lot of it, and it would seep into the grain and the very cellular structure of the wood, getting right down under the stain, and it would stay there forever, and no one could bear such a thing in their home. When she had walked away, she had walked through it. She had gotten the imaginary blood on the bottoms of her imaginary wellies and left imaginary and garish footprints across the landing and to the stairs and down the stairs, each one getting lighter and lighter the farther from the pool she had gone.

And while he did not want to, he had to. Harry took those three steps to the edge of the pool, and he put the toe of his house shoe into the pool and pulled it out again, streaking it across the floor. It did what real blood would do, obeying all the laws of physics and hydrodynamics and whatever other laws there were that he did not understand. The blood clung to his shoe, and it made a mark across the floor, and it was on him again. After twenty years, his daughter's blood was on him, and it was a very good thing that this was not real because that is the sort of thing that kills a man. Harry thought that very clearly. There was no doubt at all. If this were real, it would be the sort of thing that kills a man.

Harry was unsteady, a sort of tremble going all through him like shaking a pan of Jell-O. But he could not think too much about that right then because Becca had moved out of his sight, and that, more than anything that happened that night, scared him. Now that he had seen her, he wanted to never not see her again. And when he took the stairs after her, he took them faster than he had taken any stairs in more than a year and a half.

The next landing was empty, and this time when he put his hand to Rachel/Becca's door, it did not occur to him to hesitate.

"Becca?"

He saw the clothes on the floor and the tanks and the lights and the equipment that hummed and the electrical cords that snaked across the floor plugging into a half-dozen power strips that plugged into yet others. He saw them, but he did not see them because none of it told him where Becca was.

"Becca!"

Down again to the main floor. Shooby was waiting for him at the base of the stairs wearing the face he wore when something had gone wrong in his world—a missed walk or an imminent trip to the vet. Harry walked right past him and made a circuit of the whole floor.

Kitchen.

"Becca?"

Dining room.

"Becca?"

Library.

Parlor.

Storage closet.

Bathroom.

Garage.

"Becca?"

He tried the closet by the door where he hung his coat, and when that and all else had failed him, he went out onto the deck, leaving the door to the warm, golden, glowing house open behind him, and he yelled out to the bay.

But the bay did not answer him, and the sound of the water and the wind stole his voice so that not even the workers on the beach not so far away and just beyond the yellow tape heard any sound. There was nothing that Harry could do, but still he stood there in the cold dark until the wind-blown mist that was, he knew, the harbinger of a bigger storm soaked his shirt through and stuck his thinning hair to his head and collected on his eyelashes. He stood there until he started to shake, and a tingle under his skin—in his foot and in his hands—told him that the pain was going to come back and was already on its way. Only then did he go inside. His good sense told him to do it while he still could.

When Tip finally kissed her on the mouth, Tilda could taste herself on his lips and tongue, and she wondered if it had been an older woman who had taught him. Maybe young men had become better at things since she was a young woman. Maybe the proliferation of porn had done some good in the world, she thought, although she doubted it. An older woman, one who had come before her, made the most sense to Tilda, and if her nearly empty glass of prosecco were close at hand, she would have raised it in thanks to the unknown woman.

After the sandwiches and the wine, Tilda and Tip had not made it back upstairs. They were on the couch in the living room where she had once sat with Tip's parents and Harry playing cards. They had set up a folding table right over there, and Tip's mother had served salmon dip with crackers. Tilda had no idea why she remembered details like that from so long ago, but there it was. Salmon dip with crackers. The Feingolds had left the television on while they all played, which the men kept turning their heads to watch and which Tilda had found irritating.

The TV across the room from her now was new, a flat screen that hung on the wall, but the couch they were lying on might have been the same from that time. Tilda couldn't remember. She gave a shiver that had nothing to do with the memories, and Tip reached up and pulled the throw draped over the back of the couch over the both of them.

"Where did you go?"

"I was thinking about your mother's salmon dip," Tilda said, wondering why men always wanted to keep their houses so cold. Did they not feel it? Did they really not notice? Or was it being cheap? She felt the same way about lights. Why the insistence that the light above you be the only one on in the whole house?

"I didn't know my mother made salmon dip," Tip said.

"It was just the once."

"Okay."

"I don't have enough blood in my brain yet to make sense," Tilda said.

"I'll take that as a compliment."

Tilda let him but didn't offer up anything else. She didn't think it was ever good to let a man think he had nothing left to strive for. She had closed her eyes, but she didn't remember deciding to do that. She had just blinked, and then opening them again seemed too much trouble. It was fine with her. She was happy to stay right there with Tip under the blanket drunk with food and sex.

"So," Tip said.

"So what?" She kept her eyes closed. It didn't seem like the sort of question that required visual input.

"So what are your plans?"

Tilda scrunched her eyebrows. Was she supposed to have plans? Were they going somewhere later? She decided to open her eyes. Tip was on his side, his head balanced on one crooked arm and his other thrown over her body. It was nice, but it didn't make the situation any clearer.

"Sorry," she said. "I feel like I missed a step."

"You're going to be on Olloo'et for a while, right?"

"I assume so."

Tilda really hadn't thought about a concrete timeline. She was here for Harry for as long as he needed her. She'd given up her apartment in D.C. and sold the house in Seattle, which had become far too big for just her. Half the nights she was home, it seemed like it had grown since the last time she was in it, as if rooms were added and enlarged when she wasn't looking. She felt like a marble rolling around inside the bed of a pickup when she was in that house. Sometimes she walked into a room just to have been in it, just to check on things because it had been awhile. The house had become depressing. She was glad it was gone. Maybe she'd buy a loft or one of those little two-bedroom, craftsman-style bungalows. She'd always kind of liked those, even if the windows were too small.

All of that was in the future at some indeterminate time. Thinking about when—exactly—meant thinking about Harry's death, which she didn't want to think about at all.

"So what are you going to do while you're here?" Tip asked.

"I'm taking care of Harry."

"That doesn't sound like a full-time job."

"More than you'd think. He can't live alone—even if he would rather. That's why he called me. I was the caregiver of last resort."

"And yet, here you are with me."

"Well, he doesn't need me twenty-four seven. At least not yet."

"He will?"

"Probably. Eventually. He isn't going to get better."

"So you're just going to sit around and wait for him to get worse?"

"No, of course not."

Tip looked at her, waiting for her to fill in her plans, which ir-ritated her more than might have been reasonable. She had always been a person with plans. She had plans and planners and color-coded schedules. The plans came from goals, and Tilda had always had goals, which was why she always had plans. She'd had goals for herself and goals for her children and even goals for Harry, when they'd been married. But here she was, a woman neither young nor old, whose greatest goal—greatest success—was behind her, and if she wasn't going on to something bigger, and she really didn't think she was, then what would she plan for now? She had no idea, and having Tip point that out while he was still young and achieving with a whole mountain range full of peaks ahead of him that he could climb—well, he was just pissing her off. What did he know about anything?

"I'm fixing up a boat," Tilda said because it was true, and it was something at least.

"A boat?" Tip said it like he'd never heard of such a thing.

"A sailboat, a small one. Maybe eighteen feet."

"I didn't know you knew about boats."

"I am large. I contain multitudes."

If Tip got the reference, he didn't acknowledge it.

"What will you do with the boat once you've fixed it?"

"I'll take it out."

"By yourself?"

"Why not?"

"I just thought you might be looking to start a business or something."

"A boat business?"

"You're the one who brought up the boat."

Tilda laughed a not-real laugh. "Like what? I'm going to give three-hour tours?"

Tip didn't acknowledge that reference either.

"I'm just saying you can be something more than Harry's caregiver."

She did need to be something more than Harry's caregiver eventually. She would have to buy a loft or a bungalow and decide what to do with herself in the coming years. But deciding such a thing meant thinking about a world without Harry, and it did not honor—did not honor at all—how important taking care of Harry was. His would not be a good death. Harry would not live to eighty-five and then have a brain aneurysm while gardening. He wouldn't be one of those people about whom it is said, "He just fell over and died, couldn't even wait for the ambulance to arrive." Harry would come apart slowly. He already was. He would lose more and more movement. He would be bedridden. Then his speech would go and then his breath. He'd worked out a DNR order with Dr. Woo. Harry had told her before she moved in and had insisted that she agree. Knowing these things, it felt very important to take care of Harry while taking care of Harry still did him some good.

It was important for her, too, for the part of her that had healed after their family had come apart, healed but with a large, jagged keloid scar that, with more regularity than she'd like to admit, she rubbed up against, picked at, and wished was something other than what it was.

She'd probably been lost in her head for a while because Tip asked, "Do you mind if I turn on the *Daily Show*?"

The card game all over again.

"Sure," she said. "I need to get home anyway."

"You don't have to go."

"I think I do."

21.

It had taken a long time for Rachel to walk from the house to the tent. She'd had to be careful picking her way through the brambles and driftwood and rocks. She was having trouble judging depth and distances, so she concentrated very hard, and then it occurred to her that maybe she had been walking a long time, a very long time. Maybe an hour had passed crossing that short distance from the bottom of the stairs to the tent, and everyone had watched her do it. But she knew that wasn't true. It couldn't be true. Rachel told herself not to think about it.

Hooper, agitated, kept touching the outside of his pants pocket, patting it and squeezing the fabric like a sort of nervous tic.

"On top of everything, I can't find my damn phone," he said.

He touched his pocket again to no avail, and Rachel had the idea that they were halfway through a talk rather than at the beginning of one, which was concerning.

"When did you last have it?" Rachel asked, trying to concentrate harder on what he was saying.

"I was at the camp answering more damn e-mails from the compliance department. Maybe I had it after that. I don't remember."

The compliance department was in charge of tracking all of the grant money that came into the university, ensuring it was used only for its designated purpose and riding the researchers to turn in time sheets, data records, proof of performance documents, and whatever else the grantor decided they wanted that week. The fact that Hooper was getting more than a few e-mails from them was not, Rachel knew, a good sign.

She was sitting on a folding chair under the tent. She had taken off her shoes and was stepping into an olive green pair of waders, a combination of rubber boots and pants that came up under her armpits and was held up by suspenders. She had to be careful. They were too big for her, and putting them on was unwieldy. They would suddenly grow much longer and sprout new legs, so that they were waders for an octopus. It helped to close her eyes when that happened and feel her way into them. They were uncomfortable, even with her arms and legs in the right places. She didn't like the rubber wrapping around her, but she would have to push her kayak out a bit into the bay until the water was deep enough. She didn't want to do that in jeans.

Earlier, Rachel had told Hooper about the lock that had been broken on the pickup. She had used it to justify her reasons for moving out of the camp. The equipment would be safer with someone right here looking down on it, even during the small spaces between shifts.

He had come within a sentence of ordering her back to the camp but had stopped short. Rachel had forced her face and voice to appear calm and to offer nothing but the most well-reasoned arguments, arguments that had nothing whatsoever to do with John, even while her heart pounded and she sweated inside her clothes. If it came down to it, Rachel would outright defy Hooper, but she did not want to. And it seemed, from her end, that he did not want to be in a position to outright order something that might be outright defied, forcing everybody to retreat to their fortified positions. He tried to convince her to stay at the camp. She resisted. He became frustrated, and his frustration agitated her. Hooper had always been on her side. He valued what she valued, worked the way she worked, and overlooked shortcomings that others would not. She had relied on him, but now being around Hooper felt like putting a shoe on the wrong foot.

Rachel had finished suiting up, managing to get all of her parts in the right parts and all the buckled bits together. With a steadying breath, she collected her plankton net, notebooks, collection bottles, and all the other ephemera she would need out on the kayak. She was anxious to get on the water and to distance herself from Hooper's disappointment, to give her eyes a chance to see nothing but the darkness of the sky and the glow of the water. She just needed a little time and was stepping out of the tent, awkward in her big rubber pants, when she heard him yell after her.

"Bell! Hang on."

Rachel turned, hoping for the best but not expecting it. He did not usually call her by her last name.

"Give those waders to Marcus. I want you to preserve the catch the others bring in."

"Have you assigned anyone to check the ADCPs?" she tried. It wasn't as good an assignment as the kayak collection work, but it would be better than being stuck under the tent.

"I'll do that," Hooper said. "You do the formalin solution, and don't forget to note the information from the flow meters."

"I—" she started.

"Formalin," Hooper repeated.

"Right," Rachel said and began to unbuckle the suspenders.

Tilda held the front door open for Shooby, who was whining and pacing at her feet.

"Well, go out, if you need to go out."

Shooby looked up at her and cried but refused to cross the threshold.

"Look, pup. No one else in this house is allowed to be crazy at the moment. The crazy list is all full, so if you need to go out, go out." Tilda leaned down and gave his hind end a shove, but he dug in his paws.

"Okay fine. Don't go. But if you pee on the floor, you're going to have to figure out a way to clean it up."

Tilda shut the door and headed into the kitchen with Shooby at her heels. She put the bouquet of white flowers and wild greenery in a vase she found in the first cabinet she opened, which was where she used to keep the vases. It was a small, pleasant surprise not to have to search. The vase was a nice one, yellow ceramic with a scalloped edge. She filled it halfway with water and then decided to water herself and poured a small glass of orange juice, which reminded her she had to pee. She did that in the little half bathroom between the kitchen and the garage, which had the same soaps she'd seen earlier that day, the lavender ones in the floral paper. She had been right. She really didn't care for them that much. They made her hands smell like powdery old ladies.

When she came back out, she flipped through the mail on the kitchen table, even though it wasn't hers, and then she looked through a catalogue that had nothing but men's clothes while she drank her juice. She rinsed the glass and left it in the sink, and only when she'd done all of that and probably some other things that she had forgotten, did she pick up the vase with the flowers and carry it up the two flights of stairs to her bedroom.

Tilda remembered all of this because it seemed that all of it was horrible. Each of those was a terrible thing to be doing while Harry lay on the floor upstairs waiting for her to rescue him.

"Harry!"

Harry was on his side right in front of her bedroom door with his arms and his legs curled up like a roly-poly bug trying to close its shell. And when she went down on her knees beside him, setting the flowers on the ground, she could feel that his clothes were damp like they had not quite finished in the dryer.

"What happened?"

He opened his eyes. "You're home."

"What happened?"

"I couldn't stand up anymore, so then I sat down. I thought you'd be home soon, but when you weren't, I decided to lie down. What time is it?"

"Why are your clothes wet? Where's your cane?"

"I left it in the library."

"You walked up the stairs without your cane?"

"I was feeling better for a moment. But the moment passed. I didn't get to take a shower."

"Did you try to take a shower with your clothes on? Is that why they're wet?"

Harry turned down the corners of his mouth. "Don't be stupid."

"Why did you come all the way up here?" Tilda asked.

"I thought I saw something."

"How could you think you saw something up here?"

"I don't know. I just did. It wasn't here when I got here."

"What wasn't here?"

Harry closed his eyes again, tight this time, like the question was too overwhelming and more than a little irritating, just too much for one human to demand of another.

"Harry?"

He was still curled up, and she knew his hip and shoulder must hurt him and probably some other parts as well. Her knees already hurt, and she'd just gotten there.

"I'm going to call Dr. Woo." Tilda started to get up, but Harry's arm shot out and grabbed her leg.

"No, you're not."

Shooby let out another whine.

"Harry, something's going on. This is why you brought me here."

"I did not bring you here to tattle on me."

"I'm not—"

"I said no."

Tilda looked down at him and wondered if this show of temper meant something. She would mention it to Dr. Woo. That's how she was thinking of Harry there on the floor, like a list of symptoms that needed to be reported to the proper authorities for cataloging. There was probably some sort of software she could use for this, a cell phone application, for keeping track.

"If you don't stop that," Harry said, "you can damn well leave."

"Stop what?"

"Stop looking at me like that."

"You want me to leave? You want me to get up and leave you here on the floor? How do you think that ends for you?"

"Rachel will be back."

"Yes, of course, Rachel. Let's trust your health and safety to a complete stranger. I'm sure she'll make you a priority, much better than your family is doing."

"You're not my family."

"I'm the only damn family you've got, so shut your mouth."

"There's Juno," Harry said.

"You want me to call him?" Tilda said. "He can come out here and take care of you?"

Harry sneered.

There it was, Tilda thought. They were the sort of parents who threatened each other with the company of their only child. What a success they were. Tilda sat back and leaned against the balustrade. "So what do you want?"

Harry didn't say anything for a while, and Tilda wasn't sure if it was because he was thinking about it or because he was testing out the silent treatment. Her mind drifted to Juno and his girlfriend and what kind of parents they would turn out to be, and when Harry spoke, it interrupted her thoughts.

"I want to get in my bed."

"Fine. We can start there."

Tilda moved the vase of flowers out of both of their way, did a deep knee bend, and, from that position, wrapped her arms around Harry's chest. He'd pushed himself up to his elbow, and she got him up and over onto his butt. Once he was sitting, she went around behind him, went down deep, and braced herself again.

"When I get you up," she said, "you grab the railing there and stabilize yourself."

He made a noise that didn't mean anything to her.

"Can you do that?" she asked, still in her deep bend like a frog about to make a leap.

"Just do it," Harry said.

"Yes, your highness," Tilda said and heaved.

She got him up and standing on his own two feet, even if half his weight was on the railing. She thought about leaving him there and going to fetch his cane, but he didn't seem like he was in much shape to go down a flight on his feet. What he needed was one of those motorized chairs that go up and down along a track. Tilda promised herself that she'd look into that, but he was in no mood to discuss it then.

"All right," she said, moving around to his right side. "You're going to put half your weight on me. We'll try to go down that way."

"I can't move my right leg much just now," Harry said.

"Is it all right to drag it?" she asked.

"Unless you plan on cutting it off, I don't see a way around it."

"Okay then. On the count of three."

22.

Harry had lost thirty pounds or more since he had
gotten sick, but a grown man who had lost thirty pounds was still a
grown man. It had taken everything Tilda had to keep them both upright going down the stairs. They had taken a lot of breaks, and there
was one point when she was afraid she was going to lose her balance
and send them both ass over tea kettle. But there they were.

She'd gotten Harry down to the second floor. He needed to use the
bathroom, but he had yet to install any grab bars, which was something else Tilda added to her to-do list. His pride allowed only so
much, so Tilda left him there, holding on to the countertop while she
went to fetch his cane. It took him a while, but he managed to get
himself over to the toilet, down, and back up again. Or at least he told
her he did. She stood outside in the hallway on the other side of the
shut door.

He let her help him into bed and to remove his khaki pants and
cardigan sweater, shoes, and socks. He kept his boxers and his T-shirt
on. His right foot was turned in, and his calf and thigh muscle on that
side were already shrinking from disuse. His skin, unable to cope with
the rapid change and too old to be very elastic anyway, hung a bit
around his ruined parts. His bicep, too, was nearly gone, not any big-

ger than his forearm. His right hand was like his right foot, no longer in the shape it should have been.

Tilda thought she'd want to turn away from these things, that it would be painful to see her former husband like that—ruined, disabled, deformed. But it didn't bother her, at least not in that way. Seeing the wounds on his body rather than just hearing about the causes of them in his nervous system made Harry seem vulnerable to her. You didn't blame a wounded bird for pecking at you when you tried to help it.

Tilda covered him with a blanket and turned out the light. In the corner of his room was a wooden chair. It had one of those seat cushions that tie with little bows in back, which was not the sort of thing she would like, but just then she was grateful for it. Her body had been through enough that night. A little cushion was what she needed.

"Aren't you going to bed?" he asked.

It was dark enough that Tilda couldn't really see him, only the lumpy black outline of him and the bed, just slightly darker than everything around it. He did not want her to call Dr. Woo, and she had not. But she wasn't at all confident in that decision. She needed to see how things would go, at least for a little while, before she could close her eyes. Heaven forbid something worse than a fall happened while she was asleep.

"I will in a little bit," she said. "I'm just going to sit here and rest for a while."

"I'm fine," Harry said.

"I know you are."

Shooby took up his position by the bed, head on paws. He wasn't sleeping either.

Rachel stood up from the plastic folding chair. She had been sitting in the same position for so long, preserving and cataloguing what the others brought in, it felt like her joints had begun to rust into position. The worst of the side effects had passed. Time felt like time again.

Nothing changed shape or size or seemed more scary than before. She checked her watch. She had added the information to her secret notebook earlier, and there had been nothing but improvement since. It was something to feel good about.

Rachel threw another empty can into the waste bag. She was three diet sodas into her night, and it was time to make the trek up the beach and up the hill to the porta-potties by the road. It was enough of a deterrent that she had put it off until it could not be put off any longer, and when she finally made the dash, she made it at speed.

She could not have been gone long, she told herself, not more than five minutes. But when she came back, Hooper had returned from checking the offshore instruments. He was standing in the tent next to the chair she had occupied for two hours, and he was flipping through a notebook.

He was flipping through her notebook.

She did not stop. In fact, when she saw what she saw, she picked up speed and was still moving forward when she got to Hooper and pulled the notebook out of his hands. She kept right on going before slamming hard into the folding table with the computers and microscopes and nearly sending the whole thing toppling over in the sand.

"What has gotten into you?" Hooper demanded.

Rachel kept a steadying hand on the rickety table longer than was necessary. "That's my notebook. My personal notebook."

"It was just here," Hooper said.

Rachel had left her backpack by her chair when she had gone to the bathroom. She had forgotten it in the rush to relieve the pressure in her bladder, but she did not think she had taken the notebook out. In fact, the backpack had been zipped. She pressed her memory, and her memory agreed with her. It had been zipped. He had opened her things and taken the notebook out.

"What are we looking at?"

John seemed to come out of nowhere, but nowhere was only the darkness beyond the light of the tent. The bare bulbs powered by the growling generator—was it getting louder?—were so bright that they made everything beyond them vanish.

"Nothing," Rachel said.

"Dr. Bell is very protective of her work," Hooper said.

"We're all protective of our work," Rachel replied.

Hooper inclined his head in a way that meant nothing but seemed like a response. "I think you should try to get some more rest."

"Maybe I should," Rachel said. "Right now I have more classifications."

23.

Day Four of the Miracle

Tilda had fallen asleep in the chair. She snored. She had always snored but had been in deep denial of it since they'd been married. She'd slept there with Harry listening until three o'clock when she startled herself awake. Whether it was because of a dream or one of those jerks that come when your unconscious mind plays a prank and tells your body it's falling, Harry couldn't say. But he heard her get up and pause halfway to the door. Harry kept his eyes closed. He knew he was being watched, and he wanted to be alone.

When she was satisfied, he heard her leave the room. He heard her right-hand ring click against the stair railing when she started to climb, and he heard the creak one of the third-floor stairs always made. He could never remember which one and couldn't be bothered to have someone come fix it. Tilda stopped at the creaky stair long enough to hold her breath and curse and then continued up to her own bedroom. He didn't hear the door shut or the latch catch, and he had been listening for them. Harry, whose eyes were open now, scowled into the dark. He would have to be even more quiet.

By six a.m., Harry would have told you that he hadn't slept at all, which probably wasn't the whole truth. Probably a night-vision camera and some electrodes could've picked up thirty or so minutes of sleep here and there throughout the night for whatever good that had done. But at six a.m., he was awake. He had gotten himself out of bed with his cane and collected his pants and his sweater and put them on, along with his socks.

Dr. Woo had told him not to wear socks around the house. Harry was supposed to wear either rubber-soled shoes or go barefoot. It seemed socks didn't offer enough traction for someone in his condition. But the shoes that were out had laces, and his right hand wasn't up for tying laces. His slip-on shoes were in the closet, and sliding open the closet door might rouse Tilda. And he didn't like anyone to see his bare right foot. Its deformity was even more repulsive unshod, so socks with a chance of falling it was. He was beginning to get a little bit used to falling anyway.

Dressed, he sat back down in the dark and resumed his listening vigil. It wasn't long. By 6:15, he heard the back door open.

Rachel had decided she needed more samples, and while she still secreted away a dozen or so of the collection containers in the "food" cooler once it had been emptied of sandwiches each night, she no longer trusted that no one would find them when she wasn't looking. And if they did find them, they might take them. And if they didn't take them, they might contaminate them—either on purpose or by accident. She was betting on the former.

To guard against the possibility of sample sabotage, she had taken an X-Acto knife and a flashlight into the porta-potty with her. She had worn her puffy coat that night. The storm front that had been threatening hadn't kicked up much rain, but the winds were increasing and it was getting colder. The coat made her look like the Michelin Man. It was black, stuffed with down and quilt stitched into poufed stripes. Each one of the poufed stripes was big enough to fit one of the smallest collection containers, bigger than a flask but not much bigger.

When Hooper was away from the tent, she'd stolen eight she was supposed to be classifying and flash freezing. Just before the shift was over, she made her trip to the bathroom. With the jacket off and the flashlight in her mouth, Rachel slit open the outer fabric and pulled out as much of the down as possible. The feathers were small and light, and they stuck to everything, which wasn't something she'd planned for. Not planning for it made her angry at herself. She couldn't possibly clean all of them up, not from the inside of a porta-potty in the middle of the night. Anyone who used the toilet after her might see, and if they saw, they might guess. Either they would guess or they would think she was trapping, killing, and plucking seabirds in the bathroom.

Rachel kept going. There was no point in stopping then. She shoved each small container of specimens into the holes she'd made—one hole per quilted row of down on each side of the zipper, four usable rows, eight containers. Afraid her body heat would raise the temperature too much as it was, she couldn't risk doing it on the inside of the coat.

She made sure no feathers were peeking out of the holes and might be noticeable against the black fabric. The down that remained kept the containers secure and muffled any sloshing. Then she cleaned up the porta-potty as best she could, which involved touching a lot of surfaces she would really rather not.

By the time she was back in the beach house, her thoughts were on loading all of her samples—those of dubious security in the cooler and her secret stash—into the tanks. Any thoughts she had left were devoted to an OCD-level need to wash her hands. She was not in the mood to talk to anyone, and when she carried the cooler up the stairs and saw Harry waiting for her on the landing, leaning on his cane, she was prepared to make herself very clear.

He spoke first. "I have a report to make, and when I finish, you have to give me more of whatever that was."

Rachel sat the cooler down. It seemed to get heavier every night. "You experienced pain reduction?"

"It was so much more than that."

Rachel had still been thinking only of her samples and washing her hands. Only the smallest possible part of her mind had been engaged with Harry, but that small portion was a scout, and it sent word for the rest of her brain to suit up.

"Tell me," she said, turning and putting her cat eyes on him.

"In exchange for another dose."

"The first dose was in exchange for a report."

"I'm renegotiating."

He looked more rumpled than usual. He wasn't wearing any shoes, his pants looked like someone left them in the dryer for a week, and his hair was taking on an Einstein quality.

"I don't think you're in a position to renegotiate," Rachel said.

"I'm going to try. I have additional information."

"What information?"

"Side effects."

"What kind of side effects?"

"A second dose," Harry repeated.

A beat passed, and then Rachel nodded.

"Deal?" Harry confirmed.

"Deal."

"I saw things after I took the first dose."

"What things?"

"Things that weren't there."

"Known," Rachel said, disappointed that she'd traded more of her samples for predictable information. She should've been smarter.

"Known, what?"

"Known side effect of the active ingredient. Native people have been making up stories to explain the hallucinations for hundreds of years." Rachel picked up the cooler. "Eventually, I hope to be able to neutralize the effect."

"What kind of stories?"

She was heaving the cooler the rest of the way to her door, and her words came out strained and breathy. "They told missionaries that it opened up a path to their ancestors."

"Their ancestors, like ghosts?"

Rachel opened her door a crack and slid in with her samples. "Ghosts. They used the word *spirits*. It's a sort of curse."

"What kind of curse?"

Rachel's hand was on the door, and Harry could barely see her through the tiny opening she left.

"Sometimes angry or vengeful ancestors would try to coax men across the divide. When a man had been to the land of the spirits, no other tribal members could look upon him for twenty suns without facing terrible misfortune. Women would be struck barren by looking at their husbands before sufficient time had passed." She spoke as though she had memorized the passage from a textbook.

"The ghosts coaxed the men?" This seemed an important point to Harry that needed to be clarified.

It was not, it seemed, so important to Rachel.

"They were an uneducated people," she said and shut the door without giving any indication of whether she would open it again anytime soon.

Harry decided that she would keep her word and that he should wait. Certainly she meant for him to wait. Ten minutes went by.

Coaxed how? Seeing Becca had been unexpected. It had left him both terrified and thrilled, but she had not indicated he should follow her. This had not stopped him from trying, of course, but that was of his own volition. He did not doubt that Becca had been, as Dr. Bell said, a hallucination, but that did not stop him from wanting to see her. The pain relief, the mobility—they were wonderful, but seeing Becca was the high. "A curse," Rachel had called it. That did not seem a very apt term to Harry.

Finally, Rachel opened the door and handed him a spoon. "I really need to wash my hands," she said and pushed past him.

"Can I read them?" Harry asked, only glancing at the dose.

"Read what?" She was heading into the bathroom.

"The ghost stories."

"Do you speak French?"

"No."

"Then you would find it challenging," Rachel said and shut the door.

Harry looked at the spoon. It was a known side effect, and she did not seem worried. She wouldn't give him more than he should have. He knew that. He trusted her. She wasn't worried, and so he shouldn't worry.

24.

As project leader, tenured professor, and a man with a lot of letters behind his name, Hooper would have been entitled to marginally better lodgings than were being enjoyed—or perhaps endured—by the other members of the team, who were mostly post-doc researchers and a few graduate students, but he liked maintaining a certain "professor of the students" facade. Still, the truth was all of his years in the field had led to various illnesses and injuries, which were beginning to add up. There were those that could be measured (one case of reoccurring malaria, two bouts of hepatitis A, one seriously infected leg wound, giardiasis twice, and three or four notable cases of dysentery) along with the cumulative bodily stresses that could not be so easily measured but that manifested in aching knees, difficulty sleeping, and a back that wasn't as reliable as it once was. All of this made whatever creature comforts that could be had worth having.

Unfortunately, there weren't better lodgings available in the camp, and while he did not have to participate in the cooking and dishwashing chores that rotated among the other team members, this was not always a blessing. Hooper's own cooking skills could not be said to be wide, but they were deep. The six dishes that made up his repertoire had been perfected by round after round of experimentation, controlling for all possible variables until the ideal ratio of ingredients and precise cooking methods had been achieved. He was especially proud of his spaghetti carbonara. However, it would seem from the dinner he had eaten that night—and several of the other nights—that this domestic skill wasn't as widely developed as one might hope.

It had been Marcus's turn to cook that night. Hooper had agreed to be his thesis advisor not that long ago and had been impressed by the young man's fastidious nature and attention to detail in the lab. Hooper trusted Marcus's prep for an experiment more than he trusted his own, and given how much cooking had in common with the experimental sciences, Hooper had expected the skills to be transferrable. He had been disappointed.

Marcus's idea of dinner had been to pick up and prepare half a dozen boxes of off-brand macaroni and cheese, the kind that came with powder the color of hunter safety vests. He prepared these more or less according to the instructions but failed to cook the pasta long enough so that it stuck in Hooper's teeth, giving him the opportunity to taste it for a good long time. This had been paired with several other boxes of frozen chicken nuggets, which Marcus did have the good sense to reheat in the oven rather than the microwave. He had offered two condiments—ketchup and mustard. And because they deserved a treat, his shopping trip was topped off by a case of beer and a large box of individually wrapped children's snack cakes.

If this was how Marcus ate at home, Hooper was left to conclude that he was doing some sort of experiment to determine if consuming a sufficient quantity of preservatives could lead to immortality. Hooper did not care to offer a hypothesis on the matter, but he did feel that life wouldn't be worth living in perpetuity like this even if you could.

Those on the night shift had finished their dinner, including the entire box of snack cakes, and had left to get what sleep they could. The day shift had not yet gathered there in the dining hall, which, even clean, smelled like old food and disinfectant. Like any research trip,

Hooper had very few waking moments to spend alone, and he was spending them there. But at least he still had his beer, and that was something because Hooper was worried.

Rachel Bell had been his star post-doc. He wasn't sure he'd said that aloud to her or anyone else. Probably he had not. She was smart and meticulous, which could be taught, and she was driven, which could not be. It had not taken him long to know she would have a distinguished career ahead of her if she did not derail it of her own accord.

Rachel had constructed for herself a shell of equanimity, but it was thin and had a tendency to crack, especially when she was under stress. Things had been worse this past year. Her composure had become wobbly, and he had wondered at one point if she was ill. But he was the department chair, not her minder or even her friend, and besides, academia tended to tolerate difficult personalities that would be shunted aside in a more corporate environment. Eccentricities were, with no proof whatsoever, considered a sign of either intelligence or creativity or both.

In the cold dining room with a lump of undercooked macaroni and cheese in his stomach, Hooper knew he had been swayed by that academic fairy tale where Rachel was concerned. He had forgiven much, overlooked more, and allowed her more leash than, it seemed now, she could handle. He had, on this trip alone, allowed her to shun the rest of the team, duck out of most of the chores, and now she was staying in a beachside mansion while the others—including him—were sleeping on short-sheeted mattresses. This had led to serious disharmony among the others. Rachel was on the verge of being roasted on a spit by her peers. And more than that, he had now seen proof that she had, in nontechnical terms, gone rogue.

He had neglected some of his more basic duties as project leader, showed favoritism, and allowed a lack of discipline on his team.

"Shit."

It was a rookie mistake that he should have outgrown. Perhaps he had outgrown it once but had started to devolve. Maybe he didn't have as much business as he'd thought leading trips like this anymore. Maybe he would be better off retiring to his lab and his lecture hall. Maybe it was time to retire all together. If he had the money, he would.

Hooper wouldn't have said that five years before, but it had been a rough five years. The divorce had been difficult on his bank account, and in an overreaction, he had made poor investment decisions from which he was unlikely to recover. Current projections estimated that he would be working in campsites like this one until he was ninety-three and a half.

It was the "half" that got to him.

Hooper reached into his pocket for his phone. He had thought without thinking that he should check for messages only to remember once again that the device was lost.

To console himself, Hooper drained what was left of his beer in a short chug and wondered if there was another left in the fridge. He pushed himself up to his full height and groaned. His long limbs had been folded quite severely onto the stool, and his knees and hips creaked as he rose. With a deep breath that he pushed back out with a hiss through his teeth, Hooper shuffled toward the kitchen. If he could find one last bottle, he would have just enough time to drink it and toss the evidence before the second shift arrived and made him coffee.

Rachel sat on the floor of the bathroom with the door locked, transcribing the notebook she'd ripped from Hooper's hand. She'd rather he had never seen it, but now that he had, she couldn't risk him looking for it again.

After mixing up Harry's dose, Rachel had spent two hours going through her usual procedure. Moving as quickly as she could, she'd set up her samples in their flasks and used the pipette to allot nutrients and green algae for food. She had lowered the tank temperature slightly. The variables were set and noted.

While those cooked, she transcribed her work into a new notebook. The tile floor was hard, and the shaggy, cream-colored bathmat offered less padding than she'd hoped. The sharp pain radiating from the two points in her pelvis that ground into the floor reminded her that she had not been eating. She hadn't been on a scale. She should weigh herself to better calculate dosage to body mass. She would make a note of that. In the meantime, she had less padding, and her butt hurt, forcing her to adjust her position. She wanted to take a small dose, just a little bit, to help her get through the work, and resisting took more self-discipline than she cared to admit. She had a little self-experimentation planned for later, and she couldn't risk skewing the results. With a deep breath, she set her jaw and pushed through.

Each page was copied from English to a shorthand code Rachel had developed in graduate school. It had proved undecipherable to anyone else, and other students had stopped asking to copy her notes. It was something she should have done originally. She could only hope that if Hooper went looking for her notebook again, he would be as stymied as they had been. As each page was completed, she tore the original into sixteen pieces and threw the pieces into the toilet to flush away.

When that was done, Rachel went back to her real work. She took four samples from the tanks and prepared each for the centrifuge. While they cycled, she set up a cooler with some pilfered dry ice from the work site. When the tubes were finished spinning, she discarded the liquid that had separated and was floating at the top. Then, using a small container of liquid nitrogen, she flash froze two of the samples and packed them in with the dry ice. Finally, she gathered the other tubes and a handful of supplies to take down to the kitchen.

Sometimes you needed a little fire.

Tilda had not slept much nor had she slept well, and when she woke later than usual but still exhausted, she was forced to choose between warm sheets but lots of tossing and turning or the self-satisfaction of just getting up and on with it. It wasn't an easy call, and she spent a good twenty minutes trying to deny the question altogether before dragging herself to standing.

She pulled her swim cap, goggles, and suit off the rack in the bathroom where she'd last left them to dry and shoved them in her gym bag with a towel. She wore the same sweatpants and sweat-shirt to the pool each time, and she pulled them out of the dirty laundry and put them on before heading down to the kitchen for a to-go cup.

On the way, she stopped on the second floor and tiptoed to Harry's room. She had left his door half open along with her own. It had been the best she could do without resorting to a baby monitor. She stuck her head inside. He was a lump under the covers turned over on his side and facing away from the door. She stood there for a moment, watching him much like she had watched her children sleep those years ago, as though her presence could forestall some waiting disaster. She had learned in the most horrible way that that was not true for her children, and she knew, too, that it was not true for Harry. But still she stood there and watched.

His cane wasn't in the same place she had left it the night before. She had put it near the head of his bed, so it would be easy for him to reach. But it was now at the foot, and Tilda assumed he had gotten up to use the bathroom, which meant that he was able to get up and use the bathroom, and she was grateful for that.

Harry hated cell phones and did not own one. Tilda no longer considered that his decision, not that she would put it that way when she came home with one for him. She would keep it charged and check that he had it in his pocket whenever she left the house. Tilda was still thinking about cell phones, which to get and where to get it, as she left Harry's room and headed for the stairs.

The guest room, which was really Becca's room, was right in front of her at the top of the banister. Anyone going up or down would come face-to-face with it. The door had been shut tight ever since the woman had shown up with her fish tanks and metal suitcases of equipment, and so the thin triangle of light that spilled out of the ever-so-slightly open door couldn't help but grab Tilda's attention.

She stood at the crack and tried looking inside, but the view was too limited. She saw only the thinnest slice of the room, and most of that was the unmade bed. It was almost as useless as looking through a peephole the wrong way. Tilda looked over her shoulder, but the door to that floor's bathroom was open and the light was off. She wasn't in there.

Tilda rapped her knuckle against the frame twice, not too quiet and not too loud, formulating a cover story as she did so. Maybe something about a cup of coffee or some extra towels. But there was no answer. Tilda rapped again just a little louder but not, she hoped, loud enough to wake Harry. Still no answer, and so she did what anyone would do. She pushed the door open and let herself inside.

25.

Before doing anything, Rachel had given herself a quick tour of the downstairs, checking the dining room, the library, the parlor, the bathroom, and even opening the closets and the door to the garage. It was too bad the kitchen didn't have a door, but it couldn't be helped. A burner was something Rachel hadn't packed.

She'd filled a standard cooking pot with tap water and set it on the stove with the fire turned up as high as it would go. The two tubes from the centrifuge were sealed, and when the water came to a full rolling boil, she dropped one of them in, along with a razor blade. And then she waited.

The ten minutes were torturous. She paced back and forth in front of the stove and, when that got old, in a triangle pattern from the stove to the sink to the refrigerator, which she opened and closed twice before remembering that she was supposed to eat more food. It was a terrible time to remember. She didn't want anything in her stomach for this experiment, and knowing she couldn't eat only made her want to eat more. She decided to leave the fridge alone and went about opening all the cabinets and inspecting all the contents until her watch finally beeped.

Rachel donned an oven mitt, just to be safe, and used a pair of kitchen tongs to pull the tube and then the blade out of the boiling water and take them over to the sink. She ran cold water over them until the razor blade, the tube, and the contents were cool enough to work with.

Then Rachel pulled up the sleeve of her sweatshirt. She took a breath, closed her eyes, and before there was time to have another thought, she picked up the blade and dragged it across the inside of her forearm. She had to hold her arm over the sink. The blood was coming faster than she'd expected, and she worried for a moment that she'd gone too deep. Rachel grabbed the tea towel lying near the sink and held it to the wound until blood no longer ran but rather oozed out of the three-inch cut. Taking care not to drip on the counters and floor, Rachel opened the small glass tube that had been boiled and swallowed the contents.

And then she waited again.

The pain in her back was chronic, and like most chronic pain, the intensity changed from hour to hour, day to day. She needed something more standardized—more acute—to start logging accurate experiments.

After twenty minutes, she didn't have to palpate the wound to know the boiled sample had not worked. Her heart beat faster, and she had to take a breath and tell herself it might all still be nothing. She had to test the control to know for sure. Rachel took up the second glass tube that she had brought down to the kitchen but had not dropped in the boiling water. She unsealed that one and, just like the first, swallowed the contents.

She didn't enjoy the taste, but the solids were less rotten-fishy than the unseparated paste.

She spent the next five minutes bandaging the wound and telling herself the experiment wouldn't work. It was a superstition of hers that she'd developed during her master's program. If she believed something would happen, it probably wouldn't, and she would be disappointed. So the obvious thing to do was to decide ahead of time that the thing wouldn't work out at all, and then it would. Although you couldn't, in your mind at the time of the experiment, make that last leap to success because that would be believing it would work, which would take you back to the first condition, which was that believing you were about to be successful ensured that you would not be.

By the time she'd finished applying the gauze and the medical tape, which wasn't supposed to pull too much on hair and skin but did anyway, and thinking all of her superstitious thoughts, she knew it had worked. Her arm didn't hurt at all.

She clamped a hand down over her mouth to keep from letting out the whoop that was rushing up her vocal chords. Chemicals hold up well to high heat. Proteins and peptides are destroyed by it. That meant that her active compound, whatever it was, was not a chemical. Rachel, her hand still over her mouth, leaped up and spun around 180 degrees and then did it again just to let out a little more energy. She hadn't been this excited since she'd taken the first dose in the camp cabin.

She knew something. She knew it for sure, and it was important. It was a piece of information that she would need to synthesize the compound into something stable and reproducible.

Grinning, she went to gather up her supplies and race up to her room, remembering at the last possible moment the promise she'd made to herself. Rachel went back to the pantry and added a half-eaten package of Oreo cookies and an old-looking box of Chicken in a Biskit crackers. While she was gathering supplies, she took two sodas from the fridge, fitting one in each pocket of her sweatshirt. No one would claim these things equaled a balanced diet, but they were all high in calories. And calories were nothing but a measure of energy. The more the better, Rachel reasoned, and sprinted as quickly as her load would allow up the stairs.

High from the excitement, she didn't even notice the door to her room was unlatched.

"What are you doing in here?"

Tilda had not been paying attention. It was the first time she had been in Becca's room in—well, she didn't really know how long it had been. She had held her breath when she'd crossed the threshold, as though that might protect her or gird her or make it easier in some way. But once she was inside, she realized it wasn't Becca's room at all. Becca's room was gone. It was in some other time, and what was here instead was—this.

Tilda was absorbed by all the tanks and the lights and the tubing. My God, she'd never seen so much plastic tubing in her whole life. And there were flasks and jugs and jars full of all kinds of things she couldn't identify, but which might have been pond scum. She had opened up one of the coolers, and smoke had billowed out. She'd slammed the lid back down and hadn't touched anything after that. It was a lot to take in, which was why the voice scared the shit out of her.

Tilda spun around and put her hand to her heart like some sort of Southern heroine, which was embarrassing but not as embarrassing as getting caught snooping.

"I was looking for you," Tilda said. It came out in such a rush she knew it couldn't sound natural.

The woman, Rachel, set a cardboard box down on the bed, which was unmade and covered in papers and clothing that all looked dirty. Tilda had had to fight the urge when she'd first come in to either pick up or scold someone. Sticking out of the top of the box, Tilda noticed her stash of Oreos. They were *her* Oreos. Harry hated Oreos. He always had. It hadn't occurred to her that Rachel would be stealing them.

"Did you touch anything?" the woman asked.

"Did I—no. I didn't touch anything."

"It's important. You have to tell me if anything was moved."

"It wasn't."

The two women looked at each other, and Tilda had the feeling Rachel was waiting for her to flinch.

"It wasn't," Tilda said again.

Rachel ran her eyes over the tanks and contraptions, trying to determine, Tilda supposed, if she was lying. Tilda thought about the cooler but refused to look in that direction and give herself away.

"You can't come in here without permission," the young woman said. She said it with such authority that Tilda was taken aback.

When Tilda didn't offer a response—and perhaps the young woman wasn't waiting for one—Rachel said, "If you were to disturb something, it could taint the results. It would be disastrous."

Tilda was meant to feel like she'd bumped the arm of a brain surgeon mid-procedure. "I came by to see if you needed anything," she said.

"Harry told me to help myself."

Tilda looked down at the food. "I see that you are."

The woman looked down, too, and shifted her weight. The comment had wrong-footed her, and Tilda moved forward. It was like a game of tennis, and the advantage was now hers.

"What work exactly are you doing for the university?" Tilda asked.

Rachel avoided eye contact. "It's technical."

"I spent two terms on the senate science committee," Tilda said. "I think I can handle it."

"I'm not at liberty to discuss it."

"That's unusual," Tilda said.

The woman didn't reply.

"Under whose authority are you not at liberty to discuss your work on this very public biological phenomena?"

Again silence. The young woman removed two cans of soda from her sweatshirt pockets and set them on the bedside table, as though she were going to go about her business whether Tilda continued to stand there and jabber or not.

"If those are cold, and I presume they are," Tilda said, "please don't set them on that table. They'll leave rings."

Still no verbal response, but the woman moved the cans to the rug next to the bed, where they would surely be kicked over.

Without a good-bye, Tilda crossed the room, passing within inches of Rachel, and stepped out into the hall. Rachel reached for the door, but before she could shut it, Tilda put her hand on the frame and said over her shoulder, "Eugene Hooper—I believe that's his name—was in yesterday's paper. He gave a rather extensive interview about your team's research. I suppose no one told him it was classified."

Tilda let her hand fall from the frame, and Rachel shut the door without comment.

The skin was looser above Tilda's knees than it used to be and above her elbows and breasts. She avoided touching her neck when she sat in front of a computer. She used to rest her hand there often. It was her unconscious thinking pose, but it just reminded her of how different her skin felt now—less elastic, like panty hose about to go south. Her forearms had a bit of mottling that maybe she should discuss with a dermatologist. The veins and sinewy bits were more visible in her hands and the tops of her feet than they used to be. And that was just off the top of her head.

There were any number of reasons to feel more self-conscious about her body than she used to, and there were times she did. But pulling on her silver one-piece racing suit with its body-sucking tightness, its low leg openings and high neck, the shoulder-blade area cut out for maximum movement was not one of those times. She didn't think about her neck or her knees in her suit. The pool was her home court. In the pool, she could beat any woman her age, most of the men, and a high percentage of the younger people, too. In the pool, she didn't need anyone to grant her a position. She took it.

Tilda shoved her duffel bag into one of the half lockers in the ladies' room and walked with her cap and goggles in hand to the showers. She rinsed off in warm water, wet down her hair, and pulled on her cap, tucking the ends up inside. Last, she put on her goggles, leaving the eye pieces up on her forehead, and walked in her flip-flops out of the locker room to the indoor pool.

She was later than usual. The sun was well up, and the glass enclosure around the pool was lit like a fish tank, which only reminded her of that woman. Tilda used her name in her own mind as little as possible, as though that somehow kept the scientist in her place.

Tilda windmilled her arms in one direction and then the other, did a few deep knee bends, and then hopped off the edge into the shallow end of the pool. All of the lanes were occupied, and she'd have to split one, which did not make her happy. She chose the lane with the fastest swimmer, a man who looked to be in his early forties. She wondered, but not for long, why he wasn't in an office somewhere. Was he one of those Seattle tech millionaires who'd retired out here decades early? If he was, she thought, he'd be bored and useless within five years.

It was possible, she acknowledged, that she was in something of a mood. She would have to swim it out. She waited for the man to get to the other end of the pool. He grabbed the edge for a second-long break and nodded that he saw her. Tilda nodded back, pulled down her goggles, and pushed off from the wall.

Stroke, stroke, breathe. Stroke, stroke, breathe.

By the time she'd done two lengths of the pool, she'd passed her tech millionaire, and he'd slid over into the next lane, preferring to share with someone else.

Stroke, stroke, breathe. Stroke, stroke, breathe.

26.

When Tilda returned to Harry's house, her hair was still wet. She was carrying a plastic bag from the corner market along with her duffel and was using her one free thumb to check her text messages.

"I like you more than I should," Tip had written.

She stared at the screen. She should say something but hesitated to say too much. Emoticons were out of the question.

"I like you, too," she replied, a response she immediately felt was both sophomoric and awkward. So much about dating, including the word *dating*, felt sophomoric and awkward, and she suspected other people did it better.

She shoved the phone into her pocket and adjusted her bags. This package of Oreos she would keep in her room. Kicking off her shoes at the door, she stopped in the kitchen for a glass of milk and carried it and her things deeper into the house, following the sound of a television playing sports. Harry hated sports.

Opposite the library was the family room. A large flat-screen television took up one wall, and a cluster of leather sofas and chairs were gathered around it, making only enough room for a large traveling trunk that served as a coffee table. On top was a bottle of beer and a glass of red wine, the latter closer to Harry, who shouldn't have been drinking it—not that Tilda didn't understand the impulse.

"Juno," Tilda said. "I didn't know you were coming."

Their son was stretched out across the entire sofa with his arms crossed over his chest and Shooby, who shouldn't have been on the furniture, lying across his knees. The game she'd heard earlier was a snippet from a highlight reel playing as part of a cable sports news show, which she knew Harry would hate even more than an actual game.

Juno took his eyes off the screen, which was large enough to create a sort of black hole, increased gravity–type effect, and pushed himself up to greet his mother, dislodging the dog, who hopped down and took a secondary position at Harry's feet. Juno was taller than both her and Harry. He gave her a not-overly long hug, and when he did, she wondered how such a large man could have come from her body. He kissed the top of her head and wrinkled his nose.

"You smell like chlorine," he said.

"They only have cheap shampoo at the community center. I'll shower again in a minute."

"Whenever I smell pool chemicals," Juno said, "I think of you."

Tilda supposed most mothers would like their grown children to say they smelled of flowers or maybe homemade cookies. Tilda had managed to swim out most of her earlier aggression, so she found the space in her brain to honor his truth—or whatever bull hockey she was supposed to think.

She smiled at him and said, "Modeling a healthy lifestyle for my son two decades and counting." And then in the next breath, "Where's your car?"

"I didn't bring it. The ferries were too packed. I called last night to say I was coming," Juno said, "but no one answered the phone."

"I didn't hear it ring," Tilda said.

"You weren't home yet," Harry said. Despite the subject matter, Harry was not immune to the super gravitational field generated by the television set. It kept his eyes from following his son and ex-wife, and instead he scowled at the screen like it was doing something very rude. "She spends the night with her boyfriend now."

In her imagination, Tilda walked the three steps over to Harry's chair and smacked him upside the back of his head. As much as her private life was none of Harry's business, it was even less Juno's.

"What boyfriend?" Juno demanded.

"Your father is just being rude."

"But you do have a boyfriend?"

"I went out to dinner," Tilda said, moving around her son and the couch to put a coaster down under the bottle of beer. "That hardly makes him my boyfriend."

She had found and purchased that antique trunk at a flea market in Seattle twenty years before. She preferred it not be ruined in twenty minutes. Also it was a distraction from this conversation.

"Where did you meet him?" Juno asked.

Tilda stood up and turned to face her son. "He lives next door."

"In the Abrams's old place?"

Harry answered. "Other side."

"The Feingolds moved?"

"No," Harry said, "it's the Feingolds' kid. The parents didn't move. They died."

"God, Mom." Juno said it like someone had punched him in the gut, and the words were the last rush of air he had left. Tilda expected him to put the back of his hand to his forehead and slump down into a chair like Scarlett O'Hara. "I played with him when we were kids."

Tilda snatched the pillow he'd been lying on off the couch and fluffed it with enough force to release the feathers in one big poof if she wasn't careful. "Oh, you did not. He's much older than you are. You didn't give each other the time of day."

"He's not that much older than I am," Juno said, which did not refute the lie he'd just told.

"Where's Anna Beth?" Tilda asked with all the patience she could muster.

"At home."

"You didn't bring her?"

"We had a fight."

Juno sat back down.

"A fight about what?" Tilda asked. She glanced at her ex-husband, who seemed as surprised as anyone to hear this. Of course he hadn't asked, she thought. Why would he?

"She wants to get married," Juno said.

The obvious and unsaid ending of that sentence was "and I don't."

Tilda looked to Harry. "Would you turn that damn thing off?"

He reached for the remote.

"Did she ask you to marry her?" Tilda asked.

"She said I should have already asked."

There were a hundred things Tilda might have said, and all of them were trying to push their way out of her mouth. Anna Beth would be good for Juno; although Tilda wasn't sure the reverse was true. But the one thing Tilda did not want and would never do was to insert herself between Juno and a girlfriend. Not even now. She said this last bit to herself firmly. Anna Beth was, after all, eight months pregnant with his baby, not to mention as good a young woman as Juno was likely to attract. A stable home life would—Tilda stopped herself.

"Are you okay?" she asked.

"Not really." Juno had drained the bottle of beer and was peeling off the blue-and-silver label in little strips.

Tilda walked over beside him and put her hand on his head, smoothing his hair like she used to do. "What do you need right now?" she asked.

"A place to stay."

"I'll put some fresh sheets on your bed and lay out the towels," Tilda said.

"Thanks, Mom."

Tilda didn't think twice about acting as though this were her home to share, and Harry didn't say anything at all. Perhaps, Tilda thought, he would offer his own kind of support and comfort, something only he could do that Juno had come to appreciate. Tilda hoped so, as much because of how sad it would be for Harry as for Juno if he couldn't manage anything at all.

"What's your next step?" she asked Juno.

He shrugged and kept peeling the label.

"She's less than a month away from delivering your baby," Tilda said. "You'll have to do something."

He didn't answer, so she kissed the top of his head and went to get a set of sheets before she took that shower.

"Oh." She had almost forgotten. "We have another houseguest."

Juno's eyes shot up, and his voice was defensive. "Who?"

"Rachel," Harry answered. "Dr. Rachel Bell."

Juno's head swiveled to his dad. "Is she one of your doctors?"

"No," Tilda said, cutting off any answer Harry had planned. "She's one of the researchers working out on the beach."

"The 100-Year Miracle," Juno said.

"Yes, apparently her lodgings were less than five-star, so your father invited her in."

"You invited a total stranger to come live in your house?" Juno asked his dad.

Tilda couldn't help feeling just a little self-satisfied. Harry wasn't the only one who could turn their son like a heat-seeking missile. She left Harry to answer that question and headed for the door.

"Mom?"

Tilda stopped.

"The Feingold kid?"

She couldn't suppress the sigh as she walked away.

Tilda climbed the stairs. She was thinking about the logistics. There were the sheets and towels, and she'd need to go to the grocery store for more than just Oreos with Juno in the house. When she came to the top of the landing, it was almost a surprise to find herself just where she had stood that morning. It seemed longer ago than that. She reached out and put a hand to the doorknob. Tilda wasn't sure what she hoped to feel. Hot? Cold? Something that would tell her what was go-ing on in there? It was the hiding that made her so frustrated and an-gry. Wasn't that always true? Tilda let the doorknob go and went to the linen closet to make her son a fresh bed.

John stood outside Hooper's cabin. He had knocked and was won-dering if he should knock again when the door opened. Hooper was wearing a gray university sweatshirt with the plaid collar of a but-ton-up poking half out around the neck. The two shirts did not match, not each other and not the green, multi-pocketed field pants he also wore along with black socks and strappy sandals secured with Velcro.

"I need to talk to you about Dr. Bell," John said.

Hooper had not stepped out of the doorway or invited him in, and John's opening line did nothing to change that.

"I don't want to be the one to rat," he went on.

"But you're going to rat?"

It was the first thing Hooper had said, and his tone took the younger man by surprise.

"I think Rachel is conducting unauthorized research," he said, try-ing to plant himself on firmer ground. "In fact, I know she is."

"I know it, too."

John blinked. He had not imagined that Hooper would've allowed competing work on his site. The younger man assumed that all he needed to do was inform him, and action would ensue. But Hooper just stood there, as if waiting for John to get to the point.

"The breeding colony is sensitive," John said, shocked at having to state what was so obvious. It didn't take an ecologist to see what was happening. Any scientist at all should have been up in arms. "We must ensure that none of us takes more than absolutely necessary."

"I'm aware of the risk," Hooper said. "Any work we do is a risk, just as doing nothing is a risk."

John didn't think that was true at all, and his blood pressure was rising along with his indignation. He needed Hooper's support and had expected to get it. Now it seemed he was siding with the enemy.

John switched tactics.

"I'm concerned that it's impacting Dr. Bell's work and also her health." The last part, while true, came out sounding slightly less sincere than he'd hoped.

"Do you know what she's doing precisely?"

John hesitated. The fewer people who knew about the *Artemia lucis*'s effects the better, but Hooper was the only authority Dr. Bell recognized. Short of running her over with the research van, John didn't know what else to do.

"She's making a narcotic."

Hooper said nothing. John said nothing. There was a sudden high-pitched screech, and John jerked to look over his shoulder.

Hooper didn't flinch. "Two squirrels fighting over a tree. They've been at it all morning."

John looked back at Hooper.

"So you think Rachel is building a narcotics lab in her spare time?" he asked.

Hooper was twisting his words, putting him on the defensive. "She's a chemist," John said.

"A biochemist."

"In this case, that only makes her more effective."

"Do you have evidence?"

"Look at her!" John was losing his temper.

Hooper held up a hand. "Let's see how things develop," he said.

"I don't think—" But Hooper shut the door before he'd finished the sentence.

John knocked again. He stood on the cracked concrete pad that served as Hooper's front porch for two more minutes, but Hooper never opened the door, and then the sound of the shower running came faintly through the walls.

John was truly angry now.

It would not be, he thought, such a terrible thing if the damn woman destroyed herself, as long as it happened quickly enough. She did not respect what she was dealing with. She did not respect John or the Olloo'et, not their history, their knowledge, or their right to protect the breeding colony. Hubris had killed scientists before, and human nature being what it was, John saw no reason why it couldn't now.

27.

Olloo'et Island is shaped like a boomerang with Olloo'et Bay cradled in the center. Dr. Woo's office was on the far tip of the island not far from the ferry terminal. All the roads on the island were two lanes, and it should have taken Tilda twenty minutes from door to door to drive Harry to his appointment. With the off-season tourists clogging things up, it took twice that long, which was even more frustrating than it would have been on the mainland. There was not supposed to be traffic on Olloo'et. There was never traffic.

She had rolled down her window a crack when they'd left the house. The world smelled like rain, not just the clean, fresh smell they always had in this damp, drizzly place, but real rain. Tilda couldn't say she was looking forward to it.

The inside of the car was quiet. Harry had turned off her country radio, and she had let him. It was a sort of reward. He'd made it out of the house and to the car and then into the car without her assistance at all. He seemed to hardly need the cane. Perhaps he'd been doing the therapy exercises Juno told her he'd been refusing for six months. Perhaps he was finally taking his medications on the precise schedule Dr. Woo had written out. Whatever it was, it was working. She'd tried asking, but he'd only grunted and said something about the hills and valleys leading to his eventual and imminent demise. That was when she'd rolled down the window.

"So," she said, tapping her fingers on the steering wheel to hurry along the other drivers. "What are we going to do about Juno?"

Harry had been looking out his side of the car and turned just enough to see her out of the corner of his eye. "What do you mean 'do about him?'"

"I'm not suggesting we get involved in a lover's quarrel," Tilda said.

"We shouldn't get involved in anything at all."

"Your plan is to have him live in his childhood bedroom for the rest of his life?"

"He got here two hours ago. How about we give it another hour before declaring a state of emergency?"

Tilda knew two things. One was that she was, in fact, getting ahead of herself. The other was that Harry was in no position to question anyone's parenting. Rather than dwell on it, she turned her radio back on. Patsy Cline saves the day.

One verse in, Tilda had relaxed enough to mouth the words as they crawled around a snake-curve stretch of road. There were at least three cars ahead of her, maybe more she couldn't see, and they had reduced the functional speed limit to twenty-five miles an hour.

"There are too many people here," Harry said when Patsy faded away and a commercial took her place.

"Yes, but they'll leave at the end of the week," Tilda said over the announcer's push for over-the-counter antacids.

"I thought we might get away for a few hours."

Tilda had not been paying that much attention to Harry since he'd called her a hysterical harpy—or words that could be translated by her to that effect. But this made her ears twitch and turn toward his voice like a cat.

"We?"

"I got two tickets to the symphony. You can come if you want."

"You sure know how to sweet-talk a girl."

Harry was back to looking out his window. Their wagon train had reached a four-way stop up ahead, and other wagon trains of tourists had reached the stop from other directions, and the "is it you/no me/ no you/no ME" cha-cha was playing out. Still, Harry kept his face turned away from her, and he wasn't responding.

"How did you get the tickets?" Tilda asked.

"I bought them."

"You bought two tickets?"

"Yes, is that important? I bought them. I bought two tickets."

"When you were buying the tickets, who did you think would use the other ticket?"

Harry sighed like a teenager. "You, obviously."

"So why not just ask me to go with you?"

"I did."

"You said you had an extra I could use if I wanted, sort of like 'Hey, there's some leftover pizza. You can have it. Otherwise I'm giving it to the dog.'"

"It's not enough that I bought you a ticket to the symphony?" Harry asked. "Now I have to tell you I bought you a ticket in just the right way, or I'm implying that you're leftover pizza?"

"I'm just saying you could flat-out ask me to go to the symphony with you."

"Yes, let me do that because the whole evening sounds so great now."

"You know, I totally let you off the hook for that bullshit you pulled in front of Juno, and now you're going to give me crap about this?"

"What bullshit in front of Juno?"

"Telling him about Tip was unnecessary."

"It was not unnecessary. It was the answer to the question why no one picked up the phone. I was collapsed on the floor, and you were off with your new boy toy."

"So now I'm supposed to feel guilty for dating? I didn't know you were hurt, Harry. I didn't leave you there on purpose. You're the one that doesn't want people pecking around you all the time."

"I never told you to feel guilty. If there's anything I learned from that damn couple's counselor, it is that I am not responsible for whatever the hell you feel. I'm just saying that what I said was the truth, and if you don't want people to know it, then maybe you shouldn't be doing it."

Tilda waited her turn at the four-way stop sign and considered it personal growth when she didn't T-bone the crossing monstrous black SUV just for the stress release of it.

Harry crossed his arms and closed his eyes but then felt weird about closing his eyes, so he opened them again. His head was tilted back against the headrest, and his gaze was up at the rearview mirror. Seeing her there startled him so badly that he whipped around, bumping Tilda's arm, which caused the steering wheel to jerk and her to yell at him again.

"What the hell are you doing?"

Harry was twisted around in his seat, looking left and right and left across the back. He even peered down into the floorboard just to make sure. Becca had been there, and then she was gone.

He turned back around in his seat, and Tilda was still talking. "What is it?"

"Nothing."

Harry looked back up into the rearview mirror, but she did not reappear. The fleeting glimpse was all he was going to get, and he didn't know whether to be terrified or excited. He hadn't known after last night if he would ever see her again.

"It was clearly something. You're acting crazier than a wound-up house cat."

"I thought I saw a spider."

"You thought you saw a spider in the backseat from the front seat?"

"In the rearview mirror. I thought I saw a spider in the rearview mirror."

Tilda looked at him for as long as she dared, glanced back at the road, and then gave him another look. She didn't know what the hell was the matter with him, but that spider lie was just stupid.

"Are you having some sort of episode?" she asked.

"The episode I had was when I bought the other damn ticket. Are you going to the symphony with me or not?"

It was becoming clear to Tilda that everyone around her was losing their minds.

"I'd love to."

"Great."

"Great."

Harry went back to his perch, staring out the side window and trying not to look nuts, and Tilda allowed herself one small shake of her head. There was no way she wasn't going to bring this up with Dr. Woo. Maybe it was a symptom of the disease progression, or maybe his medication needed to be adjusted. But whatever it was, Tilda thought, it was making him weird.

After eating a handful of Oreos and washing them down with soda, Rachel had kicked off her shoes and crawled under the comforter fully clothed. When the alarm on her phone went off, she rolled over and looked at her tanks. The room was getting dark. It had been cloudy all day, cloudier than usual, and the only light came from the tanks. From the tanks. Not from the lights over the tanks. Those the timer had switched off half an hour before. The tanks themselves were glowing green.

She sat up and tried not to breathe too hard or otherwise disturb a single molecule in the room, lest it be the important molecule that had kept her arthropods alive. Because holy mother in heaven, they were alive. Rachel stopped herself. She couldn't know that. All she knew was that there was a green light coming from the tanks. Rachel stayed where she was on the bed with her sweatshirt twisted the wrong way around and her ponytail pulled halfway out. She stayed there and tried to figure out what might be happening that would make her tanks glow green but that would not mean her experiment had worked.

Rachel was a chemist. She could make something burn green if she wanted to, and so could her colleagues. Boric acid mixed with methanol and set on fire, for example. That would be green. Rachel thought about that and got out of bed. She had to stand there for a moment with her fingers on the edge, steadying herself. She wasn't feeling well, but that wasn't surprising. Little food and no sleep. She reached for the box of flavored crackers by the bed. She'd eaten some earlier and hadn't bothered to close the top. Rachel put two in her mouth, wiped her hand on her sweatshirt, and all but tiptoed to the tanks.

She pulled one of the flasks out and held it up next to a lamp she'd switched on. She could see the *Artemia lucis* floating in the water, little bright green flecks shimmering and pulsing. Their bodies were semi-transparent. Only their complex eyes, tiny black dots, were truly opaque. She concentrated on their legs, all twenty-two of them, which were so small they looked almost like hairs. Were they moving, or was it the trembling of her hand?

Shit.

Rachel set down the flask and dug out a clean pipette to extract a sample. Using the lower powered of her two microscopes, she took a quick look. The *Artemia lucis* would not survive out of the water for any significant period of time. She had not taken a significant period of time to look, but still, the creature died in front of her eyes, giving one last twitch of its legs. She watched as the green light that was strongest along its medial line faded and went out, leaving only the rust brown color of its exoskeleton. The creature had not been long for this world even before she touched it.

She backed away from her microscope, looked at her flasks, blinked, and thought that perhaps, in that microsecond of time, the glow was a little more dim. Rachel smiled. First just a little and then some more. She couldn't help herself. She did a little *Flashdance* stompy move right there in the fading glow because while it might be fading, while thousands of the creatures might be dying, they were dying much more slowly than they had before, which meant that she had done something right. Maybe not quite right enough. Some dial somewhere needed to be turned up just a little more, but she was almost there and not one moment too soon.

The adrenaline was almost too much. She was high on biochemicals. She needed to calm down. She needed to think. Rachel walked back to the bed, picked the half-empty can of soda off the floor, and chugged what was left, warm and flat. Then she had another cracker, found the spoon she'd used to take the last dose, and licked it just in case any of the compound was left.

The highest priority, she knew, was to protect her work. She had a lot. She knew a lot. She could keep the bugs alive for longer and longer. She had human subject data. The active compound was a protein, maybe a peptide. It was an incredible amount for only four days' work. It was prodigious. It was superhuman even. And she would do anything at all to protect it. To protect herself. Jesus, she thought, she'd gotten out of bed. She'd just gotten out of bed like that was something she did. If she'd had to explain to someone the miracle of that, she wouldn't have been able to. It was as though she hadn't really been alive before.

Rachel shook herself out of the reverie. She was losing time. She pulled off her clothes—just like that!—and reached into a duffel bag for something cleaner to put on. The bag was empty of anything useful. She went to the closet. Only one T-shirt was left on a hanger. She pulled that out, grabbed some jeans and a sweater from the floor, and put it all on.

With the contents of two of the flasks, she made a quick paste. She didn't weigh the amount this time, and she didn't grind it as fine as she had. She was used to it. She didn't need to count everything anymore, not for herself. She would be more careful with anything she gave Harry, of course, but she knew the right dosage. She swallowed the brown lump and chased it with an Oreo.

Tick-tick-tick went the clock.

She had her shoes and her socks in her hand when she opened the door of her bedroom.

"Hello."

Rachel clutched her sneakers to her chest and clinched everything. "Who are you?"

"Juno. You must be Dr. Bell."

Rachel didn't answer. Instead, she pulled the door closed behind her.

"I'm sorry I scared you," he went on.

"Who are you?" Rachel asked again.

"Juno."

Rachel shook her head like a horse chasing away flies, which was what the redundant and useless information felt like to her. She could almost see it in the air around her like small golden lights, trying to get in her ears and into her brain, clogging up the works and slowing her down.

"You said that already."

He smiled. He thought he was funny.

"I'm Harry and Tilda's son. That's my room." He pointed at the door between Harry's room and the bathroom. It had been shut the entire time Rachel had been in the house, but now it was open. She could see part of the bed, neatly made up, and a dresser and a rug. It wasn't that different from her own room but without all the flowers and pastels.

Rachel wasn't sure how long she looked at it, but Juno started talking again.

"My mother told me you're one of the researchers working down at the bay."

He looked more like his mother than his father. In fact, it was almost like Rachel could see Tilda floating there behind the man's eyes. They had the same straight nose and pointy chin and the same medium brown hair that fell just right, as though they'd won some sort of hair texture lottery. Rachel remembered hers was falling out of the ponytail, which meant that it was up, which meant that her neck was visible.

She reached up and pulled the elastic out with a jerk. That was a mistake she'd never made before.

"I have to go," Rachel said.

"Okay."

He stretched out the word, so it sounded like "ooooh-kaaaay." At least, that's how it sounded to Rachel with the tickles happening in her head and under her skin.

"Don't go in my room."

Juno blinked. "Why? Are you keeping monsters in there?"

Rachel tried to smile. She ordered her facial muscles to do it, but it was too difficult to tell if they were complying. "Don't go in my room," she said again.

Rachel dropped her shoes to the ground and then herself. On her butt, she pulled on her socks and tied her shoes. Juno didn't stay. He walked toward his room without a good-bye and gave her one last look over his shoulder before going inside and shutting his own door.

She needed to get to the hardware store, and there wasn't much time. The balls of her feet tapped a staccato rhythm down the wooden stairs. She was out the front door and digging the truck keys from her pocket when she saw movement out of the corner of her eye. It was the outline of a person—her occipital lobe told her it was a person even if other regions of her brain were less sure. She jerked her head around hard and fast. It was enough to hurt her neck, a little burning where the scars were the worst, but not nearly as bad as she would've expected.

As fast as she moved, she was only fast enough to catch a bit of leg disappearing at a trot around the side of the Streatfield house.

Rachel followed her eyes, running across the grass. It was slick with rain, and the pounding of her feet matted it down. She got to the corner of the house and stared down the shallow gulley that separated it from the neighbor's. She had a clear view down the steep hill to the beach and the water below. What she didn't see was a person, not anyone at all. And the ghost image, the memory of what she had seen, wasn't even enough to make a guess. Man? Woman? Rachel didn't know.

She walked quickly down toward the thick brush that separated her from the sand. She checked under the two-tier decks on either side of her, scanning along the bay in both directions. The wind had picked up, and the caution tape was snapping and twisting. Beyond it, the day shift worked, their coats zipped all the way up. Rachel stepped back, trying not to catch their attention.

The day's mist was heavier, almost but not quite drops. Already the legs of her jeans were wet and pulling down at her hips, and her hair was sticking to her head. The wind chilled her and made her squint. She shivered and shoved her hands in her pockets. The clouds were low, low even for this place, and sometimes that did things to people. Was someone watching her? Watching the house? Trying to break in? The truth was Rachel did not trust herself. She did not know if she had seen someone or if she had not, and when she turned back toward the truck, she couldn't keep from looking behind her the entire way.

28.

Dr. Woo saw patients at the Olloo'et Hospital one day a week and spent the rest of his time in Seattle. Harry was starting to wonder if Woo didn't come out to the island just for his appointments. Harry had not ever, not once, waited. He signed in at the desk, and after a minute or two, not even time to read a decent article from the magazine stack, a nurse would stand in the doorway and call his name.

Tilda stayed in the waiting room without asking, which was fine with Harry. He got up with his cane but kept his weight on his feet as he followed the woman in salmon-colored scrubs back to the exam rooms.

There was a time when most people on the island lived on the island. There were the original island families, of course, but even thirty years ago when Harry and Tilda had come along with others like them, they lived there. They needed doctors and dentists and pediatricians, and there were enough of those to keep everybody off the coroner's hands before their time. They had taken Juno to the emergency room of this hospital when he was eight and fell off his skateboard. Tilda had sat up with him half the night because the doctors had been worried about a concussion.

Now more and more buyers were picking homes they wouldn't spend thirty days of the year in. Their doctors were on the mainland, and the hospital was turning into an urgent care clinic that did little more than patch up kitchen accidents and dispense antibiotics for sudden urinary tract infections to patients the doctors would never see again.

Woo had lived on Bay Drive with the Streatfields when they were still the Streatfields, and the three of them had been friends. After Harry and Tilda divorced and property values doubled, Woo, who had never married, sold his house and bought a one-bedroom condo not far from the hospital along with a condo in Seattle, where more and more of his practice had moved.

Harry visited him in his hospital-side condo once. All of his real furniture had been shipped to Seattle, and what was left on the island looked like the sort of mismatched leftovers people send off with their twenty-year-old children to their first apartment, furniture you know will end up soaked in spilled ramen and beer. Harry had found the place depressing, and the two men had found that Tilda had been more important to their friendship than they realized. All conversations had passed through her. She was the apex point in the V-shape of their friendship, and without her, they were just two points without connection. It was the only time Harry saw Woo until he got sick.

Harry had put it off as long as he could. There had been the tingle in his hands and feet for months. Then he started to lose his balance. He tried giving up wine, not that he'd been too much of a drinker anyway, but when that didn't help and he'd started to fall, he called Woo and asked if he could have an appointment. And now here he was with monthly checkups. Harry didn't even know if Woo still had that terrible condo. Maybe he just rode the ferry in before Harry arrived and took the next one out once Harry was gone. It wouldn't surprise him, but he wouldn't ask anything to confirm it. If it turned out he was coming to Olloo'et just for Harry then Harry would have to put a stop to it. It was too much for somebody to do for him. And if he couldn't see a doctor on the island, he'd either have to sell his house and move or give up seeing doctors entirely, which would've been his choice, but with Tilda around, that got harder. So Harry never asked. Simple as that.

Also Woo always kept the good gowns, not those horrible paper ones that ripped every time you moved. Woo's exam gowns were real fabric, soft like they'd been washed a hundred thousand times, and, best for Harry, they closed in the back with Velcro. Snaps or ties would've been impossible for the past six months, not even if Harry had turned the damned thing around and tried to do it up from the front. But that day was better. That day Harry could have done up some snaps, maybe even in the back.

When the nurse pointed to the gown and left Harry alone to change, he set his cane by the exam table and took off his pants standing up, the way he used to. Then he put on the gown and hopped up on the table, hopped right up there like Juno would do it, where he waited for Woo. Woo was probably waiting in the men's room until a decent enough interval had passed so that he could knock on Harry's door, which is what happened.

"How are you feeling, Harry?"

Woo held out his hand, and Harry shook it. Woo's hands were soft but not too soft, cool but not cold. They were the least objectionable hands a man could have, which was a real bonus at exam time, as far as Harry was concerned.

"I'm feeling all right," Harry said.

"What does 'all right' mean?" Woo asked.

He was looking at Harry's chart and had taken a pen from the breast pocket of his white coat, settling himself on the rolling padded stool next to the counter with all the swabs and bandages. Under his coat, he wore a blue dress shirt, brown dress pants with a knife-edge crease, and a brown-ish/blue-ish tie with a small pattern Harry couldn't quite discern.

Woo had gone almost all gray now with just a little of his old black hair underneath, like a silverback gorilla. But his face hadn't changed at all, not since Harry and Tilda had bought the place on Bay Drive thirty years before. It was strange, and it made Harry realize just how much his own face had changed and that he didn't really know how old Woo was. Sixties? Seventies? Harry could ask Tilda.

In response to his question, Harry shrugged as if to say "all right meant all right." He hadn't decided how much he should tell Woo, and now sitting there in the faded blue gown with the Velcro in the back, that seemed irresponsible. He should have spent the time in the car thinking this exam through rather than having such a stupid argument with Tilda. She had picked a fight with him, and he had let her, and now look where it had gotten him. Harry frowned.

Woo ran through a list of questions and exercises. "Squeeze my hand with your left hand. Tight as you can. Now your right. Can you stand unassisted? For how long? Show me."

Harry was standing in his bare feet on the cold, blue-flecked lino-leum floor. He faced Woo, who was watching him for whatever Woo watched for in these exercises. Woo placed his hand on Harry's shoul-der and applied light pressure. Harry resisted and stayed upright. That was good, Harry thought, but Woo's face was as unresponsive to Har-ry's successes as it was to the passage of time.

Something was stuck to the bottom of Harry's left foot. A lot of somethings. It felt like sand, which wasn't surprising. People had been out on the beach this week far more than any winter in, it was safe to say, a hundred years. Woo was back to sitting on his padded stool, making notes in Harry's file, so Harry picked up his foot and brushed the sand off the bottom, feeling some relief that it did turn out to be sand and not some unspeakable thing only found on the floors of hospital exam rooms. When he straightened up, he wiped his hands off on the sides of his gown and caught sight of Woo.

"How did you do that?" Woo's face was impassive, but his voice had gone up an octave.

Harry tried to be nonchalant. "How did I do what?"

"You balanced on one leg."

"I was leaning on the table a little," Harry said.

"No, you weren't. I was watching."

"It's no big deal."

Woo flipped through some pages in Harry's file. "Last time I saw you, you had significant loss of mobility in your right arm, hand, leg, and foot. You were dependent on your cane for balance, and when asked to walk the length of the hall, I observed you beginning to drag your right foot. You reported difficulty at the piano and at other fine motor activities involving your fingers."

Woo looked at Harry for an explanation.

"Some days are better than others. I'm not sure what to tell you."

Harry was getting frustrated. Was he in trouble for not being a consistent-enough patient? For not continuing to decline right along the little red line on the little chart in one of Woo's textbooks? So what if he'd managed to help himself? Helping yourself was a good thing. Although the way things were going, maybe that had changed somewhere along the way, too. Maybe you were just supposed to lie around helpless.

Woo opened his mouth, changed his mind, and shut it again. They both sat in silence for a moment. Woo sat. Harry was still standing unassisted. He thought about reaching for his cane but didn't. There was a clock with too-large numbers on the face above the door and one of those too-loud second hands. It ticked so loudly Harry could imagine it echoing.

"I don't know what this means, Harry."

Woo looked like he wanted to take off his glasses and pinch the bridge of his nose, except that Woo had never worn glasses. Instead he put his elbow on the counter with the cotton ball and Q-tip jars and covered his mouth with his palm.

The prickly feeling of discomfort over this whole exam was getting worse and worse. Harry could feel it like stickum burs under his skin. He wanted to get out of there. His clothes were folded up on the rigid little guest chair, and he reached for them.

"I'd like to take some blood samples."

The last thing Harry wanted was to give a blood sample. He didn't know what Rachel had given him, but whatever it was was bound to show up floating around with the platelets and cells and whatever else was in blood. Bits from last Tuesday's sandwich, maybe.

He shook out his pants and stepped into them. This time he really did lean on the table for support before pulling them up under the gown.

"Harry?"

Harry pulled on the gown, and the Velcro gave way with little ripping sounds at each tab. It was like being in some sort of middle-aged, sick-guy version of a striptease.

"No more tests, Woo."

Harry stood there. The muscles in his arms were sagging. He was skinny, but still his stomach pooched just a little over his pants like maybe he was smuggling a large grapefruit in there, and his pecs had slid down a couple of inches, making the skin look deflated. It was cold. He reached for his T-shirt and his sweater. It was one of his plain gray ones that he liked and had been wearing for years.

"Harry, I've never seen anything like this."

Harry pulled the white T-shirt over his head.

"Your disease—it's a very difficult one. In all cases, it is progressive."

Harry pulled his sweater on over the T-shirt. He could feel his hair standing up from the static electricity.

"We administer medications to try to slow the progression, but that's all we can do."

Harry dropped into the seat where his clothes had been and reached under his butt to remove the socks he'd just sat on.

"I need you to listen to me, Harry."

"I am listening."

Harry wasn't really listening. He was putting on his socks. It had been several hours since his last dose from Rachel, and while he could still perform the standing magic trick for Woo, he could feel his right hand getting stiff. His symptoms were coming back. That's all her medicine did. It wasn't a cure. It was just like Woo had said. But what did it matter? What did it matter if he still had the disease as long as he could control the symptoms?

Harry would tell Rachel about this. He wasn't selfish. There were others who needed the medication. He knew it probably hadn't gone through all the trials that such things go through, the approval process, which was horrible and long and littered with the bodies of the wait-ing. Surely, there were trials, though. Maybe they had already started back at her university. He would ask her to add other patients like him. But he would not rat her out to Woo. He would not say anything, and he would not consent to any tests.

"You are not progressing. You are regressing. You couldn't do that a month ago."

"I probably won't be able to do it tomorrow, Woo. It doesn't mean anything. Like I said, some days are just easier."

"That's the thing." Woo was so excited that he scooted to the edge of his stool. He was leaning forward and gesturing with both hands. He really did have a sort of immovably plastic face. It was like a Ken doll.

"No one else has good days." Woo was still talking. "No one I have ever seen. It could be the combination of medications. It could be an environmental factor. It could be you have some sort of mutant form of this thing. Who knows? It could be anything. We must do tests."

Woo was so beside himself that Harry expected him to pull at his own hair. Maybe he was. Harry was doing his best not to look at his old friend. Instead, he concentrated on smoothing out the bottom of his sock, so it wouldn't crumple up inside his shoe. He had taken to wearing Velcro sneakers like the ones they give to toddlers. He had to special order them off the Internet. How would he function without Velcro? It seemed to be holding his life together these days.

When he got like this, all turned to the inside, Tilda thought he wasn't listening, that he had gone away to some other secret place that only he knew about. If there were people who could do that, he wanted to meet them and learn their secrets. When Harry did it, he was trying to pull into a turtle shell he didn't have. So instead he just rolled up like an armadillo and hoped whatever onslaught was happening would pass. He hadn't gone anywhere any more than a child goes somewhere when he covers his eyes and insists, "I can't see you," to make you go away.

"No more tests, Woo." Harry stood up and reached for his cane. "Like I said, it'll be back the way it was tomorrow."

Woo did not follow him into the hallway, which suited Harry as much as it surprised him. He needed to get going. He needed to collect Tilda. It was time to go home.

29.

"Goddammit," Rachel said to herself and then louder to the person knocking on her door, "Just a minute!"

Rachel went back to grinding another dose for herself. She had bandages on both arms from the cuts she'd been testing. She had taken a dose within the hour, just after coming home from the hardware store. That dose had been ground from the flash-frozen specimens, but the active compound had decayed. She experienced a mild analgesic effect, reducing her pain from a four to a two-point-five out of five. Not enough. Not nearly enough. The specimens needed to be fresh to be effective.

Rachel's doorknob rattled but did not give. The old one was in the trash can, along with the plastic bag and receipt. The new doorknob she had installed herself. The new key was already on her key chain. No one could get in now. No one.

There was a pause, and then the rattling started up again.

"I said 'Just a minute!'"

Rachel finished grinding and then used a plastic spoon to scrape up the dose, a little larger than before. She had learned to swallow the whole thing in a ball without smearing it all over the inside of her mouth. It did a lot for the taste. Once it was down, she shook her head to center herself and pulled the sleeves of her shirt down over her bandages.

"Who is it?" she called, wishing she had a peephole.

"It's me."

"Mr. Streatfield?" Rachel unlocked the door, opened it just enough, and then pushed her head out into the hall. She was holding on to the knob from the inside and had her foot jammed up against the bottom of the door. It would be nearly impossible for someone to push their way in. Someone like John. He could be anywhere. You couldn't know.

"You put a lock on the door?" Harry asked.

Rachel didn't answer him. Obviously she had, and obviously it was necessary. He had just tried to barge in without permission. There was no one in the house or outside of it who didn't want to get at her equipment and specimens.

"Do you need something?" Rachel asked.

"The medicine you gave me is wearing off."

"That's to be expected."

"I need some more," he said.

"The supply is very limited. I'm sorry."

Harry wrapped his hand around the door just under Rachel's chin to keep her from shutting it. It was getting harder to control her temper. If he wasn't careful, she would have to slam it closed on his fingers.

"It's very important," he said. "I think this may be bigger than you realize."

It took a large number of the creatures to make each dose, and secreting them away remained difficult. Between what Rachel needed in the tanks and what she was taking herself, there wasn't much to share, at least not yet.

"I can't risk diluting my experiments," she said.

"You don't understand. I've just come from the doctor, and I have results to report."

He had her attention, and she wanted to go fetch her notebook, write down what he said word for word—word for word in her own code, of course. There was nothing left in English. Not that she needed the notes. She'd memorized them. All of them. That she could memorize them—not just the narrative accounts, that was easy—but she had memorized the temperature readings, nutrient ratios, and animal densities of each and every flask, not to mention times, dosages, experimental conditions. Hundreds of numbers.

Everything just stuck. It was like she'd been struck with sudden-onset eidetic memory. It was incredible. She had noted that, too, in her log. Its potential as a memory and concentration aid beyond even analgesics was more than she could wrap her mind around at the moment. Students with ADHD? Dementia patients? Alzheimer's? This drug seemed to touch every part of the nervous system and the brain itself. She would not risk Harry seeing her notebook, not even in code. She would memorize what he said to her. She took a deep breath through her nose and readied her mind to do it.

"Tell me," Rachel said.

Harry shook his head. "Trade."

"One more dose," Rachel said.

"No. I want to be in your trial. I want to be a study patient."

Trial? Rachel reeled. Did Harry believe this was official? Something overseen by the university? Something that would make it all the way to the human trial phase? Rachel wanted to laugh. She supposed it was. She had simply skipped over everything in between. It was the chemistry equivalent of flying a kite in an electrical storm.

Rachel had to word this carefully. "I'll give you the doses I can for as long as I can, but that's the best I can offer."

She could see the tension in the left side of Harry's body. He was leaning on his cane, and the fingers of his right hand, those still wrapped around the door, were curling in on themselves. She didn't have to worry about him trying to push in. She didn't even need her foot blocking the door. He had little strength or dexterity left in that side at all.

Harry pulled his eyebrows down and together. He looked like he was chewing on the inside of his mouth. It wasn't what he wanted to hear.

"What I learned today," he said, "it has implications. More people like me need to be studied. They need to test this drug."

"I know," Rachel said. "People with all sorts of conditions could be helped, but there are processes."

"Whatever the steps are, you promise you will include us?" he asked.

"When there is enough of the drug, yes," Rachel said.

"And I will be one of those people? I'll get the doses you have now, and then I'll be in the trial later?"

Harry did not understand. It would be years before a trial would happen through official channels. Of course, years in chemistry was nothing. It was normal. It was unavoidable. Years to people, though, that was different. Harry did not have years. It was sad, but it was unchangeable. She started to explain, to put the words together in her mind, and then she stopped. Why not make the promise? She would know, but he wouldn't. In the end, what difference would it make but to work out better for the both of them?

Rachel started again. Yes, he would be in the trial. Yes, he could keep seeing his own doctor—Woo, was it?—during the study. Yes, as long as he saw the study doctors, too. She said yes to everything he asked because there was no reason not to.

After he had extracted his promises, Rachel asked for one of her own. He must take careful note of all the side effects and all the symptom relief he experienced. Careful note. She said it again. Times, effects on a scale of one to five, descriptions of everything, what he ate and drank and when. Anything he could think of. But he must not type it and save copies. He could only write these things down, and he must keep the notes on him at all times. He must not let anyone else see them. No one. Not even Tilda. Then he would give the notes to her in the morning. He would not keep a copy for himself.

He agreed. Rachel wanted to make him swear on his mother's grave, on scout's honor, on a bible, but she didn't. She took him on his word because she believed he would not risk being cut off.

She left him in the hallway while she ducked back inside and used what was left in the flasks to mix up another dose. It was a little more than she'd given him last time. She weighed it on her scale and made her own notes. It was a little more than a little more. It was one-and-a-half times as much. It would be good to note the difference in his symptoms and duration of relief.

Harry took the spoon from her at the door, swallowed it with a face, and handed it back. "You're going to be a very wealthy woman, you know."

Rachel did not reply. It wasn't that she didn't understand the monetary value others would place on what she had. It was that, to her, the money was entirely beside the point. She was there to save her own life, and there were only two days left to do it.

Epoxy is a mixture of resin and hardener, which are sold in separate containers to keep them from combusting. The two had to be mixed in a precise ratio, which cured through an endothermic reaction, meaning it gave off heat, sometimes a lot, sometimes, if you weren't careful, enough to boil and catch fire. The clerk, a man of retiring age, at the marine supply store had warned Tilda to be careful of the vapors. In enclosed spaces, they had been known to cause brain damage and blindness.

If it had been a sales pitch, it had worked. She threw a mask and goggles into her cart, along with a shallow pan for mixing small batches of the stuff, thick gloves, and a stiff brush for applying it, some sail tape and various other odds and ends that had seemed useful at the time. The total for not a lot of things had been staggering.

Tilda, who was wearing the grubbiest clothes she'd brought, pulled on her headlamp and gloves, along with the mask and goggles, and got to work there under the deck. Making sure each area of rot was clean and dry, she mixed the resin and hardener, along with a tint to help hide the patches as best she could. The concoction immediately let off a stench that shot through the mask and into her nose, a caustic, chemical smell that burned her nasal passages and set off a headache as quickly as lighting a match.

Hurrying, both because it would harden on her and because she wanted to get the job done before her vision started to go, she began to apply the epoxy, pressing, filling, and smoothing each area. She had decided to buy the quart rather than the gallon, and by the time she'd moved to the hiking boards, she was beginning to worry it wouldn't be enough.

When she was done, she pulled off the protective gear and wrapped up the disposable pan and brush, which would never be good for anything again. Wanting to get as far away from the stuff as she could while it cured, she grabbed the sail bag and dragged it to the other side of the deck.

It would take twenty-four hours for the epoxy to harden but far less than that to see what horrors might await within the many yards of fabric in front of her. Unlike bigger sailboats, *Serendipity* had no supplementary motor. It was wind or nothing.

Tilda unzipped the bag and began pulling out handfuls of sail. It had been shoved inside, not folded neatly. Some mariners would argue this was better, that repeated fold lines would weaken the cloth. Tilda considered this an excuse for laziness.

This section of decking was only about seven feet high, plenty high enough to work, but she found herself ducking as she spread the fabric out. It was covered in salt and dirt, was of indeterminate age, and needed, on principle, to be replaced. But when Tilda got down on her hands and knees to run her headlamp over it inch by inch, she found only two small tears.

She scrambled up and went to fill her bucket at the outdoor spigot. Adding a good squirt of dish soap, which sank down into the water like a skinny turquoise snake, Tilda plunged the brush into the water up to her forearm and sloshed it about before she had time to think about how cold it was. Working from top to bottom, Tilda scrubbed the sail, drying it with an old bath towel as best she could, before flipping it over and doing the other side. Then, careful to clear all the grains of sand from around each tear, she unwrapped the sail tape. Using a bit more than the directions called for, she finally finished and stood, running her lamp over each spot one last time. White tape on white sail, the repairs barely showed.

Tilda was feeling good about her work and was just turning to gather up her trash.

"Jesus Christ!"

The man was standing two feet behind her. She jumped back and put a hand to her chest.

He looked chastised. "I'm sorry."

Tilda put both hands on her hips and turned in a half circle to let herself settle.

"I just saw you under here," he went on, "and well, curiosity got the better of me." He held out his hand. "Hooper, UW Biology."

Tilda dropped her hands from her hips and shook. "I read the article in the paper."

She had seen him for days, of course, from a distance. He was the one she thought of as Ichabod. Up close, he looked older than she'd imagined.

"This your boat?" he asked.

"No." She shook her head. "I'm just helping out a friend."

Almost nothing about that sentence was true, but it was all the truth she felt she owed. He still had some explaining to do.

Hooper nodded. He looked down at the sail by his feet and over to the hull. She could see him looking for something else to say and not finding it. This was a man who knew nothing and cared nothing for boats, which was fine, but it underlined the question hanging between them.

She turned and squared herself to him, crossing her arms over her chest.

He fell to the power of her stare. "I believe you know one of my researchers," he said.

Now they were getting somewhere, she thought.

"I'm not sure she's a young woman who many people really get to know," Tilda said.

"I have to confess I haven't done the job I should have with her."

Tilda didn't comment.

"I was wondering," Hooper went on, "about her off hours, how she spends her time here."

"If you're concerned, you should speak to my ex-husband. He's the one who has taken her in. I'm just visiting."

"Of course," Hooper said. "I don't mean to involve you. I was just wondering if you could tell me if she's set up anything inside, anything like a lab."

Tilda, who had the ability to raise one eyebrow independent of the other, did so. "I take it her lab isn't sanctioned?"

Hooper gave a quarter of a smile, forced and meant only to avoid a direct answer. His skin was so full of folds and creases, it was as if someone had wadded up a piece of paper several times before trying unsuccessfully to smooth it back out. It was an interesting face if not a handsome one.

"Can I see it?" he asked.

"Her lab?"

"Yes."

Tilda shook her head. "She's banned me from the room. Like I said, you'll have to speak to Harry. He owns the house."

"I don't suppose you could describe it to me?"

"Her room?"

"The equipment."

30.

Harry made Tilda stop at a mailbox on the way to the ferry.

"Why don't you just put it in our mailbox? The postman will pick it up."

Tilda realized as she said it that she'd claimed joint ownership of the box. It was a slip of the tongue, but she worried Harry would think she meant something by it. Harry paid no attention to her word choice at all and, therefore, had no thoughts about any of it. He only cared about dropping his thick manila envelope in a big, blue mailbox on the corner.

"No," he said. "A public box."

"Why?"

"It's more secure."

"What's in the envelope?"

"Papers."

Tilda waited for more and didn't get it.

"Then give it to me. I'll take it to the post office myself in the morning. That'll be even more secure."

"No, the blue box."

Tilda opened her mouth and closed it. The envelope was on his lap facedown across his knees. He was entitled to his privacy, of course, but people are entitled to all sorts of things that others don't want to give them.

She sighed to release her frustration. There weren't many blue boxes on the island, but there was one on the way to the ferry. She couldn't even claim it was inconvenient, and so when they approached, she pulled up so that Harry's door was close to it. He still had to undo his seat belt and climb out, but he did that without assistance. His cane was in the backseat, and it stayed there while he walked to the front of the box, pulled down the lever, and dropped his secret envelope into the mouth, which closed with a loud, metal clang.

Then he climbed back in the car, and neither of them said anything else about it for the rest of the night.

The lower levels of the symphony hall were full. Harry no longer had season tickets, so when he'd bought them the day before, he'd had to settle for one of the upper box levels high above the stage and flat against the hall's outermost walls.

All the people who filled the hall had started out filling the under-ground garage, where he and Tilda had wound their way down, one link in a whole chain of cars looking for a spot. Then all the people had gotten out of their cars and had gone to stand at the banks of ele-vators to wait some more. The men stood with their hands in their pockets rattling their keys and change, and the women fiddled with the iridescent olive, orange, and burgundy shawls they had all purchased from museum gift shops. Then the elevators came, and through the doors of the hall they all went, flashing their tickets to the doormen and going to wait some more at the bars that sold wine in plastic cups before the performance. And after they drank it, they all went for a preemptive pee, where only the women had to wait.

Harry and Tilda skipped the wait at the bar. If he had wanted something, Tilda would nag about his medicines. He knew he needed to put his foot down about that—these were his choices—but right then, he didn't much feel like it. Maybe he'd used up all his resolve hiding the fact that what he had mailed was a new copy of his will.

There was no reason not to tell Tilda, not really. She was in it after all. He was leaving her the house. That was the big change, but there were some smaller ones. The house had been willed to Juno before, but Harry decided he'd rather see Tilda in it. She needed someplace to land, and his place had been their place before. There was no good reason for it not to be again. She'd earned it. She'd probably earned it before, but coming to stay with him now meant he could no longer deny it. Harry knew that Tilda would pass the house on to Juno when the time came. Juno could wait. All of this was reasonable, but still Harry did not tell her. He told his lawyer, who made the changes and e-mailed the documents to him. Harry printed them, and he signed them, and he kept his mouth shut. Maybe he didn't tell her because he might change his mind later. She might become unbearable. Lord knew she was difficult. It wasn't that far a leap between difficult and unbearable. They had decided that about each other before.

Then again, maybe he didn't tell her because this medicine was new, and it was doing things. Maybe it was just treating his symptoms. They came back after each dose. Harry knew that. But it was the symptoms that would kill him, after all. The motor control he lost in his foot and his leg and his hand and his arm would spread. He would become wheelchair bound. He would lose his ability to speak, and maybe they would get him one of those eye-controlled computer things, so he could tap out a word an hour. But then maybe they wouldn't because why go to the expense? Along with his speech, he'd lose the ability to swallow and would need a feeding tube. Then other muscles would go, including the ones that made his heart beat and his lungs expand.

He had already spoken to Dr. Woo. He'd done it months ago. Woo had laid out what would happen in what order, and Harry had decided what interventions were acceptable and what were not. There had been paperwork. There were far more interventions in the unacceptable category because what was the point? Except now, maybe there was a point. Maybe this new treatment could keep those symptoms at bay forever. It had been a very good decision to go out to the beach that night. Falling there in the sand on his own dog might have been, Harry thought, the best thing that could have happened, some quirk of fate that made everything different.

That was why he could buy two symphony tickets. Already that was different. He had stopped going six months before—no, it had been longer now that he was thinking about it. It was too hard to go when he knew he would only ever finish this one piece for this one orchestra. There would be no others. Just this very last one. It was so final, so limiting. But maybe not. Maybe there would be more, another chance after this one to get it right, so he bought the tickets.

Tilda went up ahead. She wanted to find their seats. Harry wanted to find the bathroom first. He told her he would catch up.

"It's going to start soon."

Already people were abandoning their empty and not-quite-empty plastic wine cups on the cocktail tables in the street-level lobby, on the edges of planters, on benches, anywhere they could find a flat surface. And they were streaming up the open staircases that switch-backed from level to level to level. Harry and Tilda's seats were almost at the very top.

"I'll be there."

Harry had been going to the symphony since he was in his late twenties. The attendees had always been stooped and graying. Some of them were middle-aged or nearing retirement, and some of them would not last the season. That was the way it had always been. It was still that way, but he was taken aback when three of the men leaving the third-level restroom had walkers. Harry had his cane, of course, but that was different, and he was only using it a little bit that night. Harry did his business, washed his hands, and did not look in the mirror where he might accidentally assess the color of his hair and the rounding of his shoulders. By the time he made it back out, he was one of the last people not in their seat.

Harry stood on the third-floor balcony just outside the inner doors to the hall. Inside the musicians would be warming up. Out here he was jutted out over the empty lobby a hundred feet below and across from the floor-to-ceiling windows that looked out over downtown. From the outside, the symphony's Benaroya Hall looked like a giant reel of film turned on its side with glass where the celluloid should be.

Harry liked the view. The other buildings that surrounded the hall had just as much glass. In fact, some of them seemed to be made up of nothing but windows—those that were dark and reflected the concert hall's visage back at him and those that were lit like little vignettes.

Harry wasn't the only one who wanted to watch the other build-ings' night-cleaning ladies go from office to office turning on and off the lights, or look at the blinking screens left on in otherwise dark and abandoned rooms, or spot the lone worker still at his desk. One other person—a woman—leaned over the third-floor balcony railing, watching the city from a safe distance. They might as well have bin-oculars, the two of them, the way they peered into strangers' lives.

But maybe the woman didn't need them. She was hanging right over the rail while Harry preferred to stand well back near the wall. He had always disliked heights, which was one of the reasons he dal-lied here rather than go sit in his suspended box. This fear—or as Harry preferred, this aversion—had only gotten worse in the last year. The more balance Harry lost, the less comfortable he became anywhere but on the most solid, most unslippery of ground. He tightened his grip on the four-footed cane whether he needed it right then or not.

The musicians finished warming up. He could hear them. The pleasant, atonal, mishmash of notes from violins, oboes, and percus-sion all began to settle down. It sounded just like a crowd stopping its vocal chatter for a speaker who was taking the stage. Although in this case, the instruments quieted down for the tuxedoed conductor, who would soon stride across the stage in as grand an entrance as a sym-phony orchestra allowed. A lone spotlight would be on the conductor's dais already, an empty pool of white light waiting for a purpose. The musicians would be in tight, concentric semicircles around it, like ripples out from a skipped rock. Subtle tension was building in there. Harry could feel it.

Tilda would be looking at her watch and making a face. She hated to miss the beginning of things, and she didn't particularly like it when other people missed them either.

The two of them really should go inside.

"Excuse me, miss," Harry said. "I believe they're starting."

The woman's back moved in acknowledgment. The muscles readjusted themselves in a slight ripple under her bare skin as she pushed back from the rail but didn't let go of it. She wore her dark hair up in a twisted knot held together with hidden pins or, for all Harry knew, a sort of invisible Jedi force. Her dress, which was green, was so long it touched the floor.

Well, if she wanted to stay out here—

The hall broke into applause. The conductor was walking across the stage toward his dais, taking the two steps up, turning to acknowledge the crowd. Harry didn't need to see it in order to see it.

Becca turned from the windows and faced Harry. If you asked him now, Harry could not have told you when he knew it was her. It was not when she was facing him. It was before then. It was not when he had first spoken either. It was after then. It was something in the way she started to turn, he supposed, that made the hallucination so real.

Just so everyone was on the same page about it, Harry said aloud, "I'm seeing things again."

He said it loud enough for her to hear it, but she didn't respond. She was no longer bleeding, that was his first thought. She scared him, but she did not surprise him. He had conjured her too many times for surprise. People confused the two.

So while he began to sweat inside his suit, he was not startled, and his brain still had enough room to see that she had no mark or blemish of any kind. But she didn't look the same. She was older. Not old but older. Late twenties maybe early thirties, but then again, it could be the dress and the hair and the makeup. Young women these days did that to themselves, Harry knew. They layered on the accoutrements of age when they didn't have enough years, and then layered on the accoutrements of youth when they had too many. It was upsetting to the eye.

More upsetting was that she'd been crying. Harry had not dealt well with her tears decades ago, and he did not deal well with them now. It really wasn't fair what his mind was doing to him.

"You shouldn't be here," he said.

She looked surprised and not at all happy that he'd spoken.

"It's not your problem where I am."

She sounded petulant, like the teenager she never had the chance to become. One of the many things she'd never had the chance to become.

He felt like he should take a step forward. That was what a father would do, but he did not do it. He hesitated too long, and the hesitation became inertia, which settled into the knowledge that he was failing her again. Again he was doing things wrong. He wanted to cling to her, to keep her—this hallucinated version of her—with him, and yet he did not.

It was not good for him. He knew it wasn't. It did not matter what a father would do for his daughter because she was not his daughter. She was, at best, a side effect. At worst, the stories were true, and she was a sort of netherworld representative sent to drive him mad. Either way, he had to stop this. He would not become this person. He would not die strapped to a bed, screaming at shadows. He simply would not.

Harry steeled himself.

"You shouldn't be here," he said again. "There's no place for you."

He waited for her to speak, but she didn't. She just stared at him. He tried again, tried to shoo her away. "No one wants you here."

"No one," he had said, not "I." He couldn't bring himself to say that he didn't want her—real or not. Better to share the blame with others, with everyone, if he could manage it.

But this difference, however much it mattered to him, did not seem to register with her. There was a fresh flow of tears, not fast, not sobbing, but the sort that pooled in her lower lashes before falling in heavy splashes to her cheekbones. She had her mother's cheekbones—high, almost sharp.

"Just leave me alone," she said.

It took all that Harry was to hold his ground. She looked so real. Everything was right from the blotchiness in her cheeks to the chip in her nail polish. This was well beyond the uncanny valley. He took a deep breath.

"Go," he said. "You have to go."

"Why do you think I'm out here?"

Her words came out too high, almost hysterical. This was not the calm, wondering girl of all the "whys" he remembered, not the girl that had appeared to him at the house. This Becca was almost as unhinged as he was. In a way it helped. Yes, he decided, it helped. She was not real. She wasn't even as he remembered her. She was twisting and morphing, just as you would expect from a brain as ill as his. Harry felt braver.

"No one is stopping you," he said.

Becca looked over her shoulder, out toward the windows and down to the lobby, and then she followed her gaze with the rest of her body, turning back around.

"I want to," she said. "I've wanted to go for a while."

She was softening. He saw it in her shoulders, heard it in her voice. Softening and weakening. Did that mean it was working? Was this all he had to do to control things? To order the hallucinations away like a child talking to the monster under the bed?

"It's time."

And it was. It was time. Harry was afraid someone would come out and find him there, talking, and they wouldn't be able to see who he was talking to, and he would be asked to explain. He would have to make up something just like with Dr. Woo. And Tilda, he was sure, was on the verge of leaving her seat and coming to look for him, unable to decide whether she should be annoyed or worried.

"How do you know?"

"How do I know what?" Harry asked.

"When it's time to go?"

"You go when there's no reason to stay, when staying hurts people."

The railing Becca was leaning against was a thin rope of wood topping the piece of glass that ringed the balcony level. Each balcony, each landing, each set of staircases had nothing but glass to hold in the people and keep them from toppling hundreds of feet to the tile below. The architect would have called it airy. Glass inside of glass. Harry didn't care for it. It made him want to climb down and spend the whole performance listening as best he could from beside the elevator banks on the ground floor.

"I hurt people," she said. "I don't mean to, but I do."

Harry didn't know what to say.

Becca stayed where she was, bent a few degrees at the waist over the edge, her arms out to her sides and her hands resting on the wooden rail. Harry stood there, waiting. He wanted to see her go and not like before. Before she had walked away, out of his line of sight. The air had moved when she'd brushed past him. He'd felt it on the fine hairs of his arm. She wasn't real. He repeated that to himself. And if she wasn't real, then she had to materialize and dematerialize. She had to fade in and out like the musical score in a big battle scene. There was a trick to it, and he wanted to see the trick.

Inside, the conductor had raised his arms and was commanding his troops, who had started to march through the first measures of Tchaikovsky. Tilda would be gathering her wrap and reaching for the purse she had stashed under her chair. She'd be begging the pardon of the patrons around her, who would be particularly irritated that she was disrupting the beginning. Their minds hadn't even had a chance to begin to wander yet. No one's foot had fallen asleep, and the wine hadn't made it to anyone's bladder.

Harry looked over his shoulder, just a quick glimpse to see if the door was swinging open, and then he stepped as quickly as he could across the balcony. The glass-enclosed edge got closer with every step so that Harry had to give his head a little shake and order his eyes to stay on her naked back. When he was five feet away, he reached out his hand. He wanted to touch her just to see, just to convince himself, just to put his hand into the air where his mind fooled itself.

She didn't even turn to look at him before she did it. He didn't see her face. Becca simply pushed herself up with her arms, lifted her feet from the floor, and pitched herself over that delicate piece of glass.

Harry garbled a scream and lunged, clawing out with both hands. He touched nothing but air. And when she hit the cold, tile lobby floor, it was a *thwap* so loud Tchaikovsky couldn't compete.

"Harry?"

"She jumped. I saw her. She jumped." Harry's voice was not his own. It was warbly and snotty, and he was pointing toward the ledge like a fool. It wasn't real. He knew it wasn't real, but he couldn't help himself, and now Tilda would know. She would know everything. She would—

Tilda rushed past him to the glass and leaned over, and the sight of her there, just as Becca had been seconds before, scared him so badly that he lost control of his own bladder.

"No!"

"Oh, my God. Oh, my God!" Tilda said.

She backed away so quickly that she nearly tripped in her high heels. She tore into her bag, ripping the dove gray satin, and had the cell phone to her ear when the first usher came out to see what the yelling had been.

Tilda conducted both conversations at once. "A woman fell. Harry saw her fall.—Yes, I'm reporting an emergency at Benaroya Hall. We need an ambulance. I think she's dead, but we need an ambulance.—Harry, did she say anything?"

Harry looked down at himself. He was wearing black wool trousers, which was a godsend. He knew the front was wet, but as long as no one touched him—he looked back up, but Tilda wasn't waiting for him. She was taking charge, ordering the ushers to get word to their troops. The musicians should stop playing. It was disrespectful to keep playing, but the patrons should all stay in their seats. No one was to leave the hall. Hundreds of people pouring into the lobby would only make things worse.

The ushers, both men and women in their drab burgundy and black uniforms, rushed to obey without demanding any further qualifications. It was Tilda's way, or maybe they recognized her. Tilda herself was still on the phone with the 911 operator while she sprinted as best she could for the switchback stairs that would take her down to the body below.

Harry was afraid to look.

31.

They heard the ambulances before they saw them.
Two pulled up in front of the hall, just outside the rounded wall of
glass with its beautiful view that no one cared about at all. The red and
white lights bounced from pane to pane, reflecting and multiplying.
The men in their navy uniforms poured out of the vehicles in one or-
chestrated troop and ran through the doors into the lobby so large and
open it could've hosted a ball. They rushed, rushed, rushed until they
saw what was left of the woman, and the urgency went out of them.

Harry was sitting on a bench with his cane in front of him. His
insides felt as though they'd liquefied. Tilda was standing next to the
body, guarding it from the looky-loos, those who insisted "please keep
your seats" did not apply to them. One of them had picked up a small
handbag lying fifteen feet or so away. Tilda couldn't guard everything,
Harry supposed. There was a wallet and a Washington State driver's
license inside, not much money, a set of car keys, a drugstore lipstick, and one tampon with a ripped paper wrapper. That's what the
looky-loo holding the purse said when she came over to him. Tilda
had instructed her, as she'd already got her fingerprints all over everything anyway, to show the ID to Harry. The body had landed

face-first and, well, none of them could really say for sure if the brunette in the photo was the brunette on the floor.

Harry had not gone anywhere near the body, and he didn't want to look at the plastic card either. The woman holding it out to him was tiny and insistent, like a bird pecking at its reflection.

"I only saw her from behind. It could've been anyone."

The bird woman twittered. "Such a horror."

Harry didn't respond, and she had to go flit and chatter with excitement to someone else.

The police arrived a few minutes after the ambulances. Harry told his version of the story, which was no story at all.

Came out of the bathroom.

Saw her from behind.

She pitched forward.

Nothing I could do.

The police officer, a young Asian woman who'd suffered from acne in her youth that no one had treated very well, asked just two questions when Harry was done.

"When you say she pitched forward, did she fall forward, or did she jump?"

Harry was still sitting on the wooden bench by the stairs, as far as he could be from the body, which no one had moved yet. He hoped she hadn't noticed his pants.

"It wasn't a jump exactly. The glass was too high to jump. She sort of lifted herself up and bent forward. It seemed voluntary."

The officer looked him in the eye and nodded while he talked. Harry wasn't sure if that was her way of encouraging him to say more or if what he said agreed with what she saw. Harry didn't know if the police could look at someone and tell if they were a suicide or an accident.

"Did the woman say anything before she went over the side?" It was the officer's last question.

"No, she didn't say anything. I don't think she knew I was there."

Tilda stood nearby while Harry talked, close enough to hear but not so close as to look like she was interfering. When they were done, she shook the officer's hand and thanked her for her work.

"And who are you?" the officer asked.

"Senator Streatfield." She said like it didn't bother her. "But please, call me Tilda."

Harry knew Tilda wanted to stay, but there were no more official duties, and if they didn't leave in the next fifteen minutes, they were going to miss the last ferry back to Olloo'et. She didn't even get to talk to the handful of reporters who had gathered outside near the ambulances. She gave them a long look before following Harry, who had metabolized every bit of the medication, as he scooted toward the elevator that led to the garage. They just beat the crowd, which was being released from the performance hall and ushered away. It took seven uniformed officers blocking off the lobby to keep all the old men and women from hurrying over to get a peek.

Down in the garage, it was Tilda who took off too fast and had to wait by the car for Harry to catch up. She wanted to beat the snake of cars that would clog up the exits for the next hour. She held the door for him, and he didn't look her in the eye as he lowered himself down butt first using his cane for support. One leg in. Then the other.

"Are you okay?" Tilda asked when she'd spiraled them up from the lower levels back to the street, waiting for the light down the block to go red, so they could turn. "You're not saying much."

"There's not much to say."

Tilda turned and made her way around the block, heading up a steep grade toward the freeway entrance. She knew the city far better than he did. Still, if he had been well, he would have insisted on driving. She maneuvered like the local she had become since their divorce. If they could keep the pace, they would make the ferry.

Harry watched the string of taillights in front of them. The farther north they went the fewer of them there were. Fifteen minutes passed.

"Did you see the woman's face?" Harry asked. He didn't look at Tilda, and Tilda didn't look at him.

"Half of it," she said. "Her head was turned to the side."

"Did you recognize her?" Harry asked.

"No. Should I have? Did you?"

"I was just wondering."

Tilda let thirty seconds go by, which was a lot under the circumstances.

"Harry, if you have something to say about what happened, for God's sake, say it."

Harry bunched up his hands in his lap. He didn't know if he had anything to say about what happened because he no longer knew what was happening, not tonight, maybe not ever again. What had he said to that woman? He wasn't sure. He hadn't thought—She looked so much like Becca. He was certain it was her, a hallucination of her. Didn't Tilda see it? She must have seen it.

"Harry." Her voice was sharp.

"She just looked—" He was halfway through the sentence, and he had lost the will to finish it. He was being ridiculous. He was a ridiculous, old, sick man who said strange things and then had to be pacified by those around him. He was becoming someone to be avoided. He could see it happening as if from a distance, and finishing the sentence would just be one more piece of evidence to hold against him.

"She looked like what?"

Harry snorted like he always did when he felt cornered. "She just bore a little resemblance to Becca."

Tilda gripped the wheel until it hurt, her hands at precisely ten and two. She would make a perfect picture for the Washington State Driver's Manual if she weren't also the perfect picture of a woman struggling for control. Every muscle around every joint tightened, drawing her into herself, as tight as she could get and still operate the vehicle. Tilda looked and felt like the only living person to have experienced rigor mortis.

This was the second time Harry had said a grown woman looked like Becca, and it was the second time that it wasn't true at all. They had all had dark brown hair, but for the love of Pete, Becca had been a child when she'd died. Neither of them really knew what she would

have looked like when she grew up, which was—Tilda supposed—
what allowed Harry to paste her face on any woman he saw.

"She did not." Tilda said it without moving her jaw.

"Like I said, it was only a passing—"

"Shut up!" A thing in Tilda—it would be impossible to say which
thing—that had been wrenched too tightly for too long gave under the
pressure. It gave with a snap, and when it did, it ricocheted around the
car interior, making them both duck and wince.

Tilda wanted to reel it back in. She wasn't sorry, and she wasn't going to apologize, even for good form, but she was going to smooth it, to
change course, to renegotiate their present circumstances. Or at least
she would have if Harry hadn't opened his fool mouth.

"Why did you do that?"

Tilda began to answer. Everyone was allowed to lose their temper
every once in a while. Just because she almost never exercised the
right, didn't mean it ceased to—

"Why did you pretend like she never existed? Why did you try to
erase Becca?" It seemed something inside of Harry had broken under
the strain, too.

The idea of neither of them being in full control would have scared
Tilda if she was in a fit state of mind to think of it that way, but the
careful series of roadblocks she had built between her mind and her
mouth were suddenly unmanned, and the next thing left her lips before
she even knew what it would be.

"Because it was the only way I could stop hating you."

The truth is a physical thing that has weight, and the truer the
thing is the heavier it is, becoming denser and denser. Tilda's truth
had the density of lead, and the weight of it pinned them down into
their respective seats and pressed the backs of their heads into the
chairs and even held their eyeballs in place, so that they could only see
the road and not each other.

"You hated me." Harry said it as a statement and without self-pity.

"Yes," Tilda said, "I did."

"I hated me, too."

"I know."

"Why did you want to stop?" Harry asked. "Stop hating me?"

The next words came a little slower for Tilda. She had to think about them and test them to be sure they were right. "Because I couldn't bear to lose anything else."

Harry's next words came a little slower, too, for all of the same reasons. "It didn't work. We fell apart anyway."

"I know."

It was almost midnight when Harry and Tilda pulled into the driveway. It was sprinkling, and the ferry ride had been choppy, which was always harder on her stomach at night when she couldn't keep her eyes on the horizon line. They had stayed in the car the entire ride. Neither had made any move to get out, and they hadn't discussed it.

Back at the house, Harry wanted to go upstairs alone and, for the first and only time, Tilda let him go without argument. She stayed at the bottom and watched as he went riser by riser. She watched until he was all the way up at the landing, and then she followed the sound of the television to the den.

Juno was in the same chair he had been in when they left. Several additional beer bottles had accumulated on the coffee table, and the open container of Chinese takeout—shrimp lo mein from the looks of it—had perfumed the entire room, which was the only evidence Juno had done anything at all. That and the channel had been changed from sports to twenty-four-hour news. They were showing taped footage of the Miracle.

"How was the concert?" Juno asked.

Tilda sank down onto the arm of the couch. She'd already taken off her shoes, and she was afraid, if she sat down for real, she wouldn't be able to get up again. She'd fall asleep there and wake up the next morning smelling of grease and soy sauce, still wearing her burnt orange silk pantsuit with mascara smeared under her eyes.

"A woman died," she said.

"During the performance?"

Juno hadn't been all that interested in her response before, but she had his attention now, even if she was too tired to want it.

"Yes."

"What? Did she have a heart attack or something?"

"She jumped off a balcony."

The conversation with Harry in the car had been so big that the woman's suicide felt further away than it was.

"Oh, my God." Juno took his feet off the coffee table, which had been a rule in Tilda's house anyway, and sat up in the chair, fumbling for the remote to mute the television. Tilda wished he wouldn't.

"Did she land on the stage?"

"It was out in the lobby," Tilda said.

"Oh." This was far less dramatic than he had been led to believe. "That was probably pretty—you know—gross."

It had been less gross than Tilda might have imagined. Some blood, of course, but she'd seen traffic accidents that were worse. She could only imagine what the fall had done to the poor woman's insides, but the bystanders had been spared the view.

"It could've been worse, but your father saw it happen."

"Wow. What's he saying about it?"

Tilda read the closed captions that came across the bottom of the screen. She wished he'd turn the volume back on, just for a few moments. It would let her mind rest, and then she could work on forcing herself upstairs and into a shower. Harry was already taking his. She could hear water running in the old pipes. When she went up, she would take his pants and underwear from the hamper and throw them in the utility sink to soak.

"He thinks the woman looked like Becca."

Tilda was sorry she said it as soon as the words were out. She really did need to repair those checkpoints.

Juno snorted. It was the same snort Harry had done in the car. It was the sort of thing you wouldn't think could possibly be genetic, and then it turns out to be. Tilda knew Juno wanted her to respond, but it was too much to ask of her that night. He had left the remote on the coffee table, and she reached for it, getting up from the arm of the sofa to do it.

"It's been like thirty years since she died, and he can still make anything about her."

Tilda shut her eyes and counted to three.

"Becca died twenty-two years ago."

"Whatever. Twenty-two. My point is he's been fixated my whole life, since I was three years old. You try competing against a dead person."

"Nothing that happened tonight was about you," Tilda said.

"I'm making a bigger point."

There was a gear shift that happened in Tilda before any debate. It sharpened her mind—at least she felt it did—but it dulled her affect. She came off cold and calculating, and there had never been anything she, or any number of image consultants, could do about it. It was as though her mind had to retreat behind the castle wall to fire the cannons, and voters had not been the only ones on the other side.

"In the future," Tilda said in her flattest voice, "it would be a good idea if you didn't use the traumatic deaths of two young women while trying to elicit sympathy for yourself, especially when one of those was my child. I pray you never know that pain."

Tilda tossed the remote down and turned to leave the room.

"Here." Juno interrupted her dramatic exit.

"What?" Tilda snapped out the word.

Juno had a folded piece of paper in his hand and was holding it up toward her. "I found this."

Tilda took the paper from his hand, resisting the impulse to snatch it. It was a ruled sheet torn from a legal pad. She unfolded it.

Dose at 3:45.
20 mins—pain (illegible)
1 hr approx—movement in hands improves
In car, hours after dose. (illegible) *backseat. She doesn't talk.*

Elevated HR. Tuna sandwich—half.
Thirsty. 2 (illegible)

It didn't make sense at all and wasn't helped by Harry's handwriting, which tended to look a lot like the tracks of a spider that had recently fallen into an inkwell.

"What is this?"

"I found it on the couch in the library," Juno said. "Is Dad taking some new medicine or something?"

It seemed that way, but Harry hadn't mentioned any changes to her. The truth was she didn't know if he would mention it. She refolded the paper and put it in her pocket.

"I'll talk to Dr. Woo," she said and walked out before Juno could respond. She'd never even had a chance to hit the unmute button.

Harry had left the light on above the first landing. If he hadn't, Tilda probably wouldn't have noticed. But the light just above her was on, and the door handle of the woman's room was so shiny, like the newest brass. Tilda looked over at the bathroom door. That knob wasn't shiny at all. In fact, it was a flat, darkened pewter. Tilda had chosen those knobs herself because they didn't show smeary handprints. This one here was all wrong.

Tilda took hold of it, adding her oily marks, and turned. It moved less than a quarter inch. If she had put all the torque her arm could manage on that knob, it would not have turned more than a quarter inch. Tilda knew the woman was not inside, but she banged on the door with the meaty side of her fist anyway. *Whomp, whomp, whomp.* Tilda gave the door one last pounding before turning sharply for the bathroom, snatching up Harry's pants and throwing them into the sink to soak.

32.

Day Five of the Miracle

Rachel's heart was tripping over itself trying to get out of her chest. She had her pen flashlight in her backpack, but using it was even more dangerous than not using it. She had snuck away from the research site, going up toward the bathroom and then walking off the side of the road along the forest's edge. She'd walked half a mile coming down to the beach, just on the other side of the bay where the shoreline fell inward, providing her position just enough cover.

If Hooper had seen her then, he would have screamed at the risk she was taking. Rachel was sitting in the sand because she was shaking too hard to stand. She was naked but for her underpants from the waist down. The ocean temperature was forty-five degrees Fahrenheit, and the ambient temperature was thirty-three. With her own work, plus what she was dosing herself and Harry, she needed to collect more samples than she could sneak away from the research site. With only one day left, the tents and the shoreline were manned every minute, and she couldn't wait. She needed these samples. Risk no longer mattered to her, not in the way it had. Nothing short of death or failure mattered. And so she had hiked half a mile, picked her way down the wooded slope, and felt her way through the tangle of brush that barricaded off the rocky sand. She had stripped off her shoes, socks, and pants and walked into the bay with her collection net and jars.

This late in the breeding the glow—the animal density—was less uniform. She needed to wade farther out to get a good sample. When she was in past her knees, she stopped being able to breathe. Every bit of her from the skin on her scalp to her lungs contracted, trying to pull away, and she didn't think she would ever be able to expand them again. It was hard not to panic, and she had to push little gasps of icy air between her teeth, in and out, just the little her body would allow. Her scars nipped and zinged and tingled. It wasn't quite pain. She'd had enough of the compound to fight pain, but even it couldn't take away all the feeling, not under these circumstances.

Just as her scars awoke, like a sleeping monster, her feet went numb, which was just as scary. There were sharp rocks that would slice at bare skin and send her sprawling face-first into the water. Hypothermia had already set in. She was losing fine motor control with each tick of the second hand on her watch. She told her arms and legs to move. She yelled at them, "Move! Move now!" but they were slow to respond, and the slower they responded the longer she stood in the water. The longer she stood in the water, the worse everything got. If she couldn't use her hands, everything would be for nothing. She pushed and pushed and pushed herself, but none of her joints wanted to bend.

It was amazing how much nature did not care. It did not care if she was freezing or if she was even there. No matter what she did, nothing stopped. The waves, small ones, stretched out all the way to the horizon. She could see them outlined in the green light of the *Artemia lucis*. The waves piled up, one overlapping the other like snake scales.

"Geyah!" Like the loud *kiai* before a karate chop, Rachel used the shout to propel her forward, leaning into it, leaning so far that her legs had to catch her or allow her to fall on her face. She made it to the brightest part of the glowing ribbon and ran her collection net over the surface, filling her jars and scattering the animals, which swirled away from her like ink dropped into a glass of water.

She didn't know how long she had been out there, but she was numb from her crotch down. Putting her legs into her jeans was like trying to stuff sausages into casings. She didn't think she was ever going to get them on, and she had to get them on. She had to get dressed, and she had to move, to gather up her jars and get them into her bag and get back. She had to focus. The movement would warm her if only she could manage it.

It took her three tries to button her pants, and she shook so hard, she dropped her backpack trying to unzip it. Rachel was getting angry with her body, angry that it wouldn't comply with her simple demands. She gave up tying her shoes and instead tucked the laces into the sneakers to keep from tripping.

With the jars in her bag and her arms through the straps, Rachel turned her back on the ocean and started toward the road. There was no moon up here for the constant blanket of clouds. There was no artificial light—no cast off from streetlamps or passing cars—nothing to show her the way. There was only the shimmer of the *Artemia lucis*, which did nothing to help and only kept her eyes from adjusting. The path she was using was a small one, a narrow track through the brambles, the sort of thing a deer might follow, which was just how she felt. She was a black-tailed deer, lifting each foot carefully, big ears rotating toward any sound.

The brambles had even begun to take back this little path. The twigs and the prickers and the thorns reached out and snagged her clothes and pierced her hands when she tried to push them away. And when she got through the brambles, there was the slope that went up, up, up to the road more than forty feet above her head. Narrow bits of railroad ties had been sunk into the sandy earth who knew how long ago. It was long enough that the earth was taking them back, pulling them in deeper, leaving only the narrowest toe holds and covering what remained with blown sand and creeping grasses that sunk in roots and rotted the ties, leaving them weak and crumbly, ready to go to splinters like something the termites had got at, and maybe they had done their damage, too.

As she climbed, the sand fell away, and the giant ferns, prehistoric things three feet across, covered the ground on either side, and the cedars grew up between them, and the moss-covered trunks of the maples grew up between them, and there was hardly any space at all. In a moment, the horizon had gone from being empty of everything but the ocean to being as dense with living things as a Tokyo subway. It was an oppressive kind of dark, a dark that made it hard to breathe and pressed in on her ears. To keep from falling on her numb feet and shaky legs, she had to bend forward, putting her hands to the crumbling ties in front of her, carefully raising up one foot and then the other. Foot over foot, hand over hand, she made her way toward the road. She thought of Harry and his fall on the stairs and then tried not to think of him. Foot over foot. Hand over hand.

Freeze.

Rachel stopped her breath and listened. She had one hand and one foot raised, a lung full of air she dared not expel. There was something. She had heard something, or maybe she had felt it, some change in something. She couldn't identify it, but she was not alone. Rachel, who believed only in the most empirical of data, knew in her bones that she was not alone. Her scars prickled.

There it was. A whisper. A *shhh, shhh* to her left. *Shhh. Sh—* It stopped, but it had been there.

Below the trees, under the outstretched arms of the giant ferns the soil was covered in dropped pine needles, short blunt ones and long thin ones that could pierce and cut. They fell and dried and matted together on the forest floor until it was a soft carpet. It was a soft carpet that went *shhh, shhh* under feet.

Shhh, shhh.

Let it be a coyote, Rachel prayed. Oh, how she wanted it to be a coyote. But she knew, even as she wished it, that it was not a coyote. The Olloo'et people believed the coyote to be the slyest and the craftiest of all the creatures on earth. They admired him even as they distrusted him. He was a politician, a mobster, an antihero, and he moved on silent paws. This was not a coyote, but he had aspirations.

Rachel had no choice but to try to deny him. She did the only thing that made sense. She had already been made. She took one breath, and then she ran.

Hand, foot, hand, foot, hand, foot up the ties to the top of the ridge. *Chhh, chhh, chhh.* Her own feet churned up the fallen needles, scattering them behind her as she kicked off. She heard the ground turn to gravel, heard the crunch of it under her sneakers. She was near the shoulder of the road now.

Shhh, shhh, shhh, shhh.

Footsteps that weren't hers. He was trying to be quiet but picking up speed, the desire for speed soon to overtake the desire for stealth. No, not like a coyote at all no matter how he tried.

Between the parked empty cars, over the gravel and onto the black asphalt of the road, she went. Rachel broke all cover in favor of the smooth surface. *Slap-slap-slap* went her sneakers now. The white of the painted lines was so bright it glowed alien in the black, charcoal, and navy of the night. *Slap-slap-slap.* She ran back toward the houses, the research site, the people, the safety. Her backpack, heavy with ocean water, slammed against her spine. *Whack-whack-whack* with each step. She felt the samples shifting and sloshing inside, the balance all off. She tried to compensate, but she heard him behind her, closer now. He, too, was running. *Slap-slap-slap.*

No air. Rachel had no air. She was not in shape for this. She had not trained. Just a lap or two around the student rec center was all she'd done in so long, and she'd gone farther than that, faster than that here. So cold. So afraid.

Rachel risked a glance over her shoulder.

Bad idea. Terrible. Someone was there. She was not imagining it, not running from some ground squirrel or bunny rabbit up past his bedtime. John? It had to be him, and he was not more than thirty feet behind her, and his legs—not recently dipped in the icy bay waters—were churning up ground faster than she ever would. She would not make it. She could not win. There was nothing she could do.

She turned her face back around, and she was blind.

33.

The headlights were so bright that her vision ceased to exist. It was like looking into a solar eclipse. Rachel knew she would never see again, and it did not matter because in a moment, in just one second, the bumper of whatever that was would impact her femurs—both of them. They would shatter, and she would fall. Just a little. Just enough for the car to eat her up and suck her under and for the tires to run over her body, crushing her pelvis and her ribs and her spine, popping organs like Jell-O–filled balloons, shredding muscle and nerve fiber and killing her, although not instantly. Almost nothing died instantly. That was something people said of their loved ones to soothe themselves. She would feel it, and it would be the last thing she would feel.

Rachel closed her eyes.

The horn sounded, and the blowback coming off such a big piece of metal moving so very, very fast nearly knocked her off her feet. She opened her eyes in time to see the taillights swerving across the road, the whole center of gravity of the small SUV shifting, so Rachel thought it might topple over, and then it righted itself and found its lane and continued around a curve and was gone.

Rachel had stopped running, but she was panting even harder than before. She was alone. No car. No John. He had cleared from the road. But not gone. No. He couldn't be gone. Only dived for cover, only hidden.

With legs so cold and so full of adrenaline, she ran. She ran and ran and ran, and nothing mattered, not the lack of air, not the invisible knife in her ribs or the pain of her scars, not the scream of her muscles and pounding in her head and the slosh of her samples and the slap of her bag. She ran until her legs were like windmills turning too fast for the rest of her body to catch up. She ran until she fell, throwing herself forward and landing on her stomach with her arms and her face in the gravel and dirt just off the road. And when she looked up, she saw in front of her the blue porta-potty set up for the team. She had made it. She was back. Somewhere, somewhere nearby there were people, and she could scream. She rolled over on the ground as far as she could with her pack like a turtle's shell behind her, braced for whatever might be above her.

Nothing.

Rachel scampered, all torn palms and scraped elbows and knees, until she was up again. She turned all 360 degrees, her knees bent, her hands up like claws. But there was nothing. Nothing but a blue porta-potty and some parked cars up ahead. There was the sound of the waves down below and the reflective road sign just before the next curve, warning drivers to slow for switchbacks.

Rachel heard herself panting like a dog. She reached up and, with bloody hands, gripped the straps of her backpack and speed-walked down the embankment, heading for the beach. She did not cross the yellow tape, did not wave or motion to her fellows or acknowledge them in any way. Maybe they saw her, and maybe they were too absorbed in this next-to-the-last day of work to pay her any mind at all. But whatever they did, Rachel did not know because all she wanted was to get to Harry's deck, up, up, up the stairs and through the sliding door that was always kept unlocked for her.

Rachel did not stop to wipe her shoes or turn on a hallway light or grab any food or drink from the kitchen. Head down, she pushed through. Through the downstairs—no Harry in the library—to the stairs, *clomp, clomp, clomp* on the honey-colored hardwood. Had they always been this steep before, this narrow? Had there always been so many of them? It took forever to get to that first landing right in front of her bedroom door. Rachel shoved her hand into her pocket for the shiny new brass key that had come with the lock. She closed her fingers around it and pulled, taking the whole lining of her jeans pocket with her hand, turning it inside out, but she didn't care. She needed to get in. She needed to get started. She needed—

"Hello."

For the first time that night, Rachel screamed.

Tilda had taken the wooden stool that served as her nightstand and carried it down the stairs to the landing. She'd brought a David Foster Wallace book with her, but she kept dozing, her back leaned against the wall. It was the *clomp* of the woman's shoes that woke her. The book sat closed on Tilda's lap, heavy as a gallon of milk, pinning her there and, as much as anything, keeping her from toppling over. Her butt was numb. She'd been there several hours, but it had been worth it. In truth, very little could make her night any worse than it had been.

Rachel was no longer capable of pulling herself together. The best she could do was place her bloodied palm over her heart to calm her pulse rate.

"You scared me."

Tilda could hear Harry rustling behind his bedroom door. Rachel had woken him, which was another good reason to be angry, and now she had turned her back and was putting her key in the lock, as though no further discussion was required.

"When Harry offered you a place to sleep, that invitation didn't include the right to make structural alterations."

Rachel blinked twice before answering. Language was slow to move from her brain to her lips. "I needed a lock."

Tilda stood. Rachel had the door open and was walking through it. There was no way—just no way—Tilda thought. Rachel went to close the door. Tilda heard Harry crossing the hardwood floor of his room.

She could hear his three-point walk, two steps and then a *clomp* of the footed cane. Tilda put her own bare foot out over the threshold. If she had thought it would come to this, she'd have worn shoes.

"I'd like to know what the hell is going on here," Tilda said.

"I have to get to work." Rachel shut the door as far as Tilda's toes, not squashing them but applying enough pressure that someone less determined would have moved.

"There is no rational excuse for a houseguest to lock out the owners unless there is something going on. What is it that you don't want us to see?"

Rachel had very few options, and all of them were bad. She could leave the door open while she worked, which was impossible. Or she could slam the door on Mrs. Streatfield's foot and break her toes. There was no time to pack up. No time to be thrown out, and if she were thrown out, there was nowhere for her to go. She couldn't go back to the camp with all the sneaks and the spies, and every hotel and guesthouse on the island was taken. She simply could not and would not leave this room. That's all there was to the matter, so one way or another Mrs. Streatfield's foot had to get moved. Rachel braced herself.

"Tilda? Tilda, what are you doing?"

Rachel could not see Harry through the crack, but she could hear him just fine.

"I'm trying to determine what sort of immoral or illegal activity is going on in this room," Tilda said. "Because it's sure as hell something, if this woman is installing locks in our house without permission. Jesus Christ, that's just insane!" Tilda was exhausted, and the pitch and volume of her voice increased with every word until she was shouting.

"What's going on? Why is everyone yelling?" Juno had opened his door and stuck his head out.

"Everyone isn't yelling," Harry said. "Your mother is yelling."

"Why are you yelling?" Juno asked.

"I demand to know what is going on in that room," Tilda said.

"Tilda, what in the hell has gotten into you?" Harry stepped, shuffled, and clomped down the short hall toward her. "Leave that young woman alone. Jesus."

Everyone was acting like Tilda was the crazy one. How had that happened?

"Don't you think her changing the entire doorknob is a little odd?" Tilda demanded.

"I think you're embarrassing yourself," Harry said.

"She changed the doorknob?" Juno asked and was ignored.

"Can you imagine the headlines?" Tilda asked. "Former senator's home turned into drug den."

Harry was right behind Tilda then. She had to twist at an odd angle to see him and her son, what with her leg stuck in the doorway like it was.

Harry lowered his voice, not so much that Rachel couldn't hear but maybe enough to keep Juno out of it. "Tilda, this is not your house. This is my house, and you will take your foot out of the door so this woman can go to bed. She's been up all night."

Harry had pulled his navy blue terrycloth robe over his pajamas, which hung on his frame like they were two sizes too big, something that had never been true before. He had gray stubble on his cheeks. Some of the hairs were dark gray, and some of them were white, and he was paler than she ever remembered him being before. He had bags under his eyes that weren't just puffy but looked purplish and bruised, like they would hurt if she touched them. He looked like a man who was terribly sick, who might wet his pants and start seeing and talking about relatives who had passed like terribly sick people sometimes do. He was that man—unequivocally that man—and he was telling Tilda that she was the crazy one embarrassing all of them.

Tilda took her foot out of the door, which shut like it was spring-loaded. She heard it lock from the inside. Harry didn't say anything else. He just executed his three-point turn and headed back toward his room. Juno, who had hardly been acknowledged, returned the favor, shutting his own door without another word.

Tilda opened her mouth, but the words didn't find their way out, and no one was there to hear what she had to say anyway.

It was the in-between hours, the little bit of time after the night shift had come back but before the day shift was to go. The closer to the end of the project they got, the shorter the in-between hours were, which meant Hooper had almost no time to himself, almost no time to be here, a condition made worse by John. He had become overly watchful and distrusting, aggressive really, and Hooper regretted bringing him.

Hooper's key, unlike those the others carried, unlocked all of the cabins, including what had been Dr. Bell's. He stood there in her space, which she had vacated several days before. The one bed that had covers looked as though someone had been in it just moments before. The sheet was pulled off to one side and dragged down onto the floor, and the blanket was kicked down in a nest at the foot. In the bathroom, he'd found nothing but hair in the sink. For a moment he'd thought the trash can would be more promising. Inside, he found packing materials and bits of Styrofoam, but none of it had labels. There was a muddy pair of socks, which was odd but unenlightening.

Whatever she had been doing, she had left little evidence behind. Hooper sat down on the spare bed. He was very tired. He had not slept more than a couple of hours at a time for a week. He had a headache, which did not respond to aspirin, and his thinking felt dull.

He moved his feet back just a few inches, moved them so that his heels were under the bed. He wasn't even aware that he had done it, but he was aware of having kicked something. It scooted a bit across the dirty linoleum floor, and Hooper could hear the sound of years of grit.

He hung his head down to peer under the bed, and then, after a moment, climbed down onto his hands and knees. He reached into the charcoal gray dimness and pulled out two shipping boxes. They had been cut open and folded flat, and they still had the labels attached to their outsides. They were from laboratory supply companies, both of which Hooper recognized. He used them himself. The recipient was Rachel, but they had been sent care of a mailbox and shipping store-front on the island.

Hooper broke the perforation of the thin plastic envelope that held the shipping label, which, when unfolded, was also the list of contents. His eyes skimmed Rachel's order. Whatever she was doing, it was clear to Hooper that it was very different than their work at the site. They were collecting, examining, preserving, documenting. Rachel, though, Rachel was feeding.

34.

Tilda had been so upset when she carried her stool and her book up to her crow's nest of a room in the peak of the house, a refuge that suddenly felt like being shut away, that she was sure she wouldn't be able to sleep. Her chest hurt, and her eyes were itchy with unshed tears. She pulled back the covers, which she always tucked in too tight, and lay down on the cold sheets. She didn't like this pillow. It was lumpy and synthetic, and she missed her down pillow that was now in storage with everything else she owned. This room just wasn't enough. She needed to have her own space, some place she knew she could run to if she wanted and needed. She would take care of it that day, Tilda told herself, and it was the last thought she had before falling into the dead sleep she didn't believe would come.

Tilda slept for five hours, woke to her alarm, and dressed without showering. She put on a ball cap and sneakers and left the house without saying anything to anyone. She had something to take care of, someplace to be.

Out on the beach, the wind had picked up, tiny bits of salt and sand buffeted her, and she let them. She had, it seemed, run out of resistance. And now, she would wait. She would stand there and breathe in the brine, and both she and the boat would wait.

It helped to think they were together in this, absurd as that sounded. It was only a boat, a thing not a person, but it was steady and predictable in a way that other things that should have been were not. And like her, the boat was stuck, tied to the house, unable to get away when it needed. There was a long list of things that Tilda could not help, but this was not on that list. This was fixable.

The boat's rudder and centerboard, like the belly fin of a fish, pivoted up, leaving a smooth bottom that could lie on a trailer or be pushed across sand, but at twelve feet from port side to outrigger, *Serendipity* was as wide as it was tall. Tilda knew her limits. Even if the beach had not been blocked off, the distance between house and water was too great. She had called up the island's largest marina the day before, explained her situation, and had been promised a small regiment of men.

The first of them walked right past her, heading toward the water, looking left and right and only turned back when she called. Behind him, in a small clump, came the rest of the men, some in better shape than others, but all boat men, boat men who were looking for a boat, which she had to turn and point to there under the deck. They squinted at it with varying looks of surprise on their faces.

When it had just been her, it felt as though the boat were a big, solid thing keeping her company, but now with a whole team of strangers around her, it felt more like it was hiding, like a wounded cat that had run under the house to heal its wounds.

The men moved toward her, forming a semicircle with her at the center. She explained again what she had on the phone. They all wore windbreakers and whiffs of their bodies found their way into her nose, pushing out the ocean brine. One of them had worn aftershave, and they had the smell of sweat and work on them. They nodded while she talked, accepted her direction and the credit card she produced for the one with the clipboard. They asked few questions, and then, without making any deal of it at all, they did what they had come to do.

With caution tape and scientists blocking the most direct path to the bay, they instead lowered the mast, lifted the small craft off the jacks, and carried it with any number of heart-stopping jerks and starts up to the road. They loaded it onto a trailer they had brought, tied everything down, and navigated the twisting half mile of road to the housing development's communal dock.

The truck, trailer, and boat had to take the road so slowly that Tilda, who would not fit in the vehicle with them, kept them in sight the entire way as she jogged along the gravel-covered shoulder. She stopped, her hands on her hips, and walked slowly from the road down to the ramp, catching her breath and steadying her words before she got to them.

The boat's design would've allowed them to push it into the water, launching and landing from the beach like a canoe. But the ramp here was concrete, and so they backed the trailer into the water just like her father had when she was a child. Tilda climbed up onto the trailer and then stepped into the boat, one leg swinging over the side at a time. She knelt there, holding her breath as the boat met water for the first time.

She was suddenly nervous. She had been nervous the whole way, of course, nervous they would drop the boat, nervous it would come off the trailer, nervous that the mast, once down, would not come back up. But now she remembered to be nervous about this, the biggest thing. Would the boat even float?

She crossed her fingers inside her jacket pockets as the bay began to take *Serendipity*'s weight, and the men pushed her off the trailer and into the water.

"How's she look?" the most senior of the men asked her. He was her age or very near it with deep gouges radiating out from his eyes and in smiling commas around his mouth that, despite the lack of a tan, spoke of a life lived almost entirely outside. He wore a frayed ball cap pulled down low over his eyes, which were green and kind, something Tilda might have taken more notice of if her stomach hadn't been attempting to turn itself inside out.

"Good," Tilda said before enough time had passed to really tell.

The men pulled *Serendipity* over to the long, slender dock that stretched out into the bay, just left of the ramp. Two other boats were moored there, and her boat—Tilda thought of it as hers even though she knew well enough that it wasn't—took its own place. Together, they raised the mast, checked the rigging, and attached the sail, raising it foot by foot as they secured the slides. It was a simple boat. She had only the one sail, and with many hands, it was a fast job.

The boat had been in the water for a while by then, and the inside of the cockpit was the driest thing for twenty miles. Even with the taped sail and patched wood, Tilda was proud of herself.

"She'll do all right," the man said, running his hand over the side.

Tilda nodded. She had something in her throat that resembled a rubber band ball that she could neither explain nor swallow.

"You want to bring her down now?"

He was asking if she wanted to lower the sail, cover it, and tie it down, maybe ride back with them to the house, which was the very last thing Tilda could imagine wanting.

She shook her head. "Gonna take her out."

The man smiled and nodded, and with her in the cockpit, he threw off the moorings.

Rachel had been up for an hour, and she had still not left her room, not even to go to the bathroom. The blinds were closed tight. Even at just past noon, the room was so dark she'd had to switch on the lamps. But the lamps weren't the only source of light. When she unplugged the UV bulbs over her tanks, the *Artemia lucis,* thinking it was night, glowed their brilliant green. The individual flasks shimmered in the darkened room. Up close it was a bright lime both beautiful and alien.

Nearly being run down by a car had been worth it. It had been worth it because here those same samples were. They were here, and they were alive. They had lived through the night and half the day, and they were glowing and shimmering and moving and mating. She was sure they were mating.

It had worked. She had done it.

She had done it all by herself, and now the possibilities were unimaginable. She would load these and all the other samples she could carry into the truck and onto the ferry. She would have to take the truck. There was no way around it. The covered bed would be big enough to hold everything, including her small generator, powering the tanks. She would set it all up in there, a mobile lab, and she would take it straight to her apartment. She would need to get started isolating the possible proteins and synthesizing them right away. Then the *Artemia lucis* wouldn't be needed anymore. She could make as much of the active agent as she needed, test it and tweak it. She was only the first patient. Thousands and thousands after her would get better. Millions even.

Rachel had to take a breath. There was work to be done before she could pack everything. Every detail of the final conditions mattered. She had to be able to replicate this exactly to keep the samples alive until the work could commence. Rachel had written down everything she could think of in her notes, coded of course. She wanted to type the coded messages into her laptop, but she was terrified to e-mail them to anyone or upload them anywhere. That's what John wanted, of course. He had been the one to chase her into traffic. He had been the one spying on her from the very beginning. She knew it. She couldn't put the secret anywhere that could be hacked. And, of course, her laptop could be stolen just like her notebook could be stolen. There needed to be contingencies.

She was making three, no four, no five—five would be better—copies of the secret notes and folding each piece of paper as small as she could make it. She shoved one into the already sliced lining of her puffy winter coat. She slid others into the lining of her bags. She pulled the footbed out of her boot. She tried to think of everything. If only she had a condom, she could have put a set of notes into that and swallowed it.

35.

Tilda sat with her hand on the tiller heading north-
east across the bay toward Carpenter's Island. It was smaller and
greener than Olloo'et with fewer full-time residents and far fewer ferry
stops, especially in winter. Harder to get onto and off of this time of
year, almost no one bothered, which was entirely the point.

With no other boats to look out for, Tilda turned her face to the
clouds. The bank hung low but was moving fast. It would cross the
sound before ripping open and then pile up against the Cascades,
dumping out its payload before floating up and over the mountains,
turning innocuous as the clouds drifted over the dry half of the state.
Olloo'et would be spared this one, she thought, but it would be big
enough that visitors at the top of Craven's Lighthouse would be able to
see the rain come down in the distance like a blue-gray sheet on the
horizon.

That same wind that pushed the clouds was pushing her. The sail
was full, stretched really, and the hull clipped along the top of the
water like a skipping stone. Multihull boats were known for speed, but
this was more than she had expected. She would make landfall in less
than an hour, making her early for her date with Tip.

She would use the time, she thought, to walk out the kinks. Even small waves batted *Serendipity*. Tilda held tight to the tiller to keep from losing her seat, the boat coming down hard with each skip and bruising her tailbone.

There was no question that it hurt. It hurt, and she was wet from the spray. She'd been squinting to keep the wind from her eyes, something that she had largely failed at, and so tears streamed from the corners. Her hands ached from holding the tiller and the side so tightly—or at least they would ache when they warmed and feeling returned. There was every reason to be miserable. Anyone else would've been miserable. But adrenaline was flooding Tilda's bloodstream. She was excited. She was proud. She was in control of something, and Tilda could not remember a time, not in months, that she had been this happy, this purely and unquestionably happy.

It was hours before her shift was to start, but Rachel had no intention of working another shift. She needed more containers from the research site. She would take them, just go in and grab them like they were hers. Then she would go back down the road to the collection site from the night before and fill every one of them with samples. She had on her boots, which she'd reassembled, and her coat, and she unlocked and opened the door.

Harry's fist was at face level. Rachel blinked, struck dumb for a moment, and then she ducked. Harry lowered his hand.

"I'm sorry. I was just about to knock."

"I'm leaving," Rachel said. "No time to talk."

Harry looked over his shoulder like he'd heard something. Rachel looked, too, and saw nothing. He turned back to her, distracted. "You know why I'm here."

Rachel stepped into the hall, forcing him to shuffle backward with his cane and make room. She closed the door behind her and pulled out her key to lock it. When she turned back around to face him, her mouth already open and ready to refuse, he was holding up a roll of money.

"This is for one month's supply," he said. "I can get you more as we go." He was wearing a gray T-shirt and a pair of khaki pants that had become too big for him and drooped around his hips. It was cold in the house. It was always cold in the house just like it was always cold outside. And still, there were rings of sweat under Harry's arms.

The money made her feel like a low-level drug dealer, which wasn't to say that she didn't want it. She was a post-doc after all, which meant she lived largely on six-for-three-dollar packages of ramen, and her equipment was not free. Still, she had to stay focused.

"I don't—" she started, but Harry held up his hand to silence her.

It would have been rude except that he looked back over his shoulder again, longer this time. "Do you hear something?" Harry spoke without turning back to her. "We're not alone right now."

Rachel knew they weren't alone. She was never alone in the house. It was bustling with people.

"I'm also making notes for you," Harry said, giving her more if not all of his attention. "I made some—I made some yesterday, but I laid them down, and now I can't—I can't find them. There are some side effects."

Harry held the roll out to her. It was everything she had not to take it.

"I don't have time to prepare another dose right now. I have to leave. I'm packing."

"Leave? Leave where?"

"I have what I need here," Rachel said. "I can continue my work back in Seattle."

Harry was becoming more and more agitated. "No, you don't understand," he said.

She went on like he hadn't spoken. "I have just a few more things to take care of. I'll work through the night and be gone in the morning." Rachel slid past him and started down the stairs before stopping. "Thank you for letting me stay. I do appreciate it."

Harry felt obscene holding the money, ridiculous and immoral all at the same time, like he'd just tried to pay her for something more than medicine. And she'd walked away from him. She was leaving.

He tried to go after her. He took a step toward the stairs even though the thought of trying to go down them scared him. He'd lost so much in the past few days—so much feeling, so much movement. His hands and his legs were weak unless he had the medicine. When he had the medicine he was all right, better than all right. He was almost as good as new. When he didn't have it, he was worse than he had ever been, and if he'd known that going in, maybe he wouldn't have started taking it. But he had started, and there was nothing for it. She had to tell him who else had access to the medicine. Someone would want to sell it to him.

He was going after Dr. Bell. Becca didn't need to get involved, but he hadn't found any logic that worked with her. He didn't need the medicine to see her now. She came to him even when it had been hours—almost a day—since he had taken anything. After he had gone to bed, she came back to him. She was wearing different clothes, and she didn't look like someone who had fallen from a balcony. And of course, she hadn't. That other woman had. That poor woman, and who knew if she had been in control? He had been so sure it was Becca. So sure. Even now it was hard to believe . . . and those things he'd said . . . he never would have if Becca hadn't made him think it was her. She had, hadn't she? Everything was so jumbled.

Becca scared him. She stayed in his room with him all night, pacing and humming and talking about things she had done as a child. And Harry knew it wasn't real. He told himself it wasn't. And he looked away and squeezed his eyes closed, and he tried to sleep, but every time he opened them again, she was there.

And here she was again. She had stood behind him the entire time, and now as he was going after Rachel, she got impatient and pushed past. He felt it. He felt her hand on his arm and the weight of her shoving him off balance. Harry fell into the small decorative table Maggie had put in the corner. It jabbed into his hip, and his hand slipped off his cane. He went down on one knee, his elbow hitting hard on the table.

"No," he called at the two backs retreating down the stairs. "Don't go!"

Harry didn't know which of the women he was talking to, and neither of them turned around.

36.

"Rachel? Are you all right?"

"Yes."

She wasn't at all all right, but she hadn't meant to yelp like that. She'd sounded like a coyote pup, and everyone had looked up, including Hooper, who was now standing over her.

"Let me see it."

Rachel set her jaw. She didn't have time for this, and at the same time, she didn't want to pique anyone's curiosity. It was a difficult call, but she held out her hand.

Rachel had come down to the site with her hood pulled up. She'd stayed in the background, ducking into the corner of the tent away from most of the day-shift workers, who were clustered around the stereo microscopes and laptops on the other side. This back corner, where the generator was, had become the dumping ground for whatever supplies weren't in use. There were still-wet waders that would mildew, half-full boxes of petri dishes, glass slides, vials and flasks of all descriptions, collection nets, and the economy-size tubs of snack mix and chocolate-covered raisins that had made up half the team's calories for the past week.

She had knelt down to go through the boxes, looking for the largest containers she could find, as many as she could find. The sand shifted under her feet, and she'd reached out to steady herself. She'd done it without thinking and without looking, and she'd put her hand on the generator, which was nothing but a combustion engine. It was like running your car five hundred miles and then grabbing some of the metal under the hood. If she'd heard her skin sizzle and stick like meat on a grill, it would not have surprised her. Everyone was concerned, but she had, of course, been through worse.

"You're down early," Hooper said. He had on his reading glasses and was holding her palm, which was bright red, up close to his face.

"Wanted to get a head start. Tonight's the last night."

"That's what the history books tell us," Hooper said, which wasn't the same thing as "yes." Scientists were raised to avoid definitive statements. Things "appeared so" and "were consistent with." Rachel was so used to it, did it so much herself, that she didn't even notice it anymore.

"The samples we're collecting now are sluggish," Hooper went on. "Definite decrease in their activity levels."

Rachel furrowed her brow. She hoped this wouldn't complicate their transportation.

"We suspect the females are laying eggs today. It would be fantastic if we could get them to do it in captivity, but they're all dying within two hours of pulling them out of the water."

Hooper was trying to keep them? When had that started? She hadn't seen any tanks or heard any talk. She almost opened her mouth, but quickly pushed the impulse aside. Hooper, it seemed, was waiting for her to comment, but when she didn't, he went on.

"It's bad," he said, rolling her hand to catch a better light. "But I've seen worse. It'll blister and hurt like hell, but as long as you keep it clean, it'll heal. John"—Hooper raised his voice and called over his shoulder—"would you bring me the first aid kit?"

Rachel's body went rigid just as if someone had poured quick-set cement into her. Hooper felt it.

"Did something hurt?"

John came over with the white metal box they kept stashed under one of the worktables. "Accident?" he asked.

"What are you doing here?" Rachel demanded.

"Probably the same thing you are," he said. "We're running out of time."

"Rachel put her hand on the generator," Hooper said, holding out her palm for John's inspection. "Can you put a bandage on it?"

John had set the kit down on top of one of the boxes and quickly undid the metal latches, revealing all manner of Band-Aids, gauzes, and ointments.

Rachel yanked her hand back from both men. "You stay the hell away from me."

John didn't answer.

"If you follow me again, so help me God."

"What the hell is going on here?" Hooper demanded.

Rachel didn't give John time to talk. "He's been following me for days, spying on me. Last night he chased me into the road."

"Last night? When last night?" Hooper demanded.

"During our shift," Rachel said. "Two—two-thirty."

John crossed his arms over his chest and shook his head. Laughter came from the other side of the tent, and he looked over his shoulder to see what was funny, making it clear Rachel wasn't so important as to demand all of his attention. When he turned, Rachel saw his tattoo clearly, each of the black dots equidistant from the others, marching up his neck like a regiment of soldiers. She wanted to scratch them off with her fingernails.

"Rachel." Hooper was using the sort of low, slow voice you use with children having a tantrum. "John could not have done anything to you last night."

"Like hell he didn't. He ran after me through the woods."

"John spent all of last shift doing classifications. He was here."

"No," Rachel said. "He left."

Hooper shook his head. "I don't think so."

Rachel cut him off. "He left. He always leaves. You can't always be paying attention. He says he's going to the bathroom or—or—something, and then he doesn't come back. You wouldn't even notice."

"Rachel," Hooper said, "I'm telling you. I would notice. Just like I notice when you leave."

She could feel a hot blush spreading across her neck. "He followed me! He chased me. He was trying to scare me. He ran after me and forced me into the road. There was a car—"

Hooper shook his head.

"There was a car!" Rachel was shouting, and she wasn't sure when that had started. "I almost died!"

"John," Hooper said, "why don't you give us a minute?"

"No! Why are you protecting him?"

John turned and walked toward the microscopes. All the researchers who weren't out in the water were staring, and Hooper put his hand on her arm, pushing and steering her out of the tent. Rachel reached down and snagged the cardboard box of containers she'd come for, ignoring the pain in her hand. It didn't matter anyway. She could take something for that.

Hooper steered her up the beach until they were against the scrub brush.

"I have to get back to work," she said.

"Rachel, I'm sending you home. I think you haven't been sleeping enough." Rachel yanked her arm away from his hand. "I should have seen the signs earlier," he went on. "That's my fault. But I see them now, and I want you to get some help. I'm going to make some calls for you."

Rachel let out a bark of laughter. She knew what he was doing. She recognized it from the instruction sheet posted on the wall of the lab back at the university. It was posted on the walls of all the labs right next to the fire evacuation route and what to do in case of an earthquake. He was walking her through what to do if a colleague has a mental breakdown, that little sheet she'd thought was so funny for years. And it was. It was goddamn hysterical.

When Rachel had gone, Hooper turned to John. "If you know anything that might help," the professor said, "now would be the time."

John flashed red with anger. He had said something. He had gone to Hooper days before and gotten the door slammed in his face. And now? What could he say that would make any difference now? "Look at the woman!" he wanted to shout. Was it any wonder that his ancestors thought men that high had crossed to another plane? Was it any wonder they feared not being able to return? He had warned Hooper. He had warned Rachel. He had warned and warned, and no one had listened until this. And now that he was thinking about it, really thinking about it, he had been doing classifications the night before, just as Hooper had said, but Hooper wouldn't know that. He hadn't been there.

37.

Tip would arrive on the early-afternoon ferry. Even after Tilda had found her way to the public docks, lowered her sail, and tied up, she still had more than an hour to kill.

Carpenter's Island had only one town, now called Cussler's Ferry. Josiah Cussler had been the first white person to settle on the island. He was a preacher who had begun his career as a prospector, at which he had failed spectacularly. When he settled on the island, he brought with him one legal wife and three others that he called spiritual wives. Together they formed a church and attempted to recruit others to move to what was then an almost inaccessible settlement. People did eventually come to Cussler's Ferry, but few, if any, joined Josiah's church. The good preacher was eventually killed and partially eaten by a bear but not before fathering nearly two dozen children, making Cussler a popular surname on the island even today.

It was the sort of local tale that Tilda loved and loved to tell to other people who had somehow gone their entire lives without hearing it. She had told Tip, who had been mostly interested in the bear. She thought that rather missed a lot, but, as they had been planning a hike, it was understandable.

The public docks were just two blocks from the main road

through Cussler's Ferry, which contained nearly every commercial shop on the island. Less affluent than Olloo'et, there were no five-dollar coffees or animal-accessory shops. The town did cater to hikers and backpackers during the high season with an outdoor outfitter on one corner and a pizza shop on the other. There was also a taco stand and a doughnut shop, both of which were closed, whether for the day, the winter, or indefinitely wasn't clear.

Tilda went into a pharmacy-slash-convenience store, which also sold fishing and trapping permits. The clerk, wearing a blue apron over a slightly premature holiday sweater, watched Tilda walk in but did not greet her. The tile under her feet was worn, the lighting some-what sickly, and the whole place smelled of iodine and the hot dogs rotating on a metal warmer near the cash register.

Tilda had eaten nothing that day, and her stomach felt hollow. But even in that state, the hot dogs, with their shriveled ends, looked terri-ble. She decided instead on a bag of M&M's, a canister of honey-roasted nuts, some raisins, and two single-serving boxes of Cheerios, being careful to check the sell-by date on everything.

Outside, she stopped at a bench and unloaded her sack. One by one, she opened each item and poured it into the plastic bag, disposing of the containers in a nearby trash can. Then she shook the whole thing. The M&M's did tend to settle to the bottom, but other than that, it was serviceable. She carried it around the outfitter store, fishing out handfuls while she looked at dehydrated ravioli packets and camp-ing bowls that collapsed flat like accordions. When enough time had passed, she wiped her hand off on her jeans and went to go meet Tip.

He walked off the ferry with a full-size hiker's pack on his back, crossed the distance between them in two steps, and took up her mouth with his. She could taste mint on his tongue.

"What's in the pack?" Tilda asked when he'd let her go.

"A late lunch," he said.

Tilda held up her trail mix. "I cooked, too."

He looked in the sack. "Are those Cheerios?"

"It felt like it needed a starch."

He laughed and wrapped an arm around her, pulling her tight to his side in a way that made her stutter-step. It was difficult to walk pinned to him, and she pulled away. He looked at her sideways but let it go, launching into a stream of chatter about a new grill man at the restaurant.

She listened, waiting for an opportunity to tell him about the sailboat. Once or twice he took a breath, and Tilda started to open her mouth, but then it would turn out that he wasn't done and more words would pour out. He continued on as they wound their way down a short residential street off the main strip, following the white arrows on the state park signs toward the trailhead. No one else from the ferry went this way, and within ten minutes they were alone.

Tilda had stopped listening. She wanted to tell him about her boat. She wanted there to be an opening to tell him about her boat, but his monologue had taken them all the way to the end of the street where asphalt became a dirt path into the trees.

The path was narrow, and he went ahead. He had stopped talking, but now talking was too difficult. He would have had to turn all the way around to see her, and she didn't want to talk to his back. This thing she had done, this big thing of fixing a boat entirely on her own, mattered to her. She wanted someone to appreciate it, to listen while she described the smell of newly mixed epoxy. She wanted him to want to see it, to ask her to take him out, maybe even right now. She had wanted the conversation she wanted when she wanted it, and she hadn't gotten it. She could have interrupted. She could have stopped and insisted he turn around right then, but she had already gone and upset herself.

It was a childish thing. She knew it was childish. She stopped for a moment, took a breath, and told herself she was letting it go. She didn't know if she was or not, but she wanted to.

Stopped, she no longer had to look at her shoes or his pack. She could see the trees that had swallowed up the two of them, swallowed them completely in such a short distance. It was like a fairy tale where the wood seals itself around the wandering children. The trail had been kept clear, but the same ferns from Olloo'et were here. New leaves sprouted from their middle, reaching up first in a perfect spiral before unfurling their fiddlehead shape into a long leafy stem. Here and there would be a fallen tree the earth was trying to reclaim. Toadstools sprouted from the rotted parts. The little funguses were every color from creamy white to pumpkin orange and looked delicate and thin, like tiny umbrellas. Tilda saw a salamander scuttle across the fallen needles. The ground was wet and covered with mulched and rotted tree bark the dark red of an Irish setter. It made it easy to spot the bright yellow banana slug that ventured across the path like a pedestrian trying to cross a freeway. Sensing her approach, it pulled in its antenna and curled into a ball.

Tilda let her feet go again, carrying her along, but she kept her eyes up. The air was cold, but it was also clean. It smelled like cedar and rain—of both storms that had gone before and storms still to come. Breathing it all in felt like drinking a big glass of water. It felt good for her, cleansing in a way no air had ever been or felt all those years in D.C.

Tip stopped on the trail ahead of her, and Tilda, enraptured, ran into him.

"Look," he breathed.

Tilda tilted her head to the sky and saw through a break in the trees a bird soaring over them. Its white head was in sharp contrast to the dark brown of its body, and its wingspan was so large it made her feel like prey.

"Bald eagle," she whispered.

She almost never saw one on Olloo'et. There were too many people, too much activity.

"This way," Tip said. "We're almost there."

The trail, already single track, had a spur even narrower. Despite his pack, Tip took off, landing only on the balls of his feet as he hopped from footfall to footfall up the trail. Tip's legs were long, and his body was young. Young enough not to know this terrain was challenging, and so within moments, he was far enough ahead that Tilda couldn't see him.

She had worn her sneakers, and she thought for a minute about running after him, an idea that was quickly discarded. She knew she wouldn't make it far before she started huffing and puffing and would have to walk, and besides, she didn't want to chase him or anyone else. She was tired. Here in the woods where no one could find her seemed as good a place as any to rest, and so she kept to her own pace.

When Tilda caught up, they were at the top of a hill. Just to the left was a small clearing where the trees made room for the sky, and the ferns made room for the little cabin. Grasses and nibbly plants that would attract deer were here, but mostly it was a thick bed of fallen pine needles that made a soft carpet under her feet as she walked after him toward the door—or more precisely the doorway, as there was no door to fill it.

A small wooden sign proclaimed this structure CAREY'S HOUSE, built and cared for by the Carpenter's Island Trail Association. At the bottom of the sign was a little wooden box with a hinged top. Tilda stopped to open it. Inside, on a thin chain was a pen, which made her think there had been some sort of guest book at one time or another, but it was gone now, perhaps filled and taken away by the trail people, perhaps stolen. Now spiders had taken over the box, crisscrossing it with their webs so densely that only a teenager on a dare would have ever stuck his hand inside. Tilda let the top drop shut and wiped her hands on her jeans.

Tip was inside and had already begun unpacking. She followed him. The cabin was empty and so dim she squinted to see into the corners. Tip was laying down a sleeping bag that he'd unzipped until it was one thick, flannel-topped picnic blanket before reaching for the food in his pack.

She'd only eaten those handfuls of trail mix that day, and her stomach made greedy noises when he pulled out the cold fried chicken. There was potato salad dressed with vinegar and capers, Brussels sprouts caramelized with bacon, and for dessert, he'd brought walnut brownies cut into little squares.

"I have a confession," he said.

Tilda was untying her shoes to keep from tracking mud onto the blanket.

"I bought the brownies from the bakery downtown."

He put a chicken leg on a paper plate and passed it to her. She picked it up and took a bite without serving herself any of the side dishes first. It was as good as she had hoped it would be.

"I'll try to find it in me to forgive you," she said, her mouth still a little full.

"I'm a terrible baker. You should know that if we go into business together."

The drumstick became less appetizing. This wasn't at all the conversation she had hoped for. "I'm not doing any business right now," she said.

"It's perfect for both of us." Tip spooned potatoes onto her plate, which she was now ignoring. "You need something to do, and I need an investor. We can run the numbers together and see where we stand."

The cabin smelled dank and musty. The edges of Tilda's mind thought about the spiders.

"I need something to do?"

"Babe, that space won't stay empty forever, and I'll need to be open by the time the summer tourists roll in."

Tilda hated nicknames, but that wasn't the point.

Tip leaned over the open containers of food and put his hand on her leg. "I know it wasn't something you'd planned on, but the opportunity is just too amazing. Downtown has Brasserie for the high-end stuff, and The Galley is an old, worn-down tavern."

Tilda liked The Galley.

"But there's nothing in the middle for the tourists. That's what I'm talking about doing here—a gastropub where people can come in their shorts, pay middle-of-the-road prices, and get high-end versions of their favorite things. *The* best onion rings. *The* best burger. Sloppy Joes made with wild boar. An oyster bar with different varieties every day. We'll get a great bartender to do spin-offs on old-fashioned drinks."

"I like burgers," Tilda said. "I just don't want to be the person selling them."

"You won't. I'm going to take care of everything. You can stay completely in the background."

Tip was running his fingers up and down the underside of her forearm.

"You're not listening," Tilda said to him.

It really was too dark in the cabin. The woods around them blocked whatever sunlight the clouds hadn't already gobbled up.

"I don't have a lot of other places to go for this." Tip was doing his best to make meaningful eye contact. "This could all slip through my fingers."

Tilda looked away from him. She was taking a moment to decide just how to word her next question.

"When did you decide to ask me for money?"

"What?" He took his hand back and made his eyes wide.

"When—and I mean exactly—did it occur to you that I might make a good investor for your restaurant?"

"What are you driving at?" Tip asked.

"Was it when I first showed up at Harry's? You came over and spoke to me at the coffee shop the next day, remember?"

"I remember."

"Were you thinking of me as a checkbook then?"

This whole thing was horrible. It was hurtful and stupid, and Tilda was fairly certain she had embarrassed herself. The longer she sat there the more embarrassed she got. She thought about being in bed with him, and that made everything worse.

"I'll still want to sleep with you," Tip said, as though her thoughts were his to look into. "Even after we're business partners."

Tilda fought the bark of a laugh that bubbled up her throat. "Okay."

"Okay, what?" Tip wadded up a paper napkin and threw it on the ground.

"Okay, nothing. Nothing at all." Tilda sniffed and told herself it was the cold. It was cold out there. What a terrible day to go boating.

"I'd like to show you the business plan I've created."

Tilda did not want to see the business plan. The only thing worse than knowing he was in it for the money would've been footing the bill and having the whole island know. She left the piece of chicken on her plate with the rest of the food untouched.

"Where are you going? Aren't you going to eat?"

Tilda was getting to her feet and brushing at her backside. "No, I'm not." She reached for her shoes and shoved her feet inside them as quickly as she could.

"Tilda." Tip got to his feet, too. "We've got something here. Let's build on it."

"What do we have here?" she asked, still bent over her laces. "What exactly is this?"

Tip opened his mouth but couldn't find the words, and Tilda didn't know if she'd won an argument or lost one.

"Thanks for the picnic," she said.

"Are you leaving?"

Tilda had her back to him. She was in the doorway and then through it, covering ground as fast as she could without breaking into a jog. A fat raindrop landed on her face, and she brushed it away with her hand before another took its place.

"Tilda!"

His voice was both angry and pleading, and she didn't answer him. She was tired of being asked for things. She was tired of being asked for things by people who didn't deserve to ask at all, and so she was keeping her things. She was keeping her money and her time and her help, and so yes, he was going to have to fend for himself. And she wasn't sorry. Another raindrop landed on Tilda's cheek, and she left it there. She was already on the trail and moving downhill. There was no one to see it.

When she got to the place where the dirt turned to asphalt, no one was around. The houses looked as though they had shut themselves up and pulled themselves in tight. Now out of the trees, Tilda looked up and saw the clouds had changed in the last twenty minutes. They were lower and darker than she remembered, and she was starting to doubt her earlier prediction. She wasn't at all sure the storm would wait until it hit the mainland to tear itself open.

The wind pushed over a nearby trash bin left by the curb, and a red plastic cup rolled out and blew past Tilda's feet too fast for her to stop it.

"Shit."

She pulled her phone out of her pocket to check the ferry schedule. It was too nasty to take her own boat back. She would have to leave it at the dock, come back for it later. She was walking fast, trying to put as much distance between herself and Tip as she could. She didn't want him to see her, to catch her, to touch her. She couldn't bear the idea of it, and she jabbed at the screen harder, trying to make the page load faster.

"Ferry Service Canceled."

"Goddammit," Tilda shouted and threw her phone to the ground. It bounced in its protective case and landed screen up, the same message still shining up at her.

"Ferry Service Canceled."

38.

It was easy not to notice the clouds when there were always clouds. So who was to say it hadn't been coming for hours? But it didn't feel like hours. It was as though a sheet were dropped over the setting sun, like the lowering of a backdrop during a play. And now when the crowds of Last-Minute Lindas raised their eyes to the sky, they saw thick swirling clouds of the darkest gray broken only with streaks of olivey green, which scared them. The clouds roiled like something was alive inside them trying to get out, and they were monstrous. They were so large they filled the sky all the way to the horizon no matter what direction you looked, and even the sky was not large enough to hold them. And so they pressed downward, lower and lower, until even the bravest started to feel the breath of claustro-phobia on their necks.

The wind got stronger, moving the clouds and pulling on the trees and on their clothes. Hair whipped into the faces of the women until they were all but blinded, but still they stayed. The assembled crowd wanted to see the miracle before the *Artemia lucis* faded, the adults died off, the eggs went into stasis, inert until something—something they still did not understand—one hundred years from now woke them and started the process all over again. People had always clustered around the research site, but now there were so many that they had to spread out, some of them going down to the most inaccessible area of the bay—just where Rachel needed to work.

Fish and Wildlife had dispatched more deputies with more yellow tape, cordoning off all of it and standing guard. The crowd, nervous now as sheep with the smell of wolf in the wind, lowered their chattering and turned their eyes to the sky. Their phones, once at the ready to capture the first glow, were lowered.

Rachel was above them looking down. She'd hidden herself off the access path in the woods. The incline was steep, and she'd wedged herself against a tree to keep from losing her footing and sliding down. She crouched there, her left foot going numb, keeping watch, a position she could not have held just one week ago. Oh, what a difference these few days had made.

She knew it would take hours for all of the tourists to leave. Two o'clock, three o'clock in the morning, maybe. That's when John would expect her to leave for her collections. She would show him. The sun had just started to set when she'd slipped out the front door of the Streatfield house. Once she was clear of the residential road, she'd stepped off into the woods, pushing her way through the ferns and the underbrush where no one would see her, and now here she was, lying in wait, watching the crowds watch the sky. She could feel the sizzle and zap in the air around her and wondered if it was the first tingle of an electrical storm or if it was something inside her, something she was throwing off.

Then the sky split in two, and all the rain came down.

"You have to speak up." Tilda was standing under the awning of the pizza shop that had closed before she could get inside. The rain was making more noise than she ever would have imagined rain could, and with one hand over her left ear, she was straining to hear Juno.

"It's Dad," he was saying. "He's really bad."

"Do you need to call Dr. Woo?"

"I'm not sure."

"Well, can he stand?"

"It's not—It's not like that."

Tilda opened her mouth to tell him where she was, explain her situation and why she could not get there, explain that he would have to care for his father tonight, but Juno's words came before hers could.

"I think he might hurt himself, and I don't know what to do. I can't—I can't even get to him. He locked the door. He's in there alone."

"Can you talk to him?"

"He's not making any sense. He hears me, but the things he's saying—" Juno let the words fall off.

"Okay." It was not okay, but Tilda was trying to buy her mind some time. "Call Dr. Woo and tell him what's happening."

"His office will be closed," Juno said.

Tilda knew that. Of course she knew that. She just didn't have another plan.

"Are you coming home? I need you to come home," Juno said.

"Yes, of course," Tilda said. "I'm leaving right now."

"Okay," he said, sounding more like the boy he had been than the man he had become. "Okay. We'll wait for you," and then he hung up.

Tilda stood there alone in the rain. Tip had not passed back this way. She did not know if he had headed to the ferry building to wait for a boat that would not come or if he had stayed at the cabin with his picnic. Either way, she supposed it didn't much matter.

She put the phone in her pocket, pulled the hood of her jacket over her head, and took off across the street toward the public docks at a run. It wasn't that far, she told herself. She could handle it. The boat could handle it. It would be fine. It would absolutely be fine.

Hooper's master key opened the camp's business office, which was a single room with two metal desks pushed together, so that their occupants would be nose-to-nose all day long. The walls were wood paneled, and something—it was hard to know what—smelled like mildewed carpet.

Hooper had not intended to scare Rachel the night before. He hadn't intended for her to know he was there at all. It hadn't been terribly difficult—between what he had gotten from John and what he read of her notebook—to figure out what she was doing. He just needed to know how she was doing it and how far along she was. He checked his watch. Tonight was the last night the creatures would glow. Tomorrow the adults would begin to die, leaving only the eggs to float out into the Pacific. There was very little time left, and he still hadn't found his damn cell phone. He picked up the landline on one of the desks and said a small prayer that went something like "please, please, please."

It worked. There was a dial tone.

Hooper punched in the number, and a receptionist picked up. "Tern Laboratories," she said. "How can I direct you?"

"Dr. Cahill, please."

Hooper had met Cahill at a conference two years before. They'd passed time in the hotel bar talking about dart frog venom. His lab was in phase II research for the development of a nerve pain treatment derived from the toxin. This had been only moderately interesting to Hooper at the time, but the two had kept up a friendly, if sporadic, professional correspondence.

"How are the frogs?" Hooper asked after they'd progressed through the pleasantries, which included a recounting of Cahill's son's broken arm.

"The research didn't progress to the third phase," he said. "The initial results were promising, but there were too many anticholinergic effects to go forward."

"That's too bad."

"It is. I had hopes."

There was a slurping noise, and Hooper imagined the other man was taking a sip of something hot, probably coffee.

"I may have something equally hopeful if your lab is interested."

There was a pause, and Hooper imagined him setting the mug down. "We're always interested. Are you planning to step away from academia?"

"I'm going to need you to sign a nondisclosure agreement before we go into detail," Hooper said by way of an answer.

"Naturally," Cahill agreed. "Can you give me some general idea of what we're talking about?"

"A painkiller," Hooper said, "unlike anything on the market. Revolutionary."

"How far are you?"

"Far enough."

"I'll get the agreement."

After hanging up, Hooper jogged to the van in a hurry to get back to the site before he was missed. With one hand he started the engine and with the other felt for the seat belt, which was too old to retract properly. His fingers brushed something hard wedged down in the small well between the bottom of the door and the base of his seat. Grabbing the edge, he pulled it out.

It was a phone, the small flip kind without GPS or Twitter, the kind that only sent text messages if you were patient enough to hit the number 2 three times to type the letter C. It was the phone of an old person or a broke person. It was his.

"Un-freaking believable," he said aloud and shoved it into his jacket pocket.

Tilda could feel it coming. She felt it in her bones as much as in the wild pitch and roll of the boat. The waves were coming up over the side and flooding the cockpit. She clung to the tiller, no longer steering but only hanging on. She knew she needed to get the bow of the boat pointed into the waves, but knowing and being able were not the same thing. It was so loud, the waves and the rain and the snapping of the sail, that she could not tell one from the other anymore. There were no lights, not from any land, not from the sky, not even a bolt of lightning. Blinded and deaf and unable to steer or even see the waves until she felt them hit her, she could barely keep herself upright, and it was hard to think of a good reason to try.

Another wave gathered. It sucked the boat down and then pushed her sideways. She went up and over, over and over. The wall of water smashed into her. Her head snapped on her neck. It was like a car accident, like being hit by a train. There was no time to recover, no time to find air. She felt herself rising up. She was riding the back of some giant creature. It pushed her portside. Farther and farther, the boat rolled and kept rolling. Tilda scrambled for purchase, for a handhold, for anything to keep from being thrown into the sea. The mast neared horizontal. Her body smashed into the hull. It felt as though her patella cracked in two, a problem so small she barely noticed.

Desperate, she clung to the boom, willing the world to right itself, willing gravity and the gods to allow the tiny vessel to drop back down toward the earth again. All around her rigging snapped and flew like cracking bullwhips. The ocean raged in the wind, and the hull groaned like a downed boxer, unknown bits splintering and cracking like bone. And then a whole sea's worth of water broke over her. It came and came, and she thought she would drown. She was sure of it. And just then, just when she was blacking out and losing her grip, all the water that could flow over her had, and the boat dropped back down, falling from a great height and hitting the roiling surface as hard as concrete.

Crouched on the floor, the water up to her waist, her head pulled into her body, she had no sense of time other than it was short, and her heart pounded while her brain screamed "hurry, hurry, hurry!" With numb fingers, she grabbed at the old-fashioned orange life preserver around her neck, feeling for the straps, pulling it tighter. She reached into the pocket of her jacket, feeling for her phone. It seemed an insane thing to hope, a signal here between islands, but she had made calls on ferries before. Maybe, just maybe, she would get this one thing, this one lifeline. She pulled it from her pocket, her arm still wrapped around the boom, the sail snapping in her face. She felt for the On switch, but the small screen seemed too dim. Was it dying? Had it been too wet for too long? She pressed the emergency call button, but she could not hear if anyone was there, could not read the tiny symbols on the screen, not with the sail and the water and the terror that clouded in front of her eyes and behind them.

The ocean was coming up below her, rising again, pushing on the hull. There was no time. Her fingers were slipping. She could only yell, scream into her phone as though it were the marine radio she did not have, hoping some dispatcher somewhere was there.

"Mayday, Mayday, Mayday. This is *Serendipity*." Tilda repeated the name of the boat two more times. "Mayday. This is *Serendipity*. Five miles south-southwest from Carpenter's Island." She choked on the tears, and her voice shook. "Sailboat taking on water. Capsize feared."

Another wave came over the deck. The boat was going over. The outrigger was directly above her, straight up in the air, like the fin of a shark. The hull had become the floor. All around her it sounded like wood being splintered apart by giants.

Tilda continued to scream into the phone at anyone or no one. "One adult on board. Immediate rescue needed. Mayday, Mayday, Mayday. This is *Serendipity*. Five miles south-southeast from Carpenter's. Mayday."

She would never know if anyone heard. The mast touched the sea. The water took it and snapped it. It had been as thick as the trunk of a small tree, and it had broken like a chopstick. And now there was nothing, nothing that could be done, no one and nothing that could help.

Tilda and the boom were loose. The roll would not stop. She was falling, falling, falling, and the world was coming down on top of her. It was as though she had jumped from the top of a building and the building had come with her. She hit the water, as solid as the earth, earth that split open and sucked her down, deeper, deeper, deeper.

39.

The only way Tilda knew she was not dead was that being dead would not hurt so much.

The cold was paralyzing. It gripped her and squeezed. It squeezed her arms and her legs and her lungs, which let out the last gasp of air she'd managed to rescue and left her without oxygen in less than a second. She was upside down in the Salish Sea. It was December. Tilda was wearing no protective clothing, no flashing beacon, nothing at all of any use but the orange life preserver. It was the upward pull of the floatation device that told her she was ass over tea kettle. There would have been no other way to know.

Down, down, down, and then, just as suddenly, up. Up more slowly but up. The life preserver pulled her, and she let it. It was impossible to have thoughts, to fight or to give up, to move or be still. There was only what happened, what the ocean allowed, what her body could do or did do. She felt things in the water, big things pass near her face, bits of the boat, maybe the mast or maybe a monster. She willed herself to move away from the debris, to protect what was left to protect, but it was impossible to know if she was succeeding.

Everything hurt, and what did not hurt was numb. Everything around her was black whether her eyes were open or closed. Her oxygen was gone, and Tilda knew that if she did not drown, the hypothermia would kill her.

She did not want to die. That was the only thought she had or could hold, a thought not so much in her head as in her limbs, in her muscles and lungs. The pieces of her, each of its own accord, did not want to give up.

Just like at the Y, she told herself, and with the last bit of strength she had, she pushed her arms and her legs. She let muscle memory carry her when her conscious mind could not, and she swam clear of the wreck, popping her head up to the surface, gasping.

Tilda's teeth chattered so hard she could barely gulp in the air. She was losing control of her limbs and, in the cold, knew she would soon lose consciousness. She spun in place, her mind doing the same, looking for what to do next. A wave picked her up and dropped her down, putting more distance between her body and the upside-down *Serendipity*. Rain was still coming down hard, and the white wooden shape was the only thing she could see. There was no land in any direction. Another wave.

When it passed, she inhaled sharply and began to swim toward the boat, the life vest floating up around her face.

Stroke, stroke, breathe. Stroke, stroke, breathe.

"Dad! Dad!" Juno had his hands on Harry's shoulders and was shaking him hard. "Dad, it's me. It's Juno."

Harry's cheeks were wet, but he couldn't feel them. Not really. He had been shouting. He knew that. He hadn't meant to wake Juno. It was the middle of the night. His own door had been closed, along with Juno's and Tilda's. Everyone had been closed up alone in their own cells. Except, of course, for Harry. Harry hadn't been alone in some time.

He had tried to keep her out. He had put the simple wooden chair—the Shaker one that Tilda had bought years before—under the door handle. He wedged it there like he had seen people do on television, but it hadn't done any good. Becca was on one side of the door, and then she was on the other, just like that. And now the chair was broken. Juno had broken it trying to get in. It had surprised Harry that he could do it. Juno had thrown himself against the door from the outside. Harry had heard him slamming his shoulder into the wood, which began to splinter and crack but did not give way, not until Juno put the sole of his shoe to it. The doorframe split, and kick after kick, the back of the chair made of beautiful old wood gave. Harry heard it all, but he did not get up from where he was, and he did not look. He was afraid to look.

Harry, fully clothed, had been curled up on his bed, his chin to his chest and both arms covering himself like someone was beating him. That was when Juno got him by the shoulders, but no amount of shaking could get Harry to uncover his face.

"Dad!"

The sobs racked Harry's shoulders, and it was hard to form the words. They came out in wet bubbles, one or two at a time. "Don't— hurt anyone—Please, don't—hurt anyone."

"I'm not going to hurt anyone," Juno said. "Why would I hurt anyone?"

Harry opened his eyes and let his arms drop just a little. "Is she here?"

Juno reeled back at the sight of his father's face. Harry knew why. He had seen it earlier in the evening—seen himself in the bathroom mirror, just a glimpse before he'd had to shut his eyes against the overhead light and feel frantically for the switch to turn it off. He was pale and drawn, but his eyes were terrifying. The pupils were enormous, so large they took over nearly all the iris. He looked like something that lived underground, something out of the tunnels and caves. He had begun to look on the outside the way that he felt on the inside.

"Is she here?" Harry repeated.

Juno was trying to rearrange his face into something less revolted. Harry could see the effort he was making as he answered. "No, Mom's not here. I called her. She said she was coming. She should be here by now."

"No, not Tilda," Harry said. "Becca."

"Becca?" Juno shook his head and leveled his voice, speaking slowly with exaggerated calm, as though Harry were quite elderly and demented. "Becca is dead, Dad. You mean Rachel, the scientist lady."

Harry shook his head. "She's not dead. She's not." Harry tried to see behind his son, to see into the corner where she had stood. Juno looked over his shoulder, too, not, Harry knew, for a ghost but for anyone he might hand this problem off to. Neither Harry nor Juno saw who they were looking for, and Juno's eyes landed on the phone by Harry's bed before coming back to him.

"Dad, Becca died a long time ago. She died when she was a little girl."

"No." Harry pushed himself up. "She came back. It's because of the Miracle. I know it is."

"Dad, you're upset. Did you take the medicine Dr. Woo gave you?"

Harry shook his head. He shook it like he was trying to clear his mind, to make a fuzzy picture snap into focus, but really what he wanted was for Juno to see. He wanted to shake him as he had been shaken, but he didn't have the strength.

"Did you take too much medicine? Did you forget you took it and take it again?" Juno was still speaking calmly. "I'm going to call Mom again, okay? And then maybe a doctor."

Harry wrapped his hand around his son's arm. "Listen to me," Harry said. "The glow that they make, it's the path of the spirits." The more earnest Harry became the more frightened Juno's face got. "Dr. Bell told me. She doesn't believe it, but I've seen her. I've seen Becca. She came on the path, and now she's here, and I don't know if she can go back. I don't . . . She's angry. She's angry, and I think she's trying to trick people into following her." Harry squeezed Juno's arm as tightly as he could. "You have to help me protect everyone."

Harry was looking into his son's eyes, leaning forward and invading Juno's space until Juno pulled his neck back, trying to get as much distance as he could while Harry was still gripping his arm harder and harder, hard enough to leave a handprint when Juno pried himself away.

Harry had to get out of bed. He pushed himself to the edge and reached for his cane.

"Dad, I think you should stay here. Get a little more rest until Mom comes home. I'm going to call her again. She'll know what to do."

Harry ignored him and used the cane for leverage, getting to his feet but not without struggle. He was weaker than he had been just the day before. His arm shook. It was hard to get his feet under himself, and it wasn't until he was standing that he realized Juno had his arm around him, that it was Juno who had gotten him up.

"Dad?" Harry heard a waver in his son's voice. "Dad, do you think maybe you're having a stroke?"

Harry did not think that. He didn't even make room for the possibility inside his mind. To do so would have meant worrying about himself, and Harry had given up worrying about himself. That was the one gift. He knew then that he was too far gone, and all that was left was to help the others.

"We have to lock all the doors and keep everyone inside," Harry said, making for the hallway. "We have to keep the others safe."

Juno followed behind him. "Okay, Dad. I'm going to do that. But you stay here."

"I'm going to check the windows," Harry said.

They were by the stairs. Juno reached for his father's arm, and Harry leaned into his son as they started to descend. For Juno the climb was slow; for Harry it felt terrifyingly fast.

The doorbell rang, and Harry froze. "Do you think that's her?"

"No, Dad. I don't. I don't know who it is. It's late."

"No," Harry breathed, "you're right. She doesn't ring."

They continued down and had just a quarter of the way to go. "When we get to the bottom," Juno said, "I'm going to go answer the door."

"We have to check the windows."

"Right, and I'll check the windows. You go in the library, and I'll"—Juno fumbled for words—"report back."

Harry nodded. "Where's Tilda?" He knew Juno had mentioned her earlier, just recently, but he couldn't fish out what he had said.

"I'm going to call her."

"You have to tell her what's happening. She's going to be angry, but we have to tell her. Becca might set a trap."

They made it to the bottom of the stairs. Juno didn't bother stopping to look through the peephole but continued on, helping Harry to his study.

"Sure," Juno said, "I'll tell her."

"She killed someone already. I saw her do it."

"Becca killed someone?"

They were almost to the library.

Harry nodded, looking straight down the hall toward the sliding glass door and the glowing beach beyond it. It was sinister, that light. Harry didn't know why he hadn't seen the danger before. "At the symphony. She made me talk that woman off the balcony. I would never have—" He shook his head. "She tricked me."

Harry could see his son thinking things that he did not say, things he was actively struggling to keep inside. Harry could see the thoughts, he could see them wiggling behind Juno's lips.

"Okay, Dad. You just go in here and stay."

The doorbell rang again.

"Be careful," Harry said, "and come back when you're done."

Juno left the room and shut the door. Harry stood there in the center of the library, deciding. He didn't turn a light on. He didn't need to. His pupils, dilated beyond what should have been possible, had no need for artificial light. The little that came in through the naked window, the green shimmer of the Miracle, was enough for Harry to see anything he might need. He was thinking about that, drawing strength from the thought, when he heard the sound. It was a terrible scraping. Awful. Awful enough that Harry put his hands to his ears.

He could not imagine what had caused such a noise. Nothing in the room had changed. Nothing had moved. He was alone, and if he was alone inside, that meant Becca was out there. He should not have left Juno alone. Harry clomped with his cane to the door, moving as quickly as he could. He reached up, turned the handle, and pushed. The door moved three inches and stopped. Harry pushed harder then closed the door and opened it again. The wood banged into something.

Harry put his face to the crack and looked out. The console table, the one that had sat for years in the hallway, was pushed in front of the library door.

Through the crack, he could hear voices coming from the front of the house. It was Juno's voice first. Annoyed. Unhappy. And then another man. Harry couldn't put his finger on the voice, but it wasn't a stranger. It was getting harder to hold thoughts in his head, leaving him with the slippery sense that there had been a time, a recent time, when he would have been clearer about things. Harry tried to listen, to pick out words. He squinted with the effort, as though his vision and his hearing were related in ways you wouldn't expect.

"It's the middle of the damn night," Harry heard Juno say.

The other man spoke. "This is an emergency."

A memory floated by Harry. He was outside on the beach. The voice was there, a tattoo, but by the time Harry had it, most of it was gone. It was like turning on the radio and catching only the last few bars of a song. He shook his head. He had gotten distracted and missed part of the conversation. His son was speaking again.

"What kind of doctor? I mean, could you take care of a person if you really had to?"

The other man replied, but his voice was harder to hold on to, harder for Harry to catch and then to work over in his mind so that the sounds fitted themselves into words and the words into ideas that Harry could understand.

And then it was gone, replaced by Juno's voice, which was not pleased. "I'll take you up."

It got quiet. Quiet enough that Harry's ears were filled with the sound of the surf outside. It was louder than usual. There had been a storm. Harry thought that it was louder because of the storm, but then he wasn't so certain. It only took two heartbeats not to be so certain. What had happened to the voices? Harry clenched. Had she done something to them?

He looked down at the three inches of table he could see in front of the door. The top was heavy marble. It had taken two men to lift that table into place. Juno might as well have thrown a bolt closed, Harry thought. But there was nothing for it, and so he opened his eyes, which he hadn't realized he had closed, and with all the strength he had left, he started to push.

Flat on her stomach, Tilda looked like she was hugging the carcass of some monster fish. Years of swimming laps at the Y had gotten her to the boat before hypothermia stole away her muscle control. She'd clamored onto the hull, getting all of herself out of the water. The boat had turned completely turtle. The centerboard had sheared off and floated away, but the body of the boat with the outrigger still attached was buoyant. And so she lay out there, her arms and legs outstretched for grip and balance. Her cheek rested on the painted wood while she stared into the darkness.

The waves had been terrible. They had been scary and nauseating. Tilda thought maybe she had thrown up a little, which seems like the sort of thing you wouldn't have doubt about, but clinging to the bottom of an overturned boat in the middle of a storm makes a lot of things unclear. The rain was hardly noticeable. Tilda was wet everywhere it was possible to be wet, and the sound of the deluge hitting the hull was drowned out by the crash and the hiss of the ocean, which behaved like a foul-tempered creature awakened before its time.

Tilda held on as best she could with her wet, splayed limbs suckered to the boat like a starfish. She breathed through the rolling of her stomach, which was moving sympathetically with the waves that lifted up the wreck and dropped it between sets. She got a little happy when her limbs started to shake. She hadn't shivered since she'd gone into the water, and she knew that was not a good sign. It was like her body had given up any hope of being able to warm itself, but as the shivers started in her arms and worked their way down, it seemed her life force was having second thoughts. Perhaps it had given up the ghost just a little too early. But more than anything, Tilda tried not to think at all.

With no way to keep time, she couldn't be sure when it was. Dark. Well past dinner. She wondered if Harry had eaten, if he was at the house or if Juno had called 911 when she didn't come home. She wondered if either of them was frightened. She was frightened.

Tilda was thinking these things when she noticed that the rain had lightened and the waves had calmed. She had not marked the moment when the worst of the storm had passed over her. She only noticed after the fact that it was so. She was disappointed by that. She had been so busy not thinking, just like the clingy starfish she had become, that milestones were passing without her knowledge.

Perhaps she would not be so afraid, she thought, if she shared Harry's faith. If she believed that there was some other place where she would go and once there would see Becca again, then perhaps this all wouldn't be so bad. But Tilda had never been a person of faith, and lying there in the middle of the sea had not changed that. She did not believe her daughter waited for her. She did not believe she would ever see her again no matter how much she wished it, and she did. She did wish it. But wishing and believing were different. Believing would have been the only reason to give up, to let herself slip down. It was her nonbelief that kept her focused. Tilda was not giving up. She said that to herself. She said it very clearly. She was not giving up.

It wouldn't do to simply cling. She needed to think. She needed to be an agent of her own rescue even though moving sounded terrifying. What if she ended up in the water again, unable to save herself a second time? She was exhausted. Her limbs were like lead from the swimming and the clinging and the cold. She tried wiggling her fingers. It felt like they moved. She was too nervous to lift up her head to check, but she was fairly certain they had moved.

With paralysis ruled out, Tilda got thirsty. Very thirsty. The kind of thirsty that drives otherwise rational people to try sipping saltwater. Tilda told herself not to think about that. Instead she thought about how hungry she was. She'd eaten almost nothing—nothing but a few handfuls of trail mix and one bite of fried chicken—all day. She got a little angry with herself over that. How could she have been so neglectful?

Tilda's eyes were closed. She noticed then that they were, but once more the milestone had passed without her marking it. She knew, no matter how tired she was, she should not sleep.

40.

The Last Day of the Miracle

Rachel, who was down on her knees, tried to ignore it, but the pounding was relentless. It was the pounding of a cop or a landlord, someone who was making it clear that they expected to be let in. She was far too busy to deal with whoever it was, but the knocking was unbearable. She cupped her hands over her ears and rocked. She couldn't think like this. She couldn't work. And she was angry, so very angry.

With a grunt, she pushed up to her feet. "What?" she demanded.

"Open the door."

John.

Her heart rate shot up. Panic. Sweat. No. No, she told herself. Breathe. She would not feel this. She would not be afraid. He could not do anything. She knew too much. She knew it all. It was hers, and he could not have it.

"Go away," she yelled.

"Open the door, or I will tear it down."

His voice was even, solid. It had form that entered the room and sat on the floor next to her, touching her.

"You have ten seconds," John said.

She believed him. The question was whether the door would hold. Probably it would not. She needed to take control of the situation. She needed a second option. She spun on her heel and spotted the box cutter lying on the floor near the bookcase. She picked it up and held it behind her back before opening the door. She allowed only a crack, just enough to stick her head out, but John was taller than she was. He could see over her head and into the room, right past her even as she stood on her tiptoes and tried to expand herself like a porcupine extending its quills.

The bed was stripped of everything but the fitted sheet. Some of the bedding was on the floor at her feet. Some of it had been dragged around to other parts of the room. Tubes and cords ran to and from the tanks. Grow lights hung over everything, and the pumps and fans were whirring. She had cardboard boxes all over the floor, along with canisters and other containers that she was preparing to pack. Small appliances sat on the rug with more cords running from them. Everything she had brought with her, shoes and jackets, shirts and jeans, were strewn across the room, and the rugs had been tracked with mud; although Rachel couldn't remember doing it.

She tried to keep her temper in check and her voice businesslike. "I'm working. Go away."

"How much have you taken?"

"I don't know what you're talking about."

"I can't help you if you don't tell me how much. When did you start?"

"Don't be absurd."

This conversation had already taken too much time. Rachel tried to shut the door, but John shoved his hand in, gripping the edge and pushing back. Rachel dropped the civility. She grimaced and shoved, but his hand didn't move. The door didn't move. John was just standing there looking down at her like a grown man looks at a child pushing on his legs.

"Hooper lied to you."

"Everyone has lied to me!" Her anger was at the surface, like simmering milk with only the top skim to keep the bubbles from bursting and splattering out of the pot.

"I haven't," John said.

"You're the worst of them! You followed me, chased me, spied on me."

"It wasn't me, but I believe it happened. I believe some of it happened."

His voice was even. His eyes were steady. They took her in, looked her over, examined her like something under his microscope. What did it mean that he believed her? She suspected a trap.

"How far down the path have you gone?" he asked her.

It was not the question she expected. "I don't know what you're talking about."

No one alive had taken the waters. There were only reports, sketches, stories passed down in families, stories told to missionaries and what they wrote down, altered and changed. John's curiosity was almost insatiable. He wanted to know what she knew, to open her mind and see what she had seen. What was a hallucination? What was real? Could she tell? Was it different for her, a white woman, than it would be for him? He had not taken any himself. He could have, but he had not. Without the proper ritual, it would have been sacrilege. Without other members of his tribe, it would have been dangerous. But still, he wanted to know. He wanted to grab her and shake the answers from her, but it was obvious, standing there, that she would not survive it.

"What have you seen?" he repeated.

"I haven't seen anything. I don't know what you're talking about."

"You do know."

He stared at her hard, stared until her muscles squirmed under her skin.

"Your hair is falling out," he said.

She made a face at him, something to convey what a ridiculous comment that was, to talk about her appearance at a time like this, but it wasn't so ridiculous. Not really. Her hair was greasy and hanging in strings around her face. She had noticed it in the bathroom. She hadn't had the chance to shower much in the past week, and so that was fine. It was to be expected, but when she had bent forward to wash her hands, she had seen her own scalp. It had stopped her. She could see the dull, grayish skin under the strings of dark hair. It wasn't visible in patches but all over, a general thinning of her hair that she was sure hadn't been there before. It had worried her, but that made her feel vain, and so she pushed the feeling aside and did not deal with it anymore.

"Why is her hair falling out?"

Rachel's head snapped up. She had not known the Streatfields' son was there. He was smaller than John and standing somewhere behind him. She had not seen him and still could not. They were ganging up on her.

"I'm fine. You need to leave. I have work to do."

"You're not fine, and you need to come back to the mainland with me. No one else can help you. Not like I can."

Rachel almost laughed. She wouldn't have trusted John to save her place in line for the bathroom, and he thought she would leave the island with him. Absurd.

John watched her thoughts play across her face. She had no mask anymore, no ability to hide anything. She had waded into this on her own, unprotected, unaware, and she had taken too much. John did not pretend to know the right amount, the spiritual amount, but anyone could have seen that she had overdosed. John could only begin, as a scientist and as an Olloo'et, to guess at the consequences—her nervous system, her prefrontal cortex. She needed help. She needed a doctor. A medicine man. Both. She was dying.

"Go to hell," Rachel said.

John smacked both hands against the door. She didn't know he was going to do it, and the force of it knocked her back into the room. The sound disoriented her. She took two skittering steps and opened her mouth to object, but before the words could find their way out, John had her chin in his hand and was forcing her face up toward his. It made her mad, and she swung the box cutter at his bicep.

He made a sound like an animal. She had stuck him but not deep. He was wearing a puffy coat, a sweatshirt, layers to protect him from the elements, and she was not strong. She would have tried again, but he had his hand around hers, squeezing. She dropped the box cutter, but he didn't let go.

"Look at me," he said, holding her face near his.

Rachel tried to twist away, but it was useless, and it tired her.

"Your pupils are huge," he said. "Are you hallucinating right now?"

"Get your hands off of me."

John reeled when her breath hit his face. It took all he had to hang on to her, his hand still wrapped around her chin. He pushed her backward into the room, taking shallow breaths to keep from retching. It smelled like rotting fish and unwashed bodies and something else, something Rachel couldn't smell anymore.

John's arm hurt. He would need stitches, antibiotic. He tried to ignore it. He looked around. He looked and did not like what he saw.

"Jesus, what are you doing in here? Are you concentrating it?"

John let her slide out of his hands. He didn't even think about it. He was concentrating on the tanks, the lights, the aerators. Then he saw the feeding stations, the algae. Oh, God—

Rachel tried to stand in his way, but he moved around her, covering the distance to the tanks in three long, loping steps. The grow lights simulating daytime were on, and the *Artemia lucis* were not glowing. They would likely not glow again. Under the microscope, Rachel had seen the cysts that, if left alone, would disperse in the water and do nothing at all for another hundred years. The animals had bred. To see, just to see, Rachel had ground a small sample of the cysts and taken it. The effect had been far stronger than with the adults and much more immediate. She was having trouble holding her thoughts together, but she knew one thing. She had to get them back to the mainland right away. She had to start experimenting with them, and she did not have time for this.

"Leave that alone!"

John had known, but he had not known. He had suspected some-thing, something like this, but to see it, to see this most sacred thing floating here, manipulated, turned into something it could not be, should not be. He reached into one of the tanks and pulled out a flask full of the *Artemia lucis* and their eggs.

He turned his eyes to her. How could she, and how did she? Both questions at the same time, questions from the scientist in him, ques-tions from the Olloo'et. He settled on just one. "What have you done?"

"Everything!" She puffed herself up, lifted onto her toes, pushed her shoulders wide, the blades coming together in the middle of her back. "Everything you couldn't."

John, with the flask still in his hand, looked at her. "I never wanted to."

"Liar!"

"We were here to observe, to learn. Never to interfere. Never to take."

"I am saving people." There was passion in Rachel's voice. "I am making the world better, bearable."

"You don't understand," John countered.

"I understand everything."

"You won't survive this."

Juno had followed them into the room, and neither of the scientists was paying him any attention. He did not matter. He was not impor-tant. He wasn't until suddenly he was.

"You gave this to my father, didn't you?"

John's eyes went wide and swung to look at Juno, who was locked on Rachel.

"You experimented on him," Juno said. "That's what's wrong with him, isn't it?"

John looked from Juno to Rachel and back again.

She pressed her lips shut like a child.

John looked as though he'd been shot. "You experimented on a person? A stranger?"

Rachel squeezed her jaw muscles tight. She would not tell them anything. They could not make her.

"How much did you give him?" John demanded.

He was still holding the flask in his hand, and she lunged for it. With his good arm, he held it up out of her reach, and she clawed at him trying to get at it.

"Tell me what you did," he demanded.

"No!" Rachel shouted.

John tossed the glass flask at the wall. It bounced once, and then shattered on the hardwood floor. Juno jumped out of the way, as though the spray might burn him. Rachel let out a primal cry, and John reached into the tank and grabbed two more.

"This is sacred. Do you not understand? Are you so blind? You perverted it. You used it. You were selfish. Now look. Look at yourself!" John could no longer keep his temper.

"I am saving people," she shouted back. "Didn't you hear me? I am saving myself!"

"You are dying!"

"I am alive! I am alive for the first time in years!"

John threw the two flasks at the wall in just the same spot. Only one broke this time, but they both spilled. The sound Rachel made was subhuman. She threw herself at him.

If any of them had been paying attention, they might have heard noises coming from downstairs, but they were not listening. John grabbed more flasks.

"Tell me what you gave that man. Tell me what you did!"

"Those are mine!"

"They are not yours. You have no right." John threw the samples to the floor.

Rachel screamed. She could not imagine losing her work. She could not imagine going back to the way things had been, the endless, terrible pain. She would do anything, anything not to go back. There were no boundaries anymore.

"Tell me!"

"Go to hell!"

Smash, smash, smash.

Rachel hit him. Then she hit him again. She pummeled him with her fists, both of them, one right after the other. Hitting and hitting and hitting. John, with his good arm up to protect his face, reached for the whole tank.

"No!"

She grabbed hold of his coat tight, so he couldn't throw her off, and she bit him. She sank her teeth into the back of his neck like a fox grabs hold of a chicken. Joy surged through her. She had him. She had him then.

"Stop it!"

The hands were on her, grabbing her. Rachel tried to fight them off, but two attackers at once were too much for her. She flailed helplessly as Juno pulled her off, yanked her down to the ground, to the ruined carpet at their feet. He pinned her there, using his weight to hold her down.

John, free, grabbed the tank and brought all of it—the flasks and the fans and the lights and the tubes and the cords—crashing to the floor in an unholy mess of fouled water, broken glass, and electrical equipment.

Rachel howled, watching helplessly from the floor as John reached up again and again, grabbing the edge of every remaining tank, bringing them all crashing and spilling to the ground around her.

Tilda opened her eyes. She'd fallen out of consciousness. Her arm was curled up close to her body. Before she'd been terrified to leave her starfish position, and now she was afraid to move back to it.

She wasn't nauseated anymore. That was something. And she had a view. She could see the 100-Year Miracle off in the middle distance. The light was so electric, so very, very green, it was hard to believe nature created such a thing. It was the kind of green that could only really be appreciated against black velvet, like those terrible sunrise paintings sold off the side of interstates. But here again, nature had provided.

The sky was nothing but black velvet. The clouds blocked the moon and the stars, leaving nothing but that beautiful ring of green. She could see the shape of it as it curled around the island, marking it as special, as the chosen spot of the chosen people. It really was something.

She looked at the Miracle—the very last day of it that anyone alive would ever see—and she appreciated it and rhapsodized about it and was all but writing poetry in her mind when it occurred to her that, yes, she could see the Miracle. She could see it now, and she could not before, and, if that were true, it meant she was nearing land. She was quite near it, in fact. There it was. Right there. Her home. Jesus Christ on a cracker.

The whole thing was so exciting that Tilda sat right up. The hull shifted and bobbed under her. She held her breath and kicked herself for being so rash, but shift and bob was all it did. She was not dislodged, but she did have to make a decision. Did she risk staying with the boat, knowing the tide could change and send her farther away again? That she could float right past the island into open water before the sun came up, greatly reducing the likelihood of anyone finding her? But how close was she really? And how cold was the water? She knew she wouldn't have a lot of time before her old friend hypothermia rejoined the party. Still. It was close. She thought it was close. The green blaze in the water threw up enough ambient light for her to make out the tops of the trees and something that might have been a house. Not her house. But a structure of some kind. Something straight and true and unnatural.

Tilda took a breath, squeezed her hands into fists, and pitched herself forward. The hit of the cold was almost too much. It was a vise around her lungs and a knife through her brain, and there was a moment—just a portion of a second—before she remembered to kick her legs and make her strokes and head for shore.

41.

The sounds Rachel made were unholy, inhuman. They made the two men want to clamp their hands down over their ears. She made a sound like she was being boiled alive. She writhed under him, and Juno let her go. They both let her go. She scrambled to her feet, shaking and groaning. And then she ran. She ran out of the room, snatching up one of the duffel bags that still held a few of the plastic containers. She ran out into the hall and down the stairs, her footsteps banging loud and fast on each wooden tread. She grabbed the end of the banister and swung herself around 180 degrees and sprinted down the center hall toward the back of the house and the sliding glass door.

It was hard to do it. The new dose—so much stronger than before or was it somehow cumulative?—was pulsing through her arms and her legs, her hands and her feet. She needed to write this down, to add it to the notebooks, but holding that thought was so hard. She could feel the effect of the tincture spreading, and everything it touched went numb. She told her legs to move, and she knew that they did because stationary things passed her, or she passed them, or something happened, and she was not in the same space as before. Artwork moved past her head, furniture. She saw Harry's library, the door wide open, the room empty, and then she was beyond it. It was hard to keep track.

Telling her legs to move was all she could do. She could not feel them take action, could not sense her feet making contact with the floor. She could not check their work because she could not look down for fear her balance, precarious as it was, would fail her.

At the door, she put her fingers to the lock. Her fine motor control was worse than her gross. Where were her notebooks when she needed them? If only she could write these things down—supposing she could manipulate the pen—then somehow it would be better, as though documenting the side effects would improve them. Observe, calculate, classify, hypothesize, test, control. These were the things that did not fail her even as her nervous system did, as her colleagues did, as everything else did. They were her refuge, her comfort.

She heard her own footsteps bang down the wooden deck stairs. There was a time gap there, and she didn't know how long it was. She was behind the glass, and then she was not. She was outside in the last hours of dark, the last hours of the Miracle, looking out from the stairs at what was left of the most important moment in her life. Nothing would ever be this. Scientists hoped their whole lives for such a thing, and most never found it. Here. Here she'd had six whole days of the miraculous, and everyone knew it. Everyone down to the last civilian experienced it, but no one experienced it like she did. No one really understood what this meant, meant to her, meant to everyone. And she was losing it.

Rachel tightened her grip on the bag and concentrated as best she could when her feet hit sand. She moved fast, ducking under the yellow caution tape. The others still worked, a slower pace, resigned to the end, and while she dared not run right through the research site, she did not take the time to return to the other inlet farther away either. Instead she followed the beach's half-moon shape ending in a rocky outcropping at the tip like a finger pointing toward the horizon.

Tilda's foot kicked the bottom. That's how she knew when she'd reached shore. She could not stand. She was too weak to stand. She was, in fact, too weak and too cold to have made the swim, but somehow she had. Now all she could do was roll over in the water and float the last few yards on her back, her life preserver still around her neck, letting the retreating waves push her up onto the beach.

She had swum through the Miracle, through the shining green ring that pulled her home like a beacon. She had swum through it, and now it clung to her. It clung to her hair and her clothes and her bare skin, so that if anyone had seen her there they would've thought her an alien. Tilda felt the sand reach up and accept her, give her something solid and firm to lie against for what seemed the first time in her whole life, and she accepted it right back with a gratitude that was as deep within her as her bones.

There was no hurry. She was safe. She could hear people. There was shouting, and it was coming closer. Someone would find her soon. They would find her, an iridescent green sea creature washed up on shore.

It was low tide. The ocean was pulling away from Rachel, taking back the Miracle it had brought, pulling the dying animals farther out to sea where they would extinguish, leaving nothing but their eggs to float in stasis who knew where for longer than she would ever live. It was terrifying to watch the water recede. She could see it happening as she ran. With each wave that the wind piled up in a neat row against the shore, it pulled one back farther than the last. Just as John had tried to play keep-away with her flask, so was Mother Nature here.

But even Mother Nature could not get the better of Rachel that night. All along the rocky outcropping were pools that had been left behind by the tide, and those pools blazed brighter than the waves the sea was pulling away. If she could get to them, she could have a far more concentrated sample. There was still time. She told herself there was still time.

Rachel climbed up on the rocks, dropping her bag at her feet, and pulled out the largest container. With it in one hand, she put her arms straight out at her sides like a tightrope walker and headed toward the tip of the natural jetty and the tidal pools. The wind grabbed hold of what dark brown strands of hair she had left, pushing them in front of her face. Rachel squinted to see the rocks at her feet. She told each foot to move, first the left and then the right. She had to be so careful, and it was difficult.

Step, step, step.

She kept her arms out, tipping one way and then the other as her boot slid, and she only just caught herself. There was a pool—the biggest, best, brightest one—three-quarters of the way down. She could see it.

Step, step, step.

It was louder out here, louder than by the protected sand of the bay far behind. Out here the wind howled, and the waves crashed against the sharp and unforgiving rocks. The rain blew sideways with nothing to protect her. With her arms out wide, Rachel looked like a zealot, a true believer.

This was good, she thought. This was helping. Her senses, her mind, her body were in such disarray, but there on the finger pointing out to sea, the wind and the rain pressed into her body, her brain focused on keeping her soft and vulnerable parts upright. Like a monk using a mantra to keep his mind from spinning off, Rachel used the forces of nature to find some center, some point to hold on to. And there she was; she had done it. The pool was just there at her feet. All she needed to do was bend down, get on her hands and knees, and reach, reach, reach.

It was then she felt it. The hands were on her back. The center she had found melted away, as her balance—never as good as she needed—crumbled. Rachel turned quick to look over her shoulder. She had not imagined it. He was there. His hands were on her, pushing and shoving as her feet lost their purchase. It was not the face she'd expected to see. It was such a betrayal, but—and this, too, surprised her—there was relief. She knew what was happening and even perhaps why. And soon there would be peace. All the pressure would be gone and all the pain, too. This was the other possibility. This, too, would end it.

She opened her mouth to speak, even just to say his name, but there was a final push. Before the word could get past her lips, her feet went, splaying out from under her. She watched as the sharp, slime-slick rocks rushed toward her head, and the growling ocean just beyond waited to take all that she had left.

42.

Tilda had to ring the doorbell just as she had the day she'd arrived. She leaned against the wall while she waited for Harry to answer, and Shooby barked on the other side. She had been dropped off by the family that had found her on the beach, her keys lost. When Harry answered, she was wet, bruised and limping, moving more stiffly even than he.

Juno tried to take her to the hospital. She told him he was being ridiculous, which made Harry angry and turned into an argument because he always had to go to the doctor, and why shouldn't she have to go? Juno stopped listening and instead made peanut butter toast because his mother had said, in between it all, that she was hungry.

Juno did not mention Dr. Bell. Harry did not mention Dr. Bell, and both of them would have continued right on not mentioning her if it weren't for the sound of the ambulance making its way to the beach.

Tilda, in no condition to do much of anything, stayed at the table with her toast, but Harry and Juno went to the door. Harry was wearing his house slippers. Another pair of shoes sat there, a pair of dark blue sneakers with Velcro straps covered in wet sand. Juno touched them, and some of the grains stuck to his fingers. Harry pretended he didn't see and went out in his slippers instead.

People were piled up half a dozen deep at the crime scene tape, which had been strung up next to the raggedy, week-old caution kind that had kept the looky-loos off the research site. The sun was just starting to come up, and the rain had stopped. Harry didn't think this many people had shown up to see the Miracle, at least not all at once.

"Do you know what happened?" a small woman asked.

Her white-gray hair was cropped close to her head all the way around, and she wore oversize black-frame glasses that marked women of that age as artistic, well-off, and likely to be NPR donors. It wasn't clear if she was talking to Harry or Juno or to anyone in particular at all.

Harry chose to ignore her, but Juno spoke. "We just got here."

"I heard one of the scientists died, fell off the rocks, cracked open her noggin," the woman said.

Harry had known that already. He knew which of the researchers it was, too, but he didn't see any reason to share that with this woman.

"I hope they roll out the body soon," she went on. "I have a yoga class in an hour."

"We're leaving, too," Juno said and took Harry's arm.

To get back to the house, they had to walk up the cliff, through the public parking lot, and along the road. It was slow going. All access from the beach had been cut off. The police had even gone to the trouble of stringing a bit of crime scene tape across the bottom of their deck stairs.

When the two made it back, they found a man standing in their driveway, fiddling with Rachel's truck—or what had been her truck.

"Can I help you?" Harry asked.

"I wish you could," the man said. "I'm Hooper. Dr. Hooper. We met a few days ago."

"I remember," Harry said.

"I'm sure you've seen the commotion."

Harry nodded.

"I'm sorry to tell you it was Dr. Bell who fell, who—passed."

Harry nodded again, and the two men held each other's gaze. Hooper broke first.

"Well, this truck belongs to the team, and we're headed back to the university today. It's horrible to have to think of logistics at a time like this."

Hooper didn't seem all that broken up about it, but Harry wasn't one to throw stones. "Some things have to be taken care of," he agreed.

"I'd like to go inside," Hooper said, "if you don't mind, for Rachel's effects. We can take them with us. I'm sure her family will want them."

Juno cocked his head. "They're already gone."

Hooper blinked. "I'm sorry?"

"The other scientist from your team, he came earlier and took everything away. He said he was working for you. I forget his name. The man with the tattoo."

A flipbook of emotions played across Hooper's face and ended on something that looked a little like fear. He did his best to cover it. "Of course, yes. This is such a difficult time. It's easy to forget what we're all doing."

Juno and Harry watched as he hurried back toward the truck, the only thing of Dr. Bell's that remained. In his rush, he fumbled with the keys, dropped them, and tried again.

"My condolences," Harry said, but Hooper had already started the engine and did not hear him.

Inside, Harry went to make a pot of coffee. Tilda had left her plate on the table, and water was running in an upstairs shower. Juno sat at her place, and when Harry was done, he sat, too, pulling the morning paper toward himself and folding the crossword section to make it easier to work.

"How are you feeling?" Juno asked.

"I need an eight-letter word for self-assurance."

The coffee was starting to brew, and Juno got up. He selected a mug from the cabinet and filled it three-quarters of the way while the coffee continued to drip and sizzle on the warming plate until the carafe was replaced.

"Chutzpah," Harry said, answering his own question. "An eight-letter word for self-assurance is 'chutzpah.' It fits."

Juno got milk from the fridge and carried it and the coffee to the table, retaking his seat. The rest of the paper was pushed to the side unread. Juno flipped through it for the sports section. "You were down at the beach," he said. "Earlier, I mean."

His father didn't answer. Instead he filled in three boxes in front of him.

"You know you're not supposed to go down to the beach by yourself. You could fall," Juno continued, this time looking at the top of his father's head. He kept looking until Harry met his gaze.

"I didn't fall."

"But you could have."

"I didn't."

They looked at each other just like that for longer than anyone else would have found comfortable.

"Six-letter word for illness," Harry said, breaking the silence. "It starts with an M."

43.

One Month Later

It was midmorning, and the sun was streaming through the library window lighting up a haze of dust motes. Sunny days were unusual in January, and Tilda was enjoying it—although perhaps not so much that anyone else would notice. Shooby was less subtle. He lay on the hardwood floor in the middle of the beam with his stomach bared.

It was still hard to be in this room. It was, in fact, hard to be in the house, but it was hers now, and to leave, even for a while, would've been wrong in a way she wasn't sure she could have explained. Ever since Harry had died, Tilda had taken to spending her midmornings here in his room. She still slept in the attic and went for her swims, but when she came back, she would make coffee and bring it in here. Shooby followed her. He followed her everywhere, but when she came in here, he seemed to stick a little closer, as though he needed to keep an especially keen eye on things.

Tilda had moved almost nothing of Harry's. The score that he was working on still sat on the piano along with his Blackwing pencils. The debris that gathered around him—minus the plates of old food—was still piled on his small side table. Tilda could see it all sitting, as she always did, at his piano, an instrument that she couldn't play.

They had had a full Christmas. Tilda had insisted on it even though Harry had taken a bad turn by then. They all knew it would be his last even though no one, including Harry, said so aloud. That was unusual for him. He had always been too frank for his own good, and Tilda suspected it had something to do with the new baby.

Juno—who had joint custody—had come with his little girl, who brought in a haul of presents that made anything Jesus got seem chintzy. Harry's eyes had watered a little over the whole thing, and everyone had pretended not to notice. It was the first and last time Harry saw her. He died on the twenty-eighth. His funeral had taken place at his church—the same one she had driven him to the day she'd met Tip, and he'd been buried in the one cemetery on the island. "Father, composer, husband," his headstone read. It seemed, to Tilda, appropriate, and no one had dared contradict her.

Tip still lived next door. Tilda rarely saw him, and when she did, she pretended that she didn't. He had tried to speak to her shortly after the accident, but she had dismissed him, and he'd made no further overtures.

Now the world had entered the lull between New Year's and Valentine's Day, and Tilda knew she would soon need to go through things. Harry's clothes would need to be donated to charity, the medicine cabinet cleaned out. Tilda had a whole household of her own things in storage, as it was, and she would need to reconcile that with everything that was already here. But all of that would have to wait. She wasn't ready to do it now.

She had, in fact, made only two changes to the house. The first was to clean up the guest room, which had taken some doing. Whatever had happened in there—and no one seemed to know what, including Harry and Juno—had ruined the hardwood. She'd had the floors refinished, the rugs replaced, and the bed disassembled and stored. In its place, she'd ordered a crib, making it known that she expected a goodly number of visits with her new granddaughter.

No one else knew about the second change. It was very small and, at the same time, not small at all. Tilda had removed the picture of Becca from Harry's side table here in the library. It was a beautiful picture. Becca had so loved that red coat, insisting on wearing it long after it truly fit her. It had been cool the day the picture was taken. Tilda remembered it. Cool but not as cold as the picture made it seem with all the clouds and the gray, which was why Tilda had allowed her to go out without her gloves. Tilda had taken the photo in the heavy silver frame and moved it upstairs. Now it sat on the small stool that served as her nightstand, and she found she quite liked having it there.

Author's Note

For however real they seemed to me during the writing of this book, the 100-Year Miracle, *Artemia lucis,* Olloo'et Island, and the Olloo'et people are all figments of my imagination.

Residents of the San Juan Islands know that oars slapped against the water will cause a fleeting bioluminescent effect, much to the delight of children. Countless creatures, from cephalopods right down to bacteria, produce this "cold light," so called because it creates no heat. However none of these animals give off quite the display described in this book.

The genus *Artemia* is real and includes arthropods, such as brine shrimp. The *Artemia lucis* in this book are very similar to their real-life brethren, although consuming them is not recommended.

Olloo'et Island is, likewise, similar to several of the San Juan Islands off the northwest coast of Washington state. I borrowed heavily from Whidbey (not technically of the San Juans) and Orcas Islands and am indebted to the various bar and shop-keepers, ferry workers, inn owners, residents, and waitresses who welcomed me. There is even a YMCA camp to be found on Orcas, which bears only some resemblance to the one the research team inhabits. Nonetheless, the 1943 advertisement quoted in chapter 7, "A training in self-reliance is a Godsend in wartime," is a real advertisement for the camp used during World War II. That said, large swaths of Olloo'et are entirely fictional and aren't to be found anywhere but in these pages.

Similarly, bits of the mainland, too, have been rearranged to my liking.

The Olloo'et people—and the character of John in particular—were inspired by historical photos, accounts, and stories of several Pacific Northwest tribes, which I reference with the greatest of respect. The Olloo'et themselves, however, do not now, nor have they ever, existed. I'm grateful to the Burke Museum in Seattle and innumerable libraries and digital archives for giving my fictional account some loose basis in history.

I am also grateful to Katharine Berry Judson for her 1910 book *Myths and Legends of the Pacific Northwest* (reprinted in 1997 by the University of Nebraska Press, introduction by Jay Miller). And while it is true that Catholic missionaries, especially from France, were working in the Pacific Northwest at the appropriate time, none so far as I know ever recorded accounts of a phenomenon like that which is described here.

A particular nod is due Brian Gilbert for his book *Fix It and Sail: Everything You Need to Know to Buy and Restore a Small Sailboat on a Shoestring* (International Marine/Ragged Mountain Press, 2005), which, along with innumerable manuals and training videos, got Tilda and me through.

And finally, I am grateful to the Seattle Symphony. For although they did not know it at the time, I was perched in third-tier seating with a set of opera glasses against my face and a notebook in my lap.

Special Thanks

Gratitude is due in untold quantities to three women, in particular. Thank you to Dr. Cheryl Van Buskirk and Dr. Ashley Wright, molecular biologists, and Beth Lenz, marine biologist, who each did their utmost to keep me from the most egregious scientific errors, answering dozens of questions, sending me literature and inviting me into the lab. I did not make it easy on them.

Thank you to Dr. Cynthia Strathmann, a San Juan Islands native, for her invaluable insights into life on the islands. Thank you also to Cameron Brown and Amy Lee, lifelong friends who welcomed me in Seattle, and the Wright family, who opened their beachfront home to me in Oregon.

And to those who rolled up their sleeves to make this book the best it could be, thank you always to my first readers, Janice Shiffler, Jessica Staheli, and Eric Stone, and to my agent, the incomparable Barbara Poelle. May your coconuts always be full of rum. I am especially grateful to the team at Flatiron Books and to my editor, Christine Kopprasch, who pushed me and the book further than I imagined possible.

And as always, the deepest gratitude is due my husband, Austin Baker, who, above all, points north.

About the Typeface

The Bembo® design is an old-style humanist serif typeface originally cut by Francesco Griffo in 1495 and revived by Stanley Morison in 1929. The original Morison typeface contained only four weights and no italics.